A
Presum
of
Murder

By

George Donald

CHAPTER 1

Susie saw Andy Brownlie answer his desk phone on the third ring and after giving his name to the caller, turned his head towards her. "DS Gibson? If you hold on, I'll see if she's in the office Missus Copeland," she heard him say and holding his free hand over the phone speaker, questioningly raised his eyebrows.

Susie vigorously shook her head and crossed her hands repeatedly. "Ah, it seems that DS Gibson isn't in the office Missus Copeland. Can I take a message, maybe get her to call you back," he grinned into the phone, then added, "So, she's got your phone number. Right, I'll pass that on."

"Wants you to give her a call about recovered property," he nodded towards the replaced handset.

Susie shook her head. "That woman has phoned me at least twice a day since we locked up the junkie housebreaker who screwed her flat, even though I have *repeatedly* told her that I need the PF to sign off on her property before I can return it, but will she listen?"

Andy smiled at Susie then standing, glanced at his wristwatch as he shrugged into his suit jacket. "That's nearly five, so if you don't need me for anything else tonight Susie, I promised her indoors I'd be home early."

"Yeah, sure, of course," Susie put her pen down onto the writing pad on her desk and sat back in her chair, squirming slightly to relieve the dull ache that had bothered her since…

She exhaled at the sudden memory of that night and returned Andy's smile. "How is Janice coping? She's what, three weeks to go now?"

"Yeah, it's supposed to be three weeks," he groaned, "but I'm hearing all these tales about first babies, that they could be anything up to two weeks after the due date. Don't think I can last that much longer," he pulled a face.

"*You* can't last that much longer," Susie smirked. "Think about your poor wife you heartless git. She's the one who has to cope with *you*."

"Okay, mum," he grinned at her and made towards the door, then stopped.

She sensed he was a little uneasy when he turned and asked, "You going to be much longer? Really, if you need me…"

"No, go home to your wife," she interrupted and waved him away, then added, "Tell Janice I send my love, okay?"

"Right boss, see you tomorrow then," he returned her wave and closed the office door behind him.

She sat staring into space and realised that by now, Andy must have guessed that something was wrong, that almost daily she sought an excuse to stay behind; any reason not to go home.

The phone on her desk rang.

"DS Gibson," she answered and then smiled at the handset. "No, I'm here for another hour at least," she told the civilian bar officer. "It's no problem, really. Bring the witness up to the CID general office and I'll note his statement here. Right, thanks."

Peter Gibson reversed his car into the driveway and using the side mirrors, saw the lounge lights switched on. Even with the doors and windows of the car closed, he could hear the sound of loud music and grimaced.

Time after time he had warned Jennifer, his fifteen year old daughter, about the volume of her music. He was sick of telling her. He climbed his six foot two inch frame from the car and angrily, slammed the driver's door, immediately regretting his action and run an almost apologetic hand across the roof of the gleaming black coloured, year-old Mercedes SLK convertible.

He fetched his suit jacket from the boot, folded it across his arm and slid a hand across his full head of fair hair, then locked the car and hurrying through the slight April drizzle, strode towards the front door.

As he suspected, the door was unlocked and added to his anger. He slammed the door behind him and saw Jennifer's school satchel lying discarded on the bottom stair and her blazer hung across the banister.

He was about to shout his daughter's name, but realised that she would never hear him above the noisy volume of Rihanna, currently her favourite artist.

He hung his jacket on the bottom post and climbed the stairs, growing increasingly irate as he neared the top landing.

Even though the door was tightly closed the noise issuing through Jennifer's door caused the glass shade on the small table lamp on the landing to reverbate.

By now he was so furious he didn't knock, but pushed open the door and angrily screamed, "*Jennifer*!"

His daughter was dancing barefooted on the floor in the centre of her room wearing only her grey coloured school skirt and bra with her tights, blouse and tie discarded on the floor. She turned fearfully towards him, her eyes widening when she saw him standing in the doorway. Quickly, almost defensively, she wrapped her arms round her small breasts, her face betraying her surprise and embarrassment. "Dad!" she screamed back at him.

He scowled and wordlessly, stepped back through the door, slamming it behind him.

Almost immediately, the music was turned off and taking a deep breath, he barked, "I want a word with you young lady, so get yourself dressed and come downstairs."

He turned and walked down the stairs, almost as angry with himself for storming into her room unannounced as he was at her blatant disregard of his previous instructions.

In the kitchen, he poured a glass of milk and sat at the table, his fingers drumming a beat on the tabletop.

A few minutes later, now wearing her blouse loosely buttoned and with her arms folded huffily across her chest, Jennifer joined him, tight-lipped and her face red with anger.

"How many times have I warned you…" he began, only to be interrupted by Jennifer, who equally with raised voice, said, "You came into my room without knocking! My private place! How dare you…"

"How dare I?" he angrily retorted. "Don't twist this on me, young lady. There would have been no need for me to even come upstairs if you had listened to me, did as I asked…."

"As you asked?" she sneered and stepped towards him, her face a mask of fury. "Asked? No, commanded; like some kind of petty dictator."

He rose from his seat and she flinched, startling him. He realised with shock that she thought he was going to strike her.

She turned away from him and fled the room.

He could hear her weeping loudly as she ran back upstairs.

Deflated, he sat wearily back down, the milk by his elbow, untouched, wondering again what to make of the two women in his life.

No, not his life, he inwardly corrected and glanced about him; his home.

His glance took in the wall clock and realised that once again, he would be eating alone.

Morven Sutherland fetched the yellow dress from her wardrobe and held it against her body, turning back and forth and admiring the stitching and softness of the fabric, the way the colour looked against her tanned skin and long, natural blonde hair. She smiled with satisfaction, knowing that worn without the hindrance of stockings or tights the dress would hug and flatter her model figure and long, shapely legs.

She tossed her head backwards, then shook it a few times to allow her hair to fall in folds about her almond shaped face and pouting, grinned self-consciously at herself in the mirror.

Not too bad for an almost thirty-eight year old, quietly sniggering at her secret and then cooed at her reflection, imitating Marilyn's famous pout, so beloved by women of all ages.

The CD of Adele's voice playing quietly in the background prompted her to unconsciously harmonise with the famous singer in her soft, lilting Welsh accent.

She startled as her mobile phone alerted her to an incoming text. Hanging the dress back in the wardrobe, she let her body fall onto the Queen sized bed and grasped at the phone, her hair billowed out behind her. She turned onto her back, holding the phone aloft to read the message.

She bit at her lower lip, smiling as she read the message. It occurred to her to respond, but he had told her quite categorically not to acknowledge his text messages, that after he messaged her, he would delete the sent text.

They had to be careful he repeatedly warned her. His wife wasn't stupid and already suspected something was amiss and he didn't want to break the news to her too soon.

Not when there was so much at stake.

She glanced about her at the bedroom, wide and spacious and wished that things were a little simpler; that he could come and live here with her in the flat in the modern, converted warehouse, rather than what they had endured for the last three months; his occasional visits.

If he lived with her, she thought, there would be no need for her to worry about him.

He had not yet spent a full night here with her and she persistently reminded him how she longed for the day when both would be together.

He had *always* agreed with her and after all, she smiled, why wouldn't he?

Just a pity when it happened they would have to travel abroad, she thought, but she had no family or friends that mattered as much as he did, so leaving Glasgow, leaving Britain would not be the heartache that he frequently reminded her he would suffer.

She smiled at the promise she had made him, her vow that when they had left everything behind, once they settled together as they had planned, she would work hard at making him forget what his life had once been.

He had believed her, believed the promise that she would hard work to make him happy and to make him forget.

Carol Meechan chewed at the inside of her mouth, a childhood habit developed when she was nervous and which she had never quite overcome.

Sitting in her narrow, but neat kitchen, she cupped her hands round the mug, the rich aroma of the coffee tickling at her nose, but her stomach was churning and the last thing she needed was food or drink.

She felt nauseous and thought she might throw up.

It wasn't going to be an easy decision to make, but it was a decision she *must* make.

She glanced at the kitchen wall clock and anxiously waited for John to return home. She needed to discuss it with someone, but could not speak with anyone at the bank.

Most definitely, she slowly shook her head, nobody at the bank.

Andy Brownlie held the small bunch of carnations behind his back, opened the door and shouted, "That's me home."

The flowers were not what he would have liked to buy Janice, but their meagre cost had been all the change in his pocket. Since moving three months previously from their one-bed flat to the three-bedroom semi and taking on the large mortgage, that and Janice having to quit work early at the supermarket because of her pregnancy, now meant that these days every penny was a prisoner.

He knew that he shouldn't complain and would never worry her, for marrying Janice had been the best decision of his life; well so far, he would grinningly remind her and earn himself a dig in the ribs when he would laughingly introduce her to friends as his current wife.

Still, he sighed, if it wasn't for the overtime that his boss Susie Gibson occasionally wangled for him, things might have been a little more desperate.

The delicious aroma of stew wafted along the narrow hallway met him at the door and he smiled in anticipation.

He hung his suit jacket on the cloakroom peg and pushing open the door into the lounge, saw his wife's auburn haired head pop out from the small kitchen.

Smiling, she blew him a kiss and her eyes opened wide with delight when he brought out the flowers with a theatrical flourish.

"Get yourself washed and change or whatever you men do when you're in from the coalface," she grinned at him, accepting a kiss and the flowers in that order. "Dinner will be on the table in five minutes sharp and I *mean* sharp, Mister Brownlie."

Palms raised in surrender he grinned and made his way upstairs to the bathroom, first grabbing a pair of denims from his closet.

With a minute to spare he was sat at the small table rolling up his sleeves when Janice, using her backside, pushed open the kitchen door and deposited a steaming plate of mashed potatoes and stew in front of her husband.

"Let me get yours," he half rose from his seat, but she waved him back down and returned with her own meal and sat opposite him at the small, gate leg table; a cast-off from Janice's parents with four matching, if slightly worn, wooden chairs.

The flowers, looking lost in the overlarge and quite ugly crystal vase his auntie Mary had gifted them on their wedding day, now sat at one end of the table.

"How's your day been?" he asked, shovelling the food away as though he suspected his wife would reach out and steal it from under his nose.

She arched her eyebrows and replied, "I'll tell you if you promise not to choke yourself to death. Slow down, you greedy pig."

"Sorry," he grimaced and then added, "This is delicious."

She cocked her head in acknowledgement of the compliment and told him, "Well, I went to the Health Clinic at Baillieston and the midwife says that everything seems to be on course. The baby's weight is as it should be and the slight cystitis has cleared, so that's a relief," she sighed.

"Ah, any indication the baby might arrive on time?"

She slowly shook her head and stared sorrowfully at him.

"Andy, this baby of ours will come when he or she decides it's time to be born. Unless you intend tripping me from the top of the stairs or scaring the wee devil out of me, we just have to be patient and wait, okay?"

He grinned at her, knowing that if anything Janice was even more eager than he to meet their unborn child.

"So," she nibbled daintily at her food, "any further update on your neighbour, what's happening in her life I mean?"

Andy slowly shook his head.

"She was still at her desk when I left," he spooned some stew into his mouth. "I mean, Susie was never one for the overtime. Let's face it," he said without malice, "with her salary as a Detective Sergeant and I'm guessing her husband's salary as a senior manager with the Caledonian, their joint income must be pretty good. If you'd seen that house of theirs out at Kylepark in Uddingston, it's not as if they're short of a bob or two. No," he slowly shook his head, his eyes narrowing, "there's definitely something going on in her life. I get the feeling she's deliberately staying late at the office."

"Why wouldn't she want to go home, though? She has a daughter hasn't she?"

"Yeah," he nodded, then half closed his eyes as he tried to recall, finally remembering the wee girl's name.

"Ah, Jenny's she's called. She's about fourteen or fifteen now and attends that private school in Uddingston. I reckon the fees there must be extortionate. No," he shook his head again, "there's no financial reason for Susie to work overtime. I think there must be something wrong at home."

"Have you met her husband?"

"Aye, just the once, about a year ago I think it was. He's quite a big guy; well, tall I mean, but not that well built. Skinny, really, but quite a handsome man, though I say so myself. Came out of the house when I was dropping her off after a late shift, sort of shook my hand, said 'hello' and that was that."

Janice stared curiously at him, sensing he wanted to add something. He smiled at her and shrugging his shoulders, continued. "It's a stupid thing. When he shook my hand, it was, how can I put this, one of those limp handshakes; a courtesy thing. The type of handshake that makes you feel there's no warmth or even interest in it, y'know?"

She smiled at him. "Handshakes," she laughed. "You're just a macho type of guy, my rugged hero," and leaning across the table or as far as her bump would allow, good-naturedly rubbed at his hair. They finished their meal and to his and her surprise, Janice burped loudly, causing them both to erupt into a fit of giggles.

"I need to be careful when I do that," she laughed, "I almost peed myself there."

She poked at her food and then said, "I don't suppose that you can ask her if there's anything wrong? I mean, just as a friend?"

"Mmm," he screwed his face, "I don't know, Janice. I know that we get on well work-wise and yeah, Susie likes me. But she never really discusses her private life; at least, not in any depth. Yes," he nodded, "she might once have mentioned what she and her husband was doing or what her daughter is up to, but only on the surface, do you now what I mean? There's never any great detail and," his face contorted as if suddenly realising, "in the recent months, she's hardly mentioned her family at all."

Janice stood and reached for his empty plate, "Well, there's no harm in asking if she's all right, if she needs someone to talk to. It's not as if she would take offense, is it?"

"I can't answer that either," he shrugged, standing and pushing open the kitchen door to permit her to walk in front of him into the tight little kitchen, "but we get on well and to be honest, I really wouldn't feel comfortable asking her. She might think I was prying."

Janice laid the plates down by the sink and turned towards him, taking his face in her hands.

"Whatever you decide," she smiled and planted a kiss on his lips, "I'm certain will be the right decision."

As she turned towards the sink and turned on a tap, his eyebrows narrowed.

What he knew of Susie Gibson's private life was virtually nothing, however, that did not mean that he didn't suspect something was seriously wrong in her relationship with her husband.

John Paterson stopped the Mini and reversed into the one available space outside the close at number 165 Lawrie Street. Locking the drivers door, he stood back to admire the gleaming red paintwork, pleased with the paint job and run an approving finger along the offside wing.

Glancing up at the flat, he could see the front light on and smiled. Carol was at home.

He pushed open the close door and bounded up the stairs to the first floor, two steps at a time.

"I'm home," he shouted, withdrawing his key from the Yale lock and closing the front door behind him. "Got some good news, sweetheart," he called out and started to wrestle his way out of his painted stained dungarees. Getting no response, he called out, "Carol, you there?"

She appeared at the lounge door, her own anxiety overshadowed by his shout of good news.

"I got the job," he beamed at her then, his dungarees halfway off, grabbed her round the waist and spun her round, both laughing and staggering against the closed front door as his unbuttoned dungarees became wrapped round his legs.

John still held her, but more for support than passion and her eyes opened wide with delight while he regaled her again with the good news. He told her about the boss of the garage calling him into the office ten minutes before knocking-off time; he nervous and pessimistically believing that the one week's trial hadn't gone as well as John had expected, only for the boss to tell him his work was better than anticipated and he would start full time next Monday.

"Better than that," he grinned at Carol, "He's agreed to pay me a full wage for this week's trial period."

She threw her arms round his neck and hugged him tightly, deciding that her worry about the issue at the bank could wait; that tonight was John's night and nothing would interfere with his good news. "So," he winked at her, "get into your party frock and we'll hit the town."

DS Susie Gibson finished the typed note and stapling an explanatory note to the witness statement, placed them both into the detective's dookit.

She glanced at her wristwatch; seven-thirty and she could find no reason not to go home.

Shrugging into her short coat, she bid the late shift detectives goodnight and made her way through the office towards the car park at the rear of Baird Street police station.

Her charcoal coloured Honda CRV, her birthday gift to herself to celebrate her forty-third birthday four years previously, was parked beneath a security light that brightly illuminated the interior of the car.

Seated in the driver's seat, she tilted the rear view mirror and critically examined herself. Her dark brown collar length hair, now slightly tinted to conceal the few grey strands that had arrived, was short and neatly framed her face, still without wrinkles but noticeably tired. Susie would not describe herself as beautiful, but she knew she had a strong face and even she would admit her grey/green piercing eyes were her best feature.

Just a pity, she sighed at the mirror, that these days they constantly reflected her inner sadness.

Standing at five feet six inches in height Susie's weight seldom fluctuated and in years gone by would laughingly describe herself as proportionately built. Even following the birth of Jenny she had, within a few weeks of the delivery gone back to the gym and soon returned to her pre-pregnancy weight. But that was then, she inwardly sighed, finding lately that her strict gym routine was becoming increasingly exhausting and tiring her more than she could previously recall.

She had always been a conservative dresser and not one to keep up with fashion trends, preferring trouser suits rather than skirts or dresses, arguing that it favoured her job to be dressed in trousers.

Not that she had any complaint about her legs that though muscled, were slim and she knew could still attract a second glance from men. However, in the recent months she had discarded a number of her trouser suits, opting instead for knee-length skirts. She had wondered if in some way, she was trying to retain a sense of her womanhood, her sexual attraction; perhaps attempting to recapture or revive her days as a single woman.

She grimaced at the mirror.

In some ways she *was* a single woman, for Peter had hardly touched her these past few months. Touched her? she sadly shook her head. He made every effort not to come near her.

Aside from the obligatory peck on the cheek and usually for the benefit of their daughter, her husband now physically ignored his wife.

At first, she thought it was because of her age and like her mother before here, the onset of an early menopause, but in her heart she knew it was nothing to do with that

The last three months had been spent alone in the master suite while he occupied the second bedroom, even going as far as moving all his clothes into the wardrobes in that room.

She had tried to discuss their lack of closeness with him, at first fearing that he was experiencing some kind of penile dysfunction and urged him to attend and speak with their doctor.

Is it me, she had pleaded with him, but any attempt at dialogue usually ended either in argument or with him in a petulant huff.

By ignoring her pleas, she gradually had come to recognise the truth. It was not a medical problem, as she had feared.

Accepting it had been the hardest part of all, but there was no other explanation.

Peter simply no longer found her desirable.

For the last few months Susie had first suspected, but was now convinced there was someone else.

There had been nothing definite such as the smell of a woman's scent on his body or his clothes, but her feminine intuition had overcome her reluctance to face facts.

Over the course of several weeks she had discreetly searched his discarded clothing, but found no unexplainable hotel or restaurant receipts nor were there any unaccountable debits on their bank statements. She almost blushed when she recalled checking his mobile phone for text message and names, even going as far as checking the mileage on his car, but she knew that was a waste of time. Peter was normally office bound other than the few occasions when he was called out of town to meetings elsewhere and those, she admitted to herself, were rare.

No, she shook her head and inwardly fumed, Peter was too smart to be caught out so easily and reluctantly Susie had come to accept that living as he did with a woman who was a detective, it had obviously taught him to be more secretive that she realised.

Yet the suspicion persisted.

Of course, she had challenged him and sitting in the car, her hands gripped the steering wheel a little tighter and her body tensed when she recalled that time. She instinctively moved her seated position, as though the pain was a reminder of that night.

The brightness of the rear yards security lamp reflected the mirror back to her face and she was surprised to see that tears were coursing down her cheeks.

She fumbled in her handbag on the passenger seat and fetched a tissue from the small pack, dabbing at her eyes and blowing her nose.

A patrol car entered the yard and stopped opposite. She saw the two young cops laughing together; the female driver and her male partner who exited the passenger seat carrying what seemed to be a bag of takeaway food.

Susie hurriedly turned the ignition key and taking a deep breath, slightly turned her head to one side and gave the cops a wave as she slowly drove out of the yard.

He watched the woman leaving the Tesco store in Dumbarton Road and dodging the traffic, she crossed to the opposite side of the busy road.

He could see that she held a plastic bag of groceries in both hands while her handbag hung by its strap, over her left shoulder.

He thought she looked about a thirty years of age, but the real attraction, he inwardly grinned, was she also looked to be overweight and likely not one for running after him.

He skipped across the road between a bus and a black hackney and now, head down, was no more than ten yards behind the woman.

The slight fall of rain made it easier and he pulled the hood of his black coloured sweat top over his head.

Thrusting his hands into the large patch pockets of the sweat top, he tightly gripped the handle of the knife in his right hand.

He could almost *feel* the adrenaline coursing through his body.

The woman turned from Dumbarton Road into Apsley Street and he quickened his pace till he was just five yards behind her. Nervously, he glanced about him but apart from some young kids skateboarding on the opposite pavement, the street seemed to be deserted.

Now was the right time.

As the woman drew abreast with a close entrance, he ran as if to pass her by, but turned and using his weight and with the advantage of surprise, bundled her into the close mouth. The close door was tightly closed and set back three feet from the entrance, allowing him to jam the woman against the door without either of them being seen by anyone walking on the footway.

"*Give me your fucking bag!*" he hissed at the woman, holding the short-bladed knife against the nylon anorak that constrained her heavy breasts.

The woman, wide-eyed with shock and utterly terrified, stared not at him but at the knife and uttered something in response, but he could not understand and grinned.

The bitch was a foreigner.

He pulled with his free hand at the handbag strap, but though the woman didn't resist and the strap slid down from her shoulder, continuing to hold of the two plastic grocery bags meant the strap became entangled on her arm.

He pulled again at the strap with such force the woman lost her balance and collided with him, causing them both to perform a shuffling dance about the small foyer area of the entrance.

"Fuck! Fuck!" he screamed at the panic-stricken woman, spraying her with saliva as he continued to pull at the strap.

As though in understanding, the woman dropped both plastic bags, but clutched her arms tightly about her breasts as a shield against the knife and unwittingly preventing the strap from sliding from her arm.

Then, to his horror, she began to scream; a high-pitched howl that sounded like a siren going off.

He almost run, but had come too far now. The blade was sharp, but the handbag strap was thick and he had to saw at it, taking precious, stomach churning seconds before it cut through.

Grabbing the bag he ran without a backward glance, but by now the woman had found a reserve of courage and ran a few short yards after him, screaming at him, the unintelligible words pursuing him along the road.

Leigh Gallagher had been born and raised in the Partick area and knew every nook and cranny. Just over one hundred yards from the woman, he breathlessly skidded to a halt, his lungs burning with the sudden exertion and turned into an unlocked close mouth in Laurel Street.

Running straight through the close, he already knew the rear back door had previously been forced open and now hung by one hinge. Pushing his way through the door, he ran across the rubbish strewn rear court and into the open back door of a close that exited onto the nearby Crow Road.

Within the darkness of the fetid smelling close, he pulled back his hood and forced himself to be still, bent over with his hands on his knees drawing breath in gasps, his legs shaking and his heart threatening to burst from his chest.

Quickly, he tore open the old, worn leather handbag and grabbed at the purple coloured PVC purse within.

"Fuck," he muttered with disappointment, staring at the single five-pound note, three one-pound coins and the loose change of silver and copper.

He bet down on one knee and turned the handbag upside down, but all that dropped onto the flagstones from it was a few receipts, an opened letter, some photographs and a small, silver coloured crucifix attached to a broken chain.

Angrily, he threw the bag to one side and feeling cheated, rifled through the handbags contents, but there were no credit cards and nothing of value. Even the crucifix looked worthless.

Worse, there wasn't even a mobile phone.

He closed his eyes in frustration and angrily fetched a crumpled yellow coloured thin nylon cagoule jacket from his denim pocket that he pulled over his head.

Now disguised and slightly calmer, he made his way to the front door of the close and first peeking out to ensure no police patrol was passing by, stepped out into the drizzling rain in Crow Road.

CHAPTER 2

Susie Gibson awoke before the alarm clock sounded and tapped at the off button. She had slept fitfully, her mind occupied by thoughts of the apparent argument that had occurred before she arrived home. It wasn't too difficult to guess there had been some sort of confrontation between Jenny and her father

Her daughter, locked in her room, had refused to open the door and other than the sound of her television changing channels, Susie would not have guessed Jenny was at home.

Of course, Peter was gone again and with no note of explanation. He had given up some months previously trying to explain his sudden absences and now both he and Susie had come to an unspoken acceptance that if he was out, there was no need for her to know where he was.

Lying there in the comfort of her bed, her mind wandered once more to consider divorce.

She had come to accept the marriage had broken down irretrievably, but recalled the first and only time almost two months ago now when she had suggested the idea, Peter had snapped at her, calling her selfish and inconsiderate and reminding her that divorce would impact on their daughter who was commencing preparations for her Higher grade exams.

With reluctance she had accepted his reasoning and dropped the issue, but recalled with a shudder what had later occurred.

Susie had prepared herself for was a calm and rational discussion about both their future's, but within a few short minutes the discussion developed into a vicious shouting match, each trying to hurt the other with language that neither would normally condone within their home.

Short as it was, the argument had proceeded from their bedroom to the stair landing and that is when it happened.

Warm as she was under the quilt, she shivered at the memory.

Exhaling, she forced herself from bed and stood up, stretching her weary body and glancing at the full-length mirror on the sliding wardrobe door. Pulling her nightdress taut against her body, she saw that while she could probably afford to lose a few pounds about her midriff, she was still in reasonable shape. She half smiled at the thought that even though Peter no longer found her desirable, maybe there was someone out there who might.

Taken aback, she raised a hand to her mouth and to her surprise, she found herself softly crying, the tears coursing down her cheeks. She sniffed and wiped at her nose with the back of her hand.

The sound of the front door closing startled her and swiftly, she moved to the window, peeking through the closed curtain in time to see Peter getting into his car.

She watched as he started the engine and drove quickly down the driveway, but curiously turning left rather than right, the route he would normally take if he were travelling to his office in the city centres West George Street.

She glanced at the clock and saw that he had departed almost a full hour before he was due to start work.

She couldn't decide whether to be sad or angry and turning from the window, made her way into the en-suite.

Jenny Gibson heard her mother's shower running and lay in bed, angry with both her parents, her hands clenched into fists and her teeth gritted.

It wasn't fair that they no longer loved each other. Not fair that they had raised their daughter to believe that they would always be there for her as a loving couple, but now despised the very sight of each other.

Not fair that they had both created the lie of a happy family, a lie that she had to perpetuate among her friends at school.

Not fair that with the stress of her exam preparations she had to contend with the atmosphere of a home that reeked of hate.

Not fair that her father could without 'a by your leave', walk into her room; her sanctuary.

The bastards!

She hated them both!

She closed her eyes tightly and her body tensed, but resisted the urge to scream out loudly.

Forcing herself to relax, she thought of her mother and knew that in her heart, she could never hate her.

Without reason, she thought again of that time, two months ago when it happened.

If anything, she felt sorry for her mum, her limited life experience still categorising relationships in black and white; no grey areas.

No, she could never hate her mother.

But her father? The memory of that night was still fresh in her mind. She bit at her lip.

Well, that was different.

Carol Meechan quietly slipped from between the sheets, turning her head to ensure that she didn't waken John who lay on his back, gently snoring. She smiled with the memory of last night, both slightly drunk when they arrived home after celebrating John's good news, their need for each other hurrying their lovemaking. She was so relieved that he had finally found a job.

Quietly, she made her way out of the room and into the bathroom and then after her toilet, leaned into the bathtub and turned on the old, creaky shower. She grimaced at the noisy rattle of the hot water through the pipes, hoping now with the extra income they might be able to fix up the flat as they had hoped.

Stepping over the lip of the bath she tilted her head to let the water run through her short, fair hair and smiled, imagining that now with John's regular wage they might even get a holiday this year; somewhere warm, she sighed. The ruins and antiquities of Rome had always appealed to her.

The prospect of extra money reminded Carol that her income from the bank had previously barely covered the mortgage and the necessities of life and again this month, their joint bank balance would be sitting at zero, if not once more overdrawn.

Thoughts of the bank reminded her of what she had discovered and again, she knew she had to tell someone, but whom? If she was mistaken, God forbid, she would not only look foolish and perhaps even incompetent, but alleging that there was wrongdoing when there was none could even invoke her own dismissal.

She sat on the edge of the bath rubbing at her hair with the towel, brow knitted and worrying again.

No, she stopped rubbing at her hair, her face grimly set,

She was not wrong. There was a definite discrepancy.

"Coffee's on the kitchen worktop," called John through the door, followed by, "Good morning my lovely lady."
She grinned at the sound of his voice and all thought of her predicament, for the moment anyway, disappeared.

The door to the Detective Inspector's room located on the upper floor of Cranstonhill police office was slightly ajar.
Seated at his desk, DI Bobby Franklin rubbed at the ache in his midriff and studied that mornings crime report's with a pen in his hand as he allocated a name at the top of each page. Peering at the reports he sighed, realising that his wife was correct; either he would need to grow longer arms or get himself new reading glasses.
The door knocked and he glanced up to see one of his junior detectives standing there, slightly hesitant, a sheaf of papers held in his hand.
"This a bad time, boss?" asked DC Ahmed.
"No, come away in son," replied Franklin, beckoning the younger man into the room while inwardly glad for any excuse to avoid straining his eyes further.
Waseem Ahmed, or Waz as he was more commonly known throughout the Division, had been with the Department for just a few months, but already impressed Franklin with his eagerness and willingness to learn the craft.
Born in the Govan area of Glasgow to Pakistani parents, thirty-year-old Ahmed had stepped away from his parents' grocery business and to his father's horror, fulfilled a lifetime ambition by joining the police. In his initial interview for the CID he had privately admitted to Franklin that his strict Muslim parents were even further outraged when two years previously he refused to follow tradition, but married a bride of his own choosing. Unfortunately, the Glasgow born Alima's own parents were just as outraged and the newly married young couple had been initially treated as outcasts by both families. However, while Waz's parents still had not come to terms with their son's marriage, his wife's parent's resistance crumbled a little over nine months previously when Alima presented them with their only grandchild, a little girl called Munawar. Just as her name meant '*bright*', little Munawar soon won their hearts and with their enthusiastic child support, Alima had just recently returned to her primary teaching job.

"I might be grasping at straws, boss," began Ahmed, seating himself in the chair in front of Franklin's desk, "but you've got a report there," he nodded to the paperwork on the desk, "regarding a mugging yesterday afternoon down in Partick. A woman threatened with a knife."

Franklin sat back in his chair and grimaced. "I hate that word mugging Waz, so let's stick to the Scottish Criminal Law and we'll call it what it is, eh? It's a robbery, straight and simple."

Ahmed grinned a little self-consciously and nodded. "Right, boss; robbery it is then."

He glanced at a sheet of paper in his own hand and continued, "A Missus Alicja Paderewski," he struggled with the pronunciation.

"We'll call her the complainer, eh?" smiled Franklin, himself unable to pronounce the woman's name.

"Aye, good idea, boss," grinned Ahmed. "Anyway, the complainer provided the uniform cops with a description of her assailant and I've dug out some other reports," he shuffled the papers in his hand, "and I came up with two other incidents within the last week where woman have been mugged…I mean, robbed, in the general area of Partick." His voice grew a little excited as he explained. "In both the other incidents, the women were returning from the shops in Dumbarton Road and carrying shopping bags in their hands and were also approached and attacked from behind by a hooded male, who threatened them with a knife."

Franklin sat forward in his chair his curiosity now peaked and quizzed the DC. "That's too much of a coincidence, Waz. Do the descriptions match?"

Ahmed took a deep breath, his face contorted and he replied, "Well, the first complainer was too upset to provide a description other than a youngish, hooded male, but *did* see a small, black handled knife. In fact, according to the cop," he glanced at the report, "in her opinion the woman apparently fixated on the knife and simply handed her bag over without any protest."

"And the second complainer?"

"Ah, well that woman," he checked the police report for the name, "a Missus Mary McEwan. She's in her late sixties, but apparently took a kick at him and swung her shopping bag, but he managed to grab her handbag and got away. However, she gave the cops that attended the call a reasonable description of the ned that attacked her."

He bent his head to read the report.

"Aged about 17 to 23, thin build, bad acne with cropped fair hair and wearing a black, hooded top and they thin jeans. You know the type of jeans I mean, boss. All the young people are wearing them these days."

"Like drainpipes, you mean?"

"Aye, like them," Ahmed grinned, then cheekily added, "Take you back to your youth, do they?"

"Get on with it," growled Franklin, unable to suppress his own grin.

"Anyway, Missus McEwan thinks she might be able to identify the guy again."

"So, what do you propose Waz?"

"If you are okay with it boss and I know that I'm relatively new to the Department, but I was wondering if you would allocate me these inquiries. Give me the opportunity to coordinate a single response rather than three detectives working towards the same goal. I'll still be able to deal with my own work, but it will mean that I can investigate all the robberies and if I'm fortunate enough to arrest the culprit, roll all the charges together into one case."

Franklin peered at the younger man. "Trying to impress me, Detective Constable?"

Ahmed blushed. "Well, to be honest boss, I'm ambitious and the only way I'll get on and learn my trade is to take on inquiries that will test me. I've investigated most of the day to day crime that has come into the office, but I've not yet had the opportunity to investigate a run of robberies that seem to be the work of the same guy."

Franklin hesitated slightly.

He didn't disclose that he was already aware of the pattern of robberies and just that morning spoken with the Detective Inspector in the neighbouring Maryhill office to inquire if that side of the city was also being targeted by this particular individual and awaited DI Charlie Miller to get back to Franklin.

Franklin's fear was the robber's use of a knife. To date, the culprit had presented the knife that, combined with his verbal threat, so intimidated the women to comply with his demand for their handbags; however, if only took one woman resisted, the DI would find himself dealing not just with a street robbery, but possibly a stabbing and at worse, a murder.

He had considered allocating the inquiry to the divisional plain-clothes unit and tasking them with hunting the robber, but now here was young Ahmed volunteering to take the inquiry on. Ahmed had already impressed Franklin with his eagerness and willingness to work, but he wondered if maybe the younger man's lack of experience would be a hindrance.

Slowing exhaling, he nodded. "Okay, Waz, the inquiry is yours, however," he held up a cautionary finger, "I don't have enough resources to provide you with a neighbour from the CID so what I'll do is ask Sergeant Cuthbertson that runs the plain clothes squad to allocate one of his cops to work with you, okay?"

Ahmed nodded, his eyes opened wide with delight and his mouth dry.

"Right," Franklin reached for his desk phone, "tell Bobby McAllister that *you're* dealing with the street robberies in the Partick area and not to allocate you any further inquiries unless I say so, okay?"

Ahmed nodding, rose from his seat and headed towards the door, then turned back. "Thanks boss, I'll not let you down."

"See you don't," growled Franklin in response and dialled the number for the plain-clothes unit office, downstairs.

The phone call was answered by Sergeant Cuthbertson.

Franklin quickly explained that he wanted one of the plain-clothes cops assigned to assist his young DC Ahmed with a robbery inquiry.

"Oh and Archie," he confided to Cuthberston. "Young Ahmed's keen and eager, but might need a sensible hand on the tiller, if you get my drift."

"How about Des Mooney?" Cuthbertson suggested.

"That old reprobate not retired yet," quipped Franklin with a smile. "Aye, Des will be a good choice. If he's there, ask him to pop up and see me, eh?"

"No problem, he's on his way, Bobby."

Jenny Gibson refused her mother's offer of a lift to school and watched as Susie carefully drove the Honda down the narrow driveway and turned right onto the roadway.

She knew she was being churlish, that she had no plausible reason to refuse, but at that time of the morning just could not face what she presumed would be the enforced pleasantness, the idle chat about her exams and worst of all, her mother's interest in her friends.

Jenny had grown up knowing her mother was a police officer, but it was only in the last year that she suspected the hidden agenda behind what had previously sounded to be a genuine interest in her social life.

Now it at fifteen years of age, her mother's questioning had taken a different approach; what kind of parents her friends had, what boy Jenny had an interest in, who was doing well at school and who wasn't.

She suffered the usual parental warnings about drink and drugs and underage sex.

At first, she had persuaded herself her mother was simply being a caring parent, but the constant badgering was driving her crazy.

Hoisting her shoulder bag, heavy with her school manuals, she folded her arms and head down against the threat of impending rain, began the ten-minute walk towards school.

Susie Gibson joined the M73 from the slip road at Uddingston and drove almost automatically towards the slip road that would take her westwards onto the M8.

The usual morning rush-hour traffic on the motorway included a death defying white van driver who on several occasions forced his way from the adjoining lanes of the M73 onto the slip road and back again, slipping between the narrowest of gaps in the line of vehicles.

A succession of drivers cursed and sounded horns and gesticulated at the dangerously selfish moron.

Startled from her stupor, Susie stamped on her brakes, coming to a halt just inches from the van in front that had somehow managed to squeeze into the space between her own vehicle and the Volvo ahead of her.

Angrily, she cursed and banged the heel of her hand on the horn, but realised almost immediately the van driver would pay no heed to the noise, that all she was doing was liberating her own frustration at his stupidity. As the single access lane became two lanes, she saw the van speed up and swerve to the outer lane, narrowly avoid clipping the Volvo as the van raced ahead and eventually disappearing from her sight.

Wryly shaking her head at the van driver's arrogance, she grinned at her own stupidity that it had not occurred to her, a bloody police officer too, to note the van's registration number for raising a formal complaint when she arrived at work.

Exhaling, she stayed in the line of traffic, watching as the 'last minute dot com' drivers raced past on the outside lane to make-up time for that precious few minutes they had undoubtedly spent at home, finishing their breakfast.

Motoring along in the inside lane of traffic at a more sedate fifty-five miles per hour, Susie's thoughts turned again to the breakdown of her marriage.

She frowned and could not imagine what Jenny was going through; aware that both Peter and she had tried on numerous occasions to get through to their daughter, explain what was happening with them, but she consistently refused to listen.

Her daughter's reluctance to express her feelings was she realised, far more than teenage angst. In the last two months, since that night, she had become withdrawn, picking at her food, spending most of her time within her room and to Susie's surprise, even managing to screw a simple bolt lock to the inside of the door.

The previous week a letter had arrived by post from Missus Kerr, Jenny's Form Teacher, expressing her concern at Jenny's lack of concentration in school and apologising if she sounded to be prying, but worried that something at home was affecting Jenny's recent loss of academic ability.

Her brow narrowed when she recalled showing the letter to Peter, who had curtly snapped, "You deal with it."

Susie had twice to cancel meetings with Kerr, citing work commitment, but the reality was she was nervous of meeting the portly and kind, but inquisitive woman.

Kerr was no fool and would quickly realise Jenny's parents were no longer a couple.

Susie's worry was that competent as Kerr was, she was also a local woman and a known gossip.

At last, just as the traffic began to back-up on the motorway and acutely aware that any lack of attention to her driving would be problematic, she managed to exit onto the slip road at the Royal Infirmary that would lead her towards Baird Street.

Almost with a sigh of relief, Susie switched off the engine in the back yard at Baird Street and, with a final glance at the rear view mirror to check her lipstick, grabbed at her handbag and got out of the car.

"Morning boss," she heard the cheerful greeting and turning saw Andy Brownlie walking from his old and beat-up silver coloured Ford Escort towards her.

"Morning Andy," she returned his greeting with as smile. "How's your better half this morning?"

"Grumpy, feeling a bit low and unattractive and very, *very* impatient," he grinned.

He punched in the four-digit code for the back entrance door and held it open while she walked through. "That said," he continued, "her back has been giving her a bit of bother so Janice made an appointment with the doctor, but being pregnant, she thinks it's unlikely he'll prescribe anything at this stage."

"What about massage? When I was having my daughter, the midwife recommended some physio to relieve that ache. It might be worth mentioning it to her."

"Will do boss," he nodded thoughtfully, then with a further grin added, "anything to stop her moaning and keeping me awake at night with all her aches and pains."

Climbing the stairs to the first floor and the CID suite, Susie smiled in greeting to Elsie, the youthful cleaner, then turning towards Andy shook her head and replied, "If you think that sleepless nights will finish when Janice delivers your baby, thing again young man."

A head popped out of the CID general office and Martin Burns, the uniformed CID clerk called along the corridor, "Morning Susie, the boss asked if you'd pop in and see him when you arrive."

She turned and pretended a grimace to Andy and with a stage whisper said, "Here we go again; another day, another dollar."

CHAPTER 3

Carol Meechan alighted from the bus in Argyle Street and head down against the light drizzling rain, stepped into a shop doorway then fumbled in her handbag for the telescopic umbrella. She unconsciously smiled that the yellow coloured brolly matched her bright yellow three-quarter length linen coat and with practised ease, joined the morning throng of office workers who in the main, silently and gloomily made their way to their firms for another day's toil.

Eyes cast down with a wary respect for the irregularities of the city's slab stoned pavements, she safely reached West George Street and waited for the elderly, but very pleasant Corp of Commissionaire doorman to unlock the ornate glass door that bore the crest of the Caledonia Banking Group.

Stepping through the door and entering the large public room, she saw that already the place was a hubbub of activity with over a dozen staff carrying money drawers, most of who wordlessly hurried between cashier tills and the offices located on each side of the large public room.

Greeting old Max, he earned a grateful smile when he raised a hand and tipped his uniform cap to her as she passed him by.

Max liked the young blonde woman, believing her to be one of the nicer individuals in the bank and not like some of the stuck-up wee arses that thought they were something because they wore a suit to work. Sighing, he turned and locked the main door, glancing at the wall-mounted clock and wishing it was time for his break.

Carol made her way to the female staff room and removing her coat, pretended to take an interest in her locker, but listening with a smile to the conversation as three of the younger tellers giggled while recounting the antics of one who related her nightmare date that occurred the previous evening with a junior clerk.

The laughing girls seemed unaware of Carol's presence and comporting themselves, left to attend at their workplaces.

Alone in the room, she shrugged and glancing at her watch, saw that there was still almost ten minutes before she needed to be at her desk.

She sat down heavily on a plastic chair under the window, her brow creased and biting at her lower lip, twisting her hands together as her mind still reeled with the decision she had made that morning.

"Penny for them," said the voice.

Startled, she turned to see Morven Sutherland, standing at the open door. Dressed in a one-piece bright red coloured, knee length dress that flattered her shapely figure and complimented with a thin gold chain round her neck and matching bracelet, Sutherland was holding a sheaf of papers and wore a broad smile on her face.

Carol guessed that Sutherland must be in her mid to late thirties, yet her expensive work attire, flawless skin, natural blonde hair and perfectly applied make-up suggested her to be a fashion model rather than the bank's Assistant Accounts Manager. Carol knew that it was jealously whispered among her female colleagues that Morven Sutherland was so good-looking she made the other women look positively dowdy.

It was also common knowledge in the bank that Sutherland was *always* first to arrive and commence work and usually among the last to depart. An ambitious and dedicated employee with proven fiscal talent, her attractiveness misled some of her male colleagues who, with predatory arrogance and to their later regret, seriously underestimated her ruthless charm.

While it was accepted by the staff that Sutherland was not one to associate socially with her work colleagues, her private life became the subject of solicitous gossip within the workplace. Human nature being as it is and with nothing other than malicious supposition, one of her rebuffed suitors had some months earlier whispered she was probably gay. However, nobody really took the suggestion seriously and most preferred the alternative story, that Sutherland had a wealthy, but married admirer.

"Ah, morning Morven," replied Carol, rising to her feet, unconsciously deferring to the seniority of Sutherland. "Just getting myself prepared for another day," she hesitantly joked.

"You take your time, Carol," Sutherland waved her to resume her seat and walked towards her own locker. "You're still a few minutes early anyway. So, any word about your young man," her eyes narrowed as she turned towards Carol. "John isn't it? Is there any news yet of a job?"

Carol smiled brightly. "Yes, as a matter of fact. He was taken on yesterday by a local garage, so that's a great relief," she exhaled, pleased that Sutherland remembered their informal chat from a few weeks previously.

"I'm glad for you, not least because I'm sure it must help with the bills," she replied over her shoulder, rummaging in her locker and bringing out a small bottle of perfume. She turned again and placing the paperwork on a nearby table, sprinkled some of the scent onto the two fingers of her right hand and dabbed behind her ears.

"Things I forget in the morning," she half grinned at Carol, displaying an even set of sparkling white teeth before returning the small bottle to the locker.

Perhaps or because of the friendly confidence that seemed for those few seconds to exist between them, Carol made her second decision of that day and inhaling, bit at her lower lip. "Morven, if you have a couple of minutes sometime this morning, would it be possible to have a word with you? In private, I mean. It's something that has been bothering me."

Sutherland stared curiously at her and asked, "Personal or business?"

Carol looked surprised. "Oh, it's business Morven, about something here in the bank," she gushed.

"Well, in that case Carol," she glanced at her watch, "I'll let you get settled into your morning so come to my office, say, midday during your break?"

Carol nodded eagerly, a wave of relief sweeping through her and smiled. "Midday it is then."

Des Mooney wearily climbed the stairs and made his way to the CID suite of office on the upper floor. His left knee continued to ache and the two Paracetamol he had popped with his coffee hadn't seemed to make much difference. Shaking his head, he was slowly coming to terms that he would need to first lose a couple of pounds from around his waist, then obtain an appointment at the surgery and get the knee attended to.

Pushing open the door of the general office, he saw Waz Ahmed seated behind his desk, his head bowed as the younger man pored over a map spread out in front of him. Pulling up a chair, Mooney sat heavily down and growled, "Coffee, milk, one sugar."

Waz looked up and grinned. "Is that you making a point, that you're the old guy and I'm the boy? I thought you were sent up here to help me, not for me to run after you, Homer."

"Less of the Homer, you cheeky wee bugger," Mooney pretended annoyance, but unconsciously run a hand across his thinning hair, "so fetch your old dad a coffee and *then* we'll talk business, all right?"

"Coffee it is," replied a grinning Waz and passed a file to Mooney. "While I'm fetching it, you might want a wee look at these crime reports and I'll explain when I'm sat back down."

While Waz walked to the table to fetch two coffees, Mooney fetched a pair of reading glasses from his plaid shirt pocket and read the three reports. Almost immediately, he understood why he had been selected to help the young detective. His eyes narrowed as he read and he instinctively knew that the threat from the street robber was very definite. If the suspect wasn't soon found and arrested, there was an increasing likelihood that some poor woman would end up getting stabbed and all for the sake of a few quid.

At the coffee table, Waz turned and sneaked a look at Mooney, pleased it was the older plainer who had been selected to assist him. He guessed that Mooney must now be in the twilight of his service and most of that service, if not all of it, working in the Anderston and Partick areas of the city. A little over five foot ten tall with a monk's tuft of hair remaining on his head and a little paunch round his midriff, Mooney was what coppers referred to as a 'take-on' in that he did not at all look like a police officer. Indeed, Mooney was more likely to be mistaken for his cartoon alter ego Homer Simpson and to his credit, suffered the nickname with good humour.

What pleased Waz, however, was Mooney's undoubted professionalism and old-fashioned beat skills. Yes, Waz was smart enough to realise that if he kept his eyes and ears open there was still a lot that Des Mooney could teach him.

Returning to his desk, he placed a mug beside Mooney's right hand and standing, pointed to the map.

"I've highlighted the three locations of the assaults, Des. The first was five days ago in Burgh Hall Street, the second the following day in Fortrose Street and then yesterday in Apsley Street. As you can see, all within a few hundred yards of each other and the commonality is that all three complainers had just left shops in Dumbarton Road and were carrying grocery bags."

"So, there is three days between the second and the third robbery then?"

"Ah, I thought that at first," replied Waz, reaching for an e-mail on his desk, but the boss phoned the DI at Maryhill, and he e-mailed me this copy crime report. Two days ago a woman coming back from the Maryhill shopping centre carrying a shopping bag in each hand got out of her car in Hughenden Drive and was mugged," he smiled, "robbed I mean. The woman wasn't injured and because the locus was just over the divisional boundary, Maryhill got the report.

According to the DI," he glanced with narrowed eyes at the e-mail, "this DI Miller, he says that if the description of the suspect matches our suspect then he's happy to assign the crime report to me. Well, us I mean."

Mooney slowly nodded his head and asked, "What about the times of the robberies?"

"All the robberies occurred in the late afternoon."

"So, you're convinced it's likely the same guy?"

Waz shrugged before replying. "You know what witnesses are like, Des. He's six feet tall in one report and five feet tall in another. He's bearded then clean shaven. But yes," he nodded, "I'm relatively convinced it's the same guy. The MO is very similar as is the status of the complainers; four women all returning from the shops and each carrying grocery bags."

"Except number three, she was in her car," pointed out Mooney.

"Aye, you're right, but that could have been an opportune crime. The culprit passes by, sees her and takes the chance to rob her. I haven't yet decided if it's the same guy. But I'm veering towards it being him."

He paused, now a little uncertain and stared at Mooney, eager for the older man's support. "So, what do you think? Is it worth pursuing?"

Mooney twisted his mouth in concentration, ignoring the ache in his knee and slowly nodded. "I think you're spot on regarding the three in our area. I'm not convinced about the Maryhill robbery, but when we catch him, we can always put it to him, eh?"

Waz nodded with a smile, then realised what Mooney had just said; *'When we catch him.'*

And that made him smile even wider.

"So," Mooney interrupted his thoughts, "how do you want to begin?"

"Well," Waz slowly drawled, "DI Franklin is of the same mind that this guy might panic or out of sheer badness, use the knife on one of his next victims, so the boss decided that we contact the media department at Pitt Street and request they do a press release. You know, warn the local's about this guy, let the public know about extra patrols in the area and ask for any information, that sort of thing. I sent them an e-mail and got this back," he handed Mooney a sheet of paper, then as the older man read it, continued with an explanation of the reply. "Basically, they told me that in the event there's no major incident in the city tonight, the media people will try to get it into either this evening's issue of the 'Glasgow News' or tomorrow's morning edition."

Mooney slowly nodded, his lips pursed and said, "I mean obviously, that's a good idea, but the only down side is that guy might read it and either quit while he's ahead or simply move on to somewhere else."

"You got any suggestions then Des?"

"Mmm, first thing I think we should do is re-interview the witnesses. It's been my experience that when somebody has had a shock and let's face it," he scowled, "somebody waving a knife at you is enough to give most people a fucking heart attack, but after a couple of days, little things do come back to the individual. It might be an idea to try and firm up on the description of this guy. What do you think?"

"Sound idea. I'll get onto the blower and try to fix up a time for meeting these women and going over their statements."

Leigh Gallagher woke with the mother of all headaches. Blinking away the desire to roll over and again try and sleep, he lay quietly in his bed staring at the ceiling. In the kitchen, he could hear his father tunelessly singing along to the radio and glanced at the digital clock radio on the bedside table. With a sigh, he reached across and switched on the radio and then, with his eyes tightly closed, thought again of Chloe.

He smiled and unconsciously reached for his groin, remembering that last time that he had touched Chloe and her reaction. He felt himself stiffen and wrapping his hand round his erect penis threw back the quilt cover, grinning in expectation of his own pleasure when the door suddenly flew open.

"Morning son, want a cuppa do you, eh?"

"Fucks sake, Da," he turned angrily away from his father, embarrassed that he had almost been caught with his erection in his hand and irate that his father opened the bedroom door without first knocking.

"Sorry, Leigh," replied Magnus Gallagher, "didn't realise you were trying to have a wee stroke there, son." His father stifled a guffaw while trying to stop himself from laughing. "So, is it a cuppa, eh?"

"Aye," Leigh irritably responded. "I'm getting up anyway," he growled. "Give me a couple of minutes."

Magnus Gallagher softly closed the door and Leigh could hear his light footsteps on the laminate flooring of the hallway, returning to the kitchen.

His penis now wilted, he pulled his shorts up over his bony hips and exhaling noisily, sat up then swung his legs from the bed onto the cold linoleum. He lifted a pair of denim jeans from the floor and pulled them over his thighs then from the bedside drawer fetched a pair of socks. From the lopsided wardrobe in the corner Leigh rummaged among the tops, finally choosing a freshly washed and ironed yellow coloured tee shirt. Slapping his hand against the side of the wardrobe he promised himself that when he got a few quid together, he would dump the flat pack crap that was his bedroom furniture and get some real, cool stuff instead. Lost in a daydream, he imagined himself getting his own place as he pulled the tee shirt over his head and shrugged into it. Glancing at the Star Wars wallpaper, he decided that the room could also use a lick of paint. Maybe bung his Da a few quid to give it a makeover, he nodded to himself.

"Grub's up," his father called from the hallway outside and knocked on the door.

Skipping across the hallway into the bathroom, Leigh peed and splashed some water onto his hands. Then with a quick glance in the old-fashioned wall-mirror above the sink, patted at his crew cut hair and pulled open the door.

In the steam filled kitchen, Magnus Gallagher, a fish slice in one hand and a frying pan in the other, grinned at his son and nodded to the small table set with two places.

Leigh swallowed hard at the smell of fat cooking. He didn't have a strong stomach and could become nauseous at any smell or taste that did not agree with him.

"Open that window there son, then sit yourself down and I'll have this ready for you in a jiffy," his father said over his shoulder.

Forty years living and working in Glasgow and Magnus Gallagher still spoke with a Cork accent so thick it could be cut with a knife.

The smell of frying sausage and eggs finally overcome Leigh's sensitive stomach and tantalised his taste buds, reminding him he hadn't eaten anything since teatime the previous day. Almost immediately, he began to salivate.

"So, what's your plans for today, son?" asked Magnus, carefully sliding two square sausages and an egg onto a plate to which he added a spoonful of steaming hot baked beans. "Is it the Job Centre at Maryhill again?"

"Aye," Leigh glibly lied, "I'll take a wander down there Da; see if anything's turned up since yesterday."

"That's the ticket son," his father nodded approvingly, "you don't get if you don't try. Bejesus, they must be tired of seeing your mug there every day, son." He sat down in front of his own breakfast and stared at Leigh. "Do they not give you any hope at all, Leigh? I mean you're in there every day. Is there nothing at all that they can offer you?"

"You know what it's like Da. Sure, how many times did you knock on their door looking for work and how many times did they actually offer you something?"

Magnus Gallagher slowly nodded his head in agreement, recalling the shame of having to attend daily at the Job Centre. The embarrassment of being interviewed by a succession of young people, mostly wee girls and finally being curtly informed that at fifty-seven and without any kind of qualification, he was unemployable in today's market; that he would be better accepting his dole money and just making the best of a bad lot. He, who had worked since his teens on the building sites and never, ever asked for a handout from any man.

He glanced up at his son, the younger of his two boys and worried that Leigh might end up like his father; unemployable.

God, what would my Mary think he wondered of his deceased wife, God rest her soul; gone now these last eight years.

He inhaled deeply and watched as Leigh devoured the breakfast then, hoping he sounded encouraging, said, "Maybe if you were to give our Patsy a wee phone, Leigh. He might know of something. It's worth a try, is it not?"

Leigh, continuing to chew at his food, stared down at his plate, unwilling to get into another fucking argument again. Without looking at his father, he gave a noncommittal nod and gulped at his tea.

"So," Magnus pressed, "what do you think? Is it worth a phone call son?"

"We'll see, Da. I'll find out first how I get on at the Job Centre then if there's nothing doing there, I'll consider phoning Patsy, okay?"

Magnus nodded in reply, picking at the slowly congealing food and unwilling to continue pressing Leigh for like his son, he did not want to get into another argument. Magnus could not know that Leigh had no intention of phoning his brother; the man whom Leigh privately referred to as Saint fucking Patrick.

"I'll wash up," he made as if to stand and smiled to his father, but knowing what the reply would be.

Magnus waved a hand indicating Leigh sit back down. "Now, what would I do with the rest of me day if I didn't have the flat to clean," he repeated the daily joke, rising to his feet and reaching for Leigh's empty plate. "You just get yourself attended to son and get off down to the Job Centre. You never know," he winked and nodded theatrically at his son, "today might be the day, eh?"

Leigh smiled dutifully at his father and wondered how his Da would feel if he knew that Leigh hadn't been near the Job Centre for at least a month, that the last time he was there he had been told not to bother attending, that if something became available, they would contact him.

Aye, right, so they will.

He watched as Magnus stooped over the sink, running the hot water into the plastic basin in preparation for washing up. Leigh didn't like lying to his father, but equally didn't like dashing the older man's hopes any more than they already had been. No, the old man had taken to many knocks in the recent years and a curious wave of sympathy swept through him for his father.

Softly shaking head as though dismissing the unaccustomed sentiment, his brow knitted and his eyes narrowed. He had learned there was other ways that to supplement the meagre cash of his the unemployment benefit cheque and thought again of the fifty-nine pounds and the knife in the small, red tin box, hidden beneath the loose board at the bottom of his wardrobe.

He glanced through the open window towards the clouds that hovered over the tenement skyline, his eyes brightening.

If as he hoped it turned out to be another cloudy, drizzly day, conditions would be ideal for taking a wee wander down to Dumbarton Road.

He inwardly grinned.

Him, his hoody top and the narrow bladed, but very sharp, black handled kitchen knife.

CHAPTER 4

Andy Brownlie drove the CID car carefully round the graffiti stained and chipped, concrete traffic calming bollards standing solidly like grey guardsmen in the roadway in Hollybank Street and risked a glance at his passenger.

"I used to work the beat here when I was in uniform," he said to Susie Gibson, anything to break the silence in the car. "It was a real dump a few years ago, but," he waved his a hand through the window, "you can see that most of the people here are making an effort to get the place into shape. It's only the few families like the McGriffin's that are bringing the place into disrepute. In fact, about eight years ago when I started working here, there was a wee shop on that corner there," he pointed with his forefinger, "that was licensed and used to sell the worst type of electric soup, the cheapest wine you could get and it was reputed to drive the local neds to all sorts of violence. In fact, the stuff was so potent, the punter's used to ask for a bottle of the 'who the fuck are you looking at?' wine," he grinned at her.

His story didn't even raise a smile

Staring out the side window, Susie, usually a cheerful and talkative individual seemed this morning to be on another planet. He had thought all morning about his conversation with his wife Janice and finally come to a decision.

"Susie," he nervously began, swallowing hard and prepared to be rebuffed, "I know it's none of my business and if you want to tell me to bugger off, I'll understand, but I can't help but notice that you're spending a lot of time at the office. Too much time, I mean. Is there anything bothering you, anything that you want to talk about?"

She turned and stared at him, surprised to see his knuckles white as they gripped the steering wheel and almost immediately realised that

Andy was nervous. She liked Andy and knew he liked her and with a gentle sigh, she smiled.

"So, am I the talk of the steamie or what?"

"No, not at all," he burst out, "it's just that, well, fuck."

He nosily exhaled. "I'm making a mess of this."

Andy steered the car into an empty parking bar, mindful of the broken bottle by the kerb and applying the handbrake, switched off the engine and turned towards her.

"We've been neighbours now for what, eight months? Firstly, I like working with you, boss. You've taught me a lot since I joined the CID, Susie and you've been good to me. Me and Janice, I mean, with the overtime and that."

His mouth was dry and he could feel himself blushing, the prepared speech slipping away as he babbled like an adolescent schoolboy.

"I know that we don't, you know, socialise or anything like that, but if you need somebody to talk to, well…" he faltered, unable to explain himself as he had earlier practised. Gamely, as he waited on her response, he blurted on. "Look, I would have to be a blind idiot to know that something's bothering you and it isn't the job. My God, you could lose half, no, most of the Department when it comes to polis work, Susie. So, what's bothering you, what's up hen?"

She bit at her lower lip, fighting the tears that once more threatened to engulf her.

A sudden banging on the passenger window startled her and turning, she saw a small boy, no more than ten years of age, his red hair tousled and wearing an oversized Celtic football top with a wide grin that revealed the lack of two upper front teeth.

"Watch your car for you, missus," the lad bellowed through cupped hands at the window. "Dodgy as fuck round here. I'll watch it for a pound and make sure it doesn't get screwed."

As one, she and Andy burst into laughter and taking a deep breath, slowly exhaled, the tension easing from her at the cheek of the wee bugger and, for some unaccountable reason, cheered by the unexpected encounter.

"Thanks neighbour," she nodded slightly to Andy, "if I do need to speak to somebody, I'll give you a shout, eh?"

Still smiling, she unbuckled her seat belt and turning to face the dwarf sized hard man, pressed the button to lower the passenger window.

"You know we're the polis and this is a CID car, don't you wee man?"

"Oh aye, missus," he grinned at her as he leaned with grubby hands on the passenger door. "Everybody round here knows *your* cars," then screwing his eyes together, knowledgably told her, "al the reggie plates start with the letters SF and you've got that extra wee aerial on top as well. Are you here to arrest somebody, missus? Is somebody getting the jail the day, eh? Is it the McGriffen's again? Is that the ones you're after, missus?"

Bemused, Susie turned and smiled at Andy's wide grin.

Janet McGriffen, at twenty-three years of age, was not just a heroin junkie, but also an accomplished housebreaker. So accomplished in fact that less than two weeks earlier, Susie had arrested her for what turned out to be a roll-up of eleven domestic break-ins that included her ground floor neighbour, Missus Copeland. Dragged screaming and kicking, from her mother's house on the second floor, fighting tooth and nail to the CID car, Janet now languished on remand in HMP Cornton Vale. She likely might have been bailed at her custody hearing, but for her for screamed threat to murder Susie, the female turnkey at Baird Street, the Fiscal Depute who libelled the charges at court and finally the Sheriff who, shocked at her behaviour, ordered her detained till time of trial.

Not a nice young woman, the neighbours whispered of Janet McGriffen, but not too loudly for Janet's mother, big Agnes was just as vicious as her firstborn.

Turning back to the boy, Susie warned him, "Stand back wee man" and opening the car door, stepped out and glanced up at the four storey tenement building. The area had previously been known for its problems with unemployment and high incidence of violent crime, but like Andy said, most of the locals were determined to turn the areas reputation about. Still, it never ceased to amaze her how the predominantly decent people managed to survive in the squalor that was this part of the great City of Glasgow. The tenants lived the life preyed upon by the minority whose complete disdain of the police and all type of authority caused so many problems for the majority.

"So, missus, what about my pound," said the voice at her side, his hand outstretched.

"Don't you be so bloody cheeky, wee man," Andy walked round the car to the pavement and finger wagging, scolded the lad. "Anyway," he cocked a head, hands on hips and stared at the smaller figure, "should you not be at school the day?"

"In-service day," was the immediate practised and cocky response.

"In-service day," Andy slowly repeated, stroking at his chin, his eyes narrowing. "So, if it's an in-service day, where's the rest of the kids round here then?"

Quicker than either detective could bat an eye, the wee redhead was off running, calling over his shoulder in a high-pitched, squeaky voice, "All cops are bastards."

Susie suppressed a giggle at his bravado, yet saddened that a small and bright lad like him should be out playing on the street during what was obviously a school day. She sighed and shook her head, then nodding towards the tenement main door, walked towards it. Already she was dismissing the lad from her thought and preparing herself for another lengthy and whining complaint from Missus Copeland, who consistently demanded her stolen property be returned while further demanding all junkie housebreakers and the McGriffen's in particular, be painfully and at length, executed.

Carol Meechan sat at her desk, munching absent-mindedly at her brown bread sandwich, oblivious to the crumbs that spilled onto her skirt, her thoughts reeling with relief that she had been able to unburden her worries to Morven Sutherland. She reached for the bottle of water, still surprised that Morven had been so attentive to Carol's suspicions and readily agreeing that she had done the right thing. She could clearly see that what she had learned and told Morven had upset the older woman. Taking notes, Morven had then sworn Carol to secrecy meantime and explained that to accuse such a prominent member of the bank and without real proof would not only provoke a public scandal and undoubtedly bring the bank to the attention of the media, but might backfire and involve Carol in a case of slander and false defamation.

Yes, Carol unconsciously nodded and almost sighed again with relief.

Morven was right; having now brought it to her attention it was wiser letting her deal with the issue.

The two women spent the next five minutes chatting, with Morven again congratulating Carol's partner John in finding full time employment. Carol boasted of the tremendous job he had made renovating the old Mini car and of her belief that it was this renovation that persuaded John's new boss to hire him.

At last, Morven pointedly glanced at her watch and taking the hint, Carol took her leave with a smile and grateful thanks to Morven for taking the time to listen to Carol's worries.

Returning to her own desk it seemed to Carol that suddenly, her day seemed a little brighter for sharing her concerns.

Rita Whyte had been born angry.

Just after four o'clock that afternoon, she angrily gave a mental two-fingered salute to the bastard and stormed out of the shop, furious that old Mohammed her boss had again rebuked her for her timekeeping. If it wasn't for the fact she and Ricky needed the money for their two weeks in Ibiza, she'd pack the crap job in tomorrow. Walking swiftly and reaching for her mobile phone, she crossed Dumbarton Road just as the pedestrian light turned red, her attention devoted to the phone and ignoring the glare from the driver forced to brake fiercely to avoid striking her.

"What!" she snapped at her mother then rolled her eyes upwards. "Can you not have gotten the messages yourself when you were out?" she hissed into the phone, then irately shaking her head, turned into the door of the small grocery shop.

She barged past the elderly woman on her way out the door who shaking her head, tut-tutted at the rudeness of the stocky-built young woman with the dyed blonde hair, the too tight short skirt and the mobile phone welded to her ear.

Eight minutes, two litres of milk, a pan loaf, two cans of beans and a large bar of Cadbury's chocolate later, Rita left the shop, struggling through the narrow door with the plastic bag in one hand and her small patent leather backpack in the other. The ringing of the mobile distracted her and hooking the backpack through the arm that carried the shopping bag, snarled, "What!"

Had she been a little more observant, Rita might have noticed the hooded figure standing across the road in the doorway of a shuttered shop whose attention was focused on the young woman wearing a black anorak jacket. But more importantly, the hooded figure guessed from the manner in which she waddled along the road, the heavy built woman did not seem to be an athletic type who might chase after him.

Peter Gibson, the New Business Investment Manager at the Caledonia Banking Group, smiled at his colleagues as the six men and two women stood and concluded their meeting.

"Got plans for the weekend, Peter?" asked Harry McPherson, the rugby playing senior Assistant Manager from Accounts as they moved towards the door of the boardroom.

"Usual stuff," he replied with practised ease, nodding as McPherson courteously held the door open to permit him to pass. "Gardening, maybe get the guttering round the house seen to. Just the same old, same old domestic duties," he sighed with a grin.

"Yeah, been there, done it," responded McPherson with a slap on the back. "Just see you don't fall off any ladders old son, not at your age," and moved away with a backward wave.

McPherson was simply being genial and not being deliberately offensive; nevertheless, he could not have guessed how the remark had wounded.

Peter, his mouth grimly set, watched the younger man walk towards his office door and clasped his file that little bit tighter. Thinks I'm fucking getting old, he inwardly seethed.

He was about to turn away when the Accounts door opened and Morven Sutherland, the Assistant Accounts manager and McPherson's deputy came through the door and almost bumped into McPherson. Peter saw them both laugh at their near collision then Sutherland reach up and in an openly proprietorial manner, gently brush some fluff from the collar of McPherson's suit jacket, her hand lingering just a little longer on his broad chest than was necessary.

It was common knowledge in the bank that McPherson, married with a recently born daughter, flirted outrageously with the younger female staff and Peter had learned in strict confidence, that McPherson had recently received a warning from HR regarding his behaviour.

Now, here he was, flirting with Morven Sutherland.

Or was she flirting with him, he wondered as a sudden jealous rage threatening to overtake him.

Turning on his heel, he strode towards the stairs that led to the upper floor and the corridor that in turn would take him to the Business Loans office.

Striding purposefully through the outer office, he ignored the startled glance of Maggie, his elderly secretary and the half dozen staff who made up his team and caught himself before he slammed his office door shut.

Forcing himself to calm down, he sat heavily at his wide desk and took a deep breath.

The framed photograph of his daughter Jennifer sat on his desktop stared accusingly at him.

He realised he was stupid to have taken McPherson's remark to heart, that the younger man was just being sociable. Still, now approaching his fifty-third birthday, Peter had recently developed a sensitivity to his age, not least since the annual appraisal interview some months previously when the HR Director had subtly suggested retirement might be an option, if Peter so desired. The inference that the bank was considering redundancies for supervisory staff and voluntary retirement for senior staff had not been lost on Peter nor had the jokes about more time for family and golf.

It was that meeting that had decided him.

His thoughts turned to that night when he was there with her, telling her of his decision; a decision that he was now coming to regret.

Things were almost getting out of hand and a sudden panic welled up in his chest. If he *was* to go through with it, they could not afford any slip-ups; not now when they were so very close.

He swallowed hard and thought again of his wife and daughter and of the betrayal he intended, but realised that while he might be able to lie and fool others, he could not lie to himself.

His eyes turned once more to the photograph and with a sigh, he softly smiled.

Just who am I kidding, he thought, slowly shaking his head and with a heavy heart, knew that he could not go through with it. The lingering doubt that plagued him since he had agreed to her scheme now beat at his conscience like a hammer.

A physical weakness came over him and he slowly sunk to his chair, exhaling softly through pursed lips and both hands placed palm down on the desk.

He swallowed hard and eyes narrowed in thought, made his final decision.

If he was astute enough, he could repair the damage he had done and with luck, no one would be the wiser.

All he had to do now was convince *her*.

Bobby McAllister answered the phone and listened for a few seconds later, then replied, "Right away boss."

Turning from his seat at the CID clerk's desk, he called across the room, "Waz, the DI wants a word, son," and message passed, bent his head to again pore over the newspaper and torture himself with The Herald's 'Wee Stinker' crossword.

Ahmed knocked on Bobby Franklin's open door and was waved inside.

"I had the Media Services on from Pitt Street, Waz. They're running an appeal in tonight's 'Glasgow News' about your street robbery inquiry. Just the usual, you know? Watch yourself missus or the bad man will get you," he chortled.

"Right boss, ah, do I need to give an interview or anything?"

"No, Waz," Franklin sat back and placing his hands behind his head, continued, "nothing like that," he smiled at the young Detective's eagerness. "You're not a film star yet, sonny. Only the big bosses get on the tele. The article will simply highlight a series of street robberies in the Partick area and request the public contact the polis, that being you I mean, if they have any information that might identify the culprit. On that point, have you and Des Mooney turned anything up yet?"

"No boss," Waz shook his head, "but it's early days yet. If you don't mind, we might change our shifts to cover the times when the robberies have occurred."

"And those times are?"

Waz grimaced. "Best I can offer is the four robberies…"

"That have been reported," Franklin pointedly interrupted.

"Remember son, not all victims come forward."

"True boss," Waz nodded. "As I was saying, the four *reported* robberies have all occurred between midday and early evening. Three of the robberies, if we excluded the one that occurred in the Maryhill Divisional area, occurred after the women had collected shopping from stores on Dumbarton Road. So, with your permission, we'd like to conduct a mobile patrol in the Partick area during those times with particular emphasis on Dumbarton Road."

Franklin's eyes narrowed.

"Dumbarton Road is a fair stretch of road son and it would mean tying up a car during those times Waz. We've only got the three inquiry cars for the rest of the guys and the Plain Clothes Squad will need their own car. They've a couple of jobs on the now, so you and Des are on shanks pony meantime."

"Shanks pony?"

"Hoofing it, son. On the beat, as it were."

Waz's disappointment was reflected in his face and the image of him and Des doing their Starsky and Hutch patrolling quickly disappeared. "Can I use my own car, boss?"

"No way," Franklin firmly slapped a hand down on the desktop. "You get caught using your own transport to patrol then it's a rubber heels issue. For one, it's not a police vehicle and for two, your insurance won't cover you if you're in an RTA or anything like that, okay?"

"Okay boss," replied a slightly chastened Waz.

"Look son, I know you're dead keen on catching this bugger. Tell you what," he almost smiled at Waz's disappointment, "let me phone over the Helen Street garage and see if the supervisor there can rustle something up, okay?"

"Right, boss." Waz turned to go and then stopped, turning towards the DI. "I'll not let you down boss."

"I know son, but here's a wee word of advice. I realise how keen you are and I'm confident you will go places if you stick this job, but listen to Des Mooney. The old guy's got a good head on his shoulders and a wealth of experience. If he tells you something, guaranteed its set in stone. Okay?"

Waz flashed a toothy grin. "Got it boss," and closed the door behind him.

Her ears ringing from Missus Copeland's whining complaint, Susie Gibson stepped from the darkness into the bright sunlight through the close door held open by Andy Brownlie. Standing in the path, she stopped to take a deep breath.

"Bloody hell, can that woman talk," Andy shook his head at her side and stepping in front of her, made his way towards the CID car.

She smiled and stepping from the tenement path onto the pavement, began walking towards the passenger. Her peripheral vision caught a slight movement and that's when she saw the small, red haired lad from before, still wearing the Celtic top, trying to conceal himself behind an overgrown hedge in the garden of the ground floor flat in the tenement across the road.

Her curiosity aroused, Susie watched him as she reached for the door handle then saw the small boy's head snap upwards to stare at the tenement behind her. Some unexplainable instinct caused her to turn sharply round and move away from the car. In that split second turning her head and glancing upwards, she saw a flash streaking through the air and then a glass bottle crashed onto the pavement, striking the ground almost where she had been standing, shattering and sending splinters like shrapnel rattling against the side of the car.

"*WHAT THE FUCK....!*" screamed Andy, racing from the driver's side of the car towards her.

Susie's eyes had followed the path of the thrown bottle, but now she quickly turned her head upwards to stare at the tenement.

She counted five lounge windows that were wide open; one on the first, two on the second and two on the third floor, anyone from which the bottle might have been thrown, but now there was no face at any of the windows.

Andy grabbed at her arm, his face pale and concerned.

"Did it hit you Susie, are you all right hen? Susie!" he shook her.

"I'm fine, I'm fine," she repeated. She turned to stare across the road, but the small lad had run off and was nowhere to be seen. She already realised he had known what was to occur and was probably there to alert whoever had thrown the bottle that Susie and Andy were about to exit the close.

The wee shite, she inwardly snarled.

"I'll get some of the glass, maybe get a print," suggested Andy, his handkerchief already in his hand.

"Leave it," she snapped at him, her voice sharper than she had meant and still staring upwards at the tenement building.

Softer now, she explained, her voice calmer than she felt. "It's no use to us unless we can state we saw who threw it Andy. A defence against a culprit's prints on the glass would be that the bottle was discarded in the rubbish bin and whoever threw it must have gotten it from there."

"It'll have been one of those fucking McGriffen's," he snarled at her, then angrily suggested, "Why don't we go and knock on their door? Fuck that, kick it in!"

She realised he had not seen or taken any notice of the small boy who undoubtedly had been acting as a watcher or in Glasgow parlance, 'keeping edgy'.

She smiled at Andy and his concern for her, conscious now that after her close escape from injury, her stomach was churning.

She softly exhaled and said, "No, there's no point in acting like bogeymen. Whoever threw the bottle will know we can't arrest without evidence, so the next time we knock on their door *or* kick it in," she added with a smile, "we'll have the evidence to arrest somebody."

"Right," she pulled open the passenger door, "We'll call it one nil to the McGriffen's for now, so let's get back to the office," and talking a deep breath, grinned, "I could do with a cuppa."

CHAPTER 5

Waz Ahmed had one arm in his anorak and was preparing to go home, his mouth already salivating by the promise of one of his wife Alima's curries when Bobby McAllister, the CID clerk shouted from his desk.

"Waz, that's a report of another street robbery, less than half an hour ago. Some woman got herself mugged down in Dumbarton Road," McAllister waved a crime report at Waz. "The boss told me you're dealing with them. That right?"

Waz sighed and slipping the anorak back across his desk chair, strode over to collect the report.

"Aye, Bobby. It's Des Mooney and me that are collating the muggings," then with a small smile, added, "I mean the street robberies."

He read the short, concise report and saw with some relief that as the complainer was uninjured she was on her way to her home address at Barshaw Road in Penilee and requested the CID contact her the following day at her place of work, the newsagents shop with an address in Dumbarton Road.

So, he mused, the curry might be on after all.

Returning to his desk, Waz continued reading the report and unconsciously nodded at the suspects description, almost certain that this was now the fifth reported robbery that could be attributed to the suspect.

He shrugged into his anorak, bade farewell to McAllister and prepared to make his way home.

Unusually for the deputy Assistant Accounts Manager, Morven Sutherland slipped on her coat and made to leave the bank earlier than most of her colleagues.

Thoughtfully, she made her way towards the exit door and began to walk through the city centre streets towards the converted warehouse in Brown Street, where her upmarket flat was located in the Anderston district.

Sutherland normally took delight in the attention her good looks received from the passing male pedestrians, but today her attention was elsewhere, for the midday meeting with Carol Meechan had shocked her.

The younger woman was far more astute that Sutherland would have guessed and her accusation against Meechan's manager completely taken Sutherland by surprise.

Her explanation as to how she had come by her suspicions seemed to indicate that Meechan was far brighter than Sutherland had realised, but how to deal with the issue; well, she unconsciously bit at her lower lip, that was another problem.

Turning into Bothwell Street, she stopped at the Tesco Express and purchased milk and a small bag of groceries, as well as that evening's edition of the 'Glasgow News.'

At the checkout till the youthful shop assistant blushed and even considered offering to carry her shopping home, so smitten was he by the glamorous Sutherland's smile of thanks.

Making her way outside, her mind too wrapped up recollecting her meeting with Meechan to even pay any attention to the youth, Sutherland continued on her way home.

First thing she would do she decided, was she would phone him and bugger anything else; they had to meet and it must be tonight.

Leigh Gallagher almost punched the air in delight, ignoring the pain in his left shin.

The fat bird's purse had revealed over eighty quid in used notes and a handful of coins. He had kept the single credit card, seeing that it didn't have 'Miss' or Mrs' on it but just an initial and the fat bird's name, 'M Whyte'. It occurred to him that it might be useful, that maybe some time in the future he might use it as an ID, pretend to be 'Martin Whyte' or something like that.

Slipping the money and card into the pocket of the yellow coloured cagoule jacket, he tucked the hood of the sweat top inside the jacket and as casually as his could, began to walk homewards towards Shakespeare Street, all the while keeping a furtive eye open for the police.

It was when he turned the corner from Hotspur Street into Shakespeare Street that he saw her. His throat tightened.

Aged just sixteen, Chloe Ferguson stood outside her tenement close chatting to a friend. With her naturally curled blonde hair and clear skin she was already displaying a body that attracted young men and was the fantasy of most of her male neighbours, regardless of their age.

A little over five feet four inches in height, Chloe's buxom fullness complimented her hourglass figure and she had quickly come to realise the sensual power she exuded.

Her loosely knotted school tie hung down on the tight, white coloured school blouse that was tucked into the short, grey coloured school skirt that barely covered her white thighs. Her blazer was draped over her left arm and her satchel over her left shoulder while Leigh could see the other hand held her mobile phone.

Before she saw him, Leigh ducked into a close and fetching his own mobile from his pocket, rang her number. He watched as she startled and throwing an empty crisp bag to the ground, licked at her fingers and answered, "Hello?"

"I can see you," he drawled, teasing her.

He watched from the corner of the close as her head snapped about, trying to spot him.

"Where are you, you dick," she replied, grinning at the phone, her head turning as she sought to find him.

"Get rid of your pal," he whispered into the phone, "and meet me in my close."

"What for?" she replied, glancing slyly at her friend, but already knowing why Leigh wanted to see her.

A thrill of anticipation swept through her.

"Come meet me and you'll find out," he replied, his mouth suddenly dry as he watched her and imagined what lay beneath the tightness of her blouse.

"Hang on," she said and saw her speak to the other girl who quickly walked off in the other direction, giving a small farewell wave as she left.

"Where are you?" she asked again, her head turning and taking a few steps towards the roadway to glance up and down Shakespeare Street.

"My close, one minute," he replied, then pressed the red button on his phone, confident her curiosity would get the better of her and she would meet him in number eighty-six.

He watched Chloe place her phone in her satchel and head still turning back and forth to find him, walk towards Leigh's close.

He hurriedly ran though to the rear of the close and into the back court of the tenements, running towards the rear of his own close and excited at the unexpected encounter. Panting slightly, he arrived at the rear of number eighty-six and stood within the close at the bottom of the stairs, trying to control his breathing and decided he would pretend surprise at her arrival.

Chloe entered the front of the close, her eyes narrowing, but smiling at him.

"Have you been here all the time?" she asked.

"Sorry, you are again?"

"Fucking chancer," she grinned at him and dropping her satchel and blazer, wrapped her arms about his neck and began to kiss him.

"Up here, quick," he bent and lifting her blazer and satchel with sudden urgency began to pull her gently up the stairs towards the upper half-landing.

"What are you like?" she teased him, pretending reluctance, but now as eager as Leigh to climb the stairs.

In the quiet of the cold, semi-dark half-landing, they clinched together, lips locked while his fingers searched for the buttons of her blouse.

Her tongue explored his mouth and with a little disgust, he became acutely aware of the pungent smell and taste of the cheese and onion crisps she had just earlier consumed, however, not enough disgust to prevent his furtive if clumsy attempt to remove her clothing.

"Don't," she sighed, pushing at his hands, but not as forcefully as she might and afraid if she resisted too strongly he might give up. He pulled her blouse free from the waistband of her skirt and his hand explored the soft skin of her stomach then crept with stealth till he touched the cotton of her bra.

"No, Leigh," she whispered, pushing her breast against his hand and willing him to continue, her own fingers now helping him undo the buttons of her blouse.

His trembling fingers sneaked beneath the constraining fabric of her bra, forcing the bra upwards until he cupped her ample breast, her nipple brushing the palm of his hand that was becoming firm and erect in the chilled atmosphere of the close.

Aroused, he pushed his groin against her thigh, growing more excited when she responded by lifting then sliding her leg around his and pulling him closer to her.

His free hand slid down her hip, over the waistband of her skirt and clumsily grabbed at the tight material to pull it upwards. Her hand grabbed at his hand and guided his fingers onto the elastic of her knickers and with her help he began to slide the knickers down. Chloe moaned lustfully and thrust her tongue deeper into his throat, causing him to gag involuntarily.

He coughed, spluttered then jerking his head back, uncontrollably sneezed, splattering her face with mucous.

"Fuck's sake!" she shrank back in disgust, instinctively wiping her face with her hand, her blouse partly undone and left breast fully exposed.

Horrified, his eyes opened wide as he sniffed and rubbed at his nose with the back of his hand.

"Sorry, Chloe," he mumbled and reached again for her.

Quickly and with unexpected modesty, she turned away from him and pulling her bra cup down, began to button her blouse.

He exhaled and stood watching her, overcome by a feeling of remorse and wilting in his trousers, uncertain what to say other than numbly repeat, "Sorry."

"Aye, well, sorry doesn't cut it Leigh, snotting onto my face like that," she replied, bending over and reaching into her satchel for a handkerchief.

Bent over from the waist as she was, the short tight skirt rode up, exposing the whiteness of the back of her thighs and his desire overtook common sense. With a grin, he placed his hands about her hips, forcing his groin into her buttocks.

His mistaken attempt at reconciliation didn't work out as Leigh expected and to his shock, her reaction took him by complete surprise.

Chloe pulled away from his grasp and stood upright, then whirled about so swiftly he had no time to avoid the hand she swung that slapped him on the face.

Shocked, he stood back and stared at her with anger then angrily raised a clenched fist.

"Try it, ya bastard," she hissed at him, her eyes shining with anger, "and my brothers will fucking chib you!"

Leigh hesitated, for Chloe's brothers, one a year younger than Leigh and one a little over two years older, were both known throughout the area as headcases and each had already accrued multiple convictions for violent assault.

"What the fuck was that for?" he backed away and whined at her, rubbing his cheek that stung from her blow.

"Don't you get it, you fucking idiot? You don't take advantage when I'm pissed at you," she hissed at him.

The seconds passed as they stared angrily at each other, each unwilling to give ground.

Leigh did not have the maturity or experience to accept his mistake and unable to reason with her, pushed roughly past her and with a final, "Fuck you," quickly made his way upstairs to his home on the second floor.

Chloe, tears stinging her eyes at her perceived humiliation, gathered her blazer and satchel into her arms and hurriedly made her way downstairs towards the close front entrance.

The bookmaker situated just off the corner of Maryhill Road and Garrioch Road was not a regular venue for Magnus Gallagher, but he had his occasional visits become known to the staff for his politeness and courtesy. The Irishman, they agreed, was always a welcome punter, though not usually a successful one. However, today seemed to be different and to his surprise, albeit that Magnus's bets never exceeded ten pounds, he walked from the bookies with over one hundred and thirty pounds in his back pocket. A small fortune to a man whose weekly income barely covered the most basic bills that needed to be paid simply to keep body and soul together.

Standing on the pavement outside the bookies, Magnus turned his head towards the skies, to the Heaven that he knew for certainty existed and with a brief but heart-felt prayer, thanked God for His kindness and his beloved Mary, who continued to watch over him and their two sons.

He took a deep breath and slowly began to walk towards the Maryhill shopping centre, unable to contain a smile for Magnus knew that what he could not previously afford, he could now purchase and that a small sum of the money was already accounted for. It also struck him that by spending the forty-eight pounds, he would, in some way repay the kindness the good Lord had bestowed upon him.

With a new found spring in his step, he covered the brief walk in a few minutes and pushed through the glass door into the centre. Smiling at the few neighbours he recognised, Magnus made his way to the cancer charity shop and nodding to the young assistant, stepped into the rear room. With a little relief, he saw they were still there and smiled even wider; since his last visit the price had dropped to forty pounds.

His eyes narrowed as a little guilt settled upon his shoulders, feeling that he was not just getting a bargain, but somehow would be cheating the charity of the eight extra pounds he had been prepared to pay. No, he would not do that; certainly not after being gifted the win.

He unconsciously nodded as he made his decision. He would pay the original price for in his heart, Magnus believed that God had struck a deal with His servant and who was he to quibble with the Almighty.

"Can I help you there pal?" asked the young assistant at his elbow.

"Aye, son," he pointed with a smile, "these two here. Do you deliver?"

The youth grimaced. "We do, but it would cost you extra, depending where you live, I'm afraid."

"I'm in Shakespeare Street, number eighty-six. What would be the cost to deliver there, son?"

"Ten quid extra; sorry," the lad added with a frown.

The younger man guessed the extra ten quid was a lot for the old Irishman to pay, but didn't have the authority to make an arrangement and sod's law, the manager wasn't in today.

Magnus chewed at his lower lip and then a thought struck him.

"If I was to pay now, could I arrange for them to be uplifted, say tomorrow?"

"Shouldn't be a problem if you pay for them," the youth hesitated, "but we can't keep them for too long, you understand. New stock is always coming in and that."

Magnus nodded, but his thoughts were already on the arrangement he would make. He didn't own a mobile and in truth just couldn't afford one, so would have to make the phone call when he arrived home.

With a smile he paid the surprised assistant, explaining the extra money was for a good cause then with receipt in hand, left the shop feeling that little better about life.

For the first time that week or in as many weeks as she could remember, Susie Gibson finished work and left Baird Street before her neighbour, Andy Brownlie.

At his insistence, he had persuaded her to let him finish the two reports to the Procurator Fiscal they were collaborating on, further insisting he needed the experience.

Rather than argue, she relented and now, here she was turning into her road and with sudden shock, unable to recall making the journey home.

Her eyes narrowed in surprise when she saw Peter's car parked in the street outside the house. It was his habit to reverse his precious Mercedes convertible into the driveway so she assumed that he was home to collect something then going out again in the evening. Not that there was anything new there, she inwardly scowled.

She parked her Honda in the driveway and getting out of the car, glanced up to see Jenny's window open and through which she could hear the muted sounds of Rihanna belting out her latest hit. Susie shook her head in wonderment, recalling that as a teenager she had needed complete silence when studying.

She opened the front door, half expecting to hear Peter shuffling about upstairs, but instead found him sitting at the kitchen table wearing his suit jacket, his mobile phone in front of him and apparently deep in thought.

He turned as she walked in and to her surprise, smiled at her. "Didn't hear you arrive," he said and then glancing at the clock, added, "You're home early tonight."

Susie dumped her handbag on the table and turned to switch on the electric kettle, replying over her shoulder, "I had an easy day of it. How was yours?"

He didn't immediately answer, then quietly said, "Interesting."

In times past, she might have queried that one word response, but of late had learned Peter no longer wished to discuss his work so let it go.

From the wall cupboard, she fetched a mug and spooned coffee into it then with her back still to him, placed both hands on the worktop and asked, "Are you staying for dinner or going back out again?" but already knowing what his answer would be.

Again, Peter seemed to hesitate than replied, "I've got an informal investors meeting to attend at one of the city hotels, but I won't be late."

The kettle boiled and clicked off and reaching for it, filled her mug then holding it one hand with the spoon in the other, turned towards him.

Before she could respond, he continued, "I won't be too late. Why don't you hold off on dinner and I'll bring something in for the both of us. A takeaway curry, maybe. Well," he softly smiled and glanced upwards to the ceiling, "for the three of us if Jennifer is speaking to me again. I shouldn't be any longer than say, an hour?"

Surprised, she was taken aback. The very fact that they were even engaged in conversation had thrown her, but now Peter was actually suggesting sitting down at a meal together. He saw suspicion register on her face and again slowly smiled, uncertainty dancing about his face.

"Maybe it's about time that you and I sat down together and had a chat, Susan. A long chat, if you're agreeable. About us I mean," and shrugging his shoulders, added, "How we might try and mend things between us."

Automatically stirring the coffee, she dared not breathe, but could only watch stony-faced as he rose from the table and gave her a slight nod then heard him walk along the hallway to the front door, hearing it close behind him.

In the distance, she heard his car engine start and he was gone.

CHAPTER 6

Waz Ahmed was fortunate to find an empty parking space not to far from his tenement close in Pollokshaws and locked his Ford Fiesta, stopped in at his local newsagents to purchase that evening's edition of the 'Glasgow News'. Scanning the paper as he walked towards his close, he quickly found the article about the robberies and appeal for witnesses on the third page then reading his own name, grinned while muttering, "Would never have guessed I'd find myself on page three."

Buoyed by the article, he raced up the stairs to his first floor flat and unlocked the front door to the mouth-watering, aromatic smell of his wife Alima's chicken curry. Softly closing the front door, he could hear the giggles of their daughter Munawar, now a lively nine months old, from the front room and found her lying naked on her back on a rug while Alima smothered her soft belly with raspberry kisses. The scene made him catch his breath and brought a smile to his face and once more, Waz thanked and blessed Allah who in his wisdom had brought Waz and Alima together.

"So," he shrugged off his jacket and walking over, dropped to his knees beside his wife, "how are my two wee Glesga birds today, then girls?"

Munawar, at first startled by her father's sudden appearance, giggled even more and reached with her arms to be lifted by him, her small fingers grabbing at him.

While he threw his shrieking daughter into the air, Alima reached across and drawing him to her, placed a sloppy kiss on his lips and grinning, said, "Have a few minutes with the wean and I'll get the dinner on."

Waz, holding the squealing Munawar over his shoulder, grabbed Alima by the back of her neck before she could rise and gently pulling her to him, kissed her again.

"Miss me?" he smiled at her.

"Always," she returned his smile and one hand on his shoulder to support herself, stood upright and made her way into the kitchen.

Later, they sat at the solid, square wooden table Alima had rescued from a charity shop with Munawar in her high chair between them, the spoon discarded in favour of her hands with which she messily decorated the chair's tray.

"How was school?" he asked.

Alima, a primary teacher at a local school, at length recounted the difficulties of dealing with a class of ten year olds, some of whom had recently arrived from the Eastern European nations and who were with difficulty, trying to not only come to terms with the complexities of the English language, but also the local Glasgow dialect.

"I mean," she sighed, "it's not the fault of the parents or, for that matter, the school. Most of the parents I've met are keen their kids learn English. They fully understand that if the children are going to survive and thrive in Scotland, they can only do so if they speak the language."

He glanced up and saw her biting at her lower lip.

"What?" he asked her, his eyes narrowing in suspicion.

Alima sighed and placed her cutlery down. "Now Waseem, don't get annoyed with me."

He sat back in his chair and like her, placed his cutlery down. Alima only called him Waseem when she was about to give him some bad news.

He saw her throat tighten as she swallowed hard and then she leaned forward and said, "I've volunteered to run an after school class for the kids who are struggling with English. It's only for two hours, two nights a week. The council have agreed that they will pay the janitor to keep the school open on those nights, but staff wishing to volunteer will be unpaid. It's only me and Missus McKenna who have volunteered."

He stared at his wife, her long, shiny black hair tied back to reveal a face that was clear skinned and, in his mind, beautiful. How he loved this woman.

Pretending to be stern, he replied, "And you think I would object, why?"

She saw right through him and grinning, reached for his hand, squeezing it tightly.

"It might mean asking my parents to babysit Munawar while I'm at the class for those two nights."

He glanced at his daughter, wide eyed and grinning with little lumps of chicken hanging from her hair and chin, her bib polka dotted with food stains. The spoon held in her right hand now used as a drumstick.

"Mmm, that might be a problem," he theatrically grimaced at the giggling toddler, but knew with certainty her parents reaction when asked to spend time with their beloved granddaughter.

Magnus Gallagher arrived home a little breathless, quietly excited at Leigh's reaction when he would discover what his father had purchased, but already decided not to tell his son; he would surprise him when they were collected and in place.

Hanging his jacket in the neatly ordered hall cupboard, Magnus could hear his son's bed creaking and first knocking on the door, popped his head in to let Leigh know that he was home.

He could not guess that Leigh was still smarting from his argument with Chloe Ferguson.

"I'll pop on the dinner," he said, then holding up a plastic carrier bag, nodded at it and added, "mince and tatties all right with you son?"

Leigh lying on his bed with earphones plugged into his mobile phone, nodded.

Magnus closed the door and smiled. He was himself a member of The Pioneer Total Abstinence Association of the Sacred Heart, the Irish organisation for Roman Catholic teetotalers, but knowing that Leigh liked a lager didn't mean he couldn't buy his son a couple of cans of Tennents to have as a wee treat with his dinner.

First though he had the phone call to make.

Magnus dialed the number and when the call was answered, "St Joseph's presbytery," he smiled and said, "Hello, Missus O'Dowd, it's myself here. Can I speak to my son?"

"Ah, Magnus," she cheerfully replied with her soft Donegal accent, "hang on and I'll shout him for you."

He listened as the phone was placed down and then her voice echoed as she called, "Father Patrick, it's your Da on the line."

Less than a minute later, his son lifted the phone and said, "Hi Da, what's up?"

Almost whispering for fear that Leigh might hear, Magnus asked Patrick to help him collect the purchase tomorrow from the charity shop. "You've still got use of the parish van, haven't you, Pat?" "Aye, Da, but not tomorrow I'm afraid. The vans out on a job, helping a parishioner move from her house to a nursing home, but I'll definitely have the use of it the next day though."
Slightly disappointed, Magnus nodded at the handset and said, "Well, that will need to do. I'll see you at Maryhill shopping centre then, say ten in the morning at the charity shop, if that suits you son."
"Dead on," replied Patrick, "I'll see you there and God Bless you, Da."
"No son," replied Magnus, smiling at the old joke between them, "God Bless *you*, son."
Magnus fetched the charity shop till receipt from his trouser pocket and with a disappointed sigh, phoned the number on the receipt to cancel the pick-up for tomorrow and rearranged it for the following day.

Morven Sutherland returned sweaty and tired from her hour-long kickboxing workout in the private gym, located in the basement of the luxury flats in Brown Street. The once seedy and derelict warehouse had a year previously been totally renovated, the building split into four floors, each of the ground and first two floors now two-bedroom apartments. The four more expensive and overly large top floor apartments, where she resided, had but one large bedroom, but with the attraction of a residents elevator from the privately accessed car park in the basement that bypassed the other floors and a balcony that overlooked the street outside.
Freshly bathed and wearing nothing other than a short, black coloured silk slip beneath her short, cream coloured dressing robe, she sat relaxing in the lounge of her flat and sipped at the chilled Chardonnay, the strains of a *Harry Connick Jnr* song playing softly on the CD player. That evening's edition of the 'Glasgow News' lay as yet unread and folded on the couch beside her.
She thought of her day at work, the meeting with Carol Meechan and the recent attentiveness she was receiving from Harry McPherson. Now, she smiled and glanced at her long fingers holding the wine glass, there was a body she could enjoy running her hands over,

recalling the firmness of his muscular arms and the faint scent of the pine cologne he favoured. She was aware it was no secret the married McPherson, to ape a male expression, liked to play away, but continued to smile as she wryly admitted that she herself was no stranger to the intrigue of infidelity.

It occurred to her that if things did not work out as she had planned, the flirtation she had instigated over the last few days with McPherson might just come in useful. It was, she thoughtfully nodded her head, always prudent to have a back-up plan.

She stroked the skin on her flawless arm, smiling that her admission to be in her mid-thirties was documented with the bank's HR Department, that she had never married nor even had a relationship that lasted beyond two years.

However, Morven Sutherland was no stranger to the ways of men or…she inwardly grinned, the sexual desires of those who bedded her.

While she liked men and in particular, men who were not only handsome, but wielded authority too, she would be the first to admit that it was the finer things in life that she preferred to enjoy.

Men might come and men might go, but money and influence; these were the real attraction for Morven Sutherland.

She continued to smile and sipped at her wine, closing her eyes and imagining what it might be like to bed the handsome and athletic McPherson, but was realistically aware that to invite him to her flat might complicate what was already proving to be a problem.

Still, she sighed, stroking at the silk material that clung to her body as a strong, sexual feeling coursed through her body her mind racing with possibilities and potential problems.

Considering these problems, her thoughts again turned to the meeting with Carol Meechan. The younger woman had proved to be far brighter than she had believed and was certainly now one more issue that she would need to consider.

Unconsciously, she ran the forefinger of her free hand round the thin gold chain about her neck. However, that particular issue would have to be discussed before she could come to a decision.

His unexpected text message to herald his visit had surprised her and so she had bathed and readied herself for more of his attention. She knew he loved to see her in nothing more than the slip and would tease him while she very slowly slipped it over her head while he watched from her bed.

The sudden noise of the buzzer sounding startled her and announced she had a visitor at the door of the elevator in the basement level of the car park. Uncrossing her legs, she arose too quickly from the couch and her hand shook, spilling some of the wine onto her dressing gown.

"Damn," she irritably muttered, placing the glass down onto a table coaster and wiping with her hand at the small spillage, uncrossed her long legs and slid from the couch towards the flat door.

With a smile she acknowledged the call on the intercom and pressed the button on the wall that allowed her visitor access to the resident's elevator.

Leigh Gallagher, still angry after his confrontation with Chloe, poured the second of his lagers into the glass and finished the drink with one swallow.

His father, slightly concerned, stared across the table at him and asked, "Are you all right there, Leigh? Is there anything the matter son?"

"No Da, I'm fine. Don't go on, please," he snapped, yet feeling slightly guilty that the old man had prepared such a nice meal and bought him the two cans.

"Look, I'm going out for a walk, I'll be back soon," he shuffled backwards, scraping the chair legs against the linoleum floor.

"Ah, right son," nodded Magnus, then reaching into his trousers pocket, smiled and handed two notes to Leigh.

"What's this Da, where d you get forty quid?"

His father tapped the side of his nose and continuing to smile, replied, "The good Lord smiled on the gee-gee's today and pointed me towards a winner, so you take that money and you go out and buy yourself a couple of pints, there's a good lad. I know that you're feeling down the now because there's no work out there for a young lad like you and I know you're trying your very best. I feel for you son, I really do," he said, reaching across the table to stroke at Leigh's arm. "Something will come up soon, I'm sure of it. In fact," he stood and began to clear away the table, "once I've had a read of my paper and a cuppa, I'm off down to the chapel for evening mass so I'll have a wee word with the man upstairs and put in a good word for you, eh?"

He almost refused to take the money and guessed that whatever money his father had won, the forty pound would probably be a good part of it, but to decline the cash might make the old man suspicious and Leigh couldn't afford for his father to suspect that his son had an alternative source of income.

"Thanks Da," he mumbled, then did something he hadn't done for some time; he bent over and gave his father a hug.

Brief as it was Magnus's chest swelled with pride that no matter what life threw at his family, they still stood together.

He patted at Leigh's arm as his son broke free and left the kitchen and a minute later, Magnus heard the front door close.

Emma Saunders had never committed a crime in her life. In fact, in her eighteen years of privileged and comfortable life, she had not even as much as spoken with a police officer, now here she was, standing in the cold dingy and smelly dark close about to buy drugs from some fucking junkie.

She shivered, but more with anxiety than the cold and wrapped her arms about her and again wondered how she had gotten herself into this bloody mess and all because of a stupid boast.

Bugger!

If only she hadn't opened her big mouth and tried to impress the others, she inwardly raged, but it was too late now. She had promised and that cow Morag Peterson, the bitch, would tell everyone in their year that little Emma was nothing but a liar and her credibility among the other sixth formers would undoubtedly be shot to shit.

To travel to this dingy part of Glasgow, she had dressed down in jeans, FKNY of course and a nondescript CK jacket that she had had for over a year that her mother insisted be thrown out to one of those charity places that take good quality clothing. On her back was a small bright yellow coloured GO backpack Emma had filled with clothing to conceal the pills. Only now, standing in this vile place, she wished she had worn something a little warmer than *chic*.

She glanced about her. Even finding this place in Partick had been a nightmare, travelling from Central Station in the back of a shabby taxi that had indescribable stains on the seats. Passing along

Dumbarton Road she imagined all sorts of horrors taking place within the pokey little flats in these awful, claustrophobic tenement buildings. The taxi driver had been no help. Could hardly even speak English, the bloody foreigner and after all, one simply does not say, '*Take me to buy eccies please*', does one?

Of course, she had known that such places existed outside her Newton Mearns enclave, but never imagined she would actually *find* herself here.

Freddy Mason-Collins had been of no use; happy enough to give her an address where he assured her she could purchase the pills, but fuck all bottle when she asked him to accompanying her here. Wanker!

Her face reddened, recalling the sneering she had endured this morning in the sixth form recreation room when she offered to collect the eccies for Saturday night's party at the home of bitch-face Morag Peterson's parent's.

She would show them, she bristled.

She clenched her fists and raised one hand, hesitantly preparing herself to knock on the badly hung front door of the ground floor flat. Some time in the past the door seemed to have incurred damage, for where the locks should have been were now bits of wood inexpertly nailed or screwed to the one remaining large, metal lock that seemed like some sort of prop from a Harry Potter film.

Gathering her will power, Emma took a deep breath, a huge mistake because of the nauseous smell in the close, and banged upon the door.

She stood back in alarm when a dog began barking furiously on the other side.

She could hear a shuffling noise and then a man's voice asked, "Who is it?"

Why is this so *fucking* difficult, she inwardly fumed.

"Ah, sorry to bother you sir," she replied, while wondering at her stupidity in calling a drug dealer 'sir', "but I was wondering if I might make a purchase?"

Now she was literally hopping from foot to foot with the sudden realisation she needed to pee.

Damn that large latte.

"Who is it?" the voice asked again, but this time with a little more uncertainty.

"Ah, my name's…" she hesitated, then with a blinding flash of inspiration, said, "Morag Peterson."

That would teach the cow if the drug dealer ever wanted to track her down and blackmail her, she gleefully thought, her imagination now running wild.

"I don't know any fucking Mary Peterson."

"No, not Mary, *Morag*," she firmly replied, but not without some frustration. "Look, I was told that I might be able to get some, ah, things from you," she grimaced, wondering how one explained the prospective purchase of eccie tablets through a closed door.

"You mean eccies hen?"

"Ah yes, eccies sir," she leaned towards the door, almost whispering her response and thinking there it was again, the 'sir' word.

"That's the flat above me, hen. Just ask to speak with Billy," said the man's voice, then she heard him shuffle away.

Dumbstruck, Emma could only stare at the door.

Freddy fucking Mason-Collins told her the ground flat door. Her eyes narrowed. Just wait till she got her hands on him.

It took Emma all of four minutes to meet and greet Billy in the flat above and conclude her purchase of twenty illicit Ecstasy tablets that with trembling fingers, she secreted in the bottom of her backpack.

Happy now, but still needing to pee, she strode from the close, already envisioning Morag bitch-face Peterson's face when Emma arrived at the party with the eccies.

John Paterson stopped off at the Tesco store in Dumbarton Road and bought a bottle of red wine to present to his girlfriend Carol, along with the large bunch of flowers.

Because it was nearing the evening, the store was selling the flowers at a discounted price and though John's first paycheck was still some days away, he believed that Carol more than deserved the flowers.

The last year had been struggle, supporting him while he followed his dream of working with and renovating classic cars. Soon, he had promised her, he would make a name for himself among the Scottish collectors of such vehicles and then they might consider opening their own service and repair station, fulfilling the dream he had nurtured since childhood.

He knew Carol loved him and though unspoken, waited patiently these last four years for him to name a date.

Standing at the check-out till, he mused that if everything went well with this job where the owner had hinted at retiring within the next two years, then if the business was available for purchasing, it might mean that date could be sooner than later.

Returning to his Mini, John carefully joined the traffic and drove to the flat in Lawrie Street, nodding at his good luck to find a parking space almost outside the close at number 165.

Locking the car, he glanced up at the bay window and smiled when he saw the light on.

In the flat, Carol Meechan heard the front door open and John call out, "Honey, I'm home," in a false American accent, parodying a US sitcom show they both enjoyed.

"In here," she replied and turned to see her boyfriend holding out a huge bunch of flowers and with a bottle of wine in the other hand.

"For my girl," he grinned at her, planting a sloppy kiss on her lips.

"They're lovely," she cooed, then wrinkling her nose and with a firmer voice, added, "you smell of paint and turps or something. Go and get a shower. Dinner will be in five minutes so you're warned."

John turned and strode into the bathroom, wresting out of the coveralls and turned on the baths taps to shower mode.

Stripped, he stepped across the lip of the bath and dipped his head under the cascading water, turning when Carol entered the steam-filled room and sat on the wicker laundry basket.

"I had a chat with one of my managers today," she said.

"What about," he began and then teasingly added, "don't tell me. You're getting sacked?"

"No," she grinned at the figure behind the nylon shower curtain, her eyes running up and down his naked torso. "A week ago, I came across something that disturbed me in the accounts I deal with. Quite a lot of money," and she repeated stressing, "*a lot of money* is going into accounts I couldn't understand. I wasn't too certain what to do about it, but Miss Sutherland, the manager I spoke with," she explained, "told me that she would be dealing with it now. Kind of takes the pressure off me."

John pulled the light green coloured nylon curtain aside and poking a forefinger into each ear to clear it of soap, stared down at her.

"Sorry love, I only heard a bit of that and besides, you know me when it comes to figures. I can't even balance my own account, let alone anyone else's. This thing you're talking about. Has it been worrying you or something?"

Carol grimaced. "Mmm, it was a bit yeah. I couldn't make head or tale of a number of transactions across several accounts. Well, a large number of accounts really and it's added up to *quite* a tidy sum."

She took a deep breath while John returned to soaping himself, half listening to her through the noise of the water falling.

"Anyway," she stood and with a smile of devilment, crept towards the sink basin, reaching out while slyly watching John's figure behind the curtain, "It's in my manager's hands now, so no longer my concern."

With that Carol turned on the hot tap and laughingly rushed from the bathroom when she heard John yelp in shock as the hot water from the shower was diverted to the sink basin while the cold water continued to cascade down upon him.

Emma Saunders left the shop carrying a plastic bag containing her purchases, a bottle of water and chocolate bar. The shopkeeper had been of no bloody use, she fumed, reaching into the bag for the bottle and then stopped. The last thing she needed right now was more fluid, not when the urge to pee was greater than ever.

She began to walk briskly towards the Underground station that the shopkeeper assured her would take her straight to Argyle Street and then a short walk to Central Station.

Across the road, Leigh Gallagher watched the young woman with the brightly coloured yellow backpack, her blonde hair tied in a ponytail and carrying a plastic bag. The girl's blonde hair reminded him of Chloe and his lip curled at the memory of their earlier tryst in the close. A rage overtook him and though the girl was younger and fitter looking than the type of woman he would normally consider robbing, in his mind he would be revenging himself on Chloe. Glancing about him to ensure there was no coppers about, he began to follow her, a short distance behind.

CHAPTER 7

He had been gone for over thirty minutes when Susie Gibson knocked on her daughter's door twice, the second time a little louder in an effort to be heard over Jenny's music.

Jenny snatched the door open, her sullen face glaring at her mother. "What?"

Gripping her hands while inwardly reminding herself to remain calm, Susie forced a smile and said, "Look, your dad has popped out to one of his meetings and he's bringing food in for the three of us." She raised her hands, palms outward and slowly continued, "I know you're not keen on the idea, but I thought it would be nice of we could sit together at the table."

Jenny blinked in surprise. "You mean after all that has happened, the three of us together? Like some fucking ordinary family?"

Susie inwardly flinched at Jenny's expletive, but wisely decided now was not the time to chastise her for her language, not when she was so wound up. Inhaling, she took a deep breath and nodded. "That's what I said, so he reckons he will be home in about an hour, maybe just over. I thought I'd let you…"

"No way! You might be prepared to forget and forgive him for what he did that night, but I'm not," screeched Jenny, slamming the door closed.

Susie swallowed hard and inwardly counted to ten, then again knocked on the door.

She waited a few seconds and getting no response, slowly turned the handle and pushed the door open.

Jenny, still wearing her school uniform, lay on her side on her bed facing the wall, her legs curled beneath her and her hands upon her ears. Susie recognised that her daughter did not want to talk, but wasn't prepared to give up so easily. She moved towards the bed and sat on the edge, her hands in her lap. Slowly, almost tentatively and fearing it would be shrugged off, she moved her hand to Jenny's back, gently rubbing it as she had done when her daughter was a child. Jenny didn't react and so Susie continued to massage her back. Jenny turned towards her, her face tear-stained and then to her mother's surprise, threw her arms about her neck.

"I can't help the way I feel," she sobbed, her head lying awkwardly on Susie's shoulder. "I just wish everything was the same, before that night."

She didn't reply, but simply held tightly onto her child, for that brief moment her arms providing the comfort and security that Jenny so craved and needed.

They stayed like that for several minutes until Jenny stopped sobbing, then Susie held her at arms length and stared into her face, with one hand brushing her fair hair from her eyes.

"I can't make the world a better place love," she softly said, "and I don't know if things will get better our worse. You're old enough now to realise that not all relationships have fairytale endings. Your dad and I might stay together and try to work things out or we might end up going our separate ways, but I can promise you that no matter what happens, nothing will ever come between us. I'll always be your mum, okay?"

Not trusting herself to speak, Jenny nodded and wiped at her eyes with the sleeve of her blouse.

"What I will ask of you is that when your dad comes home, we sit down with him for dinner like he asked us to and give him every opportunity to turn things round. We listen to what he has to say and if he wishes to speak privately with me, then you will, for *my* sake," she stressed, "give us some time together. But no matter what the outcome is, whether you hear us or not, I promise that nothing will be held back from you. If not both of us, then I will tell you everything that is said and what arrangements we make. Will you do that for me?"

Again, Jenny nodded, a little clearer headed and taking a deep breath, said, "What do you think he'll say, mum? Do you think he wants to leave us?"

It did not escape Susie's notice that Jenny had seemingly already made her mind up. '*Us*,' Jenny had said and inwardly breathed a sigh if relief. If the worse come to the worse and Peter *was* leaving, then it seems Jenny had decided to stay with her mother.

"I really don't know, darling, but for what it's worth, I got the impression that your dad might be considering some kind of reconciliation."

"But you're a mum." Now more composed, Jenny giggled, the tears for now stopped. "I thought mum's *always* knew everything and *always* knew best."

"And who am I to criticise those words of wisdom," joked Susie, giving her daughter one last hug before standing. "Why don't you go and wash your face and I'll set three places, then come downstairs when you're ready."

She glanced at the digital radio clock on Jenny's bedside table. "You're dad has been gone half an hour, so he should be back in about thirty minutes, so time for us to maybe grab a cuppa, eh?"

"Okay, mum. I'll be down in a minute."

Emma Saunders, head down against the light fall of rain that fell and regretting not bringing her telescopic brolly, wasn't aware of the presence of Leigh Gallagher till he roughly grabbed at the back of her jacket and pulled her into the close doorway. Her initial shocked surprise turned to terror when the hooded figure slammed his body against her, pinning her to the wall and shoving the knife almost into her face, hissed at her, "Give me your fucking purse, ya wee slut or you're getting it!"

She could not know that in his mind, his rage was fuelled by his treatment at the hands of Chloe Ferguson and now vented against all young women and in particular, those with blonde hair.

In the few seconds that it took Emma to come to terms with the fact she was about to be robbed, her fear turned to anger that this…this…yob, should try to steal her purse.

Well *fuck* him, her mind screamed at her and with a sudden burst of energy and strength belying her diminutive build, pushed against her attacker while screaming, "Fuck you!" at him and instinctively grabbed at the wrist of the hand holding the shiny bladed knife.

Taken aback that the wee lassie was resisting, Leigh pushed harder with both his free left hand and his body against her, but this very act swung him slightly off balance and to his horror, the girl mistakenly grabbed with her left hand not his wrist, but the sharp blade of the knife.

As if in slow motion, they both saw her clasp the blade and a sudden spurt of crimson seep from her clenched hand as the sharp blade bit into the soft flesh of her left palm.

Emma screamed in pain and unclasped her hand as Leigh, realising that the simple robbery had now gone wrong, stepped back, still staring wide-eyed at the girl's bloodied hand.

"Shit!" he bellowed and turning on his heel, ran in panic from the close.

Emma, seeing him run off and with a presence of mind that she would not have previously believed, fetched her handkerchief with her right hand from her jeans pocket and forced it into the gaping wound on her left hand, stemming the flow of blood.

She staggered from the close, the carrier bag with water and chocolate abandoned and the adrenalin now kicking in. It was her good fortune that a passing black hackney cab saw her raise her uninjured hand to flag him down.

The driver, a world-weary experienced man, jumped from his cab and, eyes narrowing at her bloodied hand, assisted the young woman into the rear of his vehicle.

"What happened, hen? How did you get injured?" he asked solicitously and with some compassion.

Emma, now shivering and pale faced from her ordeal, was about to tell the kindly man that she had just been mugged, but again with presence of mind, realised this admission would without doubt involve the police.

The last thing she needed was explaining why she was in the Partick area and certainly did not relish speaking to the police with twenty ecstasy tablets in her backpack.

"I fell on some glass," she sniffed, the tears being to flow, then for effect added, "I slipped on a puddle in the rain."

The seasoned and experienced Glasgow driver could clearly see that this was a lie and besides, if the wee lassie had fallen he reasoned her jeans would be wet. However, he simply nodded and accepting the falsehood realised for some unknown reason she didn't want to tell him the truth.

"Either way, hen, you're going to need that stitching," he nodded to her hand, "so I'd better get you to the casualty at the Western Infirmary," and with that, saw her buckled into her seat and closed the passenger door and returned to his seat in the front of the cab.

The driver started the engine and in the back, Emma's mind raced as she concocted a story to satisfy her parents curiosity as to how her daughter had come by a slash wound on her hand.

However, she took a pleasure in the thought of the tale she would tell her sixth form mates at Saturday's night party, of how she fought off a drug-crazed mugger.

In her imagination, she became the heroine who had saved the party.

Even through the pain, she smirked, already envisioning the envy on the face of the backstabbing Morag bitch-face Peterson.

Leigh Gallagher ran as though the very devil himself was at his heels, his training shoes splashing in the puddles that formed in the uneven pavements of the streets he passed through.
Breathless, he reached his close, his heart hammering in his chest, his mind still reeling from cutting the girl on the hand.
Shit!
Never had he *ever* planned on using the knife.
It was just for show, for threatening the women, for scaring them, for making them do what he wanted.
Shit!
He bent over, head down and his hands on his knees and realised to his horror that he still held the knife in his right hand.
Shit!
He had run all the way home with the fucking knife in his hand!
That's when he noticed the blood on his hand.
His fingers involuntarily opened and the knife fell to the ground with a small tinkle. He stared down at it, eyes widening; fascinated by the red staining of the girl's blood, now congealing on the shiny blade.
He rubbed at his hand, but realised the blood would need to be washed off.
He glanced about him and seeing the close was empty, stooped to pick the knife gingerly by the handle, from the ground. He fetched his yellow waterproof from the hood pouch pocket and wrapped the nylon jacket around it.
Slowly, his breathing returned to normal and with a shake of his head, wearily climbed the stairs to his flat.
He opened the front door and listened for any sound from the living room, but the house sounded quiet and he guessed his father must still be at Mass.
With a sigh of relief he went into the bathroom and running the hot water tap, first dipped the blade under the water then rolled back the right sleeve of the hooded top and scrubbed at his hand. The white enamel sink turned a faint pinkish colour as he washed away blood mixed with the water.
Finally, his hand was clean.
But still he rubbed at the hand till the skin was red and wrinkled.

He heard his father's key in the door and Magnus call out, "You in son? Are you there Leigh?"

He hadn't closed the bathroom door and called back, "I'm just home in front of you Da. I got caught in the rain. See you in a minute," then scooped the wet knife back into the folds of the yellow nylon jacket.

He heard his father walking into the lounge and the sound of the television being switched on and quickly moved across the hallway into his bedroom, closing the door behind him.

It took but a moment to return the knife to the tin box and hide it in the space at the bottom of the wardrobe.

In future, he sighed with relief, he'd stick to the old and the fat birds and leave the young ones alone.

Susie Gibson, sat with her daughter Jenny at the kitchen table, risked a glance at the wall-clock.

Peter had been gone now for over two and a half hours and there had been no telephone call.

The disappointment must have shown in her face, for Jenny reached across and squeezed at her mother's hand.

"Why don't I make us some toast and beans, eh?" she asked with a half-smile and before her mother could protest, had scraped back her chair and fetched the loaf from the breadbin.

Susie watched her, marvelling at how tall she had grown. In looks and expression, Jenny favoured her father though no one could deny she had her mother's eyes.

"Maybe he got held up at his meeting," Jenny said, startling her from her thoughts.

"Yes, that'll be it," she automatically smiled, yet both knowing it wasn't true.

Peter had simply not bothered coming home.

CHAPTER 8

Carol Meechan woke before the alarm clock radio activated and slowly reached across the gently snoring John to click the button off. She was curiously happy and realised she no longer felt the stress of worrying about the accounts, not now that she had told the manager, Morven Sutherland.

She slipped one leg out from beneath the quilt cover and was about the slip the other out when without warning John grabbed her by the wrist and cried, "Boo!"

She shrieked then laughed as grinning, he pulled her back into the bed and began to smother her face and neck with kisses and pull at the tie-ribbon that held the front of her nightdress closed.

She glanced at the alarm clock and sighed.

"Well, maybe another ten minutes," she whispered, turning into his warm body and enveloping arms.

As was his usual routine, Magnus Gallagher rose early from his bed and turned back the covers, then first wiping with his hands at the condensation, opened the window to stare out into the rear court of the tenement and glanced upwards to the cloudless sky. He smiled for it seemed to be a fine and sunny start to the day.

He took a deep breath and drew the crisp air into his lungs then slowly exhaled and turning back towards the bed, stiffly lowered himself to his knees. Lifting his rosary beads from the top of the bedside cabinet, he made the sign of the cross then head bowed and eyes closed, commenced his morning prayers.

Across the city, Waz Ahmed was kneeling on the mat in the lounge of his flat and just completing Fajr, the dawn prayer. Due to the shifts and inconsistent duties of his occupation as a police officer, Waz was not always in position to adhere to the strict observance of Salat, the practice of formal worship that all Muslims were bound by. Following a lengthy discussion and with the blessing of his Sheikh, the elderly and wisest scholar in his mosque, Waz performed the prayers when and where he could, though normally caught up with the prayers when he returned home in the evening. Even then the prayers would sometimes take a backseat until, he inwardly grinned, his daughter Munawar tired of his attention, but he figured that Allah in his wisdom would not criticise a father adoring his wee lassie.

Rising to his feet, he rolled up the mat and quietly tiptoed across the lounge floor.

The wee one had developed a temperature and Alima had twice been up through the night responding to Munawar's cries; the second time bringing their daughter into bed between them.

He had tried to rise to help his wife with their child, but Alima insisted he get his sleep and assuring him that Munawar would be fine, reminded Waz that today was an in-service day at the school, so she would get some sleep when the wee one was taking her afternoon nap.

Now, he got himself dressed and turned at the creak of a floorboard to see Alima standing in the doorway, arms crossed and wearing her school Ma'am face.

"I hope you're not thinking of going out to work without breakfast, Waseem Ahmed," she quietly said, but the rebuke didn't escape him.

"Ah, well…" he grimaced, unable to find the words.

"Ah well nothing," she stepped into the room and wagged a finger at him as she crossed towards the kitchen. "I don't want you fainting halfway though the day and people believing it is because you wife didn't feed you. You've still got another twenty minute before you need to leave, so sit down and I'll microwave some porridge and get you a cuppa."

He grinned at her and finished tying his tie, then sat down on the settee to slip on his shoes.

What would he do without her?

Susan Gibson was up, showered and dressed for work in a dark grey trouser suit. She crossed the bedroom floor and pulled at the edge of the blind. Glancing out through the crack into the bright morning, it was immediately evident that Peter's car was not in the driveway nor parked in the street outside.

But of course, she already knew that for her night had been restless and punctuated with every night-time sound, from the rumble of HGV lorries in the distant M74 to the noisy diesel engine of the occasional taxi dropping a fare in the nearby streets.

Through the open door of her bedroom, she had also heard her daughter Jenny in her own room along the hallway, sob herself to sleep.

She lifted her hairbrush and stood in front of the wall mirror, surprised to see how tired she looked.

The bastard!

Stern-faced, she angrily tugged the brush through her hair and vowed that one way or another, she would get even with her husband for the emotional heartache he had inflicted, not only on Susie, but on their daughter.

Father Patrick Gallagher finished the early morning mass and slowly walking across the altar towards the sacristy cast a glance at the eight o'clock parishioners who had made the service. He sighed for as usual it was the dozen or so regulars who in the main were mostly elderly and he grinned, recalling a conversation he had overheard a few days previous between two of his equally elderly altar servers. He had not meant to eavesdrop, but almost laughed loudly when they described some of the older parishioners as last minute dot com Catholics coming to the Lord's waiting room in the hope to accrue some of God's good grace as an insurance policy before they turned their toes up in the event there really *was* a heaven.
Still, the server's discussion it had given him a start and he hadn't been able to shake the thought that maybe this idea did run through some of his parishioner's minds and he wondered how he could approach the subject during this forthcoming Sunday mass homily. Within the privacy of the sacristy, he shrugged out of his vestments and lifted the stole from about his neck, then touching his lips to it, placed it with the garments in the wardrobe. That's when he recalled his father's request for the use of the parish van.
He sighed and glancing at his watch, realised he would need to phone his dad. He hated to disappoint him about the loan of the van and wanted to assure his Da he would definitely have the use of it if not tomorrow, then the next day.
"Father?" one of his altar servers touched at his shoulder and distracted, Patrick's thoughts turned elsewhere.

Morven Sutherland arrived at the bank doors at her usual time and ignoring the smile directed at her by old Max the commissionaire who held the door, likely would not have been pleased had she heard him mutter, "Sour faced bugger," while she passed him by.
She made her way to the Accounts office on the first floor, deciding first to see if anyone else had arrived before depositing her coat and bag in the female locker room.
The office was empty and still wearing her coat she sat at her desk and switched on the computer, carefully typing in her logon details and password.

She had never quite gotten used to computing.

Eyes narrowed and her brow knitted in concentration, she scanned the HR files that were presented on the main screen and selecting one, tapped the mouse through several sub-files till she discovered the name and information she needed. She had no need to write anything down, for what she found she could easily remember. Locking the terminal, she quickly made her way downstairs to the locker room.

Stuck in the nose to tail morning rush traffic, DC Andy Brownlie drove to work, but still blazing mad with the nameless and cowardly bastard who had lobbed the bottle at Susie Gibson.

I'll bet it was that fat mother to those fucking McGriffen's he scowled and then braked sharply to avoid colliding with the car in front.

Bloody hell, he thought and slowly exhaling with relief, glanced at the passport-sized photograph Janice had stuck with blue-tack to the dashboard. He had gotten into the habit of thinking of the photo as a good luck charm and with one eye on the car in front, reached across and touched it with his forefinger. Her voice invaded his thoughts and he grinned at her gentle, but persistent chiding of his speedy driving and unconsciously nodded in agreement with her that he should really slow down and concentrate more.

However, the near miss had given Andy more of a fright than he realised and his driving during the remaining ten minutes of his journey to Baird Street, even Janice would admit, was faultless.

Des Mooney was sitting with a cup of coffee waiting for Waz when the young Detective arrived at his desk.

"Morning DC Ahmed," he theatrically glanced at his watch, "so that will be the late shift in, eh?"

Waz grinned at the older officer and taking off his suit jacket, replied, "Some of us have a life you old fart. Anyway, I heard a rumour that you live here, that you've got a fold-up bed in the boiler room downstairs."

Mooney merely grinned in response and carried on reading the paperwork in his hand then brow furrowed, pointed curiously at Waz's jacket and tie. "I thought we were in plain clothes today?

Didn't you tell Missus Ahmed before she dressed you this morning, sonny?"

"I don't need to dress like a vagrant to be in plain clothes," Waz nodded towards Mooney and continued to grin as his new neighbour waved a sheaf of paper at him.

"I've been going through the robbery reports again, Waz and the only thing that all the complainers can agree on is the suspect is male, hooded and carrying a knife.

The statements are weak and likely we'll need to re-interview *all* the women again. I'm not blaming the cops who took the statements," he added with a shake of his head, "but it's understandable that in the short time after the robbery was committed, each women was probably still in shock after they were threatened with a knife. The last thing these women are going to worry about is providing us with a decent statement when they were in fear of their life or at best, being cut," he shook his head.

"As far as I can establish from what we've got so far, the description of the suspect ranges from mid teens to late twenties, five foot four to six feet two, thin to heavy build, clean shaven to a slight facial growth and really, bugger all else. Oh, I should add, a local accent, so that narrows it down to a few thousand suspects."

"Do you have a copy of the latest robbery, the woman from last night?"

"Aye, a Margaret Whyte, but calls herself Rita; aged twenty-nine years, lives over in Penilee, but works in a shop on Dumbarton Road. The cop says …."

"That we can get the statement today at her work," interrupted Waz, then explained, "Bobby McAllister told me last night, before I left for home, so I thought that can be our first port of call today."

"Agreed," Mooney sipped at his coffee, then slyly asked, "What about some breakfast first?"

"Breakfast," Waz pretended shock, "Oh no, old guy, breakfast will have to wait till we interview this witness. You should be like me, I *always* have my porridge before I leave the house in the morning," he glibly lied.

"Here, Waz, catch," he turned as his name was called from across the room. Bobby McAllister, the CID clerk drew back his arm and threw a set of car keys towards the young Detective. "DI Franklin

had the garage send over a vehicle for you this morning. It's down in the back yard," McAllister added then turned back towards his desk.
"Right," Waz clutched the keys and turned brightly towards Mooney, "let's hit the road and see this witness, eh?"

"You've got to be kidding me," moaned Des Mooney with disbelief. Standing with Waz in the rear yard of Cranstonhill office, both stared wide eyed at the battered Ford Transit van. Once white coloured, it was obvious the van had been a patrol vehicle, for though the police livery was stripped from it, the removed logos seemed to have been either peeled or scraped off with a chisel, if the damage to the bodywork of the van was anything to go by. It also appeared the van had suffered a shunt to the rear as bits of the bumper were missing. Walking round the rusting heap, Waz saw the two back door handles were secured together with wire and guessed from the damage to the door lock, it was to keep the doors from flying open when the van was in motion.
Mooney opened the passenger door and wrinkled his nose.
"I think something fucking died in here," he morosely shook his head.
"If the garage sent it over then it must at least be MoT'd and fit to drive," replied Waz, his confidence in the statement slightly shaken when he saw the hole in the passengers footwell through which he could see the car park tarmac underneath.
Mooney turned to stare at his younger colleague and suddenly grinned. "Well, it should get us as far as Partick anyway," and held out his hand for the keys. "I'll drive first and if it collapses on us at thirty miles an hour, we sue the polis. Agreed?"
"Agreed," Waz returned his grin.

Carol Meechan arrived at the bank and after leaving her coat in the female locker room, made her way to the Accounts office and settling in behind her desk, switched on her terminal. Morven Sutherland, she could see, was already busy in her sub-office and head down, typing at her keyboard.
Carol admired her manager's work ethos and like many other women in the bank, was also a little envious of her good looks. She didn't pay much attention to the gossip that surrounded Sutherland's private life, but had to admit to a certain curiosity and on several

occasions, had seen her Accounts manager, Harry McPherson casting more than just a covetous eye towards his deputy manager and recalled with a slight shudder, the tentative move he had made a few months earlier on her.

She smiled and acknowledged the greetings from two of her colleagues and her gaze drifted towards the other sub-office.

McPherson was as usual late. His frequent tardiness annoyed Carol, recalling the day several months previously when her bus had broken down and she arrived after McPherson, who had called her into out in to the corridor away from the other staff and warned her about her time keeping.

Yet Carol knew that being late was not the real reason he had rebuked her, but was his little revenge for her rejection of his advances at the bank's annual dinner dance in the Glasgow hotel. His heavily pregnant wife Tracey had stayed at home and McPherson, a little the worse for wear with drink, had suggested he and Carol book a room for the night. Not a common user of expletives, her face flushed when she remembered the language she had used to rebuff him.

Later recounting the story to her partner John had been a mistake, for John had wanted to visit McPherson at the bank and challenge him and it had taken all of her persuasive skill to stop him, reminding him that it would not do her career any good if he caused a scene at the bank, of all places.

Since that time, she had been wary of McPherson and made it a point not to be alone with him.

Maybe I should have brought that to Miss Sutherland's attention as well, she mused with an inner smile.

Magnus Gallagher replaced the phone into the cradle and sadly shook his head that his surprise for Leigh would have to wait yet another day. He knew that his son Patrick would not have let his father down without good reason and so with a sigh accepted the disappointment.

He reached for his coat and softly walked along the hallway to the front door, hearing his son softly snoring and with a smile, left the flat to attend morning mass.

Des Mooney reversed parked the decrepit van into a bay on Dumbarton Road, wincing at the squeaking noise coming from the brakes and wondering what the strange, burning smell from the dashboard was.

Waz Ahmed, audibly sighing with relief, got out of the passenger door and glanced at the row of shops, seeing number 1891 to be the Rite Price newsagent, 'Proprietor U. Mohammed'.

Followed by Mooney, he pushed open the door with the tinkling bell above and saw an elderly Pakistani man, who smiled and greeted him with "Assaalamu aleykum" (*peace be upon you*).

Waz replied, "Wa'aleykum assalam" (*peace be with you too*) and producing his warrant card, identified both himself and Mooney as the police.

"I'm Mister Mohammed, Usman Mohammed," said the elderly man, "and this is my shop. How might I assist you gentlemen?"

"Actually, it's a Miss Margaret Whyte we're here to see," replied Waz, glancing over Mohammed's shoulder towards the rear of the shop. "Is she here the now, sir?"

Mohammed raised his hands and his face changed from a smile to a frown. "Oh, you mean Rita? That lazy good for nothing girl; I tell her be here on time, but she listen? No," he irritably shook his head, "never listens."

No sooner had he complained that the door tinkled behind Waz and a red-faced, heavy-set young woman burst through the door.

"Bloody bus was late again Ussy," she huffed, pushing past Mooney and Waz in the apparent belief they were customers. "Sorry," she continued, pulling her jacket off and making towards the rear of the shop.

"Wait there young lady," Mohammed called out to her. "These policemen, they are here to see you. What have you done now?"

"Fuck all," was her response, then added, "Is it about me getting mugged? Is that why you're here, eh? Tell me you got the bastard. Do you know that he's away with my holiday money, eh?"

Waz raised a hand to stem her verbal outburst, telling her, "Whoa there, miss. We are here to get your statement, okay?"

She glared at Waz and replied, "But I told that big polis yesterday what happened."

"I know, I know," he kept his hand raised to placate her, not wanting to start an argument and guessing that the large, young woman could be confrontational.

"We got the report, but my neighbour and I are here to get your formal statement."

Before she could argue, he turned to Mohammed and asked, "Is it okay to use your rear room for ten minutes sir?"

Mohammed nodded and waved them through to the rear of the shop, turning when the bell tinkled to greet a customer.

Waz and Whyte settled themselves on the only two chairs round a small folding table while Mooney stood leaning against the doorframe.

While Waz wrote her statement in his notebook, Whyte chewed at her fingernails huffing and puffing like a petulant teenager.

"So," he asked at last, "you reckon this guy was about twenty to thirty years of age, five foot nine tall, dark hair under the hood and looked like a junkie?"

"Aye, that's right. He had these evil eyes like you know, that guy that was in that film, what do you call it again, eh…?

Pan-faced, Mooney asked, "John Wayne?"

"Smart-arse," snorted Whyte, "I *know* who John Wayne was and it wasn't *him*. No, that guy … bollocks, I cannae remember his name, but it will come to me. I can always phone you later with it, can't I?"

Waz inhaled and asked, "What about the knife. Did you get a good look at the knife, hen?"

"A good look?" her eyes narrowed and then she snarled, "Fuck's sake pal, he waved it in my face. Of *course* I got a good fucking look at the knife. It was a wee narrow one, you know, the kind that you use in the kitchen, with a black plastic handle."

She held her hands six inches apart and said, "About this long. Sharp as fuck, they are too. Hang on a minute," she said then getting up from her chair, stepped over to a corner of the room where the sink and a small cupboard was located. Pulling open a drawer in the cupboard, the officers watched while she rummaged in the drawer among the cutlery and brought out a small knife.

"Here, this is it. This is the same kind of knife that he shoved into my face," she triumphantly brandished the knife at Waz.

Mooney stepped forward and cautiously took the knife from her outstretched hand. He turned the knife back and forth and said, "A boning knife, for cutting meat," then asked, "Can we take this with us?"

"Aye, just don't mention it to that old bugger," she whispered, nodding out towards the front of the shop. "Miserable sod wouldn't part with breath if it cost him."

"Right, anything else," Waz turned to glance at Mooney.

"No, I think you got it covered other than," he turned towards Whyte. "Will you be able to identify this guy again if you see him?"

"Oh aye, but I'm telling you this, if I see him before you catch him, he's getting fucking battered," she grimaced between clenched teeth. Waz, staring at her thick forearms and hoped for the suspect's sake the police got to him first.

Andy Brownlie answered the phone and with it still held against his ear, glanced across the room to where Susie Gibson sat at her desk. "Yes, Missus Gibson is here now, if you hold on sir," she heard him say then saw him press the Secrecy button.

"Susie, it's a Mister Brewster from the Caledonian Bank; says it's a personal matter." He glanced at the other officers seated at their desks. "Do you want to take the call here, in the office I mean?"

Her brow knitted with curiosity. Brewster, whom she had met briefly on a few occasions at the bank's annual dinner dance, was the HR Director with the bank and one of its senior officers. She nodded that Andy transfer the call to her desk phone.

Lifting the receiver, she felt a curious sensation in the pit of her stomach, but asked, "Hello, Mister Baxter, how are you?"

Andy saw her face turn pale and shake her head several times then heard her say, "No Mister Brewster, I have no idea at all. If you or I hear anything, I can assume we will inform the other, yes? Of course I will; goodbye."

He watched as she returned the phone to its cradle and turned towards him, her face ashen. He watched her rise from her chair and walk towards him, then stand and lean down, their heads barely inches apart.

"It's Peter," she began in a low voice, "he didn't turn up for work this morning, for a meeting that they were having; an important meeting, according to Brewster. They, the bank I mean, tried calling the house, but," she hesitated and instinctively trusting Andy, bit at her lower lip and confided, "he wasn't home last night and he's not answering his mobile phone. They thought I might know where he is."

She took a deep breath and shaking her head, continued, "The thing is Andy, I haven't a bloody clue where he might be."

CHAPTER 9

By mid afternoon, Susie reckoned she had tried her husband Peter's mobile phone at least a dozen times and each time her call was forwarded to the messaging service. On the last three occasions she left messages, venting her anger in the final message and accusing him of being heartless and by his silence, not giving a damn about the worry being experienced by Susie or their daughter and concluded by asking if Peter had contacted Jenny?

She refused to admit even to herself that the plain truth was, she really *was* worried.

Andy agreed to cover for her and so at three o'clock that afternoon, she quietly slipped away from Baird Street police office and travelled home, arriving at the house just as Jenny, walking with two school friends, was waving them goodbye and turning into the driveway.

"Hi mum," she greeted Susie with a bemused smile. "You're home early? Something up?"

She smiled and tried to be cheerful, but knew that Jenny was bright and would easily detect the lie, albeit a lie designed to protect her and so decided on the truth.

"Have you heard today from your dad, sweetheart? Has he phoned you or left you a message or anything?"

"Why, what's wrong? Has something happened to him?"

"No, nothing like that," she replied, dearly hoping it was true, "it's just that for some unknown reason, it seems he has taken the day off work and not told anyone in the office. So, has he been in touch with you at all?"

"Ah no, I haven't spoken with him," Jenny replied, head down as she fumbled in her blazer pocket for her mobile phone and quickly glanced at the screen. "No new messages either," she added, her face now etched with concern rather than curiosity.

The phone in the hallway begun to ring and swiftly Susie, closely followed by an anxious Jenny, unlocked the door and grabbed at it.

"Hello?"

"Is it dad," mouthed Jenny, her eyes widening, but her face fell when Susie shook her head.

"Mister Brewster, yes, it's me. No, not yet. I've just arrived home and Peter's not here either. I take it you haven't had any word then?" Jenny was literally hopping from foot to foot, eager for any news.

"Yes, yes," she saw her mother nod her head. "Of course Mister Brewster, the minute I hear from him. I assume he has your home phone number, then? Okay, yes I'll do that, goodbye."

Susie slowly replaced the phone and glanced at Jenny.

"That was Mister Brewster, one of the directors at your dad's office. He still hasn't contacted them yet. They were calling to see if he had arrived home."

Her eyes narrowed as thought suddenly struck her that even though Peter's car wasn't outside, he still might be here, in the house.

A sickening thought occurred to her.

She felt her chest constrict and her stomach turning. She glanced towards the stairs. What if he has…no, please God, not that.

"Wait here," she curtly instructed Jenny, wagging a forefinger at her. Biting at her lower lip, she walked towards the stairs, one hand on the wooden banister and slowly walked upstairs. Susie was not a stranger to violent death or suicide but here, in her own home?

She began to breathe in short spurts and steeled herself for what she might find. Nervously she reached the top hallway landing and first checked the bathroom and almost sighed with relief it was empty.

The two spare rooms, one used as an office and Jenny's room were next, but all three were empty.

At last, with a trembling hand, she pushed aside the partially open master bedroom door, but the room was also empty. Her head turned towards the closed en-suite door and her brow knitted, for she could not recall closing over door when she left that morning for work. She took a deep breath and slowly pushed the door open, by now almost certain what she would find.

The small bathroom was empty and legs shaking, she stumbled backwards and sank heavily down onto the bed, almost crying with relief.

"Mum," Jenny's voice startled her and she saw her daughter standing at the bedroom door, her face betraying her curiosity and wearing a smile.

"Did you think he might be hiding upstairs or something?"

She smiled in return, thankful her daughter had not guessed the real reason for Susie's fearful search of the upper floor. Calmer now she reached for Jenny who sat beside her and awkwardly, threw her arms around her mother's waist and buried her head into Susie's shoulder. "Yeah, something like that," she agreed and again wondered where her errant husband had got to.

The gossip grapevine within the Caledonian Bank was in full swing when word circulated among the hundred plus staff that the Business Loans Manager Peter Gibson had not only failed to attend an important meeting, but Mister Brewster, the HR Director, had been overheard by his secretary speaking on the phone to Gibson's, wife trying to contact him.

Within ten minutes, the word was out and simple fact became salacious fiction with the favoured rumour that Gibson, who according to some of his staff had in recent months been unhappy at work, had run off with another woman.

It was unfortunate that the rumourmongers were unaware just how close to the truth their inventive stories were.

Parked on the corner of Purdon Street with a clear view both east and west onto Dumbarton Road, Des Mooney sitting in the drivers seat exhaled loudly and lifting one cheek of his buttocks, expelled a noxious fart.

"Bloody hell," whined Waz, turning to stare at his neighbour and using the evening edition of the 'Glasgow News' to fan the smell towards Mooney. "I wouldn't want to clean out your stable at night, you smelly bugger."

Mooney grinned then almost as quick, his smile faded and he glanced at his watch.

"Time's getting on Waz. That's nearly an hour we've sat here and no show by our suspect. Why don't we move along Dumbarton Road a bit, see what's happening there, eh?"

Waz sighed and agreed. "Really, it's a hit and a miss, isn't it? Whether or not we get this guy, I mean."

He turned again towards his neighbour. "You've got a lot of surveillance time under your belt Des. Is it always like this? I mean, sitting about?"

"It's mostly like this young man. Ninety-five percent of the time doing nothing, but watching and then five percent running around like a headless chicken."

Waz grinned and inwardly thought that a full time job with a surveillance unit just would not suit him. No, it sounded too boring for a young guy keen to get on in the job.

"What about the CID," he asked. "Have you never fancied doing something like that?"

Mooney shrugged. "Too much paperwork and besides, you need your exams to get into El Cid."

"You're bright though, Des. Why haven't you sat your exams?"

Mooney turned to stare at Waz. "What is this, Mastermind? Look Waz, you seem keen enough to get on and likely you will progress through the ranks and maybe, just maybe, you will end up being a boss some day. But you need to realise that not everybody that joins the polis wants to be a supervisor or a manager. Some of us still like the honourable profession of being a police office, out there mixing with the public, catching and locking up the bad guys and being the face of the police."

He blew through pursed lips.

"Look, let me explain and the best way I can think of is if you imagine the police as pyramid," he used his hands to demonstrate, the fingertips together and shaping a pyramid. "At the top of that pyramid is the beat copper; man or woman, it doesn't matter. The beat cop is the first to attend at most incidents. It might be that the beat cop has been out in the rain or the cold for hours; maybe needing fed or maybe even needing a pee. Then the call to assist the public comes over the radio. Arriving at an incident where the public need him or her, that cop has seconds or if he or she is lucky, maybe minutes to decide if a crime or offence is committed; who to arrest or who to treat as witnesses. Once the cop's decision is made then that decision will be questioned and pored over, not just by follow-up detectives or support services, but maybe even at court by the judiciary who have the luxury of hours, days, months even, to decide if the correct decision was made at the time."

He paused, seeing he had Waz's full attention and continued. "Then, the cop's actions within those few vital seconds or minutes might be questioned at length in a courtroom, with the cop sweating in the witness stand, asking himself or herself, did I make the right decision?"

He shook his head. "So, again, at the top of the pyramid is the beat cop and every other department, whether it be CID, Traffic, Serious Crime, Drugs, Forensics, ballistics, senior management or whatever, are there to support him, for it's the poor bloody beat cop who in the *first* instance, makes the *first* decision and *that* decision *needs* to be the correct decision."

He smiled at Waz. "Now tell me, who's the first guy to be blamed for any fuck-up?"

Waz slowly nodded, for some unaccountable reason feeling a little guilty. "The beat cop I suppose; the guy taking the crime report."

"Correct, give that man a coconut. The beat cop," Mooney repeated. "Now tell me, who's the guy who has the most basic training in police work?"

Waz slowly exhaled, feeling like a rookie on his first day of duty. "I suppose again, the constable on the street."

"Correct again. The constable on the street receives the most basic law training, yet he is usually the first individual to arrive on the scene when an incident occurs and to whom the public turn to when they need assistance; not management, not the detectives or fancy departmental wallah, not the lawyers; the poor, bloody beat man." He sat back with a self-satisfied smile.

"I've a bit more, no," he corrected himself, "a *lot* more time under my belt than you young Waz, so if I can advise you of anything, it's this. When, as I hope you do, you achieve some supervisory or managerial rank, don't think promotion makes you brighter or smarter than the beat man. Treat him or her with respect and you will be surprised just how much they can help you, okay?"

Waz suddenly grinned and nodded. "Okay Da. So, lesson over?"

Mooney returned Waz's grin and turning the key, started the engine then carefully inched out into the traffic on Dumbarton Road. Inwardly he knew that his two-minute rant wasn't really needed or justified, for young Waz was a decent enough guy, but again it didn't do any harm to keep the CID on their toes and remind them that they weren't God's gift, like some of them believed themselves to be.

Jenny Gibson got to the phone and lifted it before the third ring.

"Hello?" she breathlessly asked, her mother standing anxiously watching her.

"Oh, it's for you," she handed the phone to Susie. "It's an Andy Brownlie, he says."

Susie took a deep breath and said, 'Hello Andy, I'm guessing you're calling about Peter, but no news yet I'm afraid."

"I've just arrived home and first thing is that nobody noticed you were away early. Now, is there anything I can do for you, do you need me to come over and maybe go and knock on a few doors for you?"

Touched by his concern, Susie assured Brownlie that if she did need any help in looking for Peter, he would be her first call.

"Who's Andy Brownlie mum?" asked Jenny when she had finished the call.

"He's a young officer I work with. A nice young guy," she reached across and stroked at her daughter's cheek, "and soon to become a parent too. Maybe even with a daughter as lovely as you," she smiled.

Leigh Gallagher stood a few feet back from the entrance of the close, watching through narrowed eyes the entrance to the charity shop, his right hand in the pouch pocket of the hooded top and gripping the knife. He could clearly see middle-aged woman in the black jacket through the large shop window, browsing among the second-hand clothes and saw her select what looked like a short dark coloured dress and holding it up to inspect. He watched as the woman took the garment to the till and saw her take a purse from her red coloured shoulder bag, smiling at the elderly assistant and handing her a currency note.

The assistant placed the garment into a plastic bag that she handed across the counter as the woman returned her purse to the shoulder bag and made her way to the door.

A bus drove slowly past the shop, obscuring his view and he moved out from the close entrance, fearing that he might lose sight of the woman.

"Shite!" he muttered. The woman had gotten into the passenger door of a parked car with a man in the drivers seat.

He saw the man turn his head and then ease the car out into traffic and drive off.

He hadn't realised he was so tense and let out a breath.

But it was still light he thought and time enough yet to find someone else.

Pleased to be going home at the end of her working day, Carol Meechan buttoned her coat and prepared to leave the locker room, nodding a farewell to some of the typists who with hushed voices were crowded together and discussing the curious absence of Peter Gibson.

Like the rest of the bank, Carol had heard of Gibson's no-show at the important meeting, but unlike her colleagues in the Accounts office, Carol had no interest in adding to the gossip surrounding Gibson's apparent disappearance.

Leaving through the main door, she smiled and nodded to old Max the doorman and joined the throng making their way along West George Street.

Her thoughts turned to her partner John and a warm glow surged through her body. The day they met some four years previously had been the best day of her life so far and now, she could not imagine life without him.

She glanced at the busy traffic and quickly crossing the road between the stationary vehicles stopped at a red light, headed towards St Vincent Street and her usual bus stop where she joined the half dozen or so regulars who like Carol, were wearily making their way home.

The five-minute trip to Partick took almost fifteen minutes as the bus crawled through the heavy traffic. Sitting in an aisle seat on the lower deck, Carol decided that she would not get off at her regular stop, but stay on to the next stop at the railway bridge on Dumbarton Road; the stop next to where the small delicatessen was located that sold John's favourite cheese.

She smiled as she imagined his pleasure at her thoughtfulness.

At last, the bus arrived at the stop and skipping lightly onto the pavement, made her way towards the shop to make her purchase.

Leigh Gallagher watched the blonde haired woman carrying the plastic bag over her forearm and followed her at a discreet distance with his hand on the knife handle, almost as if to reassure himself that he could do this.

Fucking blondes, he inwardly raged, still angry with Chloe Ferguson.

Carol Meechan decided against risking life and limb on the busy Dumbarton Road and crossed as the pedestrian lights turned green. Gently swinging the plastic bag containing he cheese, she hummed to herself as she walked up the slight incline into Gardner Street and then turned towards Lawrie Street.

Leigh Gallagher closed on the woman and now she was a mere twenty yards ahead.

Carol reached the close at number 165 and glanced about the roadway, but John's Mini wasn't to be seen. She smiled and entered the half-light of the close and walked towards the stairs, her high heels clicking on the concreted ground and pleased that she was first to arrive home. She had already decided to hide the cheese at the back of the fridge and surprise him after their meal.

She raised her foot to step onto the stairs, but some intuitive sense of danger befell her. She started to turn to her left, suddenly aware of a hooded figure coming from the shadow of the ground flat doorway, behind her.

She gasped as the figure plunged something sharp downwards into the top of her back, the sudden, awful pain like nothing she had ever before experienced.

Then again, more pain as the figure withdrew then plunged the knife a second time into Carol's unprotected back.

She tried to scream, but could not know that the first stabbing blow had punctured her back between the shoulders, just below her neck and in doing so sliced into her spine and effectively caused an immediate paralysis, not only of her limbs, but of her vocal cord.

In a heartbeat, her legs jerked spasmodically and she felt herself falling, but having already commenced to turn towards her assailant, Carol's momentum carried her round to face her attacker. She grasped with her hands, her fingers clawing at the hooded figure as she fell forwards, her eyes widening and with a quiet sigh, died with a surprised expression on her face.

CHAPTER 10

The police office located in Old Glasgow Road at the east end of Uddingston still had Lanarkshire Constabulary etched into the stonework above the door.

Susie Gibson knew that the office operated during daylight hours only, but rightly guessed the officers patrolling the area would be in for their break around six o'clock.

It had been with difficulty she persuaded Jenny to stay at home and explained if her father phoned, it might be on the landline.

Parking her car on the roadway outside the office, she ignored the sign on the door that suggested for emergencies, the public use the phone located in the box attached to the wall and instead hammered with her fist on the door.

After several minutes and at her third attempt, the door was angrily pulled opened by a young constable, a half eaten sandwich in his hand.

"I hope this is an emergency, missus. I'm at my piece," he complained and took a bite from his sandwich.

"Yes, I can see that," she replied, "but I'm here to report a missing person. My husband, actually, so I'm sure you can make allowances for that, eh?"

"If it's not an emergency hen …" he began, shrugging his shoulders as he chewed.

Susie, by nature a civil woman had never been known to pull rank other on a colleague; however, in her present state of mind, the last thing to concern her was whether or not this young upstart finished his sandwich.

Gritting her teeth, she interrupted him and sternly replied, "Firstly, I'm not a '*hen*'. If anything, I'm a Detective Sergeant so perhaps as I'm in the job you might do me the courtesy of taking my missing person report, please?"

The young cop swallowed with difficulty and began to choke, overtaken by a coughing fit and stepped to one side to permit Susie to step past him into the foyer of the office.

A policewoman came from an inner office into the foyer, her face expressing puzzlement at her colleagues coughing fit and stared curiously at Susie.

However, the younger woman had the presence of mind to realise that by letting her into the foyer, there must be a good reason and stepping behind the uniform bar said, "Good evening madam. Is there a problem I can help you with?"

Susie took a deep breath and produced her warrant card that she placed on the wooden top of the bar.

"My name is Detective Sergeant Susan Gibson. I reside with my husband and daughter at 188 Kylepark Drive, here in Uddingston. I've come in to report my husband Peter Gibson as a missing person.

DI Bobby Franklin arrived in Lawrie Street in his own car from his home to see that the uniform shift on duty had already taped off the area around the close entrance at number 165.

The Scene of Crime and Forensics vehicle, along with two marked police vehicles and an old, ugly and battered looking Transit van were closely parked near to the entrance.

An ambulance was pulling away from the kerb and as it passed him by, startling him as quite unexpectedly the driver switched on its blue lights and activated its siren.

Getting out of his car he watched as Des Mooney, dressed in a white overall paper suit with blue disposable overshoes on his feet, saw Franklin and walked towards him.

"Bad news boss, young lassie stabbed twice in the back. Fucker let her bleed to death in the close," he spat out, physically shaking with anger.

Franklin knew that Mooney was an old and experienced cop and no stranger to sudden and violent death. Odd though, he thought, for this to rattle him.

"Who else is here?" he asked as he walked towards the Forensics vehicle to grab a paper suit and overshoes. Passing the close entrance, he saw the flash of a camera from inside.

"Young Waz Ahmed, who was with me when we got the shout and the two backshift CID. Waz is up the close at 165 and the other two guys are up the close on either side, banging on doors, trying to find witnesses. The duty casualty surgeon has already attended and pronounced life extinct."

"That was quick," Franklin dryly remarked.

"He was at Partick office, called there regarding a drunk driver, so stopped by on his way home," replied Mooney.

"That will be about two hundred quid for an hours work, eh? Good money if you can get it," huffed Franklin, hinting his opinion of what he considered to be overpaid medics retained by the police for such incidents.

"Did Waz or the backshift make any arrangements?"

"Aye, Waz notified the Duty Fiscal Depute, so she should be on her way here. The backshift have called out some of the dayshift and I'm almost certain that they asked the duty officer at Force Control to arrange for the Traffic Department to deliver the Incident Caravan too."

"Good," replied Franklin, his mind working at considering any details the attending officers might have missed, but pleased that for the time being, everything seemed to be covered.

Preferring to let the Forensics finish their examination before he entered the close, Franklin asked, "Who discovered the body?"

"A Missus Violet Cairns; she's one of the neighbours that lives in the one of the ground floor flats. She's in her late seventies, poor old soul. Popped out to the shops for some message and came home and saw the body, thought it was a drunk."

He saw Franklin's curious expression and explained, "The old biddy's half blind, boss. Then she realised it was a young woman and when she saw there was blood on the body and on the ground, she started screaming and run from the close into the street. Well, when I say run," he shrugged his shoulders. "Anyway, Missus Cairns run into that lad there," he pointed to a figure sitting hunched with his head bent low, in the rear of a patrol car. "John Paterson, he had just arrived home in the Mini over there," Mooney pointed towards the parked car. "He went into the close and…" Mooney took a deep breath, "The lassie, the dead girl that is; she's his girlfriend, his partner. They live in the close, up there on the first floor," he pointed towards a window. "It was him that phoned us, 999 I mean. Waz and I were first here. We secured the scene as best we could," he tailed off.

"Who's away in the ambulance?"

Mooney shook his head. "It's Missus Cairns, the old woman who discovered the body. She took a bad turn and collapsed on the street just after Waz and I arrived, so not only did we have the distraught boyfriend, but then we had a medical emergency to deal with as well."

"What did the ambulance crew say about her condition?"

"Not good, I'm afraid. One of the ambulance crew recognised the old woman and told us that she's got angina, so they think it's an attack. Given her age, it could be touch and go, boss."

Franklin shook his head. That a murder should occur was bad enough, but for an old woman in the twilight of her life, a witness no less, to become a victim simply for being in the wrong place at the wrong time; that was even worse. What was it the Americans called it again, collateral damage?

He nodded towards the figure in the rear of the patrol car. "Any chance we could be looking at a suspect there Des?"

Mooney screwed up his face as he considered the question and then slowly shook his head. "His alibi, he says he was just returning from work, will of course need to be checked boss, but if you want my humble opinion, the young guy seems genuine. It took Waz and me all our time, between the old woman collapsing and him going into shock, to seal the scene for the SOCO team and the Forensic people." He shook his head again. "You guys in the CID will need to interview him, I realise that, but to answer your question, I don't think he's involved."

Franklin's experience of murder was by the book; start with the victim as the centre of the spider web, then work outwards from spouse, family, friends and associates. However, he had known Des Mooney for many years and respecting his opinion, realised that though there was no medical term for it, a coppers gut instinct was a belief that could only be trusted through years of experience.

Both men patiently waited outside the close for the SOCO and Forensics to complete their examination of the locus.

Franklin asked, "How about you Des, any ideas at this time?"

Mooney turned towards the DI and replied, "Obviously boss, I had to check the body to ensure there was no sign of life. From what I could see the wee lassie was dressed for work and from the few details Waz and I could elicit from her partner, he told us she is …" he hesitated, "was I mean, employed in a bank in the city."

His brow wrinkled and he continued. "The funny thing, is being a young woman you would expect her to be carrying at least a handbag, but all that was lying there was a plastic bag. I could see that a bit of cheese she had presumably bought had fallen out of the bag. So," he sighed, "I can only guess that as the victim was stabbed in the back and with her handbag missing, there is a strong likelihood that the guy you set Waz and me to track down has upped his game."

He shrugged his slowly shoulders and said, "I think the guy committing the street robberies must by a prime suspect, boss."

The Divisional outdoor patrol Inspector Andy Buchan and his young Sergeant arrived in their unmarked police car outside Susie Gibson's house less than thirty minutes after she reported her husband Peter missing.

With the barest of facts to hand, Buchan was a little uncertain if he had sufficient information to be calling at Gibson's house, but sighed; the Duty Inspector at Hamilton had contacted Buchan on his mobile phone and his suggestion was that maybe the inquiry be dealt with by an Inspector, so here he now was.

The Duty Inspector had also confided that Missus Gibson had apparently been a little shirty with the young cop at Uddingston office, but Buchan was not too concerned about that; he knew the cop to be a lazy bugger and it wasn't the first time Buchan himself had rebuked him.

Knocking on the door, it was pulled open by a teenage girl who turned her head and over her shoulder called out, "Mum, it's the police."

The girl stood to one side and invited the two officers into the house. Buchan removed his cap and stood waiting, conscious that the Sergeant, following his Inspector's lead, had also removed his cap.

A woman stepped from a doorway, the lounge it proved to be and said, "Good evening sir, I'm Susan Gibson. This is my daughter Jennifer."

He saw the young girl sharply turn towards her mother and could not know that to her parents, she was Jenny to her mum and Jennifer to her dad.

Buchan introduced himself and his Sergeant and invited by Susie into the lounge she indicated they should sit.

"I have to tell you Missus Gibson," he paused, "I understand from the little I know that you're a Detective Sergeant?"

Seating herself in the armchair opposite Buchan, her hands clasped together in her lap and Jenny hovering in the doorway, Susie nodded and replied, "Yes sir, at Baird Street. My boss is DCI Ross McConnell."

"I have to tell you Missus Gibson," he paused again while fetching a pen and notebook from a pouch on his utility belt, "are you all right with missus rather than DS?"

"Susie would be better," she quietly smiled, then turning to her daughter said, "Jenny, couldn't switch the kettle on and maybe put some mugs together, please?"

Jenny would have preferred to listen to what her mother intended telling the two officers, but recognised a dismissal when she heard one. With a petulant sigh she about turned and disappeared towards the kitchen.

"I've got a teenage daughter myself," Buchan said with a smile of sympathy. "Right, then Susie, I'm Martin or Marty if you like. So again, I have to tell you that I was on patrol when I got the shout and while I'm aware a form has already been raised by the cop at Uddingston, I have no further details, so maybe you could start at the beginning?"

She took a deep breath and began to bare her soul, in short, terse sentences, telling these two strangers of the apparent irretrievable breakdown of her marriage to her husband Peter, their separation within the same house with her in the master bedroom and him occupying a guest room.

"I hesitate to ask this," said Buchan, uncertain how to phrase it without upsetting her and conscious that Gibson herself is in the job, "but was there any domestic issues? What I mean…"

"Violence, is that what you're asking? No nothing like that, but…" she slowly exhaled, "just about two months ago, we were arguing at the top of the stairs. It was a stupid thing; an accident really. I…" she swallowed deeply and then continued. "I accused him of being involved with someone else. He turned to walk away and I grabbed at his arm. He tried to sweep me off, but somehow I lost my balance and I fell backwards down the stairs. It was nothing…"

"That's *not* what happened mum!"

They had not noticed Jenny at the door, a tray with mugs in her hands, her eyes wide and face pale. "I *saw* it," she insisted again. "His face, I saw his face. He meant to hit you."

"*Jenny*!" snapped Susie, rising to her feet, her hands outstretched. Buchan had also gotten to his feet and said, "Missus Gibson," his voice a little sharper than he intended, then softer, "Would you mind if maybe my Sergeant could speak with Jennifer in the kitchen?

Please, Susie," he reverted again to her forename, "it might be better if I got both sides of the story, eh?"

She sat heavily back down in the chair and watched as Buchan took two mugs from the tray and with a nod of his head, ushered the Sergeant and Jenny out through the door. Handing one of the mugs to Susie, he turned to close the door and said, "You know what young people are like. Sometimes they can turn nothing into a drama, eh?"

Seating himself back down, he asked, "Did you report the accident; I mean, were you injured at all?"

"It *was* an accident Marty," she softly replied. "Jenny just didn't see it like it happened and no, I hurt my back a bit, but nothing that Paracetamol couldn't fix."

Buchan reckoned that from the manner in which she sat upon the chair, her back was still hurting, but decided not to press the issue. He knew that though the cop at Uddingston had already completed the form that recorded all the personal and salient details of Peter Gibson, he needed to learn more about the man so asked, "Tell me about Peter, where he works and why you think he might have been having an affair?"

Susie spent the next five minutes describing her husband's employment, the anxious phone calls from the banking staff and a further ten minutes relating her suspicions about his occasional late nights out with no explanation as to where he had been. However, the more she spoke, the less she herself believed. In her retelling and thinking like the cop she was, Susie knew that none of her suspicions would ever convince a jury.

In fact, she suddenly startled, I sound like a jealous shrew of a wife. "Do you have any idea why your husband might have taken off or," he was almost afraid to ask, "…why someone might hurt him?"

"No, none at all," she shook her head, yet fearful and inwardly admitted the real reason was he was gone out of both Jenny and Susie's life *because* of another woman.

"Even if he has gone off with someone else, I presume that he would have informed you Susie, and if not you, then his daughter perhaps?"

She nodded her head and replied, "Peter doted on Jenny. No matter what problems or issues we might have as a couple, he would never, never abandon Jenny. Yes, they had their father daughter arguments like any other family, but he loved her," she half laughed, "sometime I think even more than he loved me."

She exhaled and added, "That's the reason I was so quick in reporting him missing. His absence today from the meeting and nobody being able to contact him; it's completely out of character."

She closed her eyes tightly to fight the tears that threatened to spill from her and opening them, was surprised to see Buchan handing her a clean, folded white coloured handkerchief.

"My wife always insists I carry one for ladies in distress," he softly smiled at her.

He took a deep breath and glanced down at his notebook. "Peter's job, at the Caledonian Banking Group, does he have direct access to cash? I mean, is he a vulnerable person that someone might be able to pressure or coerce into…"

Susie smiled and dabbing at her eyes, interrupted him. "No, he works in an office and deals with the bank's investors, organising business loans, that sort of thing. His job is purely advising and suggesting new openings for investors. He doesn't even *see* the money so to answer your question I can't think of any reason why he would be targeted by a criminal."

Buchan nodded and snapped his book closed.

"There's just one final question for now, Susie. You know I have to ask it. Is there any chance, any possibility whatsoever that Peter might self harm?"

She shook her head. "I loved my husband," then sighed, "or at least I *thought* I loved him, but he could be a selfish bastard at times. I put up with it, his selfishness I mean, because I thought I loved him. No," she finally and with some sadness, shook her head, "I don't think Peter would ever consider hurting himself."

It occurred to Buchan that rather than being objective, he was involuntarily siding with Susie and that, he inwardly decided, was completely unprofessional.

He stood and grimaced at her. "We both know that I don't need to explain the rules. Protocol requires that the Sergeant and I have a look around the house to ensure you don't have your husband hidden in a cupboard somewhere."

She stood and nodded her head in understanding, both aware that since some time previously, two highly publicised missing person cases in England where the MP's were discovered within the parental home, it was now standard procedure by police forces throughout the UK at the report of a missing person, to first search the MP's home address.

Buchan and his Sergeant took less than five minutes to satisfy themselves that Peter Gibson was not secreted within the house and bidding Susie and Jenny goodnight, returned to their patrol car.

"What do you think, sir?" asked the Sergeant, switching on the engine.

"Well, it doesn't help that the MP is the husband of a serving officer and when the hint of scandal because she thinks he might have been playing away from home hits the media, as undoubtedly it will," he shook his head. "What I think is that I'm glad some other bugger will be conducting this inquiry."

In the original plans for Cranstonhill office that were sometime in the 1960's submitted to the Glasgow District Planning Department, clearly indicated the room be utilised for use as recreation by the station's officers. However, the reality was the room hardly saw any use of its dartboard, table tennis or snooker table simply because from the outset the long and wide room was more frequently used by the Division as an incident room for the investigation of serious crime.

Pushing open the door, DI Bobby Franklin saw that within three hours of the discovery of the body of Carol Meechan, the smooth apparatus that was the HOLMES Unit with their dedicated personnel and computer equipment was already set up. Seated at their desks the dedicated incident room team quietly prepared themselves to receive the first of the information and witness statements that they would later file, cross-file and catalogue. As the Senior Investigating Officer, Franklin was confident that all the relevant data since the discovery of the victim would soon be computerised and readily available to both him and the inquiry team.

HOLMES, he inwardly mused at the acronym. Just a pity it doesn't solve fucking murders, he thought as he glanced at the baffling array of computer equipment.

"Boss?" said a voice behind him.

He turned to see Waz Ahmed handing him a handwritten statement form. "I've just interviewed the boyfriend, well, partner I should say, John Paterson. I've taken what details I can, but the poor guy is pretty cut up and to be honest, I think we should maybe consider giving him a bit of time to come to terms with what's happened to his girlfriend," his face fell slightly, "if that's okay with you I mean?"

"Where is Paterson the now?"

"He's with Des in the interview room, having a coffee. I think he's in a state of shock, to be honest. Paterson, not Des," he half smiled.

Franklin glanced at the statement without reading it then asked, "Where does he intend staying tonight? In the flat?"

"No," Waz shook his head, "he's going to his parents. In fact, they're downstairs in the waiting area at the uniform bar."

"Des Mooney is of the opinion that Paterson has nothing to do with the murder. What do you think?"

Waz shrugged his shoulders and replied, "I think Des is right. I mean, I can't be certain, but the guy seems genuine enough. His alibi sounds to be easily checkable, so if you want, I can get right on that now."

Franklin glanced at his watch. "No, leave that the now. You and Des have had a long enough day as it is. Hand Paterson over to his parents and remind him that we might need to speak again with him tomorrow, so get their telephone number and address and he is to let us know where he will be at. Once that's done, you and Des get yourselves home for the night, but I want you both back here sharpish in the morning, say eight o'clock, okay?"

"Right boss," said Ahmed and was about to turn away when Franklin called him back.

"Just one other thing, Waz, Des is also of the opinion that the murder suspect might be the guy you're after for the street robberies. What do you think?"

"Not beyond possibility, boss." His eyes narrowed. "Are you thinking about running the two inquiries together with the mugger, I mean the robber as a suspect for the murder?"

"No," Franklin shook his head, "not at the minute anyway, however, it's worth considering. Right get yourself away home and Waz, good work at the locus in Lawrie Street. You and Des did well son, getting the place secured and the support agencies contacted."

"Thanks, boss," grinned Waz and left to hand the distraught John Paterson over to his parents.

A phone rung in the incident room and was answered by a portly analyst who called out, "DI Franklin, that was the Duty Officer at Pitt Street. Says to tell you that Force Control received message from the Cardiology Unit at the Western Infirmary about a Missus Violet Cairns?"

Franklin was at first bemused and then remembered the elderly lady who discovered the body and was removed from Lawrie Street in an ambulance. He nodded his head and answered, "What about her? Is there an update?"

"Aye," the woman frowned, "she succumbed half an hour ago. According to the consultant that attended her, it was a massive heart attack that the consultant considers was apparently brought on by shock."

CHAPTER 11

Magnus Gallagher awoke and turning towards the alarm clock, saw that it was not yet seven. Conscious of his increasingly aching back, he slowly arose from bed and pressing one hand on the sagging mattress, shook his head. What he needed was a more firm mattress, but baulked at the cost of such a luxury. A thought occurred to him. Perhaps if he was to lay a board across the springs to support the mattress then that might help.

Kneeling beside the bed, Magnus spent a few minutes at his morning prayers, but his thoughts were elsewhere.

He stood upright and with his arms raised, stretched his back and smiled. This morning after mass, if nothing else cropped up, he would be meeting his son Patrick at Maryhill shopping centre where they would collect Magnus's purchases from the charity shop. He walked to the window and pulled aside the curtain, seeing that the sky was overcast and threatening rain.

However, he decided the prospect of bad weather would not dampen his spirits and quietly opening his bedroom door, stepped into the hallway. He made towards the bathroom but hesitated outside Leigh's closed bedroom door, smiling in anticipation of his son's surprise. With almost childlike pleasure, he rubbed his hands together and went into the bathroom.

Glasgow, like most UK cities of a similar size and population during its long history, experienced its fair share of serious crime, including murder.

Throughout the ages the increasingly rapid advancement in both IT technology and the understanding of human physiology has contributed immensely to the arsenal at the disposal of the Senior Investigating Officer; that often lonely soul tasked with solving such crimes. However, no matter what tools are available to the SIO, the indisputable fact is that if the crime is to be solved it is the detective who wearily tramps from door to door, clipboard in hand, collecting information by interviewing witnesses or suspects and, who using his or her knowledge and experience, is the SIO's best asset.

DI Bobby Franklin, still weary after a late night but refreshed by a hot shower, arrived just after seven that morning in the incident room and saw that two of the HOLMES team were already at their desks. He acknowledged their nodded greetings and smiled when one with her hand, indicated the table in the corner where he saw the tea and coffee fund was already up and running.

Pouring himself a coffee, he learned that no new information had come in through the night and then mug in hand, settled himself at his desk with a printed timeline summary of the murder and prepared himself for what the day might bring.

Waz Ahmed arrived at work by bus, having persuaded his wife Alima that rather than their car sit all day outside the office, she could use it to visit her parents, an offer she gratefully accepted. Walking the short distance from the bus stop to the front door of Cranstonhill office, he was surprised to see Des Mooney dropped off from a newish, gleaming, black coloured four by four BMW, then lean back into the vehicle to deliver a passionate kiss farewell to the driver, a much younger and good-looking redheaded woman. When Mooney closed the passenger door, the woman shot off at speed.

"Morning Des, nice looking daughter you've got there," Waz greeted him with a grin, tongue in cheek, but nevertheless, his curiosity peeked. He couldn't explain why, but had presumed Mooney to be married, though never actually asked what his domestic situation was.

"Hi Waz, didn't see you there," smiled Mooney, smartly dressed in a navy blue two-piece suit with white shirt and blue polka dotted tie.

Mooney didn't explain who the woman was and Waz had the good sense not to ask.

"You look the dog's bollocks," Waz again grinned while they pushed their way through the entrance door into the foyer of the office. "That's a sharp suit for an old guy. You attending court today, are you?"

"No, smart-arse, as I've already been seconded to the CID for the robbery inquiry, the DI told me that I'm now part of the murder inquiry team so that, my cheeky upstart of a pup, means I'm your neighbour for the duration."

Making their way to the first floor, they continued their good-natured banter and upon entering the incident room, found that most of the officers designated to the inquiry had already arrived.

DI Franklin, seated at his desk, saw them arrive together and with his reading glasses in his hand, waved them both towards the tea and coffee table. "Briefing in ten minutes lads, so get yourselves a cuppa first," he instructed and then head bent, slipped on his new specs, courtesy of the twenty-four hour supermarket, and returned to reading the summary.

Susie Gibson, though having slept fitfully, woke later than she anticipated and jumped from bed, immediately regretting the action for her head was thumping. She took a deep breath and opening the curtains, saw the overcast sky and eyes narrowing, stared out into the roadway and wondered, Peter, where the hell are you?

Leigh Gallagher finished his breakfast and slipping off his chair, told his father that once more, Leigh would head down towards the Job Centre, "Just in the off chance there might be some new employment vacancies posted, Da."

His father could not know that though the staff had informed Leigh there was no need to attend the Job Centre, he had decided to collect some pamphlets to show his father and give credence to his continual lie.

With a knowing smile, Magnus nodded and when he heard his son bang the front door closed, hurried to clear the dishes and get to mass, but his thoughts were elsewhere; fixed firmly on his meeting later that morning with his son, Patrick.

The continuing absence of Peter Gibson from his office at the Caledonian Banking Group was still the subject of much gossip and speculation. Much to the consternation of the senior management and in particular, John Brewster, the HR Director, rumours regarding Mister Gibson's whereabouts continued to circulate throughout the building.

Settling himself behind his large, ornate and highly polished desk, Baxter reached for the phone and dialled the number that now was beginning to irk him.

"Ah, good morning Missus Gibson, it's John Brewster here," he began. "Is there any news yet of Peter?"

He listened intently, his brow furrowed and face turning to a deep frown when Susie Gibson informed him that no, there was no news and because of the unusual circumstances surrounding the disappearance of her husband, she had the previous evening reported Peter to the police as a missing person.

Brewster was astounded.

"My dear Missus Gibson; was that wise?" he blustered. "I mean, after all Peter has been gone what, just about twenty-four hours or so, isn't that right? Surely the police will not deem him to be missing after such a short time?"

"Peter has been gone now over forty hours Mister Brewster and has never at any time during our marriage, been out of touch for such a lengthy time without informing me of where he is. Besides, it is not the time that matters, but the circumstances. You have known Peter for a number of years, have you not Mister Brewster. In that time, have you ever known him to conduct himself in such a manner; to miss meetings, not return phone calls or inform his wife or colleagues where he might be? I have to consider that there might be a reason he is not in touch with me or anyone at the bank and so, as his wife I took the decision to report him missing to the police," she firmly stated.

It occurred to him to question if perhaps there was some domestic reason that Gibson had fled the marital home, however, he shirked from entering such a discussion, reasoning that what he did not know, might not therefore return and bite the Caledonian Banking Group firmly in the arse.

Besides, from their former though brief encounters, he was astutely aware that Missus Gibson, a police detective he recalled, was a formidable woman and might not take lightly to any prying into her and her husband's private life.

He decided that there was little more he could say on the subject and requesting that if there be any word from his errant colleague, she have Peter contact the bank immediately.

Replacing the handset in its cradle, he sat for a moment and a ghastly thought struck him like a hammer blow.

Quickly he lifted the phone again and dialled the first of the internal numbers for his fellow Directors.

Sitting in the lounge of her home, Susie Gibson stared at the phone, willing it to ring if only for Peter at least to let her know he was okay.

"Mum?" said Jenny from the doorway, her school satchel over her shoulder and her blazer across her forearm. "I'm just going now. Will you be all right?"

She forced a smile and nodded, not trusting herself to speak.

"Are you going to work?"

Susie swallowed hard and taking deep breath shook her head and said, "No, I've already phoned in and spoken with my DCI. He's told me to take the day and besides, she waved a hand at the phone, I want to be here when your dad calls."

"Do you think he will call? I mean, that he's all right?"

"Yes, of course," she firmly replied. "I think… well, the last couple of months have been a strain on us both love and I think your dad just needs some time to get himself together. I don't think he will have gone to any of our family or friends. He's probably embarrassed and likely lying on some hotel room bed, trying to pluck up the courage to phone and admit what an idiot he has been," she smiled bravely at her daughter, but even Susie hardly believed what she was saying.

Jenny held up her mobile phone. "I'm in exam revision all morning. Will you text me when you hear something?"

"Course I will, love. You try not to worry," but could see that the advice was falling on deaf ears. Jenny had also suffered the through the last months; the niggling and the arguments, the tense apprehension when Susie and Peter were in the same room. As if suddenly realising what Peter and she had put their daughter through, Susie got up and quickly crossed the room, wrapping her arms about her daughter and holding her tight.

Jenny's satchel and blazer fell to the floor as she hugged her mother to her.

At last, they pulled apart and placing her hands softly on Jenny's cheeks, Susie stared at her and with a lump in her throat, pretended surprise and asked, "My God, what have you done with my daughter? When did such a lovely young woman take her place?"

Jenny blushed and smiled then stepping away from her mother, lifted the satchel and blazer from the floor and closed the front door behind her.

Susie, standing in the lounge, watched her walk along the driveway and turning out of sight.

Sighing, she went to the kitchen and brewed some coffee.

Waz Ahmed pulled the passenger seat seatbelt across his body and clipped it into the housing.

Des Mooney glanced with distaste across to the wreck sitting in the corner of Cranstonhill yard and starting the car, said, "Well, at least it's not that bloody van again."

Waz read the Inquiry Action delegated to them by the HOLMES office manager after DI Franklin had concluded his briefing.

"Says here that we have to attend at the premises of the Caledonian Banking Group at 148 West George Street and obtain a statement regarding the victim's employment there. Shit. I thought we might get something a bit more interesting," he exhaled with disappointment. "The Murder Investigation Team guys, they seemed to get the best Actions."

"Stop whining, you moaning faced git," grinned Mooney, "and consider yourself lucky that you are working on the murder and not covering the day to day crime reports like some of the rest of the office. Besides, how many murders have you previously worked on and when have you been involved in a HOLMES inquiry, eh?"

"Okay, so this is my first," Waz spat out, feeling a little petulant and shrugged, "but I suppose if I'm going to be in the CID for a number of years, I have to start somewhere, don't I?"

"Agreed, so think about that," Mooney nodded, stopping at traffic lights and then when the lights changed to green, turned the car left into North Street and joined the slowly moving, early morning commuter traffic that drove towards the city centre. "But you have to understand young Waz that Bobby Franklin can't use the murder of a young woman just to train you. He has a responsibility to the deceased and her family to get this solved as soon as he can and *that's* why he's ensuring the priority Actions go to the big boys, the detectives that are trained in this type of major inquiry. These guys are all seasoned detectives who have cut their teeth as divisional CID and done it before and know what they are doing, so in the future when you get the opportunity to be part of a murder inquiry team, you will have the previous experience of having worked on this inquiry, yeah?"

Waz nodded, glancing out of the passenger window at the throng of pedestrians making their weary way along Sauchiehall Street.

"Sorry, Des, you're right of course. I'm just a bit too keen to get as much under my belt as quickly as I can."

"It will happen, wee pal. Just take a minute to look at the big picture. For the first few days, unless we get an immediate break, we're doing the groundwork, building up a picture of the deceased and her movements prior to her murder."

He braked sharply to avoid running over an elderly woman who, without a backward glance, hurried across the road in front of the traffic, a mobile phone clamped to her ear.

"Bloody idiot," he seethed and then, picking up speed, continued. "Groundwork, like the foundations of a house; it's the basis of solid police work. The Action we've been handed will hopefully tell us something about the deceased, what she was like at work, who her pals were. Maybe even be an insight into her private life at home if she's confided in some of her workmates, yeah?" he turned to glance at Waz.

Waz nodded and sighed.

"Okay Da, lesson over," and his brow narrowed. "Have you worked on a murder before?"

"Not as an inquiry officer," he shook his head. "The odd occasion as a plain clothes officer when for example, the boss needed a suspect's house watched or maybe standing guard at the scene of a murder, but even with my lengthy service, this is my first time actually being part of the inquiry team," he grinned.

"Well then," Waz returned his grin, "we'd better get it right then, eh?"

The dark coloured, heavy fabric curtains, tightly drawn over the six large windows cut out the bright light of the morning, though the sound of light rain was still heard rattling against the old fashioned, single glazed panes.

In the dim light, the four Directors sat quietly waiting within the wall panelled boardroom on the second floor of the Caledonian Banking Group headquarters, in West George Street.

In complete contravention of not only the Scottish Government edict on the issue, but also the banks own rules, three of the men sat smoking, one with a highly expensive Cuban cigar that polluted the air with a thick, sweet, sickly smelling fog.

For the time being, all the men ignored the silver coffee pot and four china cups and saucers that lay upon a nearby occasional table, at the side of the room.

The only non-smoker of the quartet, the HR Director, John Brewster sat at the top of the highly polished table watched by his three colleagues who fortuitously were in the bank that morning and who, responding to his urgent call, were readily available to attend the hastily convened meeting.

A loud knock caused Brewster to press the small switch located under the table by his right hand that in turn activated the green light on the wall by the oak doors, outside the room.

Harry McPherson, bereft of his customary confident and slightly arrogant demeanour, hurriedly entered the room, closing the door behind him.

"As you instructed sir," he said to Brewster, handing the older man a single sheet of paper.

McPherson stood deferentially to one side, his hands clasped in front of him and swallowing hard, nervously licked his lips.

Brewster put on his reading glasses and slowly scanned the written script.

Then his face paled and he turned towards McPherson.

"This can't be correct?" he gasped.

"It's just a preliminary examination of the files sir," McPherson quietly replied, bending slightly towards Baxter. "I have my staff, sorry," he swallowed hard again, recalling Brewster's instruction, "not my staff sir, Miss Sutherland checking further, as we speak."

"But this figure," Baxter held the paper in one hand and from the other, pointed a bony forefinger at McPherson's conclusion, "this can't be right surely. How could he possibly have…" his voice stuttered to a close and he shook his head as though disbelieving what he read.

His fellow Directors glanced uneasily at each other, unconsciously leaning forward, keen to hear the update yet reluctant to disturb Brewster's concentration as he continued to scan the report.

"When will you have a definitive result?" he snapped at McPherson.

McPherson, believing himself to be the focus of Brewster's silent rage, gulped and with grimace, replied, "We have to check each individual reference that was forwarded sir and that takes time, then of course each account will…"

"Don't give me excuses, give me a time," Brewster again testily snapped, then realised he was being unfair and briefly closing his eyes against the sudden onset of a headache, with a slight but courteous nod, added, "If you please, Mister McPherson."

"At the earliest sir, I can have a preliminary result within five figures by the close of business today."

"Thank you, Mister McPherson. Please, do not allow me to detain you any further," Brewster responded with a further nod of his head, dismissing the younger man.

He waited till McPherson had left the room then glanced at each of his Directors in turn and calmer now, said, "Gentlemen, it seems we have a problem."

CHAPTER 12

Sitting on the single bed in his parents' home in what had once been his own bedroom, John Paterson had had a restless night, his mind reeling and still unable to accept that Carol was dead. No, not just dead, but murdered.

He lowered his head into his hands and again silently wept; his shoulders heaving as unabated, his tears flowed.

Standing silently and unobserved in the shadow outside the doorway of the room, his father slowly shook his head and reaching for the handle softly closed the door to permit his son the privacy to grieve in peace.

The morning news on the radio had simply disclosed that a woman's body had been found the previous evening in Lawrie Street and police were treating the death as murder, but thankfully, poor Carol had not named.

A knock at the front door startled him and recalled the detectives warning that the press might come calling, but then he heard his wife say, "Come in officers," and descending the stairs, saw his wife showing two suited and sombre faced men into the front room.

DI Bobby Franklin shrugged into his suit jacket and with his Detective Sergeant, Emma Ferguson, made his way from the incident room, through the office and downstairs to the car.

"You okay with post mortems Emma? I mean, you will have been to a few when you were with divisional CID and the Serious Crime Squad, yeah?"

"More than a few," she replied, getting into the driver's seat while Franklin climbed into the passenger seat, then with a smirk added, "and some I even enjoyed."

She saw his curious expression and smiled. "I mean, when the victim was a bad guy and no loss to society."

"Aye," he agreed in understanding, "there's been a few worthies that the Mortuary has seen pass through there, eh?"

She drove the car expertly out of the yard and joined the traffic on St Vincent Street, travelling east.

"The briefing this morning," he opened, "do you think I did the right thing? I mean, placing so much emphasis and resources on finding this street robber?"

He flinched slightly as with a sudden burst of speed, she drove the car through a changing traffic light and continued eastwards.

"I understand your reasoning boss and there seems to be little doubt that the current crime reporting seems to indicate the street robber is a likely suspect and particularly as it seems the victim's handbag was stolen, but I agree with you that you are not going to pursue just the one line of inquiry. Who knows what the door to door will turn up and when the guys have interviewed the partner …John Paterson isn't it?"

"Aye, apparently they've been together for several years."

"Well, once we've got Paterson's statement we might have an idea if the lassie had any enemies; I mean anyone vicious enough to stab her twice like that."

Never a comfortable passenger, no matter who was driving, a moment passed while Franklin decided to permit her to concentrate on her driving.

Stopped a traffic light, he turned slightly towards her and asked, "What's your thoughts on the old woman dying; Missus Cairns, the heart attack victim."

She shook her head, her mouth tightening. "To live your life then in your twilight years see a sight that so horrifies you that it causes your death? How the hell can you explain that one, eh?"

He flinched again as Ferguson narrowly scraped the car between a parked bus and an oncoming truck.

"Why do you ask, boss?" he saw her brow furrow as she concentrated on her driving or was she thinking like he was?

"Are you thinking that if we get a result for the murder, you might somehow include libelling some sort of charge against the accused?"

"Well," he slowly drawled, "if I was able to prove that the sight of the heavily bloodstained deceased was a direct result of Missus Cairns heart attack, I might consider a charge of breach of the peace."

"You're kidding me on!" she burst out with a half laugh. "The Fiscal, let alone the Crown Prosecution Service, would never go for it!"

She half turned towards him, but her eyes on the road ahead. "Wait a minute is there some sort of stated case about this, a previous conviction? It's that what you are on about?"

"None that I'm aware of," he smiled, "but there's always a first time, isn't there?"

"Do you not think that libelling a charge like that against an accused might get laughed out of court?"

"Don't see why," he huffily replied, then with a grin playing about his own mouth, said, "If Missus Cairns' doctor can provide a statement that as long as she took her prescribed medication, the old woman was relatively healthy and if her own consultant, not the guy that pronounced life extinct, is able to swear that in his opinion the shock brought about the heart attack. Well, think about it Emma. The Law says that if an individual's conduct is severe enough to cause alarm to ordinary people and or threaten serious disturbance to the community and in Missus Cairns case, actually caused death, I *might* have sufficient medical evidence to prove the accused actions of murdering and leaving the deceased for Missus Cairns to discover resulted in her heart attack. And let's face it, my doubting young sceptic; you won't get anything more breaching the Queen's peace than leaving a dead, bloodstained body lying about, will you?"

"Boss," she stopped the car in the Mortuary courtyard and switching off the engine, turned towards him and shook her head, "you are one fucking chancer, so you are."

Magnus Gallagher had arrived at the Maryhill Shopping Centre half an hour early and buying the morning edition of the 'Glasgow News', unaccustomedly treated himself to a bacon roll and cup of tea in the small café in the Centre while he waited.

Now he was quite literally hopping from foot to foot, his eyes darting back and forth as he searched among the shoppers for his son Patrick.

A few minutes later than agreed, he saw the tall young priest strolling towards him, his priestly clothes abandoned for a pair of worn jeans and a plaid shirt under a worker's black coloured donkey jacket, one hand waving in greeting and a large grin on his face.

Magnus saw with pride that his handsome young son, who some likened to a young Gregory Peck, turned more than a few of the women shoppers heads and almost grinned, wondering what their reaction would be if they learned Patrick was a devout and celibate priest.

The two men briefly hugged then Patrick said, "Right Da, I've parked the van at the rear of the charity shop so let's go and collect the stuff."

Coincidentally, while his father and brother were meeting within the Shopping Centre, Leigh Gallagher was a little more than fifty yards away and was about to depart the Job Centre with a handful of pamphlets that he stuffed into the back pocket of his denims.

A member of staff who recognised Leigh noticed his brief visit and, this being Maryhill, left the relative safety of the wire grilled back office to suggest that Leigh might wish to make an appointment to discuss his job prospects.

Not wishing to provoke a problem with his unemployment benefit handout, Leigh pretended interest and spent a boring ten minutes arranging an appointment that he already knew he would not attend. Pushing through the door with its plywood replacement for the glass that once had been there, he started to walk towards Shakespeare Street, already planning that later that evening he would spend an hour or two in the Partick area and this being Friday, hoped that whatever woman he robbed might have a weeks wages in her purse.

Susie Gibson had hoped that a shower might make her feel a little better, but it was to no avail. Wrapped in a bathrobe, her hair still wet, she wandered though the empty house.

So far, she had fielded three phone calls; the first from the HR Director John Brewster, no doubt worried about any adverse media publicity Peter's disappearance might bring, she bitterly thought and shortly after that a call from her DCI, Ross McConnell; a decent enough man who kindly told her to take as long as necessary, but with a request she keep him apprised of any developments. The last and most recent call was from her CID neighbour, Andy Brownlie, insisting she phone him if there was anything she needed or that he could do to help.

"So, what's the word in the office there, Andy? Am I the talk of the steamie," she had tried to joke.

"Nothing but good things said about you Susie. I mean," he pretended a growl, "would I let any of these sods say something bad about my neighbour?"

She heard him sigh then, he continued, "It would be naive of me to try and kid you that people are curious. I've had a few questions directed at me about you and Peter; you know, the nosey bastards wanting to know if he's run off with another woman, that sort of thing."

He had meant it as a joke, but no sooner said it than she heard him inhale and say, "Sorry Susie, that was a bit insensitive, I didn't mean…"

"No, don't worry Andy," she quickly interrupted him, "if they're talking about me, they're leaving everybody else alone. Besides, who's to say that Peter *hasn't* run off with someone else?"

There was an awkward silence and then he said, "I take it Susie you have no idea where he might be, where Peter's gone to, I mean?"

She shook her head at the phone. "None whatsoever," she replied. "I'm probably correct in guessing he wouldn't go to any of our family or friends, simply because he knows that they would tell him not to be stupid and to get his arse back here and talk through whatever problems we have. He's too much of a bloody coward for that," she said, unable to prevent the bitterness in her voice.

Any awkward silence fell between them, broken when, trying to sound a little more cheerful, she asked, "So in other issues. How is Janice?"

The next few minutes of the call was taken up with a discussion about the pregnant Janice. Then Susie said, "Look Andy, I might not be in for a couple of days, maybe longer. I've got some inquiries …"

"Right, stop there Susie. You know that I'm on top of it, so the last thing you need to be worrying about is what's happening here. I've already been through your basket on your desk and done what's needed, okay?"

She smiled and took the mild rebuke, simply replying "Thanks, Andy. I owe you one."

"You owe me nothing, boss," he immediately replied and concluded the call by insisting again that if Susie needed him for anything, she only had to phone.

In the kitchen, she made yet another mug of coffee and tried made toast, but buttering it her stomach heaved and nauseous through lack of sleep, knew she wouldn't be able to eat it.

Her mobile phone activated and eagerly, she scrolled down, but almost with disappointment saw that it was a text from Jenny, asking if there was any news.

She quickly typed a reply then leaned against the kitchen worktop and for the hundredth time that morning, wondered again where he was.

Magnus Gallagher and his son Patrick, with some difficulty, heaved the solidly built double door wardrobe up the tenement stairs and at last, to the older man's relief, arrived at the landing outside his flat.

"Maybe be an idea to get the old furniture out first Da, and while we're doing that, how about a cuppa, eh?" suggested Patrick, worrying at the sight of his father's flushed face.

"Aye, right you are son," replied Magnus, breathing heavily and ignoring the tightness in his chest. "We'll leave this here the now," he waved a hand at the wardrobe, "and I'll get the kettle on to boil." In the street below, Leigh Gallagher stood in the entrance of a close and wondered what was going on. He had seen his father and brother lifting the wardrobe from the back of a van and almost cried out a greeting, but stopped. The last thing he wanted was to have to speak to that pious bastard Patrick, he snorted. Angrily, he turned on his heel and began to walk away; deciding he would go to the corner café on Maryhill Road for a coffee and hope by the time he returned home, his brother would have fucked off back to his church.

Back in his own department, senior Accounts Manager Harry McPherson locked eyes with Morven Sutherland and with an almost imperceptible nod of his head, indicated she join him in his office. As she followed him through the door, he turned and closed it behind her, but the curious expressions of his staff seated at their desks, did not escape his attention.
"What's going on Harry?" she asked with a puzzled expression.
"Fucked if I know," he snapped back and then contritely raised his hands. "Sorry, sorry," he repeated and then seating himself at his desk, waved that she sit opposite.
She could see that he seemed anxious and upset.
"Those accounts you checked for me," he began. "John Brewster and the other Directors are in the boardroom as we speak discussing them. All I know is that the accounts were all recommended by Peter Gibson and the sums that Gibson allocated to each account as business loans…" he hesitated, at a loss how to explain it. "Well, it seems the money has not been invested after all."
Sutherland stared at him. "What do you mean, not invested? Why ever not? I mean, if Mister Gibson hasn't invested the money, what has he done with it then? Where *is* it?"
His face paled.
"That, Morven, is the real question, isn't it?"

Magnus Gallagher breathing more easily, now felt slightly better and fetching some screwdrivers and a hammer from a cupboard in the hallway, led Patrick into Leigh's bedroom.

"Right son, we'll get the wardrobe and drawers emptied first, Just put his clothes onto the bed for now."

"I don't think you'll need those tools, Da," replied Patrick with a grin, shaking the rickety wardrobe. "This thing looks like it's about to fall over," he joked.

It took the two men just a few minutes to pull the wardrobe apart, stacking the wooden sides against the wall.

"I'm going to keep two of those," said Magnus, pointing to the MDF shelves and thinking they might serve to bolster his sagging mattress.

It was when Patrick bent down to lift the base of the deconstructed wardrobe that he saw the tin box. He smiled and with a joking whisper, said, "I think I've found our Leigh's secret trove of treasure."

"Ah now, don't you be looking in there, boyo. If your brother has some knick knacks he wants to keep private, then it's not for us to pry."

"Okay, Da," smiled Patrick and still down on one knee, held the tin box out to his father. Magnus made to take the box from Patrick's hand, but stumbled and reached to steady himself on his sons shoulder. However, by doing so the box fell from Patrick's grasp to the floorboards, causing the lid to come off.

They both stared in surprise at the bundle of currency notes and the credit card that fell from the box, but the object that really took their attention was a long, thin bladed, black-handled kitchen knife.

Max the commissionaire pointed Waz Ahmed and Des Mooney towards the inquiry desk situated within a corner of the large, ornate foyer of the Caledonian Banking Group with the whispered caution, "Watch her lads, she's a sullen faced harridan, that one."

The old man's warning wasn't far off the mark.

Declaring themselves to be police officers and requesting they speak with a manager in Personnel, the haughty young woman curtly told them to take a seat, that she would try to ". get someone in Human Resources," to speak with them.

"*In Human Resources,*" aped Mooney in a falsetto voice as they turned towards the bench seats. "Well, that puts us firmly in our bloody place, doesn't it?"

The young woman, one hand holding a telephone to her ear, called across to them in a disapproving manner, "Exactly *what* is the inquiry about?"

"Sorry love," Mooney cheerfully answered, "we really need to speak to someone a lot more senior than a wee snooty receptionist like you."

It took all of Waz's willpower to control himself and even then, he almost choked trying to stifle his laughter.

The young woman, her face reddening and lips tightly closed, glared at them but then visibly startled as the person on the other end of the line reminded her that he or she awaited a response.

"They'll no tell me," she stuttered in broad Glaswegian, her practised accent for the moment forgotten.

"You've to wait there," she hissed at them both and slamming the phone down into its cradle, turned away with her head down, pretending to busy herself at her desk.

Less than five minutes passed before a young man wearing a dark suit arrived and politely invited them to accompany him.

He led them towards a door at the side of the foyer, but Mooney didn't miss the opportunity to give the young woman a parting smile and rudely blew her a kiss.

"Who are we seeing in your, ah, Human Resources then?" asked Waz as they climbed the richly carpeted stairs.

"Oh, I'm not taking you to HR," the young man turned to Waz with a curious expression and then continued, "I've been told to take you to meet with Mister Brewster. He *is* the HR Director."

"Okay, fine," answered Waz without giving it any further thought, but walking slightly behind him, Des Mooney considered it odd that two cops turn up out of the blue and are taken straight to meet with a Director.

Arriving on the second floor, the young man stopped outside a set of double oak doors that bore a brass plate, declaring the room to be the 'Boardroom'. He knocked firmly on the door and glanced upwards.

A green light flashed and he opened the door then stood to one side and ushered the officers through, but did not follow them into the room.

The door closed behind them.

In the dimness of the room, they saw four men who stood around a heavy wooden and highly polished table.

The fug of tobacco hung heavily in the air and seemed to permeate throughout the room.

"Gentlemen, I'm John Brewster and these are my fellow Directors," he waved a hand at the men who each in turn nodded to the officers. Waving Waz and Mooney towards chairs on his left, Brewster resumed his seat at the top of the table while his three colleagues sat on the chairs to his right.

"Thank you for being so diligent in this matter, though I have to admit I did fear that Missus Gibson was a little too quick in reporting her husband Peter to be missing."

Waz snapped a glance at Mooney, who shrugged his shoulders.

"As you must realise, gentlemen," continued Brewster, "the media implications for the bank will be," he paused, seeking the correct word, "troublesome, so I must insist on your discretion in this matter."

"Mister Brewster," Waz began, feeling a flush rise to his cheeks, "there seems to have been some sort of misunderstanding. We are not here about a… Peter Gibson, did you say the name is?" Brewster in turn looked confused.

"Yes, Peter Gibson, our senior Business Loans Manager, so if you are not here about Mister Gibson, young man, why exactly *are* you here," he thundered.

Mooney gritted his teeth. He wasn't about to let this old idiot bully his younger colleague and interrupted with a snapping reply. "We are here about one of your employees, Mister Brewster. A Miss Carol Meechan who we understand from her partner was employed in your Accounts department."

Brewster sat stiffly back in his chair and slapped both hands down on the table.

"Really," he huffed condescendingly at the officers, "we have no time to discuss one of our employees. We have rather more pressing issues to deal with at this time."

Later that afternoon, relating the story to his DI, Waz insisted that Des Mooney really enjoyed the moment, for according to Wax, Mooney locked eyes with the older man and leaning forward, ever so quietly replied, "What? More pressing than murder, you mean?"

DC Andy Brownlie slowly worked his way through the pile of paperwork that had somehow mysteriously accumulated within a working day. Sighing, he created a pile of reports for urgent attention and one for not so urgent attention. He was about to commence on the most pressing issue when he heard his name called.

DCI Ross McConnell stood at the door of the general office and beckoned Andy to follow him, then turned away into the corridor and towards his office.

Andy could guess what the summons was about and closing the DCI's door, he sat in the chair that was indicated opposite McConnell's desk.

Promoted just two months earlier into his current rank and though nobody had really gotten to know McConnell, his reputation from his former Ayrshire division as a fair man had preceded him. The word was that the DCI, who was just over a year from retiring, had been promoted to enhance his pension as a reward for previous service rendered, as well as his close personal association with the former Chief Constable; golf partners, it was rumoured.

"No word yet then," said McConnell, already knowing the answer to his own question.

Andy shook his head. "You know she's reported him missing, boss?"

"Aye, and there's a problem, Andy. I had DI Bobby Franklin from Cranstonhill on the phone just now. You heard about the woman's body being found yesterday, over in Partick?"

Andy's eyes narrowed and his stomach lurched, fearing that he wasn't going to like this; not one little bit. He slowly nodded, though slightly confused.

"According to Bobby Franklin…" then McConnell smiled. "Bobby's a good guy, one of the old school. Anyway, in confidence, Bobby's gave me the heads up. So just to be clear, you and I are not having this conversation. Do you understand?"

Even more confused, Andy again nodded.

McConnell took a deep breath and said, "It would be remiss of me to warn you that you are not to become involved in anything that I tell you, however, in the short time I have been here, I have been impressed by Detective Sergeant Gibson's work output. She strikes me as being a dedicated and tenacious detective and you, young man, seem to be following in her mould. That said, though admittedly I am not conversant with all the facts of the case, I learned earlier this morning that the young woman who was found murdered worked in the same bank as DS Gibson's husband." He leaned forward and stared at Andy to stress his statement, "I am *not* at all suggesting there is any connection, however, coincidental as this might be, there is a *strong* likelihood that the murder investigating team could call upon DS Gibson if indeed they make any connection between the dead woman and her husband. Do you understand what I am saying, Andy?"

"Aye sir, I do."

"Then there is nothing more for us to discuss other than *might* I suggest that you leave off dealing with your paperwork, take a car and perhaps consider leaving the office to go and follow up on some inquiry or other?"

Andy took a deep breath and nodded. The message was clear and unequivocal.

Ensure your neighbour gets forewarning of the storm that is about to descend upon her and do not let Susie Gibson face this alone.

Father Patrick Gallagher sat with his father in the kitchen of the flat, the tin box and its contents on the table between them.

"Look, Da, it might be completely innocent. I mean, it might be money that Leigh has saved from his benefits and he could have found the card, eh?"

Magnus took a deep breath and with a forefinger, poked at the knife. "You could always see the good in people, Patrick. I always believed it as being a blessing, not a failing, but not this time son," he sadly shook his head, his eyes wet with unshed tears. "I can see no explanation other than Leigh has stolen this money and…"

His face paled as a recent memory struck him like a hammer blow, something he had read. He tried to rise from the chair, but his legs failed him and he sat heavily back down. "The paper, this morning's paper; the 'Glasgow News'," he croaked, pointing out the kitchen door into the hallway, the pain in his chest returning. 'It's in my jacket pocket, in the cupboard, Pat. Fetch me the paper son."

Patrick could see his father was in distress and hurrying through to the room, brought the paper back and placed it on the table before his father.

With shaking hands, Magnus turned to page two and stuttered, "There," pointing to the article about the discovery of a woman's body within a close in Lawrie Street in the Partick area.

Leaning over his father to read the report, Patrick gulped and unconsciously placed his hand on his father's shoulder.

Though the police, he read, did not confirm the cause of death, local residents had disclosed the victim was stabbed to death.

Slowly Patrick's eyes rose from the newspaper and staring at the knife, he said in a hushed voice, "Oh God, oh no, Leigh. What have you done?"

CHAPTER 13

DI Bobby Franklin stood in the centre of the room, the inquiry team ranged about him seated on chairs or standing, leaning against the walls. He glanced briefly at the notes he held in his hand and began his briefing.

"DS Emma Ferguson and I attended at the Mortuary and were present when the PM was conducted upon the deceased. As you will all be aware, Carol Meechan was stabbed twice to the back, both wounds inflicted with a sharp, narrow bladed weapon with the first blow puncturing her back between the shoulders, just below her neck and this stabbing blow sliced into her spine and effectively caused an immediate paralysis to her limbs. The first blow would undoubtedly have killed Miss Meechan. The second blow," he glanced at his notes, "pierced her aorta and caused massive internal haemorrhaging with her blood almost immediately filling her lungs and, according to the pathologist, would certainly have resulted in death even if she had received immediate treatment."

He paused, allowing the shocked men and women about him to appreciate the savagery of the attack upon the young and defenceless woman.

Turning towards an older detective, he said, "Eric, see that the productions, the clothing, etcetera, that Emma and I brought back for the PM are lodged and get the blood and tissue samples up to Forensic soon as you can.

"Yes boss," Eric replied.

Taking a deep breath, Franklin turned towards DS Gary Thomas, the Incident Room manager and asked, "Gary, what's the position regarding the door to door, so far?"

"There's only one statement of any relevance at the minute, boss. A woman returning from her work saw a hooded figure hanging about in a close near to the murder scene, but could only provide a very, very rough description." Thomas nodded towards a statement form he held in his hand and said, "Dark coloured hoody, dark trousers and nothing else, I'm afraid. The witness says she got a bit of a fright and hurried into her close and up to her flat. No chance of an identification, I'm afraid," he concluded with a shake of his head.

"No other witnesses?" asked Franklin, the disappointment in his voice evident.

"None," Thomas again shook his head.

"Right," Franklin slowly acknowledged, exhaling at the bad news. "Okay, as you are aware, I said at this morning's briefing I was going to concentrate our inquiries upon the street robber who in the last week has committed five robberies that we know of. The partial descriptions we have indicated a male wearing a dark hooded top and dark trousers, who threatened his victims with a long, sharp bladed knife similar to this one."

He held up the knife given to Waz and Mooney by Rita Whyte then handed it to the nearest officer indicating it be passed about the room.

"However, there has been a spanner thrown into the works, guys and gals. Waz Ahmed and Des Mooney there," he nodded to the two officers, "were Actioned this morning to make inquiry regarding Carol Meechan's employment with the Caledonian Banking Group. Waz," he beckoned him from his chair to the DI, "give the team an overview of how it went, please," then Franklin stepped to the side of the room.

Waz cleared his throat and began. "Des and I interviewed the HR Director Mister John Brewster. He initially thought we were there regarding another employee, a Peter Gibson who is the Business Loans manager for the bank. When we explained the purpose of our visit, it turned out Brewster didn't really know Meechan," he half smiled, "kind of inferred she was just a lowly employee and told us the bank employs over one hundred people in its head office and that he couldn't be expected to know them all."

Several of the inquiry team caught the sarcasm in his voice. "Anyway, it turned out that our deceased works, I mean worked, in the Accounts Department and there is nothing to suggest that she has known Gibson either through work or socially, though it *is* highly likely that their paths must have crossed many times because the Business Loans personnel work closely with the Accounts staff."

"Tell the team what you learned about Gibson, Waz," interrupted Franklin, keen to move the briefing on.

"Right, boss. As I said, Mister Brewster, the HR Director thought we were there about Gibson and got a bit shirty when we told him no, that we were there regarding Carol Meechan. Anyway, it turns out that the bank is in a bit of a panic about Gibson's disappearance because though at the time of our visit they hadn't completed their accounting, it seems that Gibson, as the Business Loans Manager had somehow or other managed to divert a considerable sum of the bank's money that was supposedly loaned to a number of companies for business purposes."

A hands was raised by a young female MIT detective who asked, "What, stolen the money you mean?"

"Seems so," agreed Waz. "The bank is still trying to trace where the money is."

"How much are we talking about here?" the young female detective asked.

"As I said, the bank is still trying to collect all the information, but when we were there, Des and me, I mean, Mister Brewster told us that the bank couldn't account for two point eight million pounds and they were still checking further loans issued by Gibson to these companies."

A gasp went round the room and at least one comment of, "Fuck me!"

"I take it that you haven't had time to check with the companies?" the detective persisted.

Nobody missed the glance that Waz gave Mooney before he replied, "It's speculative at the minute, but it seems that the companies apparently don't exist."

Franklin held up his hand and walking to the middle of the room, with a nod dismissed Waz to his chair.

"As you will rightly guess, this new information provides the inquiry with a further motive for the murder, other than my first assessment of street robbery."

He paused and glanced down at his feet, reluctant to continue because he was aware that what he was now about to tell his team would not just surprise some of them, but some might be personally known to DS Gibson.

"Waz and Des learned that while there does not at this time," he stressed, "seem to be any personal contact between our deceased and Peter Gibson, we must keep an open mind that Meechan and Gibson are somehow implicated in the missing money from the bank. I also must inform you and, ladies and gentlemen, what I am about to say *must not*," he stressed, "be discussed outwith this inquiry. Do I make myself clear?"

He glanced around the room at the nodding heads and continued. "The MP Peter Gibson is the husband of a serving officer, who some of you might know; Detective Sergeant Susan Gibson of Baird Street CID. If you are socially acquainted with DS Gibson, I must ask you to see me after this briefing and declare your relationship. I must stress this is still a murder inquiry and we have not proven any link between our victim and Peter Gibson. So again, this inquiry is not about the husband of DS Gibson. I am simply being cautious and trying to cover all angles, okay?"

He licked at his lips and hands extended as if in unconscious empathy, continued. "My understanding is that DS Gibson reported her husband missing and has no knowledge of his whereabouts, so she is as much a victim as anyone. Do I make myself clear on that issue?"

Again, there was a nodding of heads.

"Is there any questions?"

A number of hands were raised and he pointed to the young female detective who earlier had quizzed Waz.

"I don't know DS Gibson, boss. I take it that because of the *coincidence* of her husband being an MP from the same bank as the deceased and in particular with the missing money being investigated, we will inherit the MP inquiry for her husband?"

He shook his head. "Not at this time. However, we will have a watching brief and I will be in discussion with Detective Superintendent Lynn Massey regarding this issue. However, if a relationship of any kind between our deceased and Peter Gibson is proven, then of course, we will include him in our investigations."

He pointed to a grizzled Detective Sergeant from the Murder Investigation Team.

"If the inquiry expands, Bobby, like it seems it might, you could be looking at drafting in more officers. Do you want me to contact my boss and forewarn him?"

"Leave it for now Sandy and we'll see how we get on meantime with what we've got, eh?"

Sandy nodded and Franklin pointed to the last hand raised, a young analyst who was part of the HOLMES team.

"In the event Peter Gibson overlaps the murder inquiry sir, do you wish me to contact the local division from where he is reported missing and commence the creation of a separate index and an Actionable inquiry?"

He drew a deep breath as he considered her question and then shook his head. "It's too early to make that kind of decision," and turning towards DS Thomas, said, "Am I correct in thinking that if the two inquiries do overlap, you will be able to merge the MP inquiry into our system, Gary?"

"Only if it's already on the HOLMES system, boss, but if it's still just on the Police National Computer, then at the minute the two systems are not compatible. That said," his brow furrowed, "I don't think there should be too much information other than the MP's details, where he's missing from and the initial inquiry made to trace him. It wouldn't take too long to include the details into our inquiry."

"Good, then we'll leave it as it stand," decided Franklin. "Any more questions, no?"

Before the briefing broke up, he held his hand in the air and said, "There's one more thing ladies and gentlemen. I just want to remind you that a fall-out of the murder of Carol Meechan was the unfortunate demise of an elderly lady, Missus Violet Cairns who according to her cardiologist suffered a massive heart attack. As you will be aware, Missus Cairns' discovery of the body is what apparently brought on her attack. I want you all to remember that while we cannot libel a murder charge when we undoubtedly arrest the culprit, please do not forget that the killer's actions resulted in *two* deaths."

The silence in the room was almost deafening.

"Right then," said Franklin, "DS Thomas has further Actions for you guys so line yourselves up and collect them from him and one further thing," he smiled as almost as one, the team all hesitated. "Gary Thomas told me that *anybody* failing to contribute to the tea fund will be getting the Actions for checking dustbins and skips."

The smiles satisfied him that so far, morale was good.

A few minutes later, in the privacy of his office, he dialled the Pitt Street office number for Detective Superintendent Lynn Massey and left a message on her answer service, requesting she contact him as soon as possible.

That done he phoned home and with a wistful sigh, asked his wife to put the dinner in the dog.

Seated behind his desk in his office, Harry McPherson, with his jacket off and hung on the back of his chair, tie undone and shirt cuffs rolled up onto his strong forearms, sat back in the chair and stared at his desk that was heaped with ledgers and paperwork. A nearby table, for convenience pulled across from its normal position against the wall, was similarly stacked. Crumpled notes were inside or lying on the floor around the wire mesh waste basket where they had been carelessly tossed. His shirt felt damp under the arms and he realised he had been perspiring in the warm office and was conscious of a faint odour of sweat.

Across the desk, Morven Sutherland, her jacket similarly draped across the back of her chair, finished typing on the laptop and pushing the portable adding machine from her, also sat back, twisting her neck to relieve the ache that had developed from almost five hours of concentrated checking and re-checking.

McPherson blew through pursed lips and said, "Well, that's it then. That's the lot, as far as we can tell. What's the final tally?"

Sutherland, her face expressionless, nodded and tearing a slip of paper from the adding machine, leaned across the desk and handed it to him.

He stared at the figure and his face paled. "Are you certain?"

"According to the files that we have," she wearily replied and unable to hide the sarcasm in her voice, "the total sum that Peter Gibson has *supposedly* granted as loans during the preceding two months from the fourteen client accounts that we know of is what I've printed out on the adding machine. Unfortunately, we have no record of those loans actually being *collected* by the clients."

"These client files," he indicated the heaped cardboard files with their printout paperwork that lay between them, his forehead furrowing with suspicion. "Just how many of these clients are genuine?" He rubbed his hand across his brow and wondered at the dampness, then realised he was perspiring even more and realised how stressed he was feeling.

Her silence prompted him to ask, "Are any of them real, genuine I mean?"

She slowly shook her head.

"The paperwork, our files here in the bank I should say, all seem to be in order and also *appear* from the signatures and references, to be perfectly legitimate, but when I check the web," she flicked with a perfectly manicured nail at the laptop, "I can't find any of the businesses that the details provided are supposed to relate to. The addresses of these firms," she picked up a file and let it drop again to the desk, "they *do* exist. The addresses I mean, but the firms listed in our files are *not* the firms listed as those at each address. It seems to me," she continued, "that a cursory check of the addresses would stand up for verification, by that I mean for example a road map check. But unless a more thorough check has been carried out, actually visiting the locations I mean, then these files," she disdainfully pushed with her hand at them, "seem to me to be a load of shit."

She sighed and stared into his eyes, then leaned forward, her elbows on the desk and her clenched fists supporting her chin.

"If you want my opinion Harry, I believe that while the addresses are easily checkable on the web, the companies for whom the loans were issued are *not* located there and, if you want my further opinion, I do *not* believe these companies in fact exist. Somehow or other, with deliberate intention or mistaken confidence in the information he was provided with, Peter Gibson has issued massive business loans to what I can only describe as ghost companies."

Those two words, 'ghost companies' almost caused him to shudder. He didn't need an explanation of her chosen description; bogus companies created for the purpose of deceiving the lender and in this case, his bank.

He stared back at her and raised his hands to clutch at his head.

"These massive loans and all that money; where did the money go, where was it deposited by us, the bank I mean?"

She glanced down at her handwritten notes. "All the loans were transferred at different dates throughout the two months by the bank to the same account number and sort code. The only problem as I see it and I apologise for stating the obvious, but the clients issued the loans simply don't exist."

As though a thought occurred to her, she said, "Hold on," and standing, fetched a reference book from a nearby shelf. She glanced again at her notes and flicked through the book, finding the page she sought and run her finger down the page. "The sort code refers to a…." she stopped and stared at him again, her eyes widening. "The sort code refers to a bank in the Cayman Islands, the McMurray Bank of Cayman."

"My God, Morven," he burst out, "how the *fuck* did he get away with this and we didn't… I mean, nobody noticed?"

She closed and dropping the book into her lap, shrugged her shoulders and replied, "I can only assume that because of his position of trust, any transaction he authorised was deemed by his staff to be acceptable and in the interest of both the client and the bank. Further, I think we must assume he couldn't have done this alone; he must have had someone helping him with the paperwork, someone he trusted."

Neither of them wished to openly say the word, but both guessed what the other was thinking.

Peter Gibson had somehow blatantly and without most of his staff realising, colluded with a colleague and perpetrated a massive fraud against the bank.

He stared at her as she run her left forefinger across her bottom lip, her mouth slightly open revealing her even, white teeth. His glance fell to the swell of her breasts straining against the thin material of her white blouse; the top button of the open neck blouse now undone and revealing a tantalising glimpse of the bright whiteness of her bra. His saw a soft sheen of perspiration at her cleavage and felt a stirring in his loins.

"How will you break the news to Mister Brewster and the rest of the Directors? Do you want me to come with you?" she asked, breaking into his train of thought.

God, even her voice sounded sexy. He breathed hard, briefly distracted from the task in hand and worried that she might have sensed his desire for her.

"Not unless you want to witness the messenger being shot," he tried to sound jovial, but the joke fell flat.

Resigning himself to his fate, he stood and shrugging into his jacket, straightened his tie.

"How long do you think it might take? To inform them of the bad news I mean?"

He shook his head. "I think we have done as much as we can for tonight. I know its Friday, but I'm guessing you and I will be told to come in tomorrow, probably Sunday too. I take it that won't be a problem?"

"No problem," she smiled at him, a beguiling smile. "Do they need to know today? About the Cayman account I mean? Why worry them over the weekend? Maybe we should keep that information till we know a little more?"

"How… why… I don't understand? What do you mean?" he asked, confusion evident on his face.

"It's just, well," she paused, her eyes narrowing as though in thought, "I'm wondering if we can somehow find out more, maybe even work out how to recover the money. Wouldn't that sort of make you the hero of the day, so to speak?"

He didn't want to ask more of her and worried a little where the conversation was leading to, but as she stepped closer, all thoughts of the urgency to inform the Board of the Cayman account seemed to fade as he stared at her; her beauty and her beguiling smile, her moth slight open and her tongue darting out to lick at her upper lip.

Then, as though uncertain and it just occurred to her, she narrowed her eyes and said, "It's just that it's been a long day. I was thinking if you're not in a hurry to get home I mean, we could grab some takeaway, a bottle of wine perhaps. Maybe discuss what's happened and try to come up with an idea how Gibson thought he might try to get access to the account and the money. My place isn't too far."

His eyes widened and he felt his mouth dry. "That's an idea," he replied, suddenly eager to get the meeting with the Directors over and done with.

"Right then," she stood up from her chair and moved in close to him, her breasts lightly playing against his chest as she reached up and straightened his tie.

So near to him, the discreet scent she favoured swept across him and he held his breath, afraid that the wrong move might startle her into changing her mind.

"I'll leave my address on your desk for you and maybe you can grab some wine while I get home to freshen up a little and wait there for you," she cocked her head slightly to one side and biting at her lower lip, coyly smiled.

Andy Brownlie parked the CID car in the street adjacent to Susie Gibson's house, conscious that by now, neighbours might be wondering at the number of police vehicles coming and going from the Gibson household.

Susie saw him walking up the driveway and was at the front door before he rang the bell.

"It's me, the bad penny and all that," he joked, slightly taken aback at her appearance, seeing the dark patches under her eyes and face devoid of make-up, her normally neat and tidy appearance gone and her hair in disarray, though it had been just over a day since they had last met.

He correctly thought she hadn't slept much the previous night.

Inviting Andy in, Susie led him into the kitchen and switched on the kettle.

"How's Janice?" was her opening remark.

"Like me, she's worried about you, boss," he replied.

Susie shook her head and sat wearily down on a chair, leaving Andy to spoon coffee into two mugs and watched as he fetched the milk from the fridge.

"I'm guessing you haven't eaten anything," he stared at her.

She shook her head and blew a soft raspberry. "I just can't face food, not now anyway," she replied.

He decided to be hard on her, to put a little pressure on, but knew he would find it difficult. He inhaled and said, "Well, Susie, with all that's going on, you need to eat," handing her a mug. "You have to keep up your strength. I can't imagine what you must be going through, but you've got a daughter to consider and she is going to need her mother to be fit and well, not wasting away. You have a duty to Jenny, so get some grub into you, missus. I don't want you taking more time off than is necessary and leaving me to do your cases because you've decided to become a fucking anorexic."

She stared open-mouthed at him, then burst out laughing, a laughter that turned to a fit of the giggles.

"Andy Brownlie, *you* are a headcase," she finally said and smiled at his grin. "Thanks, neighbour, I needed that. It might not persuade me to have a curry or fish and chips, but I really did need a laugh."

She sipped at her coffee and then her brow wrinkled in thought. "What do you mean, with all that's going on?"

Leigh Gallagher returned to Shakespeare Street and cursed loudly when he saw the van still parked outside his close and that could only mean that Saint bloody Patrick was still in the flat.

He was undecided whether to stay out until Pat went away or return home to collect his hoody and the knife.

Jesus! His eyes opened wide. The wardrobe, it must be for him. His Da was always going on about getting him some new furniture and if they move the old wardrobe, they had to find the tin!

He clenched his fists and beat at his forehead. What the fuck was he going to do now? Would they tell on him, grass him up to the coppers?

No, he reasoned. His Da wouldn't do that, but his holier than thou bastard of a brother Patrick; he just might.

What Leigh couldn't guess was just then, his father and brother were both on their knees, their hands clasped together in prayer as they sought guidance from their Lord on what to do.

After a few minutes of silence, Patrick helped his father to his feet and again tried to persuade Magnus to inform the police.

"No, I want to see him, speak with him before I make my decision," his father firmly said, shrugging off his son's hand as he stumbled through to the kitchen and sat heavily down on a chair, his mind still reeling at their discovery of the tin box contents. God, he gritted his teeth, but his chest *did* hurt.

"Look Da, if he is innocent, then Leigh has got nothing to fear. It might be there is a perfectly logical explanation for the money and the knife," but in both his head and his heart, Patrick knew that his brother was not innocent; that the money had to be stolen and as for the knife; well, there was no excuse for its presence in the box. He inwardly seethed that the little shit was once again taking advantage of their kindly and trusting father.

Without warning, Magnus started to breathe heavily and clutched at his chest, the excruciating pain overtaking all other concerns.

"Da, Da! Are you all right, Da?" asked Patrick, bending over his father, worry now creasing his forehead.

"Da!" he reached to catch him as Magnus drooped forward and began to slowly fall from the chair, his face screwed tight with pain and his hands kneading at the awful agonising ache in his chest.

"Oh, God, oh God, please no!" cried Patrick, laying his father on the kitchen floor and scrambling in his trouser pocket for his mobile phone.

"Da!" he patted at his father's cheek, the other hand frantically pressing the three digits on the keypad that would call the emergency service.

Staring up at his son, Magnus opened his eyes and tried to smile, but then quite suddenly, a heavy darkness engulfed him.

CHAPTER 14

The recently promoted Detective Superintendent Lynn Massey, her shoulder length blonde hair pulled back into a tight ponytail and sitting in the comfortable swivel chair behind the desk, run a forefinger along its polished top and smiled. Never in her wildest dreams would she have imagined herself at this rank so soon. With a sigh, she lifted her pen and again tried to concentrate on the reports that lay in front of her.

The telephone on the desktop rang, startling her. Bloody ringer's too loud she shook her head, reminding herself to get the thing sorted and lifted the handset.

"Ma'am," said the voice on the other end, "DI Bobby Franklin here from Cranstonhill. Are you busy or can I have a few minutes of your time?"

"No, I'm not too busy Bobby. How are you these days?"

"Aye, getting by, Lynn," she heard him sigh. She was aware that Bobby, a much experienced and competent detective, was investigating the young woman murdered in Partick, but if he needed some of her time, there had to be a problem.

"So, what's on your mind?"

"Bit of a problem here," he slowly began, but she detected a slight hesitancy in his voice. That decided her.

"Give me a minute, Bobby," she interrupted him and glanced at her desk calendar, a freebie advertising a local Chinese takeaway in Sauchiehall Street.

Each calendar day was sectioned off into hours and she saw that other than poking a head into the office of her boss, Frankie Johnson for a quick update on the circumstances regarding the suspected paedophile ring in the North Lanarkshire area, for the remainder of that afternoon she was free. Besides, she inwardly reasoned, Cranstonhill wasn't too far off her route home.

She glanced at her wristwatch, a wedding present from her husband Greg.

"It's just gone three o'clock, Bobby. Stick the kettle on for say four and I'll be in your office about then, okay?"

Susie Gibson watched Andy Brownlie get into the CID car and drive off and was about to turn away from the window when she saw her daughter Jenny turning into the driveway, her head turned to watch the car drive off. A lump formed in her throat and pulling the curtain to one side, she attempted a smile and waved as the teenager glanced up at the house.

Jenny returned her wave and in the brief time it took for her to reach the front door, Susie had taken a large breath and forced herself to be calm.

"How did the prelims go?" she closed the door and smiled at her daughter, who simply responded by shrugging her shoulders and grimacing.

"Time will tell," was all she could say and then added, "I didn't see his car, so no news then?"

Susie shook her head and replied, "No, nothing so far."

There seemed little point is trying to be brave or positive. Even from a young age, Jenny had always been a bright and perceptive child and would see right through any lies or half-truths her mother would tell her, even if the falsehoods were told to protect Jenny.

"What would you like for dinner," smiled Susie, trying to appear cheerier than she felt.

Jenny dropped her satchel on the floor of the hallway and stared at her mother, then said, "Whatever we have, mum, we have to eat together. Don't think I haven't noticed you not eating. You've hardly touched food these last couple of days, so if you intend making dinner it has to be for both of us."

"Well, in that case," Susie inhaled at her daughter's unexpected reasoning, wondering when this young woman arrived without her noticing, "as I don't *really* feel like making anything, I'll order us something in, okay?"

"Okay," replied Jenny and with a sudden rush across the few feet that lay between them, clasped her arms about her mother's neck. They stood there together, fiercely hugging, almost afraid that to let go might mean the end of their family.

The ambulance driver narrowly scraped the vehicle past a spotlessly clean and polished Nissan Micra reversing his from a hospital car parking space, driven he saw by an elderly woman. The driver muttered an obscenity under his breath and shook his head, thinking the blue lights and the siren should have been a clue for the old besom.

"How we doing in the back there, hen?" he shouted to his crewmate, afraid to turn his eyes away from the narrow road that led to the canopied entrance of Gartnavel Casualty Department and was filled with pedestrians, visiting their family and friends. He grimaced as a young man skipped across the road literally yards in front of the ambulance. Fucking idiot, he snarled through clenched teeth.

"Stable so far," replied the young woman, holding the oxygen mask on the patient's face while a younger man, his son apparently, sat pale faced, fearfully staring at his father. She didn't fail to notice he was a good looking man and tall, too. Kind of reminded her of one of they older Hollywood movie stars, but couldn't quite recall the name.

"Magnus, can you hear me love?" the woman softly asked, stroking the limp hair from the forehead that was soaked in perspiration.

"That's us here love, we're at the hospital; Gartnavel, okay?"

"Da," said Patrick Gallagher, his voice choked with emotion as he reached across the woman to holds his father's hand, realising that Magnus was oblivious to her attention.

The doors swung open and the driver pulled out the vehicle steps. In a well-rehearsed routine, the two crewmates pulled the stretcher from the rear of the vehicle and unlocked the wheels underneath, creating a gurney that they then quickly steered through the glass doors and into the department.

Patrick had never experienced such a feeling of helplessness and following the gurney, almost strode over the small Philippians nurse who held a firm hand up to stop him progressing any further into the ward.

"Please," she indicated with a toothy smile and her free hand, "you sit there, sir. I come and get you when I need some details and tell you what is happening. You let us do our job, yes?" she said in her accented and slightly singsong English.

He nodded at her, but his eyes followed the gurney into the room where the door almost immediately closed behind the ambulance crew.

"Please sir?" she persisted.

He hadn't realised the young nurse was still at his elbow, guiding him to a plastic chair at the side of the ward.

Numbly, he sat down and began the long wait.

Harry McPherson returned through the now deserted corridors of the bank towards the Accounts office, still shaking and worried that the Directors might indeed carry out their threat of, "…heads will roll." Bastards, he vehemently spat. Pushing open the door he saw Morven Sutherland had not yet left but was standing with her back to him, a small powder compact in her hand as she stared into the mirror and repaired her make-up. She turned towards him, concern etched upon her face.

"I decided instead to wait," she began and then added, "How did it go? What did they say?"

He paced up and down the carpeted floor, angry at the humiliation he had suffered at the hands of that bastard John Brewster; him and his three fucking cronies.

In short, terse sentences punctuated with expletives, he told her of the meeting, of Brewster's rants, virtually accusing him of ignoring the drip theft of the money from the bank.

All three million, two hundred and sixty thousand *fucking* pounds! He disclosed the threats that had been made against him; that he would not just be ignominiously sacked from the bank, but that Brewster would ensure he never again would be employed in the financial industry.

"But you're not sacked, are you?" she interrupted him, her hand on his arm as she stood close to him.

He took a deep breath and once more inhaled her scent. "No, not for the time being," he scoffed, "at least not till I've found out how to recover the money; if I can."

"Of *course* you can, Harry," she smiled up at him, "and I'll help you. We'll work together and anything we learn, we'll keep between us and we'll ensure *you* get the credit. Peter Gibson wasn't *that* bright a man. He must have left some sort of clue where he hid the money, some kind of way to access the cash. Once he's found, the police will persuade him to admit what he's done and if he has any sense, he will cooperate and you'll be the hero, won't you?" She moved close to him and quite unexpectedly stroked his cheek. "I'll help you find out how we can get the money back. Like I'm telling you, Harry, all we have to do is *work* together. Wouldn't you like that Harry?" She stared into his eyes. "You and I, spending together I mean?"

He was captivated by her and staring down at her felt himself again become aroused. He hadn't realised that they now stood with their arms entwined and he bent his head to kiss her, surprised how delicious her moist lips felt against his own.

His heart beat faster when she thrust her body against him and suddenly startled when her fingers lightly stroked his groin. He drew his head back from her, his face eager with expectation.

She smiled up at him and softly said, "Like I told you before, Harry; I don't live too far away."

Lynn Massey refused Bobby Franklin's offer of his own comfortable chair and instead sat opposite him, placing her coffee cup on the desk between them.

"So, to summarise Bobby; the dead girl, your victim Carol Meechan; she worked in the Caledonian Banking Group Accounts office. Today, your guys visited the bank and discovered that one of their senior managers in the Loans Department has gone missing along with… how much again?"

Franklin glanced down at the statement noted by Waz Ahmed and read out, "Two point eight million, but that figure has still to be ratified. As I understand it the bank staff is still checking the final total and we expect to have it any time now. Certainly by close of business today, I hope."

"Right, so that's about what you earned last year in overtime, eh?" she joked.

"I wish," he grinned back at her.

More soberly, she said, "Shame about the elderly lady, Missus...?"

"Missus Cairns, Violet Cairns," he replied.

"To live to that age then stumble across a murder that so shocks you, it causes your death; dreadful," she shook her head

"The missing man, this Peter Gibson," she continued. "He's the man married to one of our own?"

"Aye, she's DS Susan Gibson who works out of Baird Street CID. Do you know her?"

Massey shook her head, her lips pursed and eyes narrowing. "Maybe the face, but the name is not familiar. You know what the job is like, Harry, the number of people we meet through the years. How about you, have your paths crossed?"

"The name isn't familiar with me either, boss," he replied and then raised his head when the door was knocked. Waz Ahmed poked his head inside.

"Boss that was…" he saw Lynn Massey and stopped, "Sorry sir, I didn't realise that…"

"It's okay Waz, come in," then turning to Massey, formally said, "This is Detective Superintendent Massey. Ma'am, this is one of my younger officers, DC Waseem Ahmed."

Waz was dumbstruck when the good looking blonde woman in the navy blue pinstriped trouser suit uncurled herself from the chair and standing, reached out to shake his hand.

"Pleased to meet you DC Ahmed," she smiled at him, conscious that he seemed to be uncomfortable, inwardly guessing the reason why and pleased that she could still turn a young man's head. "So, is this your first serious criminal investigation?"

"Ah, yes Ma'am," he nervously replied, his mouth suddenly dry and not just because Massey was his boss's boss, but more because she was a right stunner.

Lynn Massey wasn't blind to the attention she received from men and like most women, enjoyed the occasional flirtation, but only if it wasn't taken too seriously. However, the young man was a subordinate officer under her command and she knew it would be unseemly to even acknowledge his attention of her.

She fought hard to keep a straight face and said, "You have something to bring to the DI's attention then?"

"Eh, yes Ma'am, it's, ah..."

"Some news, Waz?" asked Franklin, similarly aware of the younger man's discomfort and struggling to refrain from laughing.

"I just had a phone call from the bank's Director, John Brewster. Here boss," he leaned across the desk with a sheet of paper, "the final total of the stolen money."

Franklin took the paper from Waz and read aloud, "Three million, two hundred and sixty thousand smackers, Ma'am," he unconsciously shook his head and remarked, "A right tidy wee lift, eh? Right thanks son," he nodded a dismissal to Waz who almost fled the room. He smiled at Massey. "I think you made a fan there, Missus Massey. What your new hubby say to that?"

"He'd be pleased to know I've still got it, you sarcastic old sod," she sat back down and coyly grinned back at him.

He sipped at his coffee and more soberly asked, "So, Lynn, what have you decided about the murder and the missing man, Peter Gibson? Do you have any ideas yet? Do you want me to run the inquiries in parallel or as the ranking officer, do you want to take over?"

"I haven't had time to take it all in yet, Bobby," she shook her head, "and before I *do* make a decision, I think I had better discuss it with our new Detective Chief Superintendent."

He grinned at her. "How is Frankie Johnson taking to his new rank?"

"Hates it," she returned his grin. "Says it's the politics that is doing his head in, but let's face it, as operational CID officers in managerial roles, we couldn't have a better representative when it comes to fighting our corner when we need more resources or a bigger budget."

"Agreed," he nodded. "Anyway, back to my original question regarding running the inquiries as one or two," he held a hand up to cut short her protest. "I understand why you have still to make a decision, but as the MP inquiry impacts on my murder inquiry, do I have your authorisation to interview his wife?"

"Bloody hell, Bobby, that's a tricky one," she inhaled, not having given it any thought and then replied, "You said his wife is a serving officer at Baird Street, so that will be Ross McConnell then, who is her boss."

She chewed at her lower lip and frowned. "I hate to have to say this, but being a serving officer and also the wife of a man who is currently reported as an MP and now seems to be suspected of fraud *as well* as possibly implicated in a murder, DS Gibson is likely to find herself suspended and dependent on what Frankie Johnson decides, might well be subject to interview by the Police Standards Unit."

"What?" he was taken aback. "Hang fire there, Lynn. Just because she is married to a guy that is a suspect doesn't necessarily mean that she is involved in his shenanigans."

She held up both hands defensively. "You're preaching to the converted Bobby, but without evidence to the contrary, we the polis have to assume that she might have some knowledge of her husbands…" she paused, choosing her words carefully. "How can I put this without actually putting him completely in the frame? His *activities,* let's just say for the time being. We need to err on the side of caution. You know the rules as well as I do; without fear or favour and that *does* include colleagues. If DS Gibson is innocent, well, hopefully that will be quickly obvious. If not…" she left the rest unsaid.

"Anyway," she bent to collect her handbag from the floor beside her chair and then stood up, "I know that Frankie will still be at his desk, so I'll pop back to Pitt Street and apprise him of our conversation." She glanced at her watch to check the time, but the watch also reminded her of another appointment. "After I've spoken with him, I'll phone you, hopefully within the next hour. Will you still be here?"

He sighed and waved at the files on his desk. "What do you think?" Grinning, she bade him farewell and walking along the corridor towards the rear door of the office, fetched her mobile phone from her handbag. Scrolling down the directory, she stopped at 'Greg' and pressed the green button.

"Hi darling, guess what? Yeah, maybe an hour later than I thought, so you and Louise go ahead and eat; just don't scoff the lot, you greedy buggers," she smiled at the phone and opening her car door, gently laughed at her husband's reply.

Leigh Gallagher was surprised. The van his brother had brought over was still parked in the street, outside the close. Sod it, he decided and started to walk towards the close and with teenage bravado, determined that if Saint Patrick started any of that *have you found yourself a job yet* shite, he'd punch his head off his shoulders, big as he was.

With more bluster than sense, he entered the close only to be ambushed by Missus Murphy, the elderly and very nosey neighbour who according to local legend, reputedly could hear a mouse farting outside her door. Coming out of her ground floor flat, she quickly shuffled on her NHS issued walking sticks and arthritic legs and stood in his path. He exhaled at the old woman's determination not to let him pass as she asked, "How's your Da, son? Is he all right then? Did they keep him in?"

He stared curiously at her. What the fuck was she rambling on about now?

His sullen silence provoked more questions.

"I mean," she sniffed, "at his age, these things can be fatal, can't they?"

"I don't know what you're on about Missus Murphy," he shuffled past her and started to climb the stairs.

"Well," she huffed; annoyed that young Leigh wasn't paying her any attention. She raised her voice and it followed him up the stairs. "I was speaking to Missus Linden in the next close and she heard it was a heart attack."

He stopped dead. Heart attack? What was she saying, heart attack? He turned and slowly walked back down the stairs where to his dread, he learned of his father being taken away in an ambulance and, delighting in being the bearer of bad news, the old woman shook her head and sniffed again as with common gossip authority she added, "He didn't look good, son, not good at all. Wouldn't surprise me to hear he's dead by now."

CHAPTER 15

Outside Cranstonhill police station, Waz Ahmed cheerily waved goodbye to Des Mooney and turning, readied himself to skip across St Vincent Street between the evening traffic. Standing at the edge of the pavement, he turned his head to check on the speed of the passing vehicles and saw a large, black coloured BMW vehicle pass him by, then stop outside the front entrance of the station. As he watched, Des Mooney climbed into the front passenger seat and the vehicle sped off west and away from Waz.

He hadn't seen the driver, but guessed it was the same woman who had dropped Des off earlier that day and recalling her good looks, smiled to himself and thought, you lucky, lucky bastard, Mooney. The forty minutes it took for Waz to travel home gave him time to reflect on how his day had gone. The inquiry had taken an unexpected turn with the DI's revelation at the evening briefing that there existed the possibility that the murder of Carol Meechan and the disappearance of Peter Gibson, the banks New Business Investment Manager, might be linked. That thought carried on and caused him to recall his and Des Mooney's attendance that morning at the bank.

He knew now he had not handled the initial interview with the Director John Brewster, very well. The older man had a bearing and presence that garnered respect and demonstrated an authority that had obviously been nurtured through his long years in the banking industry. Brewster had been close to intimidating the younger Waz with that authority, but for Des intervening. Glancing out of the window, he sighed. Being a detective in the CID was all Waz ever wanted, but he was quickly coming to learn that not everyone was impressed by his rank. In those brief seconds verbally sparring with Brewster, he had almost been at a loss for words and experienced a self-doubt, wondering if he had the confidence to be a police officer, let alone a detective.

Des interjecting had saved him the embarrassment of being tongue-tied and he gave silent thanks to his colleague's recognition that Waz was floundering in front of the banks Directors.

Yes, he inwardly thought, there was much he could learn from his streetwise partner; much about attaining the confidence to be a good police officer, let alone a good detective and realised with a smile he really did like Des.

Frankie Johnson rubbed with a forefinger at his brow, his right hand holding a pencil with which he doodled under the notes he had made on the writing pad. He glanced up at Lynn Massey, seated in front of his desk and sighed. Things had seemed to be so much easier before they lumbered him with his new rank, he thought to himself, for now he not only had to oversee even more officers and departments, but deal with the politics of acquiring resources to support these responsibilities.

"So," he said at last, "the sum of it all is that you think it will be a good idea to coordinate both inquiries, but run them separately? I don't quite follow how you mean to do that Lynn."

"I was thinking that Bobby Franklin continues with his murder incident room at Cranstonhill office while I have a watching brief from my own office here at Pitt Street. The officers I designate to the missing person inquiry will work out of a separate room in Cranstonhill office, but report directly to me and I will provide such information as I deem necessary to Bobby's inquiry; that is, anything I believe to be relevant that might assist in solving his murder investigation."

"You realise of course…." he stopped, interrupted by a knock at his door and irritably called out, "Come in."

A young woman, a hesitant smile on her face, entered the room with a cardboard file clutched in her hand. "Sorry, Mister Johnson, I'm from the HR Department. You wanted this file?"

"Ah, yes my dear," he smiled graciously and taking the file from her, dismissed her with a courteous nod. Laying the file on his desk he glanced at it then said to Massey, "DS Gibson's personnel file. Now, as I was about to say, I'm thinking, Lynn that the interviews you will have to conduct with those involved in the MP inquiry will quite obviously need to include DS Gibson," he indicated with a wave at the file. "I don't have to tell you that if this man Peter Gibson *is* the main suspect for the stolen money, we cannot discount that his wife, police officer though she is, might have colluded with him in some way or other. Neither of us need reminding of our own accountability as police officers and we both know of occasions …." he paused and bit at his lower lip, "well, let's just say that not all of our colleagues walk the straight and narrow."

He paused and taking a deep breath continued. "That said, I must insist that any interview with Detective Sergeant Gibson be conducted firstly at her home, then if for any reason it is suspected she might be prevaricating, under formal condition at a police office. If necessary, the Police Code of Conduct is to be invoked if she resists *any* attempt to avoid interview. Obviously at this stage I *don't* wish her to be treated as a suspect, but nevertheless, we must not discount the possibility of her involvement in her husband's disappearance."

"You've something planned, haven't you?" she smiled at him.

He nodded and said, "To ensure complete impartiality and negate any later allegation made against us that we favour our own, it's my intention to arrange with the Detective Superintendent in charge of the Police Standards Unit that the interview with DS Gibson be conducted by two of her officers and they be assigned to you, for the duration of your inquiry. Of course, you will instruct them what you want asked and knowing you," he grimly smiled, "they will be told that *complete* fairness is to be extended to DS Gibson at all time, yes?"

"Oh yes," she drawled in ready agreement, stony-faced while she briefly recalled her own verbal mauling by the rubber heels after her involvement in a rooftop shooting.

He exhaled and quite suddenly grinned.

"I sound like a *real* bloody senior officer now, don't I?"

Massey returned his grin and replied, "Well, that's why they pay you the big bucks, Frankie."

He smiled, but again a tightly grim smile and she guessed there was something else.

"I actually know Susie Gibson, Lynn. She was a DC on a couple of inquiries I supervised. One was a murder in the Dumbarton area, as I recall and then, a year later those CIT, the cash in transit robberies we had about eight years ago, over in the south side of the city. As I remember, it was *me* that recommended her for promotion."

"Don't sweat it Frankie. There's nothing yet to say that she's guilty of anything other than reporting her husband missing," she grinned at him and added, "There's a few women I know that wouldn't mind seeing the back of *their* husband's."

Digressing, her eyes narrowed, she asked, "How are you adapting to the Chief Super rank then?"

He grimaced and said, "There's a lot more paperwork, but fortunately," he waved towards the door, "I've got a wee lassie out there dealing with the clerical side for me. It's the morning staff meetings with the Chief and the flunkies that surround him. Some of those gits have never seen an angry man, yet pontificate as though they are old sweats. That's the *real* pain in the arse; forgive me my expletive, Lynn. You wouldn't believe some of the antics my peers get up to, trying to ensure that they are noticed by the Chief. Fortunately, he's as wide as the Clyde."

"I haven't met him yet, only know him by reputation," she replied.

"I wouldn't say he's the brightest police officer I've known," Johnson admitted and cocked his head to one side, screwing his face as he sought to describe the newly installed Chief Constable, "but his strength lies in that he recognises bright guys and is slowing surrounding himself with them. Okay, he might use their ideas and maybe pass them off as his own, but nobody seems to complain. He's a likeable man and I've noticed he rewards effort and commitment, but equally he's quick to slap down stupidity and self-promotion. Aye," he nodded, "all in all, I think he'll do a good job."

Privately, Massey agreed for hadn't one of the Chief's first acts been to promote Frankie Johnson?

Selflessly, it never occurred to her that she had also featured in that promotion parade.

Then quite unexpectedly, Johnson softly growled and added, "Just as long as he keeps that moron MacPhail off my back."

Massey's eyes widened. Shortly after the new Chief was appointed, the incumbent Assistant Chief Constable (Crime) John Moredun had transferred from Strathclyde to a surprising appointment as the Deputy Chief to a regional English force. As far as Moredun's CID subordinates were concerned, Moredun was no sad loss to the Force, adding strength to the rumour that the new Chief had been vocal in his dislike for Moredun.

However, the Chief held little sway over the Police & Fire Committee that almost immediately appointed Jonathon MacPhail to replace Moredun. A young, but dour man originally from Shetland, as far as she could recall, he had spent his probationary period of two years with Strathclyde, serving in a Glasgow based division then married and transferred to the Metropolitan Police where it was said he had spent most of his service in various administrative roles.

The rumour factory added fuel to the flames when it was disclosed MacPhail's older cousin was a Glasgow Councillor who currently served on the appointing Police and Fire Committee.

"I haven't yet had the pleasure of meeting the new ACC," said Massey, her curiosity piqued at the normally amiable Johnson's comment.

"Well, don't have to high an expectation of our new ACC. He's already set his cap at saving money, no doubt following the tradition and values of his penny-pinching cousin, so if you think Moredun was tight, wait till this new boy sets your budget for next year," he shook his head.

"Right," he slapped a hand on the desktop, "back to business. You have my support to run both inquiries in tandem; so what's your first move Lynn?"

"While Bobby Franklin continues running the murder, I'll arrange statements to be noted from everyone connected with the MP and," shrugging her shoulders, "without any evidence to the contrary, consider him my prime suspect in the theft of the money. Needless to say, the first statement will be from his wife, DS Gibson."

"What about Forensics," he asked. "Have you thought about bringing in the Fraud Squad?"

"Yeah," her eyes narrowed, "I know a DS Laura Scott who works in Fraud and who has a Forensic accountancy background. I had her attached to an inquiry I conducted last year and she proved to be *very* capable. At the subsequent trial, she provided expert opinion regarding the confiscation of property that was proven to be the proceeds of crime," then grinned. "The bugger thought he had gotten away with it, signing the properties over to his family members, but Laura traced the property through several holding companies and we recovered most, if not all the goods."

"Right, any problems having her attached to your team, contact me. Is there anything else?"

"No, that seems to be it for now, Frankie," she stood and arose from her chair. "I won't get anything done tonight, so it's off home for now, but I'll make a few phone calls first and get the ball rolling for tomorrow morning."

With that, she left the room and in the corridor outside, reached into her handbag for her mobile phone.

Leigh Gallagher, his face red and breathing heavily after his long run to the casualty ward of Gartnavel General Hospital, pushed open the glass entrance doors and roughly barged past a young woman, ignoring her protest as she pushed a wheelchair upon which sat a child with bandaged legs. His mind raced in panic, already convincing himself that he was too late.

Pushing aside an already irate older man who stood at the glass enclosed reception window, Leigh gasped, "My dad's been brought here, in an ambulance. Magnus Gallagher. Is he okay?"

The receptionist had been employed within the casualty for almost ten years and prided herself on her ability to remain calm under the worst of circumstances, having through those years dealt with the panic-stricken relative, the slobbering drunk, the angry and confrontational, the weeping and the recently bereaved, all or most of whom had the inalienable belief that their need was greater than that of everyone else.

With a patience borne of experience and wisdom, the receptionist smiled apologetically at the irate older man and turning towards a clipboard upon which was listed the most recent admissions, replied, "Okay, son, tell me again. What's your dad's name?"

Had Leigh taken a few seconds to consider, he might have realised that dealing with his anxiety first, the woman was being kind, showing that she understood his concern and he might not have reacted as he did, but at the age of nineteen years, he had yet to display any kind of maturity or sense of propriety and snarled in response, "I told you, you stupid bitch. Magnus Gallagher. Are you fucking *deaf* or something?"

It was the wrong attitude to take with the helpful woman, whose smile froze on her face. Continuing to smile, she discreetly pressed at a button located beneath the counter that she knew would summon the porters who also acted as the department's security.

"If you would please take a seat," she calmly replied and pointed behind him towards a row of plastic chairs, tiered like soldiers on parade, "I'll see what I can find out."

"Aye, watch your language pal," interrupted the elderly man beside him, deciding the young upstart needed a lesson in manners, "the lassie's only doing her job."

Turning, Leigh was about to stick the head on the old fart when he suddenly became aware of a presence at his shoulder. Two burly porters dressed in NHS Nato style pullovers had quickly arrived, one of whom leaned into Leigh and who asked, "Is there a problem here, then?"

"Leigh!" called out a voice from behind the porters. All of them turned to see a tall, good looking but pale-faced man striding towards them from through the door marked 'Treatment Room.'

"Patrick," said Leigh with relief and walking towards his brother. "How's my Da?"

The porters, realising the issue seemed resolved by the arrival of the tall man, nodded towards the receptionist, but made the unspoken decision to hang about for another few minutes, 'just in case.'

The older man, relieved his near confrontation with the young thug was over, swallowed hard and realising his legs were shaking, walked towards his seated and anxiously waiting wife, his back a little straighter for having stood up to the thug and with a proud smile, sat down and held his wife's hand, his query for the receptionist now forgotten.

The receptionist, well used to such incidents, carried on with her work, the minor drama almost immediately forgotten… or at least, till the next time.

Within the treatment room, Patrick indicated they sit on a row of six plastic chairs that were lined against the corridor wall and explained that the casualty doctor suspected a heart attack and that Magnus was undergoing treatment, adding the prognosis was good and the prompt arrival of the ambulance crew meant treatment could be immediately applied. With a tight smile, he repeated the doctor's assertion that their father was a lucky man. "In all," said Patrick with a nod of his head, "with God's help Da will pull through and survive this difficult time."

Leigh stared at his older brother. "God's help?" his lip curled in disgust. "If there *was* a fucking God," his voice began to rise, "this wouldn't have happened in the first place."

Patrick closed his eyes and slowly shook his head, his hands clasped in his lap.

"I don't think this is the time to be testing your faith in the Almighty, Leigh," he opened his eyes and softly replied, aware that his brother was now attracting the attention of passing hospital staff. "Perhaps we should discuss this…"

"Discuss nothing," Leigh leapt from his seat and stared down at Patrick. "You," he sneered, shouting now, "holy Father *fucking* Patrick."

Neither man noticed the door open nor the quiet entry of the same two porters, their arms hanging loosely by their side and preparing themselves to haul the mouthy younger man from the room and throw him out of the casualty department.

"Mister…sorry, Father Gallagher," called out a nurse, drawing aside a curtain and obviously having heard the raised voice, stared hesitantly at Patrick and Leigh.

"Yes, nurse," Patrick stood and now ignoring his brother, stepped towards her.

The porters closed in on Leigh and as one, grabbed him by the arms. "You're out of here pal," said the older porter and bundled the protesting, but unresisting Leigh towards the door.

"Patrick!" he called out for support, but his brother continued to ignore him and stepped behind the curtain then drew a chair close to the bed and sitting, took his unconscious father's hand in his own and bowing his head began to pray, but not for his father's recovery or his brother's soul.

Instead, Patrick had already decided his father's fate was now in God's hands and instead sought his Lord's guidance in the issue of an apparent stolen credit card, a sum of money, a black-handled knife and the newspaper report of a murdered woman.

Harry McPherson pulled on his trousers and zipping them closed, glanced down at the sleeping form of Morven Sutherland, the firm roundness of her buttocks creating a soft mound under the sheet while her legs splayed wide and perfectly shaped. He stared in open admiration at the flawless skin of her naked back, her head on the pillow turned slightly away from him, both arms slightly raised as though in surrender, her eyes closed as she softly breathed. He thought about waking her, but decided it better that he slip quietly from the flat, his mind already concocting an excuse to explain to his wife Tracey his late arrival home.

Never in his wildest dreams did he think he would bed the Ice Queen, as Morven was known to some in the bank, and inwardly grinned at his good luck.

Bending over, he grabbed his clothing from the chair in the corner then his socks and shoes from the floor and with the bundle in his arms, tip-toed from the bedroom, softly closing the door behind him. In the bed feigning sleep, eyes still tightly shut, she listened for the click of the door lock and a few minutes later, heard the front door of the flat close. Turning, she sat up with her back against the headboard and pulled her knees up, her hands clasped around her shins and rested her naked breasts against her thighs.

Slowly rocking back and forth, she grinned and thought that it had been easier even than she had planned while inwardly admitting that Harry's seduction *did* have its benefits.

Susie Gibson spent that night sitting alone in the darkness of the lounge, the television on but hardly aware of what she was watching. Both her mobile and the house hand-free phones lay on the couch beside her, but other than a couple of calls from family and friends, uncertain of how to reassure her, there had been no word either from or of Peter.

Earlier that evening, Jenny had been invited by her best friend for a sleepover, ostensibly for the purpose of both girls collaborating in their studies for the forthcoming exams, though in reality such nights usually involved practising the art of applying make-up, pizza, loud music and DVD's.

Susie suspected that with the worry and concern about her father's disappearance, Jenny would need the comfort of her friend's shoulder and so thought it might do her daughter some good to get out of the house; at least for the night.

As the minutes ticked by, a terrible dread overcome her and with a start, she realised the central heating had not come on, that she was shivering.

She arose from the couch, her body aching from sitting so long in one position and made her way to the thermostat on the hallway wall. She turned the dial, hearing the click as the boiler fired up and standing there in the twilight of the night, her arms about her, felt so terribly alone.

Leigh Gallagher had wandered home, still angry at his treatment at the hands of the porters who had unceremoniously ejected him from the casualty department with the threat that if he returned, the police would be called.

He grimaced with embarrassment, recalling his petulant dance in entry area in front of arriving and departing patients at the front of the glass doors, his goading and threats to batter the two men, calling all sort of curses down upon them, but they had not reacted, simply stood with their arms folded and stared at him, shaking their heads.

In his mind he imagined how he would hurt and degrade them and revenge himself upon them both for his perceived humiliation of him.

As he walked towards Shakespeare Street, he scowled at the passers-by; well, the women and the elderly or those males whom he believed would not return his challenging eyes, wordlessly daring them to stare back.

A large plastic waste bin, not yet collected by the council refuse department, stood on the pavement outside a doorway and seemed to invite him to attack it. With a solid kick, he knocked the bin over causing the lid to fly open and the contents to spill on the ground. A shouted cry form an upper window of, "Hey you, ya wee shite!" prompted him to flee, giggling as he ran.

He stopped several hundred yards further on and feeling a little better for it, arrived at his close. A sudden thought occurred to him and he hurried up the stairs. In his anxiety, he fumbled with his key at the Yale lock, finally with a curse getting the door open.

In his bedroom, he stared open-mouthed at the dismantled wardrobe, the pile of clothes lying on his bed that he quickly rummaged through. His heart sunk. It wasn't there.

The tin box was gone.

The teenager was angry. Angry with his boss for hinting at the promotion that had now been given to that stuck-up tart he worked alongside; angry at his perceived humiliation of now having to call her 'Miss'; angry that the bloody Inland Revenue had docked his pay at Basic Rate; angry with his mother for insisting he pay more each week towards his keep and angry that the bloody bus was late as usual; just *fucking* well angry.

Standing among the other grumbling passengers at Buchannan Street bus station, he leaned against the glass panelling and fetched the 'Glasgow News' from his coat pocket. Turning the pages, he happened upon the hotline phone number and e-mail address that urged readers to contact the paper with their news items.

He smiled grimly, recalling the whispered gossip that currently held the bank staff in its grip, the rumours that abounded about the Investments Manager, Peter Gibson and glancing again at the newspaper's hotline number, reached into his coat pocket for his phone.

DI Bobby Franklin rubbed wearily at his eyes and was considering calling it a night. He really should make that eyesight appointment his wife kept harping on about.

The day hadn't gone well and no information, nothing to progress the murder investigation, had come to light. Although it had been such a short time since the discovery of Carol Meechan's body, there was no imminent arrest and the tentative suspect, the street robber, had not been active since then. The only other source of inquiry was the link between Meechan's place of employment and the missing banker, Peter Gibson.

Franklin felt no resentment that Lynn Massey had now assumed overall charge of both inquiries. Indeed, quite the opposite in fact. He liked Massey and valued her insight and experience and believed they could work well together, running the inquiries in parallel. Tired and lost in thought, he startled when his desk phone rung.

Nicotine Mary, the elderly, heavily built civilian bar officer who worked the front desk of Cranstonhill police office and was so called because, regardless of the amount of strong cologne she used, still smelled like a Woodbine factory, informed him in her rasping voice that there was a man at the desk, "…and really cute," she whispered through the phone.

"What's he want, Mary," sighed Franklin, checking his watch and hoping the Friday night traffic had by now eased off.

"Says he has information for the man in charge of the murder of that young lassie, Bobby and that's you, is it no?"

"You know fine well it is, you old bugger." He glanced again at his watch then added, "Hold on a minute."

Franklin popped out of his office and peeked into the incident room, sighing when he saw it already deserted and the last of the team gone home for the night leaving just one civilian nightshift operator to man the hotline phone. Returning to his office, he lifted the phone and said, "Right, I'll be down in a minute."

Shaking his head at the misfortune of being caught just before he got out of the door, he made his way downstairs.

The tall, dark haired man sat patiently on one of the plastic chairs that were bolted to the floor, opposite the bar and was clearly uncomfortable being stared at by the smiling Mary.

Franklin saw him to be casually dressed in a cotton plaid shirt, denim jeans, working man's boots and wearing a dark coloured rain jacket. He was holding a white plastic carrier bag that lay on his lap. "Hello, I'm Detective Inspector Franklin. You requested to speak with someone in the murder inquiry team. How can I help you?" The man stood and reached out his hand. Franklin's initial impression was of a man who clearly seemed to be worried. "My name is Father Patrick Gallagher," he replied in a soft, but weary sounding voice, "I'm the parish priest at St Joseph's." He held up the plastic bag and said, "I think I have something that might be of interest to you. Your inquiry, I mean."

CHAPTER 16

Lynn Massey stepped from the en-suite shower and began to roughly towel herself dry. Walking into the bedroom, she saw the bed was empty. She grinned knowingly and began to dress, stepping into her underwear and selecting a pinstriped navy trouser suit from the wardrobe she laid it on the bed alongside a clean white blouse. She was standing in bra and pants when the door opened and her husband Greg poked his head in.

"Tea and toast downstairs when you're ready," he said, his eyes taking in her still slim body and grinning wickedly, added "unless you've still got ten minutes to spare."

"It'll take you more than ten minutes to satisfy *me*, Mister Campbell," she returned his grin and then pretending annoyance, said, "wasn't last night enough for you?"

He stepped into the room and she saw he was barefoot and dressed in his old raggedy jeans, a *Che Guevara* T-shirt. He stepped into the room and closed the door carefully behind him lest he awaken his daughter Louise, still asleep in her room further along the hallway. Reaching for his wife, he wrapped his arms around her from behind and nuzzled at her neck. She placed her hands on top of his encircling forearms and again wondered at her luck in finding such a good and loving man.

The bleeping noise from a downstairs smoke alarm activating prompted him to cry out, "Shit! The toast!" and he hurried from the room.

Giggling, she continued dressing and was buttoning her blouse when a light tapping at the door was followed by a sleepy-headed Louise, who sticking her head in smiled and said, "Good morning, Lynn. He's burnt the toast again, hasn't he?"

She nodded with a grin at her step-daughter as Louise sighed and rubbing at her long, tangled hair, said, "Well, as long as I'm up at seven o'clock on a Saturday morning, he might as well burn me some too," and headed downstairs to join her father.

A few minutes later Massey joined them both at the table and snatching at some freshly made toast, sipped at her tea as she reached for the delivered morning edition of the 'Glasgow News'. The headline literally jumped out at her: '*Police Search For Killer Banker*' with a smaller by-line underneath that read: *'Love Tryst Ends In Murder.'*

"Shit!" she angrily exclaimed, startling both her husband and step-daughter.

"Oh, oh," said Louise pulled a face and glanced at her dad, "somebody is going to get hell today, that's for sure."

Waz Ahmed, arriving at Cranstonhill office in the mistaken belief he would be the first to arrive in the incident room, was surprised to see his Detective Inspector already seated at a desk and head bowed, writing on a pad.

"Morning boss," he greeted Franklin, "coffee?"

"No, you're all right, son," Franklin replied without looking up.

Waz helped himself to a mug and was pouring the boiling water in when the phone by Franklin's elbow rung.

"Yes Ma'am," he heard Franklin say and then add, "He came in last night, just turned up with a tin box and a story. Aye, he's a Catholic priest right enough. No, what he said doesn't seem to be any conflict with his religion. What he told me was that the information he provided didn't come through the confessional or anything like that, but he believed he had a duty to inform us." He shook his head. "I think it tore him up, the guy being his brother, I mean, so as soon as possible, I'll have a team dispatched to Shakespeare Street."

Waz thought that whoever the DI was talking with must be on a mobile phone, probably travelling in a car and on the hands free car. He guessed, from the number of times that Franklin said 'Ma'am', he was probably speaking with Detective Superintendent Massey.

He saw Franklin nod his head and turn towards the younger man. "One of my lads has just turned up so when his neighbour arrives, I'll brief them both and send along a couple of uniforms as back-up and have them go hunt for the suspect."

Listening to Franklin, Waz inhaled and felt his pulse quicken. The suspect, he'd heard Franklin say. Was this a break-through, he wondered?

"Yes, Ma'am" he listened as Franklin continued, "I did read this morning's edition of the 'Glasgow News', but I see that the by-line is by that wee weasel Ally McGregor who is also the author of the article, so going by his past record he's obviously had a snippet from somewhere," then seeing the curiosity on Waz's face, threw the younger detective a folded copy of the 'Glasgow News. "What I *can* assure you is that nobody in my team has provided McGregor with any information, but of course I can't obviously speak for anyone at the bank."

He nodded his head and continued, "That's likely it, then. The murder of Carol Meechan working in the bank is common knowledge now, so someone must have told McGregor about the MP Peter Gibson also working in the same bank and he's put two and two together to make five."

Waz turned from reading the headline and saw him grin and agree, "Aye, he's a wee shite right enough. Bye."

"What's happening?" said the voice at his back. He turned to see Des Mooney standing with two male and one female uniformed officers, curiosity written all over his face.

"These guys," he thumbed at their colleagues, "were told to attend at the incident room. What's going on," he asked again.

"What's going on, Des," interrupted Franklin, waving Mooney and the uniformed officers to gather round his desk, "is that last night, we had a walk-in witness, a Catholic priest who fired in his younger brother as a possible suspect for Carol Meechan's murder. They have still to be sent to the Lab and given a going over by Forensics, but on the desk over there," he pointed to a corner of the room, "is a tin box with cash, a credit card in the name Margaret Whyte and a knife that is very similar to the one the witness Whyte gave you as the type used to threaten and rob her. The knife seems to be remarkably clean, but I intend having it examined anyway."

"So boss, where do we find this wee brother?" grinned an obviously delighted Mooney.

Father Patrick Gallagher, dressed in his cassock in preparation for that morning's early mass, sat on the old, wooden chair in the vestry, elbows on his knees, his head bowed and held in his hands, full of self-reproach.

He rubbed at his forehead and stared at the floor between his feet. He was weary from lack of sleep, worrying that he had made a huge mistake in contacting the police and given them the tin box. His head reasoned that he had did the right thing, but his heart ached with the knowledge that poorly as his father undoubtedly was, should Magnus learn he had informed the police of what seemed to be Leigh's obvious criminal activities, it could inhibit his Da's recovery or worse, exacerbate his condition.

He thought again of his interview the previous evening. Upon hearing Patrick's story, the detective Mister Franklin had first tried to cajole him into revealing Leigh's name and address and when that had not worked, to bully the younger man with all sort of dire legal threats, but Patrick had held firm and flatly refused to cooperate; at least, not till a deal had been struck.

After almost ten minutes of being harangued by Franklin, the detective had finally agreed that he would hold back on the information and permit the worried priest the opportunity to urge Leigh to surrender himself to the police before they came searching for him, but firmly warned Patrick that their highly unofficial and confidential agreement would end at eight o'clock, the following morning.

Shaking from his encounter with Franklin, he left the police station and immediately returned to the flat in Shakespeare Street to speak with his brother.

He had almost forgotten about the van that was still parked outside the close.

He was first puzzled then realised why he had been unable to gain entry to the flat. His brother's key was in keyhole on the inside of the locked door. Banging on the door and shouting Leigh's name had been to no avail, other than disturbing the neighbours, one who was not known to him and had turned nasty, threatening to contact the police because of the racket Patrick was making.

Phoning Leigh had also proved to be of no use for the house phone had rung out while Leigh's mobile had gone straight to the answer service.

Finally, he had given up and returned to the chapel house to worry through the night.

His sleepless night had been spent in meditation sat in the old, comfy armchair in the lounge of the chapel house, his thoughts full of reproach at his own actions between bouts of praying for his father's recovery and forgiveness for his brother's sins.

He had with deep reluctance come to his decision just after seven o'clock that morning and phoned Mister Franklin on the mobile number the detective had given Patrick the previous evening, admitting his failure to speak with let alone persuade Leigh to surrender to the police.

He shook his head, recalling how his voice had broken and his shame when at last, he provided the detective with Leigh's full name and the flat's address.

"Father?" said the quiet voice.

He turned to see the elderly, white haired man dressed in the robe of the altar server staring at him.

He smiled and drawing a deep breath, nodded his head. "Just coming Eamon," he replied and rising to his feet, prepared himself preach the Lord's word to those hardy few who waited patiently for his sermon.

The five officers arrived in two vehicles outside the close at 86 Shakespeare Street, Waz and Des Mooney in an unmarked CID car while the uniformed officers within the liveried police van, parked behind them.

Bobby Franklin's short briefing had been quite specific.

"The suspect Leigh Gallagher resides on the second floor within the tenement," he had told them, "so unless he is prepared to jump out of the window to the street or the back court, if he's at home he's going nowhere. If you can't immediately gain entry to the flat, wait there till I organise a warrant and I'll have the Support Unit with their door entry team meet you there, okay?"

Waz had been a bit uneasy that no supervisory officer was to accompany them, but Franklin had explained, "I'm staying here to organise things, so as soon as I get a DS in, I'll send the first one up to join you guys. The priority is to find the suspect and preferably persuade him to come voluntarily to the office, but if that doesn't work, detain him and that will give us the six hours to sort things out."

Sending them on their way, his last instruction had been that they maintain contact with him and he would update them as necessary. Now here they were. Waz glanced up at the tenement building, turning as he heard Mooney instruct the female officer and a male colleague to maintain a vigil within the tenement entrance and that nobody, regardless of whether they resided there or not, was to get into or out of the close.

"We're only up the stair," he added, "so if there's a problem, just holler and I'll be down in a jiffy."

It occurred to Waz to ask Mooney who made him the boss, but he held his tongue and inwardly realised that the older and vastly more experienced Mooney was the obvious choice to take charge and besides, he reasoned, it was clear the uniformed guys looked toward and accepted Mooney's instructions as he *was* the senior man.

With Mooney and the remaining uniformed officer, they quickly made their way up to the second storey landing and he watched as Mooney first pressed an ear against the door for a few seconds, turning and shaking his head to indicate no noise from within.

Taking a deep breath, he banged at the door with his fist.

Still, there was no reply. Mooney bent down and peeked through the letter box, then moved his head to peer with one eye through the keyhole.

"I don't think there's anybody home," he sighed and again banged at the door.

"What the fuck's going on here!" shouted a man's voice from behind them.

Waz turned to see an unshaven obese neighbour, wearing a stained white vest stretched across his beer belly, pyjama bottoms and barefooted, peering at them from the opposite door and thought the presence of a uniformed cop *might* have been a bleeding clue!

"Morning sir," the uniformed cop cheerfully replied, "just giving the young man who lives in there an early morning wake-up call. How are you today then?"

"How the *fuck* am I?" the man stared in bewilderment at the officer, uncertain if the piss was being taken and shook his head. "Me, I'd be fine if you bastards would let me get my Saturday morning lie-in, so I would. And as for that wee Fenian toe-rag," he pointed with a stubby finger at the closed door, "I heard him banging the door earlier on, so I think he's fucked off out of it. Must have known *you* people were coming, eh?" he sneered.

The cop, a fixed smile plastered to his face was about to retort when his female colleague climbing the stairs breathlessly called out, "Hey guys," and beckoned towards Mooney and Waz. They could see from her reddening face she must have rushed up the stairs.

"The wee woman that lives on the ground floor flat," she cast a thumb over her shoulder, "said that she saw Leigh Gallagher leaving the close about half an hour ago."

"She certain it was him?" asked Mooney.

"Oh aye," the cop fought for breath, "it was him right enough. If you want my humble opinion, that wee woman doesn't miss a trick. I'd be surprised if anyone gets in or out this close without her knowing. She's the street's nosiest bugger, so she is."

Mooney inhaled and biting at his lower lip said, "Waz, can you give the DI a bell and update him that the suspect is out and about and that we will take a turn round the area, just in case Gallagher is hanging about watching for any police activity." Turning to the female officer, he continued, "Will you and your mate there stand by the door hen? At least till the warrant gets here, eh?"

It was more a request than an instruction, but to her credit, the young woman grinned and nodded. "Aye, just don't forget we're here," she replied then added with a grin, "I've not had my breakfast yet."

The two men began to make their way downstairs when they heard her ask the grumpy neighbour, "So, what's the chance of a cuppa then, sir?"

A few seconds later they heard a door being loudly slammed.

Usman Mohammed carried the metal shutter from the front window into the close entrance beside the shop and using a short length of chain, padlocked the shutter against the ring bolt that was secured to the wall. It didn't do to take a chance and leave the shutter insecure; too many damned metal thieves in the area, he shook his head at the thought. Exiting the close, he glanced at his watch. That bloody girl's timekeeping was getting worse and unlocking the shop door, was about to close it behind him when Rita Whyte burst through, almost knocking him down in her haste to get inside.

"Sorry, Usman," she gasped, "the bus was late again."

Without waiting for him to respond, she shrugged out of her coat and headed towards the rear of the shop, calling over her shoulder, "I'll stick the kettle on. Do you want a cuppa?"

He sighed and his shoulders slumped, the annoyance of her lateness and his opportunity to chastise her now gone. Oh, but she was a fly one, he thought and inwardly grinned at her cheek, having to admit to himself that yes, he *did* like her.

"Yes please," he heard himself call out and as the door opened behind him, turned with a smile to greet the first customer of that day.

Detective Superintendent Lynn Massey arrived at her office to find two detectives sitting in the corridor outside her door, awaiting her arrival.

Her anger at the 'Glasgow News' headline had dissipated during her car ride into the office and confident as she was that nobody in Bobby Franklin's team had spoken with that little shit Ally McGregor, she reminded him that the point must be made that anyone found to be providing information outwith the inquiry team would be harshly dealt with. Franklin, she knew, would disseminate her anger and while it was not in her nature to hover over her subordinates, she also knew that as senior management it was her duty to remind her people where their loyalties lay.

The two detectives stood as she approached.

"Good morning Ma'am," said the male detective in a clipped, yet surprisingly high pitched voice, who standing at a little over six foot, had short, thinning brown hair gelled back from his forehead and sported a neatly trimmed, pencil moustache. His sharply defined facial features were even more outlined by an overlarge nose upon which rested wire framed spectacles.

He reminded her of a school teacher she once had and suppressed a giggle at the nickname the man endured; Poker-arse, due to his erect style of walking.

Massey could not know that lenses were plain glass and that the tall man wore the glasses because he believed they made him appear even more intimidating.

Wearing a three piece navy coloured pin stripe suit, pale blue shirt and maroon coloured tie, her first impression was of a man with military bearing who took fastidious care of his appearance.

"Our Superintendent at the Police Standards Unit has sent us over to assist you with an ongoing inquiry. I'm Detective Inspector Alex Cameron and this," he waved a hand towards the slim built, fair haired woman without looking at her, "is DS Baxter."

Massey saw his colleague to be a slim built woman in her early thirties, her short fair hair fashionably cut and framing a face that though devoid of makeup, was remarkably clear skinned with her most notable feature, her piercing blue eyes that fashionable wire-framed spectacles couldn't hide. Baxter wore a two piece dark green coloured skirted business suit and carried a tan coloured leather handbag and matching short heeled shoes. At a little over five feet six inches tall, the neat and tidy younger woman stood demurely at Cameron's side, her hands clasped in front of her.

Lynn Massey had never been an individual who was quick to judge, yet almost immediately took a dislike to Cameron and mainly due to his curt and disdainful introduction of Baxter that had annoyed Massey.

For some reason she could not quite place, his name struck a chord and seemed to ring a bell.

Graciously, she smiled at them both and extending her hand, shook Cameron's then turning to Baxter, asked, "I'm sorry, what's your first name?"

"Arlene, Ma'am; Arlene Baxter," the younger woman smiled and stared directly back at her, yet Massey sensed her eyes conveyed the message that Cameron's attitude towards her didn't at all faze Baxter.

"Right guys," she smiled brightly at them both and said, "Let me have five minutes to get myself organised and prepare to brief you, but in the meantime," pointed further along the corridor, "there's a small kitchen along there if you want to grab a coffee or tea."

She was turning into her office doorway when Baxter asked, "Ma'am, can I get you something too?"

"Yes, Arlene," she smiled with pleasure at Baxter's thoughtfulness, "a coffee if you please; milk only."

It didn't escape her attention that Cameron cast a scowl at Baxter, but why, she couldn't quite fathom.

Susie Gibson, lying in bed, stared at the sunlight streaming through the crack in the curtains, creating a brilliantly lit slash on the bedroom wall. She turned her head slightly toward the bedside digital alarm clock and groaned. It was almost nine o'clock and having lain awake for most of the night, her body ached for sleep. Wearily she threw back the cover and swung her legs over the side of the bed, slipping her feet into the pink coloured, fluffy mules, last years Christmas gift from Jenny. Her nightgown was soaked in perspiration and she worried that she was coming down with a cold or worse. Through the closed door, she heard a noise from the kitchen downstairs of a metal pan being banged and for a brief instant her heart raced, thinking that maybe Peter had returned home. She stood and fetched her dressing gown from the hook behind the door and wrapping it about her, hurriedly made her way downstairs. Jenny, her eyes red rimmed and dressed in her brightly coloured 'onesie', turned as her mother waked through the door.

Susie saw her daughter had raided the fridge, the worktop now resembling a battle scene and loaded with bacon, sausage, eggs and an open can of beans. A loaf lay opened as the kettle boiled on the hob.

"Sorry, I woke you when I dropped the pan, didn't I? I wanted to surprise you, make you breakfast," she sniffed at her mother, her lips trembling as she fought back the tears.

Susie swallowed hard and unable to trust herself to speak, simply opened her arms, into which rushed Jenny, her body shaking as she sobbed into her mother's shoulder.

They stood for a few moments, hugging each other, with Susie gently caressing her daughter's hair. Then more composed now, she whispered into Jenny's ear, "That'll be the low calorie fry-up, then?"

Jenny's body wracked with sudden laughter, the tension of the moment eased. Drawing herself from her mother, she smiled and replied, "Maybe we could cook this together, eh? Sit down like normal people and eat something, mum."

Her hands still clutching her daughter's arms, Susie smiled and nodded.

"That's my girl, my brave, brave wee lassie. Yes, let's do that. Together," she added

They both startled when the house phone resting on the worktop loudly chirruped.

Leigh Gallagher's nerves were on edge and who would blame him? His brother, the sanctimonious bastard who was supposed to keep peoples secrets; he had fired Leigh in, grassed him right up to the fucking cops. Now he was a hunted man, imagining the cops all over the place looking for him.

Eyes darting back and forth like a rabbit on speed, he walked warily along Dumbarton Road, every passer-by an informant, every passing car containing the CID searching for him. Twice already he had run through tenement closes, once thinking that he had been spotted and a second time when he saw a police van cruising in a nearby street. Now, legs trembling, he stood in the sheltered doorway of a shuttered shop, a mere ten yards away from the stop, impatiently waiting for the bus that would take him into the Buchanan Street Bus station in the city centre. His head swivelled back and forth and again, back and forth, searching for any tell-tale sign that he was spotted, preparing himself to run and abandon the small backpack into which he had stuffed the few clothing items he needed. Just enough clothes till he could get across the water from Cairnryan to Belfast and then to the South, where he knew his father had family. He regretted having taken the money from his father's hidey-hole, but since Patrick had fucked off with his tin, it was the only cash available to Leigh and hoped it would be enough for a one-way ferry ticket. He'd pay his Da back, he promised himself.

His brow furrowed as he thought of his Da.

He slowly shook his head, the overwhelming feeling of guilt causing his legs to shake. He would phone the hospital when he had gotten clear of Glasgow, find out if his Da was getting better. He'd understand why Leigh couldn't hang about. Yes, he convinced himself, his Da would understand.

The female customer stared curiously at the tall, heavy-set assistant. "Are you listening to me, hen?" but the lassie just stared through the shop window, her mouth open and eyes narrowed, the can of peas she had fetched from the shelf clutched in her hand.

"You're not listening to me, hen," the woman angrily persisted, turning with a curious look at the shopkeeper, Mister Mohammed who with equal curiosity, stared at his assistant.

Des Mooney drove while Waz Ahmed spoke with DI Franklin on the mobile phone.
"Aye boss," Mooney heard Waz say, "The uniform guys will stand by the locus till the warrant arrives. Des and me, we're taking a wee turn through Partick but to be honest, without a photograph of the suspect, we're chancing our arm. All we know is he's nineteen and probably shitting himself knowing that we're looking for him."
Mooney stifled a grin at Waz's description of the suspect and turned the car onto Dumbarton Road.

Leigh Gallagher was becoming increasingly anxious and wondering if instead he should have made his way to the underground subway station near to Byres Road, but to do so would mean either walking exposed along Dumbarton Road or taking a roundabout and lengthy route using the backstreets and like it or not, time was critical to him getting away.
He glanced at the heavy-set woman wearing the apron that had just exited the shop across the road and was now walking towards the bus-stop. Bloody idiot, he thought, watching with surprise as she ignored the traffic and nearly got herself run over by a van.

"Look at the clown!" fumed Des Mooney, staring at the woman wearing an apron walking across the road and who was nearly struck by a white coloured van that had to swerve sharply to avoid her. Waz Ahmed stared too, his eyes narrowing as the CID car got closer and he slowly said, "Isn't that…"

Leigh turned back just in time to see the woman, who he saw wore a white coloured apron that bore the log 'Shop Rite Price' printed upon it in large, red letters. His eyes narrowed because….yeah, she *did* look vaguely familiar. Now she was past the bus-stop and walking directly towards him, her face a mask of fury. Surprised, he tried to take a step backwards, forgetting he was already hard up against the closed shop door.
"You, ya bastard," screamed Rita Whyte and drew back her arm.

Waz Ahmed's eyes opened wide. "It is her, that's our witness Margaret Whyte and she's…" his eyes opened even wider. "Fuck me, Des!" he shouted as he saw her suddenly attack a youth in a shop doorway, "Stop the car! Quick!"

Mooney spun the driving wheel and cut in front of an irate Hackney taxi driver who waved a fist, then stamped on his brake to stop his vehicle and stare at the two men who jumped from the car, now recognising it as a CID vehicle.

The driver watched as the two men leapt upon a stocky built young woman who was lying on top of a skinny teenager, wrestling with her as she battered the young guy with something she held in her hand.

"Let me at him! The bastard! Mug me, would you?" screamed Rita Whyte, straddling the unfortunate Leigh Gallagher, both her arms now restrained by Waz Ahmed and Des Mooney who were vainly trying to haul her off the terrified teenager.

Together, the officers managed to drag Whyte to one side and while Waz struggled to maintain his hold of her, Mooney went to aid the fallen Leigh, who lay moaning and bleeding slightly from a wound to the left side of his head.

While Waz attempted to calm the enraged Whyte who continued to scream abuse and issue dire threats towards him, Leigh was pulled by Mooney to his feet who with a grin asked him, "Mister Gallagher I presume?"

Dazed, Leigh could only at first only nod and then realising the officers would not allow any further assault upon him, spat out, "Keep that mad bitch away from me or I'll fucking do her properly the next time," then shrunk away as the maddened woman lunged once more towards him.

Mooney continued to grin and said to Waz, "I think we should take that comment as an admission of a previous assault, Detective Constable, what do you think, eh?"

Waz grinned in return and still holding the struggling Whyte, watched as Mooney slammed Leigh face first against the wall and handcuffed his wrists at his back. Turning his prisoner and backing him against the wall, his eyes narrowed as he glanced at Leigh's wounded head and then at the weapon held in Whyte's hand and grinned even further.

"Well, well. Looks to me like an assault with a deadly can of peas," he chortled.

CHAPTER 17

Morven Sutherland, dressed once more in a fashionable two piece suit, arrived at the bank's front door, but mounting the marble stairs and before she could ring the buzzer, was admitted by the elderly commissionaire Max McFarlane, dressed in his best blazer, crisp white shirt with regimental tie, sharply creased flannel trousers, highly polished shoes as befits an old soldier and delighted to be earning double time for turning out on a Saturday morning.

"Morning Miss Sutherland," he cheerfully greeted her, but received a blank faced nod in return.

Not even worth a bad thought, he inwardly sighed and was about to lock the door when he saw the Accounts Manager Harry McPherson striding purposefully towards the bank.

"Morning sir," smiled Max again and then sighed as once more he was ignored.

This time, however, he gave in and muttered under his breath, "Stuck-up twat.' Locking the heavy wooden door, Max settled into the padded chair at the reception desk and fetched his morning edition of the 'Glasgow News' and his old flask from beneath the counter, the two rude bank staff already dismissed from his thoughts.

"Morven," McPherson called out, seeing her turning as he said her name and racing up the stairs to draw abreast with her. "Glad I caught you before you went into the office," he quietly said and taking her by the elbow, drew her into an alcove. "About last night…." he began, but she reached up and placed a forefinger against his lips.

"It was… no, *you* were amazing," she smiled benignly at him and without another word, drew herself away and walked towards the office, her high heels clicking loudly with each step on the polished wooden floor and the sound reverberating throughout the high vaulted and empty hallway.

He stared after her, hesitant to call out and tell her that was not what he wanted to hear, that he what he really needed to tell her was that it couldn't continue, that because of his previous affairs, his late arrival home had caused his already suspicious wife Tracey to question him again.

He needed to end it here; tell Morven their all too brief fling was simply that, a one night stand but afraid not just of her reaction, but if word got out....well, he sighed, knowing that no matter how much the banking industry tried to persuade the public it was tolerant of such issues, a married man caught philandering with a female colleague could well and truly kiss his arse and his career goodbye. He had to tell her, but staring at her graceful figure as she walked off, could not deny the desire that arose within him and besides, he inwardly knew that he lacked the courage for such a confrontation. He glanced at his watch and straightening his tie, used both hands to slick back his hair and taking a deep breath, followed her towards the Accounts Department.

"Who was it mum, was it Dad? Was it the police? Have they found dad? Was it him? Mum! Tell me, please," Jenny almost begged her place faced mother.

Susie gently returned the phone to its cradle and turning shook her head.

"No, it's not fresh news, darling. It *was* the police. They just phoned because they want to interview me." She glanced at her daughter. "You too, I should imagine."

"Are they coming here?"

"Yes," Susie nodded, "they did ask if I would prefer to meet them at the police office in Uddingston, but I thought it would be better if we spoke here."

What she didn't tell her daughter was her experience told her that if there was to be any interview, particularly in light of the suspicions now raised against her husband Peter, she wanted to be on home ground, not sitting in the sterility of a small interview room and definitely not having her daughter interviewed in that type of environment.

"When will they be here?"

"I've agreed that eleven o'clock will be fine, so," she smiled, but a smile without warmth, "let's you and I first have some breakfast and then get ourselves tidied up, eh?"

Lynn Massey turned at the sound of her open door being knocked to see a young, slim woman standing there, one hand in the pocket of her denim jeans and the other holding the strap of a bulging, flowery decorated canvas bag that hung over her shoulder, the bottom of which indicated by the sharp corners that within was probably carried a laptop among others things. Dressed casually in a sleeveless, loose fitting, brightly coloured yellow sunflower-print top, she wore an array of beaded necklaces as well as a variety of wristbands and scuffed open toed sandals on her feet. Both ears sported a number of stud earrings while her short red hair was spiked with gel and a cheery, almost infectious grin plastered to her pretty face and highlighted by a splash of deep purple lipstick.

"Hello boss, you looking for me?" she winked at Massey.

Massey sat back in her chair, her pleasure at seeing the younger woman evident by the wide smile she returned to and waved her through the door. "Come in Laura, thanks for coming out on your day off."

"No thanks needed," she replied, drawing a chair over from the wall and flopping down into it. Massey had long ago realised that Laura Scott, the most unlikely Detective Sergeant she had ever met, was the most pleasant of young woman who treated all her colleagues, irrespective of their rank, and the public with the same easy going courtesy and charm. Some colleagues and most suspects she dealt with mistook Scott's laid back, casual manner for apathy and later come to seriously regret underestimating the razor sharp mind behind the smile.

"I figured that if you needed me, then something is going on and nobody calls the Fraud Squad's *top* Forensic accountant unless it's either a really interesting case or the investigating officers are out of their depth," she nodded towards Massey, grinning at her own boast. "So, what's up, boss?"

It took Massey almost thirty minutes to brief Scott on the known details of Carol Meechan's murder and the disappearance of Peter Gibson, the Investments Manager with the Caledonia Banking Group.

"I read the 'Glasgow News' on the bus on the way in here," Scott's eyes narrowed. "The paper has him figured for the murder, sort of inferring that both Gibson and Meechan were colluding in the theft of the money and that he done her in before getting on his toes. Any chance that wee shite Ally McGregor might have got it right, boss?"

Massey sighed and slowly exhaled. "Obviously, we can't discount there might be a connection between Meechan and Gibson and of course, there's the additional problem that Gibson's wife is one of our own, DS Susan Gibson. Do you happen to know her?"

"As it happens, I do," she nodded with a sigh, her eyes narrowing as she remembered. "It was a couple of years ago, before I was promoted, I was working as a desk officer in the Squad when I assisted her and her neighbour with a fraud in one of the Council's museums. Long story cut short, the kitchen supervisor was claiming salaries for over a dozen ghost workers and divvying the extra wages up between herself and the other five staff. As I recall, DS Gibson had gotten the sniff of the fraud from a disgruntled staff member, but was uncertain how to research the National Insurance numbers and needed to speak with someone from my office who had contacts within the Council and that's where I came in."

She sniffed at the memory. "Back then, the Council's auditing system was worse than pathetic, so the suspect and her cronies had been getting away with it for almost two years. It worked out to be quite a tidy sum they had managed to steal. Gibson and her neighbour, with my assistance of course," she smiled, "locked the six of them up, but the Council worked a deal with the Fiscal and the accused defence team and the buggers all walked; minus their jobs, of course."

"They walked?"

"Aye, boss. Seems the Council were embarrassed at getting taken for thousands of the ratepayers money, so rather than risk a scandal for the sitting Labour Party councillors, the accused all signed a non-disclosure agreement that they would not talk or otherwise discuss with any other party and, in particular the press, their part in the cover-up. Saved face for the Council and the poor unfortunate ratepayers were none the wiser that thousands of pounds of public funds, a high five figure sum in fact, had been stolen."

"That'll be where the road repair money went, then," quipped Massey, not at all surprised at the deviousness of local government.

"I'm interested in what you said, though, about the ghost workers," she continued. "In essence, that seems to parallel how Peter Gibson has managed to cream off the money with the false investments; creating ghost companies, I mean."

"Mmmm, but from what you told me, Gibson's scheme is a lot more involved than the relatively simple scam his wife dealt with boss, but once you let me get into the paperwork and the banks computers, I should be able to unravel how he achieved it. Will there be any problem with the banking industry, me getting involved I mean? You know how close-knit and secretive that mob can be."

"You leave them to me, Laura. If they want their money found and their bloody incompetence kept quiet, I imagine they'll be more than happy to assist with whatever information you might require to conduct your investigation. Anyway, you haven't told me yet about how you got on with DS Gibson."

"Oh, right, but you have to understand my involvement in her case was purely advisory and it was she and her neighbour who conducted the investigation?"

Massey nodded.

"Well, I can't admit to knowing Susie Gibson that well," she slowly said, "but I thought she was a good cop and she took my advice when offered. As you can see," she waved both hands at herself, "I don't fit the image of a big city 'Tec, so it was nice to work with a supervisor who didn't judge what they saw, but listened without prejudice. Aye," she gave a nod of approval, "she seemed okay to me, but as I said it was just the one inquiry so I can't comment other than that. Sorry."

"Well, there's nothing to suggest at this time that DS Gibson is implicated in either her husbands alleged fraud nor of his disappearance. We might know more when the two PSU officers I sent to interview note her statement."

"Who are the PSU guys, boss?"

"They're a DI Cameron and a DS Baxter."

"Ah wee Arlene," Scott nodded. "She's all right. I worked with her when we were both divisional CID in Easterhouse. Tough wee lassie, though you wouldn't think it to look at her. She's got a mind as sharp as a razor. Not somebody I would like to underestimate either."

Exactly what I was thinking about you, Massey inwardly thought as she stared at Scott.

"DI Cameron, you said. Would that be an Alex Cameron, boss?"

"That's him," nodded Massey, "do you know him?"

Scott ran her tongue inside her mouth, pushing her cheek out, but failed miserably in trying to stop a grin from spreading across her face. "Well," she drawled, "not personally, but if it's the same guy, he was known in his last division as Ben Dover."

"Ben Dover?" asked Massey and then fought to restrain her own grin. "Ah, I get it. Not a popular man, then?"

"Let's just say if the rumours are true, he wasn't just a management tout, oh," she suddenly went pale. "No offence intended boss."

"None taken," replied Massey, now grinning widely and waving her hand, then added, "Continue."

"Well," Scott leaned forward, "it's rumoured that Cameron was a direct line to our former ACC for Crime …"

"You mean John Moredun?"

"Aye, that sleaze-ball," she shook her head. "I didn't like home at all. Anyway, it was said that any rumour or complaint that a cop uttered went straight back to Moredun and that as a reward for firing in his colleagues, Cameron was promoted to DI as a parting thank you for all the back-stabbing he did as Moredun's tout. I heard he was shifted into the PSU because no divisional CID wanted him."

Massey was surprised she had never previously heard of Cameron and a sudden doubt swept through Massey, wondering if Cameron would adhere to the strict instructions she had issued prior to sending him and Baxter to interview DS Gibson.

She forced a smile and lifting a handwritten note from her desk, said, "Right, Laura, first things first. Can you get yourself down to the bank in West George Street? I understand that the two I mentioned, McPherson and a Miss Sutherland are working there today. By now they should have been told to extend to you every courtesy regarding our investigation. Any problems …."

"I've still got your mobile number, boss," Scott interrupted her and standing, lifted her bag and slinging it across her shoulder, nodded cheerio and left Massey to her thoughts.

Waz Ahmed and Des Mooney really had no need to handcuff Leigh Gallagher, for the younger man was going nowhere now, however, both later agreed a strip of masking tape for his foul mouth might have been appropriate.

Sat in the rear of the CID vehicle with Mooney beside him while Waz drove, the teenager, with a liberal use of expletives, whined and moaned during the thankfully short ride to Cranstonhill police office, demanding that his attacker be arrested and he be taken to the casualty at Gartnavel Hospital.

Turning into the rear yard, Mooney had had enough and turning to the younger man, whispered with quiet menace, "Shut the fuck up, you excuse for a hard man or I'll…."

"You'll what?" Leigh sneered, his face a mask of hate as he stared at Mooney. "You can't touch me or I'll make a complaint."

With considerable tolerance, Mooney simply stared back and to the teenager's surprise, grinned. Then, with a voice so low that Waz was unable to hear, again whispered, but on this occasion said, "Let's see how tough you are when you're charged with murder, hard man."

Watching Leigh Gallagher's face turn pale, his eyes widen and his mouth drop open as he silently mouthed the word 'murder?' was, Mooney later told Waz, worth suffering the five minute car ride and sneering abuse.

The two detectives travelling in the CID car eastwards on the M8 towards Uddingston did not have the same rapport as their Cranstonhill colleagues.

DS Arlene Baxter, sitting the passenger seat, had in the five weeks she worked with DI Alex Cameron come to accept that the morose bastard was the worse type of bigot. Being the most recently appointed member of the tightly knit group of PSU detectives, it was her inopportune luck to be assigned as Cameron's neighbour, a partnership that neither he nor she was happy with, but one she would be forced to suffer till some other poor unfortunate was posted into the PSU.

She miserably accepted she had a long wait.

In the short time they had spent together, she had come to realise that Cameron wasn't just chauvinistic and loudly opinionated in his intense dislike of Catholics, women police officers, Muslims, Irish and yes, women again; he just about hated everybody who wasn't a card carrying member of the Wee Free Church of Scotland.

However, if the rumours were true, the Wee Free's weren't too happy either about him as a member of their flock.

She had already learned that her colleagues within the PSU weren't averse to occasionally setting him up, whispering stories among themselves that were blatant lies for the purpose of permitting him to overhear and then to find some gaffer or other to impart his gossip, only to have it rebound when it proved to be a load of rubbish.

He just didn't learn, she inwardly sighed.

"When we get there, I'll do the talking, DS Baxter," he told her, turning from the motorway onto the off-ramp that led indirectly towards Uddingston.

It was the same story every time. She turned her head away to stare out of the passenger window, a mounting anger within her, recalling the numerous occasions she had to step in when his incompetent interview and bullying technique failed to achieve the information that they sought. Worse, the majority of the complaints they had to date investigated as neighbours against their fellow police officers, with just one exception, had so far all proven to be malicious and invariably concocted for some purpose or other.

Even often with the knowledge that a complaint against a colleague was so blatantly contrived as to be completely ludicrous, Cameron still persisted with his sneering behaviour towards the accused officer.

Baxter did not profess to be an expert on human behaviour, but had accrued sufficient experience to realise that Cameron enjoyed the feeling of power he could wield over the unfortunate individual, though sometimes the more experienced officers they dealt with would easily turn Cameron's blustering interview technique against him.

And, she again inwardly sighed, that's when she *had* to step in.

Yet still he insisted that he take the lead in their interviews, using his rank to demand first crack, as he termed it, when interviewing their suspect, all of whom so far had been cops and some vastly more experienced that Alex bloody Cameron.

At home her partner Stephen had listened to her moans about Cameron and first suggested, then insisted she complain, that she bring to her bosses attention Cameron's incompetence, if not his bigoted and racist comments.

But that wasn't Baxter's style. She wasn't the type to run to bosses, whining about a colleague, no matter that the skinny git was a complete dunderhead. No, she would deal with it in her own way, but inwardly forced to admit she was now nearing the end of her tether.

"What was the address again," he snapped, intruding in her thoughts.

"Ah, Kylepark Drive, sir. Number 188," she replied, glancing down at the Glasgow A to Z map that lay open on her lap. It irked her that even alone in the car he still insisted she defer to his rank.

"Directions, if you please," he snapped again at her, his concentration on the road in front.

She took a deep breath and pointed out the junction into which he turned the car.

DI Bobby Franklin listened with an increasing smile as Waz Ahmed related his account about the detention of their suspect, Leigh Gallagher who now languished in the detention room downstairs.

"Where's Des Mooney?"

"Eh, he's sitting in with the suspect, just keeping an eye on him boss," replied Ahmed.

Franklin didn't press the issue, but suspected that Mooney wasn't so much keeping an eye on the young lad as priming him up for his tape recorded interview and guessed when the wily Mooney had finished speaking with him, when the time came for the formal tape interview, Gallagher would be desperate to tell his side of the story.

"First things first," Franklin began to write a series of notes on the pad in front of him.

"Has he been offered the services of a solicitor yet?"

"Nicotine Mary at the uniform bar is informing the duty brief as we speak, boss."

"Okay, that's one issue ticked off. Right, you," he poked his pencil at Waz, "get yourself a phone and organise an identification parade for our street robbery victims. Have them attend here pronto."

"What kind of ID parade boss," asked Waz, then sheepishly added, "I've never really been involved in one before."

"Okay, no matter, son. On second thought, here's what we'll do. Did you receive VIPER training when you were on your detective course at Tulliallan?"

"Aye," replied a relieved Waz. "The instructor took us through the system, but told us that it was a specialist team that run it."

"Well, he was correct. The team are based at Pitt Street, so liaise with them and have one of their team meet you and either get the witnesses in to the office or, if they can't make it, interview them at home or their workplace. What I want is a speedy response," he explained, then added, "If we can get the suspect identified for the robberies then that will at least give us a holding charge and time to permit us to work on him for the murder."

"On it boss," nodded Waz and turning towards the door, was called back by Franklin who asked, "The young woman that caught Gallagher. She was a robbery victim, yeah?"

"Aye, boss."

"Good, that means you have your first identification, so get one more for now to corroborate her statement and we can charge the now him for at least two of the robberies."

Waz hurried from the room to find a phone and make his arrangements.

His first call to the VIPER team at Pitt Street proved relatively simple and the civilian analyst who took the call agreed to attend whatever location Waz arranged with his first witness. The youngish sounding man would await Waz's second phone call wit the address. However, Waz's second phone call proved not to be as straight-forward.

English was not Alicja Paderewski's first language and a couple of minutes explanation took Waz almost ten minutes, but finally the nervous sounding woman agreed that he could meet her at her flat where, he laboriously explained, she would be shown a series of video clips of the man who had mugged her.

His third consecutive call was again to the VIPER operative who agreed first to attend at Cranstonhill and take a short video clip of the suspect, Leigh Gallagher and then meet Waz in about one hour outside the witnesses flat at 29 Lawrie Street, coincidentally, thought Waz with a frown, the same street where Carol Meechan resided and was murdered.

One flight below Waz, in the small and damp smelling detention room, Leigh Gallagher sat hunched on a wooden chair, his head bowed and arms tightly folded into his chest.

Des Mooney, sitting on a similar chair on the opposite side of the graffiti scarred table, stared at the teenager's head and said, "Do you want a drink of water or anything, son; or maybe a coffee or cup of tea?"

Leigh, the arrogance from before now gone, shook his head, unable to speak for fear that his voice would break and the unshed tears would fall.

Murder, the detective had said. He was to be charged with murder. His first thought was of the wee blonde bird, the one who had fought back.

The sudden memory of the incident caused him without thinking to blurt out, "I only cut her hand. I didn't stab her or anything. It was only her hand," he again mumbled.

Mooney's eyes narrowed. There had been no report of any of Gallagher's victims being cut with the knife. What the hell was he on about? Was this a robbery that hadn't been reported or was he talking about the murder victim?

His voice deliberately soft, he folded his hands on the table top and smiling at the anxious teenager, said, "Okay son. Tell me about it, about what happened."

CHAPTER 18

Susie Gibson sent her daughter into the kitchen to prepare a tray of coffee while she led the two PSU officers into the lounge and bade them take a seat. She saw the DI chose the prominent single seat armchair while the DS sat on the opposite side of the couch, distancing herself from him. Being an experienced detective, Susie realised that the two officers had chosen their seats to their advantage; that she would either need to sit beside the DS and that position would place her between them, forcing her to turn her attention between them both or instead, she could fetch in another chair.

I won't be intimidated in my own home, she irately thought and fetching a straight back dining chair from the nearby table, placed it against the wall so that she could see both officers together. Though she didn't then know why, she felt it would somehow be better for her gauge their reaction to her interview.

"I regret having to call upon you here at your home," DI Cameron formally began, "but given the circumstances of your husband's," he hesitated, "disappearance and the allegation that a large sum of money from his bank is currently unaccountable…"

"Stolen, you mean. Let's not beat about the bush, Mister Cameron," she interrupted him.

"Yes, that seems to be the case," he slowly replied, "as you say Susan, stolen."

Her eyes narrowed and she glanced at each of them in turn before saying, "I assume that you are both here to treat me as a witness and not a colleague?"

Cameron's eyes opened wide. "Ah, yes, of course."

"Then it's Missus Gibson. My forename is for use by family and friends and people I like and, as I do not know you, you are neither, so I would prefer it if we keep this interview formal, if you please."

Cameron's face turned pale at the rebuke and she saw his Adams apple bouncing in his skinny throat.

"Indeed," he simply replied.

Baxter fought to stop herself from grinning widely and thought, good girl. Stick it to him.

He fetched a notebook from his inside jacket pocket and opening it, removed the stub of a pencil and to Susie's surprise, licked the leaded end before asking, "Now, your husband *Missus* Gibson. When did you last see him?"

"Haven't you done your homework and read the missing person report? I have already provided that information and I'm sure you must have some rather more pertinent questions, Inspector."

"*Detective* Inspector," he slowly replied, believing that he himself was now scoring points. "Just as you say Missus Gibson; yes, we have more pertinent questions such as did you know that your husband was stealing money from his bank?"

He had convinced himself that a straight forward question would perhaps educe if not a confession, then perhaps throw her off her guard.

Baxter unconsciously shook her head and drew a sharp breath. His first bloody question and he's already knackered the interview, she thought, wondering at the stupidity of Cameron.

His eyes opened with surprise when he saw Susie smile.

"By that statement, I assume you have irrefutable proof that my husband is a thief and is responsible for the theft of the money?"

"Yes, well the circumstances seem to indicate…"

"The circumstances seem to indicate?" she parodied him. "To hell with the circumstances," she spat at him, her anger now overtaking the promise she had earlier made herself that she would remain calm. "You are sitting on *my* chair in *my* home accusing *my* husband of being a *thief?* Where is your proof? Are you here to obtain my statement regarding my missing husband or badger me into some sort of false confession?"

Rising now to her feet, her hands clenched into fists, her eyes filled with rage and all restraint now gone. "Who the *fuck* do you think you are coming into *my* home with this nonsense?" she snarled at him.

He stood awkwardly, pale faced and speechless with no defence against her onslaught, knowing that he had almost immediately underestimated her.

The door opened to admit Jenny who responding to her mother's shout was white faced and close to tears. "Mum!" she called out.

"Missus Gibson!" snapped Baxter at her, then quieter, "Please," she asked, her eyes conveying the message that Susie calm down.

Susie turned to stare at the younger woman and took a deep breath, realising that this was getting out of hand.

"*You!*" she pointed at Cameron, her hand shaking. "Get out of my home *now*. If you want your statement, I'll speak with your colleague, but *you* are not welcome. Get out!"

Cameron snapped his head towards Baxter who, still seated, suggested, "If it's okay with you sir, I'll note Missus Gibson's statement and join you in the car."

His lips tight together, he stormed from the room, almost bowling Jenny over in his haste to go.

Susie, still on her feet turned towards Baxter and frostily asked her, "Do *you* have anything *pertinent* to ask me, Detective Sergeant?"

Baxter slowly smiled and eyes almost twinkling, shrugged her shoulders before replying, "Only wondering if you have Sweetex for the coffee. I'm on a low-cal diet plan the now."

The she grinned widely.

DS Laura Scott arrived at the Caledonian Bank and pressed at the old fashioned bell push button.

Pulling open the heavy wooden door, Max McFarlane, the elderly commissionaire stared with curiosity at the spiky haired young woman and even after she had produced her warrant card, was still slightly suspicious of Scott until with a disarming smile, she commented on his regimental tie and continuing with an even wider grin, disclosed her husband was also a former military man.

"Right hen," he admitted her and learning who she sought, pointed up the stairs. "Turn left at the top and follow the corridor till you see the Accounts office on your right. Oh and hen," he lowered his voice and winking at her, conspiratorially whispered, "watch yourself with that pair. She's a stuck-up cow and he thinks he's God's gift, if you know what I mean."

Scott returned his wink and with a tactile rub at the old man's arm, said, "Thanks Max. It's always good to be forewarned, eh?"

He watched Scott wind her way up the wide stairs and staring at the tight jeans she wore, sighed with an unaccountable urge to be young again, before returning to his seat at the reception desk, his flask and the 'Glasgow News'.

In the Accounts office, Harry McPherson was sitting opposite Morven Sutherland, both examining the loan documents that had been completed by Peter Gibson and making notations on their respective pads.

The door was knocked and a spiky haired redhead popped her head in and smiled at them both.

"Hello, you'll be Mister McPherson and Miss Sutherland?"

McPherson nodded and in a harsh voice asked, "Who are you?"

Scott pushed the door fully opened and with a wide grin, entered and introduced herself.

"You'll have some identification I presume?" he asked.

Again, she produced her warrant card and he held it almost with some distaste between his forefinger and thumb, as though its very touch was somehow infectious.

"Yes, very well. So, how can we assist you, Detective Sergeant?" he asked, slightly incredulous that this hippy like creature was really a police officer.

"May I?" grinned Scott, dragging a chair for a corner and sitting down beside a slightly suspicious Sutherland who by her facial expression, very obviously disapproved of Scott's attire and pulled her chair a few inches further from the DS, distancing herself in what Scott perceived to be a definite declaration of a border between them both.

Scott, however, was no stranger to disapproving looks and ignoring Sutherland asked McPherson, "I work for the Fraud Squad, Mister

McPherson. My understanding is that you and your colleague here," she flicked a thumb at Sutherland, "will provide me with assistance in tracing the alleged theft of a substantial sum of money from your bank."

"Alleged theft? My God isn't it obvious?" he almost sneered at her. "Peter Gibson, our Business Loans Manager has stolen over three million pounds," he stared at her with incredulity. "What's alleged about that?"

"If indeed it *does* go to a trial with Mister Gibson as an accused then Mister McPherson, that *court* will decide if Mister Gibson is indeed guilty," she continued to smile at him. "It's my job to provide evidence of guilt and try to establish whether or not the culprit is in fact Gibson or perhaps some other individual."

"What do you mean some other individual?" asked Sutherland, speaking for the first time.

Turning towards her, Scott caught the faintest whiff of a scent that though she didn't recognise it, was astute enough to know didn't come off the shelf of the local pound shop. Her first fleeting impression of Sutherland was of a relaxed cat; lovely to look at, but stroking it might provoke a scratch from razor sharp claws.

Now, why do I think that, she wondered?

She inhaled and replied, "By another individual, Miss Sutherland, what I mean is that we the police must keep our options open. We have to remain objective until such time we have overwhelming proof that Mister Gibson or any other individual is responsible for the theft."

"I thought that you also suspected him of the murder of that young woman who worked here, Carol Meechan? I mean, didn't the newspaper say that they were in on the theft together and he killed her? A sort of lover's tryst?" she persisted.

"No, Miss Sutherland. The *media* suspect Gibson of the murder, not the police. Did you know Meechan?" she suddenly asked.

"Ah, yes, slightly. I mean," she shrugged, "in the passing, that is." Scott saw Sutherland glance sharply down to her left and recalled in her detective training to watch out for tell-tale signs when being told a lie. She was admitting knowing the dead girl, thought Scott, but what *wasn't* she saying?

"What information do you require from us?" interrupted McPherson, his eyes darting from one woman to the other.

Scott took a deep breath and replied, "Am I correct in thinking that these files on the desk," she waved a hand at the paperwork, "all relate to the fraudulent company loans completed by Peter Gibson?"

"Yes, this is as much as we have discovered so far."

Scott glanced at her watch. "Here's a suggestion," she smiled at him, but without humour. "Why don't you take the lovely lady here for a coffee or maybe some lunch? Give me three….no, make it four hours to study these files and decide what I require for my investigation, what documents I need to take away with me."

He was aghast. "You can't just take files from the bank," he gasped.

She smiled at him and with some tolerance, replied, "Mister McPherson. Not only are you instructed to assist me in this investigation, but yes, I can seize *anything* I believe is relevant to that investigation. Need I remind you that unless there is proven to be evidence to the contrary and as I have just explained, while there is no *definite* link between the murder of Carol Meechan and the theft of money from your bank, we are keeping all options open, so this isn't just about the theft of money; this is also about the murder of a young woman. Believe me," she continued with a steely edge to her voice, "if I have to put a padlock on the beautifully carved wooden front door of this establishment and close the building while I seize *every single item within*," she drawled, "then I *will* do so and with the full and considerable backing of my boss. So, unless you have some viable protest or information about the theft and murder that might make me consider otherwise, I suggest you do as I ask and take this nice lady for a walk. Do we understand each other, sir?"

McPherson tried to stare her out, but realised he was on uncertain ground and glancing towards Sutherland, could only dumbly nod. Sutherland, without a backward glance, stood up from her chair and shrugging into her jacket, made to walk with him from the room; he opening the office door and she following him through and leaving the door ajar behind her.

A few minutes later, old Max McFarlane unlocked the front door to permit them both to leave and about to lock the door behind them, watched with surprise as walking down the steps, he saw Miss Sutherland slip her arm through Mister McPherson's and lean into him, her head turned and whispering as he bent low to hear.

Just like a couple he thought, then remembered the gossip; the gossip that said Mister McPherson was married, but still liked the young women.

A slow grin creased the old man's face.

Waz Ahmed watched from the driving seat of the parked CID car as the small, white coloured van drove up and stopped in front of the close at 29 Lawrie Street.

Waz got out and locking the car, then joined the thin, bespectacled young man with collar length blonde hair, wearing the dark coloured sports jacket who exited the van carrying a laptop bag and who introduced himself as Neil Traynor from the VIPER team.

Together Waz and Traynor walked up the tenement stairs to the first floor flat where they were admitted by Alicja Paderewski, a slim, pretty woman who Waz knew from her statement was aged thirty-eight and who lived in the flat with her seventeen year old daughter and a younger son.

At the witness's request and to Waz's relief, Mrs Paderewski's daughter, who was bi-lingual with slight accented English, had returned from her local college to be present to both support and interpret for her mother.

"Mrs Paderewski," Waz began, glancing at the daughter's nod to ensure he wasn't speaking too quickly and acutely conscious he was also speaking with his hands, "my colleague here will show you a number of video clips on his laptop computer. It is a system we the police call VIPER," and turning towards the daughter, explained, "it means Video Identification Parade Electronic Recording," then waited a few seconds while the daughter interpreted the acronym and the purpose of the device.

The next few minutes were spent with Traynor slowly explaining and demonstrating, while the daughter interpreted how he would display the six clips, one of which would include the suspect referred to by Mrs Paderewski in her statement to the police.

Waz worried that the technology might be too much for the nervous woman to take in, but the daughter assured him her mother understood.

Seated on a chair to one side while Traynor worked his magic, Waz held his hands clutched in his lap and with a start, hadn't realised how tense he was.

Traynor activated the display and one by one, the clips soundlessly were displayed on the laptop screen. Waz knew that Leigh Gallagher featured as clip number four and carefully watched the seated Mrs Paderewski for any sign of recognition of her assailant, but when the short fourth clip ended and moved to clip number five, not a flicker of emotion passed across her face.

Waz felt his gut wrench and at the conclusion of the sixth clip, the woman turned towards him and shook her head.

"I not see man who rob me," she slowly said, shaking her head while her hand was held by her daughter who kneeling slightly behind the seated woman, rubbed comfortingly at her mother's back.

"That's okay, Mrs Paderewski. Don't you worry about it, we'll try with another witness," Waz tried to give her a reassuring smile, but his disappointment must have been evident on his face, for the woman began to softly weep.

"Look," he stood and addressed the daughter, his hands open as though in a plea, "my colleague and I will get on our way. I'm sorry that your mum's distressed. Tell her not to worry too much. The guy's locked up and we'll be keeping him for some time, okay?"

The daughter stood and bending to kiss the top of her mother's head, showed them to the door.

In the landing outside, Waz asked Traynor to wait a few minutes and dialling the Cranstonhill office number, was put through to Bobby Franklin.

"Sorry, boss. Mrs Paderewski didn't pick the suspect out," then listened as Franklin spoke in his ear.

Turning towards Traynor, Waz asked, "Do you think you could hang on for ten minutes? My boss might be able to contact another witness for us."

"Is it the same case, the same suspect I mean?"

"Aye, he's trying to track down another complainer and requests that you give us a few minutes."

Traynor glanced at his watch. "If I'm marching, I'm not fighting," he grinned at Waz, then added, "I don't mind hanging on for a while if your boss could do me a favour and authorise the overtime with my supervisor, if that's okay. Besides," he held up the laptop bag and grinned, "it's not that often I get let out of the office to play with my toys."

Dressed in his familiarly recognised black suit and white priest collar, Father Patrick Gallagher sat at his father's beside, his bible lying open but unread in his lap.

Magnus's condition had so deteriorated that the Gartnavel consultant had with some foreboding authorised his move to the fifth floor Cardiology Unit at the Western Infirmary; a move that had necessitated a specially equipped cardiology ambulance and the assistance of the police Traffic Division, who provided two uniformed motorcyclists to pass the ambulance safely and smoothly through the busy junctions between the two hospitals.

"Father," said the whispered voice behind him. Turning, he saw a ward nurse beckoning him from the room. "That was your housekeeper calling for you," said the young nurse. "She left a message that you have to phone a Mister Franklin," and handed him a piece of paper with a phone number scribbled on it.

"Thank you," he smiled at the nurse as she pointed to the Ward Sister's office and added, "You can use the phone in there."

As he turned away, she stared after the broad-shouldered young priest, her hand to her throat and blushing at the thought that rushed through her mind. Such a good looking big guy and what a waste, she sighed. Damn those Catholics and their celibacy rules.

In the office, Patrick dialled the number and heard the voice say, "DI Franklin."

A few, short minutes of conversation later, he replaced the handset, now knowing that his brother had been arrested and not just suspected for a number of street robberies, but was also a suspect for the murder of a young woman.

Arlene Baxter finished scribbling in her notebook and returned it to her handbag that lay at her feet.

"Another coffee?" asked Jenny.

"No thanks, hen," smiled Baxter. "More than two cups and I'm peeing for Scotland."

"Wait till you get to my age," grinned Susie, "one cup of tea is four visits."

She was now a little more relaxed and pleased that the younger DS had turned out to be a much more amenable interviewer than her crabbit faced neighbour.

Jenny lifted the tray with the empty cups and left the room.

"So, you worked at Easterhouse then?" asked Susie.

"Aye, four years at Baird Street in uniform, a stint in the plainclothes unit and then four years in Easterhouse CID. I was transferred on promotion to the PSU five weeks ago and lumbered with that idiot Cameron," she sighed, shaking her head.

"Not the sharpest tool in the box, is he?" agreed Susie.

"No he's not. So, now that the formal part of the interview is over, *Missus* Gibson," grinned Baxter, "tell me Susie; what *exactly* do you think is going on with your man? Is Peter capable of deceiving you like this, I mean, stealing all that money and disappearing?"

"I can see you're not wearing a ring, Arlene. Are you in a relationship?"

She nodded. "Five years now. He works in insurance."

"Five years," Susie sighed. "Well, I've been with Peter twenty two years, nineteen of them married to him and yes, I thought I knew him; everything about him, I mean. But now this," she shook her head. "It begs the question, just how well do we know our men? Like I told you, I had my suspicions these last few months that there was somebody else, but never any of the signs; at least nothing obvious, nothing that suggested he was fooling about and let me tell you, I'm an experienced detective. If there *had* been any evidence of it, I would have found it."

"Has it occurred to you, Susie, that perhaps because you *are* a detective, Peter might have been that little bit extra careful, knowing you would be looking?"

"Yes," she slowly nodded, "it crossed my mind, but if he was seeing someone else then just as he was being careful to hide it, I had to be equally careful not to make him aware of my suspicions."

She saw the curious frown that passed across Baxter's face and explained, "Look at this way, if he wasn't being unfaithful and I challenged him, it might have put a further strain on a marriage that was already showing signs of falling apart."

She stifled a sob and covered it by taking a deep breath then slowly exhaled, suddenly embarrassed that she was opening her heart to Baxter who was, after all, a virtual stranger to her. Yet the younger woman, she sensed, was no fool and equally sensed unlikely to impart anything she told Baxter that fell outside the remit of the interview.

"The thing that worried me most," she hesitantly began, "was that Peter had *not* fallen in love with anyone else; that I could have understood and fought for him against another woman. No, what worried me most was that Peter had fallen *out* of love with me."

A silence fell between them while Baxter waited for Susie to compose herself, watching her rub with the forefingers of her right hand at her eyes.

Taking a deep breath, she said to Baxter, "I know the procedure, the inquiry regarding the stolen money and the murder inquiry for that young woman." Her eyes narrowed. "It's Lynn Massey you said who is in charge of both inquiries. It's quite obvious that she will likely run them separately, but keep a watching brief and likely because the murdered woman worked in the same bank as Peter, so he must be the obvious suspect."

"You've read this morning's edition of the 'Glasgow News'?" asked Baxter.

"No," drawled Susie, detecting a wariness in Baxter's voice, "it's not a paper we normally buy. Why? Is there something in the paper I should know about?"

"Does the name Ally McGregor, the reporter means anything to you?"

"You mean the wee fat bugger who is always ringing the CID offices, looking for something to lie about?"

"That's him," agreed a grim faced Baxter. "You might want to have a look at the newspaper on the web when I've gone. He's got a front page story reporting that we are looking for your husband and not just about the large theft of money, but the murder too because they both worked at the same bank; in short, without *any* evidence or comment from the polis, the wee bugger is linking Peter to the murder of Carol Meechan."

"Oh my God," replied a shocked Susie, her hand to her throat, her first thought for her daughter. "If Jenny reads that…"

"I'm sorry, Susie; I thought you might have seen it."

Once more, a short silence fell between them as Susie came to terms in this latest shock.

"I have a final question, Susie; one that I hope won't upset you."

"Go on."

"Peter," she said by way of introduction, unconsciously running her tongue over her upper lip. "Is there *any* likelihood at all do you think, that he *might* have taken off with the money and that he *might* have, in some way, been involved with Carol Meechan?"

"Honestly," she shrugged her shoulders and exhaled, "I don't know the answer to that other than saying if he *did* steal the money and if he *did* know the dead woman, he did a remarkably good job in hiding it all from me."

"One thing I should have asked," Baxter hesitantly started, "you didn't seem too surprised to receive a visit from us and I'm guessing that you knew your husband was a suspect for the theft from the bank." She put her hands up in a defensive pose and added, "I take it that you've a source who gave you the nod and, don't get me wrong, I don't want to know who it is, okay? But, am I right?"

Susie nodded. "Loyalty to my colleagues, when they deserve it, that is," she again nodded, but this time at the front lounge window towards the roadway outside, "is something I've always believed in. Let's just say that loyalty has been returned and yes, you're correct. There's no need for you to know who tipped me the wink, as it were."

"Okay," Baxter stood and brushing at an imaginary thread on her skirt, smiled at Susie.

"Needless to say, I'll report back to Lynn Massey and provide her with your official statement that summarised is, you had no idea your husband Peter Gibson might be implicated in any theft or wrongdoing at his bank, that to your knowledge, he has *never* mentioned any association with a bank employee called Carol Meechan and currently, you have no idea where he might be."

"About our domestic situation…."

Baxter lifted her hand to silence Susie.

"As far as I'm concerned and from what Massey instructed before we left Pitt Street, your domestic issues with your husband is your business, Susie. We both know that once my statement is typed up it goes into the system and who knows what nosey bugger might have access to it then. No, I'll be typing up the facts regarding the brief the boss gave me. You have my word on that."

She glanced at her wristwatch. "Right, that's over an hour the crabbit git has been sitting waiting for me, so I'd better not be keeping him any longer. Thank your daughter for the coffee and I'll see myself out," and with that turned and left.

Susie heard the front door being closed and sat wearily down on the couch. From Jenny's room upstairs, she could hear the faint strains of music and stretching her neck, decided that she would have a bath. However, before she rose from the couch, the doorbell rung. Curiously, she wondered who was calling and opening the door, saw a red-faced and extremely angry Baxter standing there.

"You're not going to believe this," the younger woman vehemently spat out, "the bastard's only gone and driven off without me!"

Mary McEwan shuffled along Argyle Street, favouring her right leg and wishing to God the doctor would refer her to the hospital for the long awaited hip replacement that she badly needed. She worried that the strong medication she was more frequently taking might ruin her liver long before the operation and taking time off work to recuperate from the hip replacement was already worrying her, let alone taking more time off because of a bloody liver complaint. She stopped for a breather, grimacing at the aching pain and switched the shopping bag from her left to her right hand then started out again. The mobile phone in her handbag activated and resting her body against a wall, she laid down her shopping at her feet and fished in her handbag for the phone. Glancing at the screen, she didn't recognise the calling number.

"Hello?"

"Is that Missus McEwan?"

"Aye, who's this then?"

"My name's Detective Inspector Franklin at Cranstonhill CID. Can you talk right now?"

"Aye, was it you want?"

"We've arrested a suspect for robbing you and want to know if we can show you some photos, but we are in a bit of a hurry. Are you available right now? It would be a tremendous…."

"That's great son," she interrupted him, "but I'm out the house the now. I'm in Argyle Street in the city centre the now."

"Where about?" snapped Franklin.

She glanced around her. "Just near to the Hiellanman's Umbrella, son. Walking towards the old Anderson bus station," she gasped, wondering what the bloody fuss was about.

"Can you wait there Missus McEwan and I'll get my lad to pick you up? Bring you to the station?"

"Will he take me up the road when I'm done?"

"Aye, I'll see you get a lift home," agreed Franklin. "What are you wearing so he'll recognise you?"

"I've got on my good navy blue coat and I'm right pretty," she laughed into the phone, and smiled with relief at avoiding a long walk home.

Less than ten minutes later, Waz Ahmed stopped the CID car opposite the elderly, red-faced lady wearing a blue coat and leaning against the wall. Winding the driver's window down, he grinned and cheerily called out, "Taxi for a *right* pretty lady called Missus McEwan?"

Leigh Gallagher had regained some of his composure and alone now, paced the confines of the narrow detention room, racking his memory for details of the young blonde girl who had grabbed at the knife.

He couldn't have killed her. For fuck's sake, it was her *hand*, not her throat or her body or anything like that, he sought to convince himself then the horrifying thought that maybe the girl had *bled* to death!

The copper, the older one, had pressured him for details of the girl, trying to convince him that she was a woman, not a teenager like him, but he wouldn't budge.

"No," he had said, "she was about seventeen, maybe eighteen and no. It wasn't in a close, it was on *Dumbarton Road*!" he had finally shouted.

The copper had left him alone then, hurrying out the room.

He could not know that just then, Des Mooney was rifling through recent crime reports in an effort to find a female complainer who had been assaulted and robbed in the Partick area.

Nicotine Mary turned on her best smile for the young priest and thought to herself there was definitely something sexy about a man dressed in black. Like a Catholic Johnny Cash, she sighed and let her imagination run riot.

"Hello there, Father, you'll be wanting to see DI Franklin again, eh?" she simpered with a flutter of false eyelashes.

"If I might," Patrick Gallagher tightly smiled and turning away, tiredly seated himself once again in the uncomfortable plastic chair and prepared to wait.

Lynn Massey glanced at her watch and decided that she would take a turn along to Cranstonhill office and find out exactly what the story was about Bobby Franklin's suspect. If anyone needed her, the control room had her mobile number.

Just as she shrugged into her jacket, Laura Scott knocked on her door.

"How did you get on?" she asked.

"So so, boss. I've two plastic shopping bags in the boot of my Micra filled with files, so if it's all right with you, I'll knock off for today and take them home, maybe make a start on them tomorrow. If I work through Sunday, I might have a tentative result for you by," her eyes narrowed, "say lunchtime Monday?"

"That's fine by me, Laura," she replied and then her eyes narrowed, suspecting because Scott hadn't left that she might not be finished. "Was there anything else?"

Scott's eyes narrowed and she chewed at her lower lip before responding, "Nothing I can put my finger on."

Massey stared at her, then giving in to Scott's intuition, shrugged her jacket off and indicated the younger detective sit down and returned to her own seat behind her desk.

"There's obviously something bothering you or you would have phoned me, rather than popping in and seeing me, Laura. So, what is it?"

"Look, boss, it's just a feeling and you're going to think I'm being silly."

Massey smiled. In her experience, Laura Scott was a very intuitive young officer and if she could be persuaded to adhere more to the dress code, would likely find herself shooting through the ranks. However, right now Massey needed her as she was; the tenacious and clever young fraud detective.

"When I got there, two of the bank staff was trying to sort out the mess that was the fraudulent loans, the two whose names you gave me…"

"McPherson the Accounts Manager and Sutherland, his deputy, right?"

"Right, that's them. McPherson seemed to be what he likely is, a bit of a chancer and I'm guessing, from the way he dressed and his attitude, one of the lads, so to speak. Perhaps even a bit of a ladies man, but to be honest that's just supposition on my part," she hastened to add.

"What about this woman, Sutherland?"

Scott shook her head and pursed her lips. "Something about that woman I just couldn't put my finger on. Let's just say I wouldn't trust her to work with *my* man, if you get my meaning."

Massey smiled and replied, "But that doesn't make them bad people, Laura."

"No boss, you're right," she shifted uncomfortably in her chair and then continued, "but you know the old saying, the one about a vamp; a woman who uses her sex to exploit men?"

Massey nodded and wondered where this was going.

"I didn't see Sutherland wearing any kind of ring. Not in itself anything to go on, but I just couldn't shake off this feeling, you know?"

Massey smiled and the smile turned to a grin.

"I think Laura, the best thing for you right now is to get yourself home and order in a curry, then you and your hubby polish it off with a bottle of wine, yeah?"

"Yeah, you're right boss," replied Scott, and with a cheery wave, stood and left the room.

Lynn Massey sat on and thought over what Scott had told her. She didn't dismiss the younger detective's suspicion; on the contrary, it had given her something to think about.

DI Bobby Franklin was in his office with a priest seated on the opposite side of his desk when Lynn Massey arrived at his door, but assuming he was busy, turned to walk away when he called her back. Both men rose to their feet as Franklin introduced the priest, "Ma'am, this is Father Gallagher, brother of the suspect, Leigh Gallagher."

With a formal shake of the hand, the priest made to leave, but not before Franklin wished him well, adding he hoped the priest's father's condition improved.

It was only when they were alone that he explained to Massey the young priest had just arrived from the Western Infirmary where his father was a patient in the Cardiology Department.

"Is his father's condition got anything to do with his other son being arrested?"

"No," Franklin shook his head, "apparently it occurred before the arrest, however, his son, the priest I mean, told me that both he and the dad discovered the tin box with the knife, money and stolen credit card, so whether that's brought on the heart attack, who can say."

"Seems like your suspect has more than just the robberies and the murder to answer for then; what with that poor woman dying from a heart attack when she found Carol Meechan dead and now his own father."

"Just a pity we can't liable more against him," he bitterly retorted.

"Now, what's the latest on your murder inquiry and are you convinced that you have the correct suspect?" she asked, seating herself in the chair just vacated by the priest.

He inhaled and clasping his hands behind his head, sat back in his chair and said, "As we speak, young Waz Ahmed is along the corridor with a robbery witness who is viewing the VIPER parade of clips. We already have a witness's positive identification for one robbery and if this witness comes through, that will be sufficient corroboration for us to charge and hold the suspect and then we can work on him for the murder."

No sooner had Franklin imparted this information than a grinning Waz Ahmed appeared in the doorway and gave his boss the thumbs up.

"Positive ID sir," he said and then nodding at Massey, added, "Hello Ma'am."

Franklin exhaled with relief and instructed Waz to run the witness home and rubbing his hands together, said to Massey, "Well, that's one piece of good news anyway, eh?"

Her mobile phone rung and, reaching down, withdrew it from her handbag and pressing the green button, said "Hello?"

He watched her frown and then heard her say, "Arrange to have a Scene of Crime officer attend there and have it preliminary examined at the location. I also want the immediate area searched for anything that might be connected to it and any CCTV footage that might be relevant, understand? Once that's done, have the Traffic remove it to Meiklewood Road garage for a more extensive examination. Yes, keep me apprised and inform me or if you can't get me, contact DI Cameron of the PSU when it's done. Thank you, Inspector."

She slowly replaced the phone into her handbag and he remained silent, allowing her to gather her thoughts.

She took a deep breath and then said, "Seems the lookout for Peter Gibson's vehicle worked out. That was the Duty Officer at Force Control. Gibson's vehicle has been discovered in the open air, long stay car park at Glasgow Airport."

CHAPTER 19

Susie Gibson received the phone call from DS Arlene Baxter with mixed feelings; a sense of bewilderment that Peter had dumped his car at the airport and taken off for God knew where without so much as a second thought, though not for Susie, but for Jenny.

She had to know *why*. Why would Peter - she hated to even use the word, but there was no other way to describe it - why he would *betray* her and their daughter? What possessed him to steal so much money and flee like the thief he was now proving to be?

She slumped back into the armchair, listening to Jenny's music coming from upstairs, her mind racing with possibilities and the constant question of why, why, why?

She closed her head against the onslaught of the sudden headache and reluctantly accepted why Peter had done what he did.

It was another woman, of that she was now certain.

That had to be it for there simply was no other conclusion. Whether an obsession, a fling that had turned to love, a middle-aged crisis or whatever, she could not ignore the truth; he had become ensnared by someone else.

She reasoned that if he had simply fallen out of love with her, he would have left home and found himself elsewhere to live, but continued to see their daughter.

No, she knew that had he remained in Scotland, he would maintain his relationship with Jenny, for Susie didn't doubt he loved their daughter, sometimes even believing his love for her far outweighed his love for his wife, but a fatherly love for which she was never envious.

Her thoughts turned to the women that they both knew, their friends, neighbours, Peter's female colleagues, some of whom Peter had introduced to her at the occasional bank social events.

Tight lipped, she angrily shook her head, but unwittingly brought on another wave of pain.

She was torturing herself, listing in her mind the women he knew as the cause for his betrayal.

And yet, no single individual came to mind.

Arlene Baxter had asked her not to disclose the phone call, that all she knew at this time was that Peter's Mercedes had been discovered, locked and secured, that the scenes of crime people were being tasked to attend at the airport to examine it and promising if she learned more, she would contact Susie.

She knew the young DS was acting out of kindness, perhaps even compassion and if it became known she had made the call, she would immediately be removed from the inquiry.

She sighed, pleased that at least *someone* believed she had no knowledge of Peter's disappearance.

She hated sitting about, doing nothing; it just wasn't in her nature to be idle.

But like it or not, all she could do now was wait.

The Duty Officer, on this occasion the shift sergeant at Cranstonhill police office, stood with the civilian male turnkey behind the charge bar and nodded towards Waz Ahmed, who stepped forward, notebook in his hand.

Between Waz and Des Mooney stood a much subdued Leigh Gallagher, his hands tightly folded in front of him and his head bowed.

Mooney glanced down and saw that try as he might, the young man could not stop his legs from shaking.

Directly behind Leigh stood the duty solicitor, a freckle faced young man wearing his best suit in preparation for a night out on the town.

The lawyer, with extreme reluctance, was there at his boss's bidding to observe that Leigh, his client for now till one of the senior partners took the case on, was treated with fairness and not railroaded as, believing the stories he had been told, were so many of his firm's innocent clients.

Beside and slightly to one side of the solicitor stood DI Bobby Franklin, who insisted that as it was Waz Ahmed and Des Mooney's arrest, they should be the officers charging Leigh Gallagher with two counts of street robbery. Further charges, Franklin heard Waz inform the Duty Officer, are likely to be libelled at a later date and requested that the accused be detained in custody meantime, citing the need for an identification parade to be held and the likelihood the accused might flee if released.

The suggestion the accused might flee, Waz continued, was evidenced at the time of his arrest when he was discovered to be in possession of a bag containing clothing.

"I was on the way to get my washing done at the laundrette!" Leigh angrily interrupted.

"Aye," said the cynical sergeant, "I'm sure you were son," he waved a scrap of paper taken from Leigh's pocket in the air, "and you had the times of the Cairnryan ferry to Belfast for no other reason than idle curiosity?"

Turning, the sergeant nodded to the lawyer and said, "I intend detaining your client in custody in the meantime because the arresting officers will require him to participate in a formal identification parade and," he then turned towards Leigh, "I'm making that decision to have you held for court this forthcoming Monday, okay? Any questions?" he again directed his glance to the solicitor, who simply shook his head and turned nervously towards Franklin.

"Further charges Mister Franklin? Might I be permitted to know what these charges are?"

"At least two counts of robbery and your client is also to be interviewed regarding a murder," Franklin laconically replied.

The young man paled. He had been due to meet one of the firm's cute young secretary's that evening for a curry, a drink and then, with some luck, back to his new, rented waterside pad for a bit of how's your father, but this was now getting a bit out of his league. He needed to get to a phone and call somebody more senior. Taking a deep breath, he asked, "Ah, yes, very well. Might I ask when do you intend interviewing my client regarding this, ah, murder?"

The wily old detective smiled at the young man's discomfort, knowing fine well that he had been sent to represent Gallagher because his bosses were either winding up on a golf course somewhere and heading for a boozy night at the bar or just too bloody lazy to come out on a Saturday evening themselves.

"Well, my young friend," he placed a fatherly arm about the solicitor's shoulder and led him towards the interview rooms further along the corridor, "let's just say you have time for a quick pee."

A weary and utterly miserable Father Patrick Gallagher returned to the hospital from the police office to find that yet another message had been left for him, however, on this occasion there was no need for him to phone anyone. The Ward Sister caught him just as he was getting out of the fifth floor lift to inform him that his Bishop had phoned and instructed he was to take as much time as he needed at his father's bedside, that his parish and parishioners would be looked after by a fellow priest until such time Patrick believed himself free to return.

"Oh and one more thing," said the Sister, herself a practising Baptist and mother to twin sons the priests age. "Your father's fine for now young man, so you get yourself into my office. I've a plate from the canteen just been delivered and it's piping hot, so off you go now. Don't be wasting my charitable intention," she added, pretending to be stern while waving her hands at him and ushering him before her. He sighed and his shoulders sagged. With a smile, he nodded and gave in to her gentle persuasion, surprised that the thought of food made his mouth water.

Ten minutes later, he sat back in the chair at the Sister's desk, the plate cleaned and a mug of tea in his hand, turning when the Sister hurriedly entered, his eyes opening with fear until he saw the smile on her face.

"Good, you're finished. Your father's awake and asking for you," she simply said.

Sitting at her desk within the Police Standards Unit office on the fifth floor of Pitt Street police office, DS Arlene Baxter read through the statement she had typed on the computer, correcting her grammar prior to printing it out, still smouldering with rage at her DI, Alex Cameron, for leaving her stranded at Susie Gibson's house.

It was kind of Susie to suggest running her back to Glasgow, but Baxter declined the offer and pointed out that the nearness of Uddingston railway station meant she would be in the city and at her office while Susie was still fighting the Saturday afternoon traffic.

It had been her intention to confront Cameron upon her return to Pitt Street, but the slimy bugger had signed off duty early, mentioning to the duty detective he had to attend a dinner dance that night at his bowling club.

Baxter guessed it was a lie, the real reason the weasel had left early being he was a spineless git with no balls, too scared to get into an argument with the fiery Detective Sergeant and obviously now conscious that by abandoning her to find her own way back to the office, leaving himself open to criticism not just from the boss Lynn Massey, but also from the other members of the Unit.

Nobody ditched their neighbour, regardless of what department of the police they served.

She shuffled the two pages of the statement together and was about to staple them when the phone on the duty detective's desk rang. Her head turned when she heard him say, "Aye, she's here. Hang on," and saw him holding the phone towards her, a quizzical look on his face. "It's some guy from the Scene of Crimes, something about a car found at Glasgow Airport. The guy asked for Alex Cameron, but he's gone home. Can you take the call?"

Baxter strode the short distance to the detective's desk and identified herself as Cameron's neighbour, then listened carefully, jotting a quick note down on a pad in front of her.

Replacing the handset, she called Lynn Massey's mobile number, but the call went straight to her answer service. Biting at her lower lip, she decided that if Massey wasn't available, the next best thing would be to inform DI Bobby Franklin at Cranstonhill and rung his office number, surprised when the call was answered by Lynn Massey.

"Oh, hello Ma'am, it's DS Baxter. Sorry, I was looking for DI Franklin…" she began, but was interrupted by Massey who told her Franklin was interviewing a suspect for the murder.

"No, sorry," Baxter said again, shaking her head at her foolishness, "what I should have said was I was really looking for you, but your phone went straight to your answer service. DI Franklin was my second choice," and grimaced, knowing she wasn't make much sense, that she was rambling like an idiot. She took a deep breath. "The thing is I've just taken a call from the Scene of Crime officer who is at the airport examining Peter Gibson's car."

She couldn't help herself, for her voice betrayed her excitement. "The Traffic managed to get the car opened, Ma'am and the SOCO has discovered a knife in the thingy, the wheel space, you know, where they keep the spare wheel I mean."

On the other end of the line, Massey could almost feel her own pulse quicken, yet couldn't help but smile at Baxter's description. "What kind of knife?"

"Ah, he didn't say Ma'am, but to be honest," she gripped the phone a little tighter at her stupidity and admitted, "I didn't ask for a description. Sorry. But he did say that the knife seems to have dried blood on it."

Massey took a breath and said, "Right. Get in touch with the SOCO and have him take it directly to the lab at Pitt Street. Contact the Duty Officer at the control room and have the on-call Forensics attend immediately. I don't care where they are, but get someone in to examine the knife. I want the blood matched against that of the deceased, Carol Meechan. Once you've done that, call me back and let me know," she instructed and then added with a smile, "Good work, Arlene. Can you let me speak to DI Cameron, please?"

She realised almost immediately from the hesitancy in the younger officers voice there was a problem.

"Ah, sorry Ma'am, he's indisposed at the minute. Can I get him to call you?"

"No, it's okay. Just go ahead with what I've told you and we'll speak later," and ended the call.

She couldn't guess what the issue was between Baxter and Cameron, but God help him if it in any way interfered with her investigation.

The dull lighting and sickly green painted walls added to the claustrophobic atmosphere in the interview room.

Leigh Gallagher, his legal representative sitting beside him, sat facing DI Bobby Franklin and his Detective Sergeant, Emma Ferguson, who scribbled notes on the pad in front of her.

The red light of the machine screwed to the table between the suspect and his lawyer and the two detectives glowed eerily as the tapes turned silently on their spindles, recording every word and sound made within the room.

Leigh was already charged with two counts of robbery and the Scottish Criminal Law, as it currently stood, forbade Franklin from attempting to elicit any further information regarding the two incidents. However, that didn't mean he couldn't quiz Leigh for information regarding the other outstanding robbery reports and in particular, the murder of Carol Meechan.

The sudden enormity of his predicament hit Leigh like a hammer blow and an overwhelming panic overtook him. Against the advice of the young lawyer, Leigh was suddenly more than willing to admit the two outstanding robberies that had been reported to the police, one of which was that committed against Alicja Paderewski. When Franklin then informed Leigh about the microscopic traces of dried blood on the knife discovered within the tin, a panic-stricken Leigh confessed to the attempted robbery on the young, blonde woman who had resisted his assault and tried to wrest the knife from his hand.

"Honest to God, sir," he pleaded, now close to tears, "she cut her hand. I didn't stab anybody. For *fucks* sake," his hands pressed down on the table and he rose to his feet, "you have to believe me! I'm not a killer! It's the lassies blood, not the woman that got murdered!"

"Sit down Leigh!" Franklin sharply instructed, watching as the younger man slowly sunk to his seat. Then, in a quieter voice, continued. "My officers have checked the files for this young woman you claim to have assaulted and tried to rob on that date in Dumbarton Road, Mister Gallagher and there's no trace of anybody having reported being assaulted by you. Are you sure you're not making this up, son, that the young blonde woman you cut wasn't in her close in Lawrie Street? That you didn't stab the blonde woman in the back? After all, Mister Gallagher," his voice dropped to a more conciliatory tone, "you do know Lawrie Street, don't you? That's where you robbed Missus Paderewski."

To the officer's surprise, Leigh burst into tears and collapsed against the shoulder of his lawyer who in horror, tried to move the young man's head away from his expensively cut suit jacket before Leigh snotted all over it.

Franklin discreetly coughed while Ferguson's face contorted as both tried in vain to stop smiling at the lawyer's discomfort.

"I'm going to switch the tapes off for now, give your client a couple of minutes to compose himself," Franklin addressed the lawyer and reached for the machine, then turning to Leigh, added, "and DS Ferguson here will fetch you a glass of water, Mister Gallagher." No sooner had he said that than they heard a sharp knock on the interview room door.

Excusing himself, Franklin opened the door and stepped out into the corridor to be met by Des Mooney as Emma Ferguson squeezed past them to fetch the water.

"Sorry to butt in boss, but two bits of info for you that might be relevant. The Detective Superintendent says to tell you that Peter Gibson's car has been found; apparently it was parked up at Glasgow Airport somewhere. Ma'am has arranged for it to be taken to Meiklewood Road. She's going home, said that's not much more can be done this evening regarding Gibson, but asked that you call her with an update of your interview with the suspect."

Franklin didn't miss Mooney's sigh and his eyes narrowed. "What's the second thing?"

"Forensics phoned regarding the knife that was discovered in the tin box. They've managed to extract some DNA that they run through their database and they got a hit, but it's not Carol Meechan's blood on the knife," he shook his head. "The lassie that called says the DNA they lifted wasn't a definite hit on their database, but something called," he glanced at a scrap of paper in his hand, "familial DNA?"

Franklin grinned as he nodded. "That could be useful in tracing the unknown complainer. It means that the DNA they got from the knife is very similar to a family member. What are the details of the hit they got?"

"Sorry boss, the woman was under a bit of pressure. She had just been called into the office to deal with another issue, something about Peter Gibson's car, but I don't know the details. What she did say was that the paperwork regarding Gallagher's knife will be dispatched to us first thing tomorrow morning and all the details will be on the report."

Ferguson was walking along the corridor when Franklin made his decision. Glancing at his watch he told them, "It's getting on, so not much more we can do tonight."

His face contorted in thought as he asked Ferguson, "What do you think, Emma? Figure him for the murder?"

"No boss," she shook her head. "The robberies aye, no question, but I don't think he's our killer."

"Right then, the forensic report regarding his knife seems to dismiss that as the murder weapon," he replied and turned to Mooney. "Des, you and young Waz charge him with the two further robberies he's admitted and lock him up. Emma, wind up the interview and lodge the tapes, then get the team together and stand them down for this evening, but instruct all of them that they're back here no later than eight, tomorrow morning. I'll be in my office if you're looking for me, on the phone to Lynn Massey."

As he made his way to his office upstairs, he could not but help feel that solving the murder of Carol Meechan had just become that little less certain, as was the likelihood of him getting home in time to have dinner with his wife.

Harry McPherson sat alone in the lounge while his wife Tracey was upstairs in the nursery feeding their infant daughter, her tears and accusations still ringing in his ears. The television was switched on, the sound turned low as a game show host, teeth sparkling for the camera, encouraged the pack-like audience to scream at a heavy-set, reluctant and clearly embarrassed female contestant, trying to persuade her to cross a narrow bridge that swung unsteadily between two ladders, below which was a huge tub filled with some kind of green coloured, nauseating liquid. Visibly shaking, the woman began to fearfully cross, only for the inevitable and obvious outcome as on cue the bridge collapsed and, to the screaming hilarity of the mindless morons in the audience, tipped the unfortunate victim into the tub.

But none of this interested McPherson, his eyes glazed as his fingers beat a tattoo on the arm of the chair, his mind remembering a naked Morven Sutherland stretched lazily on her bed, his breathing becoming deeper, his fingers now involuntarily twitching as he recalled the firmness of her breasts, her frantic desires when she tore at his shirt and he felt himself become aroused.

He swallowed hard and made his decision. Glancing at the open door, he could hear Tracey upstairs, cooing at their daughter. Rising from his chair, he quietly tiptoed to the hall and fetched his mobile phone from his jacket pocket.

She had said she had nothing planned for Saturday evening, her voice lingering in his thoughts, that if he could get away, she would be at home.

He exhaled and blew through pursed lips and scrolled down the phone's directory, stopping at his own house number and pressed the green button. A few seconds later, the phone in the hallway rung and he snatched at it, calling upstairs, "I've got it."

He pretended to be speaking and a minute later, replaced the handset and climbed the stairs to the nursery.

His nose wrinkled at the smell when he entered the room and saw Tracey sitting with the crying, florid faced baby on her lap, wearily changing the soiled nappy. With blank eyes, he stared at the bags under her eyes, her pale once pretty features now lined with fatigue, the limp hair that needed washed and the milk stains on the front of her blouse and wondered what he ever saw in her, what had caused him to marry such an insipid woman.

"That was my boss, the HR Director, Mister Brewster," he flatly told her. "He wants me and some of the senior staff to go in tonight. Seems there's a bit of a flap on because of the money Peter Gibson stole."

She stared with incredulity at him, her eyes opened wide. "It's Saturday night, for fuck's sake Harry."

He cringed at her language, her use of the occasional expletive that had once seemed amusing and even a little sexy when they were making love, but was now simply vulgar.

"I *don't* make the rules," he hissed at her. "If heads roll because of this fiasco, then I don't want to be one of them! For heavens sake, we've a mortgage and bills to pay. Do you want me sacked? I need to demonstrate to the management that I'm a team player."

She stared at him, tight-lipped. In her heart, she knew he was lying, that he was going to meet one of his floosies, but sitting there, tiredly cradling her baby, she came to a shocking realisation.

She really didn't care anymore.

Five minutes later he was in his car, driving towards the city with one wary eye open for any police vehicles as he thumbed through the mobile phone directory to the new number.

"Morven, it's me," he gushed. "I'll be with you in fifteen minutes."

"Hello boss," said Bobby Franklin, hearing crockery rattling in Lynn Massey's background. "Have I caught you at a bad time?"

"No, you're fine Bobby. I'm sitting in my kitchen having a coffee while my hubby rustles up the dinner," she replied, smiling at Greg Campbell who with his back to her wore a brown coloured apron with a massive yellow sunflower as its centrepiece. Greg was bent over the sink emptying the water from a pot of boiled potatoes and engulfed in steam from the hot water.

"Are you still at the office?" she asked Franklin.

"Aye, another ten minutes though and I'll be packing up. I've sent the rest of the team away for the evening. Right, first things first," he began. "Our suspect Leigh Gallagher has admitted two further robberies, for which he has been charged and detained, but unfortunately I don't figure him as the murderer. Added to that, I've verbal confirmation that the Lab has obtained some DNA from Gallagher's knife, but it's not Carol Meechan's and I should be able to have that firmed up tomorrow when I receive the Lab's report." He didn't think it necessary to go into too much detail over the phone.

"I hear that Peter Gibson's car has been found?"

"Yes," confirmed Massey, shaking her head as she spoke. "At Glasgow Airport. The SOCO discovered a knife, possibly bloodstained, in the spare wheel area in the boot, so it's on its way to the Lab for analysis. Hopefully, we should have a report tomorrow some time."

"You think it might be Carol Meechan's blood?" he asked.

"If it is," she sighed, "then that wee shit Ally McGregor from the 'Glasgow News' might have struck gold after all." She shook her head at the thought that McGregor had stolen a march on the police by correctly guessing the link between Gibson and Meechan.

"Can I ask what type of knife it is that was found?" he said.

"Ah, let me see," she thought, "it was described as a black handled knife with a serrated steel blade and two steel rivets welding the wooden handle to the metal. The SOCO thought it was a domestic kitchen knife. You know; the kind of knife that you use for steak meat."

"Yeah, I think I know what you mean. That would seem to suggest if it *is* a domestic knife, maybe it was grabbed from the kitchen in a fit of anger?"

"Not a bad suggestion, Bobby," she thought about it, wondering if like her own kitchen steak knives, the bloodstained knife might be part of a set and now considering it might be worth having a look in DS Gibson's cutlery drawer.

"If the car was at the airport," Franklin interrupted her thoughts, "then there *is* a likelihood Gibson has caught a plane somewhere."

"That's what I was thinking. I've the Ports Coverage Unit trawling through what CCTV they have for the last few days starting at the approximate time and date Gibson was last heard from."

"What was it again that he told his missus, I'm just nipping out for a takeaway curry? Where was he going for it, Islamabad?" he joked.

"Not so funny Bobby if he *has* flown the coop from the airport." She glanced up as her husband gave her the one-minute signal and said, "That's me getting my orders for dinner, Bobby. What time are your troops mustering tomorrow morning?"

"I've said to be at the incident room for eight and I'll brief them shortly thereafter."

"Well, if it's okay with you, I'll attend your briefing and have the two PSU's come along as well." Almost thinking to herself, but speaking out loud, she added "I'll leave off contacting Laura Scott and wait till she phones me."

"Is that the Fraud Squad lassie?"

"Aye, with some luck and hard work on her part, we should have an idea by tomorrow how Gibson worked his fraud. Right Bobby," she grinned at Greg's wagging finger, "I'm getting told off here, so I'll speak with you tomorrow."

CHAPTER 20

Sunday morning opened with a low overhanging cloud threatening to disperse its water laden load on Glasgow below, but first heralded the day with a fine drizzle that required frustrated drivers to use their windscreen wipers. The drizzle was not enough to soak the screen, causing the rubber blades to squeak nervously at each stroke.

DS Arlene Baxter, responding to the text message from the previous evening from the duty detective at the Police Standards Unit, parked her car in the narrow lane behind Cranstonhill and grabbing her telescopic brolly, made her way towards the rear door of the office. Still seething at Alex Cameron for abandoning her at Susie Gibson's house, she had determined during the journey from her home in Alexandria to vent her wrath on the git and rehearsed what she intended telling him, that five weeks of his sullenness and overbearing attitude was over; she had had enough.

Steeling herself for the confrontation, she made her way upstairs to the incident room, finding that half a dozen of the inquiry team was already present, though none of the faces were known to her.

An older man smiled at her and moving towards Baxter, introduced himself as Bobby Franklin, the Detective Inspector and when she identified herself, suggested she grab herself a coffee, that the briefing would commence in a couple of minutes when Lynn Massey arrived.

He saw her casting a glance about her and eyes narrowing, said, "If you're looking for your neighbour, hen, he's called in sick. Something about a dodgy chicken meal, I gather."

Inwardly she sighed, a little relieved that the expected confrontation would not occur that morning, yet still angry the bastard had copped out and convinced herself the stomach complaint was an excuse not to face her.

She saw one or two of the detectives glance towards her and inwardly grinned, for she recognised the suspicion on their faces that usually occurred when officers from the 'rubber heels' department were in the room.

As more staff arrived, she watched as Lynn Massey stepped through the door, immediately walk to Franklin and then converse with him almost head to head. The few minutes of whispered conversation over, she surprised the younger detective when she detached herself from him to walk and stand beside Baxter.

"I hear that you're on your own today Arlene, but don't be worrying. I've got a job for you," Massey said folding her arms across her chest, but didn't elaborate.

"Right lads and lassies," called out Franklin as a subdued hush descended on the room. "Here's the latest on our murder inquiry," and proceeded to recount the circumstances of the interview with Leigh Gallagher.

"The sum of all that," he finally said, "is our suspect Leigh Gallagher has been charged with four counts of robbery with a fifth count pending and let me explain that one. The Lab did manage to extract DNA from Gallagher's knife, but according to him, it belongs to another victim. The Lab has tentatively identified the DNA as familial, which for you who are unaware simply means the DNA is similar to an individual who is *already* on the database, but is not an *exact* match. Simply put, as Gallagher has confessed the victim is a young female, we've assessed the DNA on the database is likely be a sibling, perhaps a parent or maybe a close relative. Later this morning I expect to be informed that a report confirming the identity of the individual on record is available and once I receive word," he pointed with a forefinger at each of the two officers, "I'm sending Waz Ahmed and Des Mooney to Pitt Street to collect the report and they will try to track down the fifth victim."

He took a deep breath and glancing briefly at his notes, continued. "I regret that having been present at Gallagher's interview and bearing in mind the tentative negative evidence of the knife, I believe it is highly unlikely that Gallagher is our killer."

A soft, but disappointed sigh went round the room.

"In consequence of the interview with the suspect and after consultation with Detective Superintendent Massey, though he is not entirely dismissed, Gallagher is no longer the *primary* suspect for the murder of Carol Meechan. However," he held up a hand for silence and paused till the murmuring died out, "as you are already aware, the workplace proximity of the deceased with the missing banker Peter Gibson cannot be dismissed. We have an update for Gibson, for those of you who haven't yet heard. Yesterday evening, his vehicle was discovered parked at Glasgow Airport."

The room as one inhaled and listened attentively at this new development.

"The vehicle, a Mercedes SLK, I understand, was locked and secured, however the Traffic managed to get it open and a bloodstained knife was discovered in the boot; not quite hidden, yet not where it could be easily seen by a casual glance. Let me explain that one," he again glanced at his notes, "it seems the knife *might* have slipped down the inside of the car wall and the carpeted area. The knife is now at the Lab and we expect a comparison report by the earliest, midday today. Needless to say, regardless of what that wee shite Ally McGregor writes in the 'Glasgow News', it is obvious that Gibson is now tentatively crossing over to our murder inquiry and depending on the result of the blood on the knife, looks increasingly like he will feature as a suspect, perhaps even the *primary* suspect for our murder," he added.

"So, in the meantime, we carry on with the day to day inquiries, but if you are out of the office, I want you all to maintain contact with the incident room because when the Lab report is completed I want you all back here because there *will* be a further briefing. Questions?" he raised his eyebrows, but to his surprise and apart from the odd shake of the head, there were none.

"Right, go to it," he finished and then waved for Waz and Des Mooney to join him.

"Okay, lads, you know what is to be done. I'll trust in your judgement regarding where the Lab report leads you, but try and come back with something. If we can hit that wee bugger Gallagher with another robbery charge, that should settle his hash, at least for a while."

Nodding their dismissal, he joined Lynn Massey and walked with her to his office.

"Thanks for coming out so early, Lynn," he courteously pushed open the door for her to enter. "It adds a wee bit of impetus to the team and improves their morale to know that senior management are not lying in bed while they're doing their damndest to solve the murder."

"And what about you, Bobby," she sat in the chair in front of his desk, watching as he seated himself. "How's your morale this morning?"

"To be honest, I was disappointed that Gallagher isn't the murderer. It would have tied the case up nicely; a street robbery gone wrong, case solved. Then you and your team could have concentrated on your MP, Peter Gibson." He took a deep sigh and run a weary hand across his face. "Now with the discovery of Gibson's car at the airport and the bloodstained knife and Gallagher *apparently* out of the frame, we're back to investigating a whodunit," he paused and opened both hands wide. "That throws the whole thing open and seems to tie both inquiries solidly together."

"Yes, *if* the knife proves to be the murder weapon," she replied, then leaning forward with one hand on the desk, asked, "Are you so *sure* that Gallagher didn't kill Carol Meechan?"

He took a few seconds to respond, but then said, "Granted, the lad's got no alibi for the time of the murder, but the MO is *so* wrong, Lynn. Every other robbery was to present the knife as a scare tactic, grab the bag and run, but on this occasion, to stab our victim in the back? No, it just doesn't seem to fit. Besides, the blood on the knife isn't Meechan's," he reminded her, "and if you want my opinion based on interviewing suspects for the last twenty-five years?" Tight-lipped, he slowly shook his head then quietly replied, "No, he's not our killer."

"But you'll not completely write him off as a suspect?"

"No," he smiled tolerantly, "not unless you have hard evidence that Peter Gibson is your man and that," he glanced at his watch, "should be confirmed in a little over four hours."

Agnes McKenna strolled along her dockland beat area, lost in thought about her sister's birthday party due to kick off next Saturday night at the Counting House in George Square. It was always the same, she sighed, an excuse for her bloody sister and dispy pals to get plastered, then end up in a night club with some greasy bastard hoping to get a punch in their knickers.

Wouldn't be so bad, she huffed, if they were young things, but the her sister and pals were all now touching fifty and all of them married with weans…or with weans anyway, she inwardly grinned. Well, all except Agnes, she sighed again.

Her thoughts turned to the new guy that had just started last week who, she had quickly noticed, wasn't wearing a wedding ring. Not a bad looking man either, she mused with a smile, thinking he must be about her age, mid-forties. But the problem with guys that age, she sighed for the third time is they *always* come with baggage.

Her nose wrinkled with disgust and as she skipped round a pile of vomit that some dirty bastard had chucked up onto the pavement instead of trying for the roadway. She adjusted the belt to a more comfortable position on her hips and moved the machine in its holster to her front to stop it bouncing against her arse while her eyes casually roamed across the windscreens of the parked cars, just a little disappointed that they all displayed residents parking permits. Since the new revenue initiative introduced by the council that expanded the restrictions for the city centre parking to include Sunday, if nothing else it meant some overtime for Agnes and her

parking attendant colleagues and who, she inwardly grinned, is going to knock back time and a half for an early morning stroll?
She had almost passed the silver coloured Nissan Qashqai when she glanced back and smiled.
Come to mama, she inwardly grinned and chalk yet another one up for the yellow peril.
Smirking at her good fortune, she tilted her cap back on her head like the cowboys in the films she so loved and lifted the machine from the holster on her waist.

Harry McPherson awoke alone in Morven Sutherland's bed a happy man, the sheets beneath him wrinkled and smelling of her scent. He grinned with pleasure. The sex had been incredible, the woman insatiable.
He lay on his back and stretched his body, emitting a small grunt as he wriggled into a more comfortable position on his back. From through the open door, he listened to the sound of a kettle whistling in the kitchen.
A few moments later, wearing a sky blue coloured, short silk robe loosely belted at the waist, she stepped into the bedroom, a steaming mug of coffee carried in each hand. He watched her almost glide towards him, savouring her perfectly toned athletic body, the muscles in her legs rippling beneath the robe and her breasts shuddering beneath the fine material.
"Morning, lover boy," she smiled at him, walking to the side of the bed and placing the mugs down on top of the cork mats on the bedside table. That done, she pulled the belt apart and let the robe slip from her shoulders and fall to the carpeted floor and then leaning across, pulled the sheets from him, exposing his nakedness. She smiled down at him and sliding her pink tongue across her upper lip, climbed onto the bed and sat astride him with one hand on each of his shoulders, pinning him to the bed.
She folded her legs behind her and sat on his thighs, feeling him grow erect beneath her. Almost breathless, he watched her hair fall loosely over her shoulders, framing her face. He could feel the pressure she exerted against him and again wondered with surprise at her strength, then and during their lovemaking.
His mouth was suddenly dry and swallowing hard, he lay unresisting, staring wide-eyed at her full breasts swinging in a soft

rhythm before his face and fought the urge to grab her and turn her onto her back.

She smiled, aware of his arousal and gently moved her buttocks against his thighs to excite him further. She leaned forward and lowered a breast towards him, teasing him as her cherry-red erect nipple brushed at his lips.

He felt his breathing become more rapid, his chest heaving and reached his head forward to take her nipple in his mouth, but she pulled back and gave a soft laugh, her hands now about his wrists, still holding him firmly to the bed.

"I'll do anything that you ask of me Harry, *anything*," she whispered, again running her tongue seductively across her upper lip.

A number of ideas crossed his mind as she added, "But what would you do for me?"

"Anything," he replied with a wide grin, staring into her eyes, his need for her almost overwhelming him.

"Does that include leaving your wife?"

"Wh…what?" he stuttered, eyes narrowing and at first confused by her question.

"I said," she stared fixedly into his eyes and softly repeated, "Will you leave your dowdy little wife for me, Harry?"

"Morven, are you serious?"

He knew immediately it was the wrong answer.

With a suddenness that took him by surprise, she was off him and standing by the bed, her back to him and arms folded.

"You pursue me and you fuck me," she said, her voice flat and emotionless, "but you don't *dare* consider committing to me. Is that it, Harry? Is that what I am to you? A good lay then you're back to your wife?"

"Morven," he began, but standing perfectly still with her back to him, she raised her hand and hissed through gritted teeth, "I'm going for a shower. I trust you will be gone when I get out."

With that, she walked to the en-suite and slammed the door closed behind her and then he heard the sharp snick as the lock was applied.

Susie Gibson, wearing her much loved, but faded dressing gown sat on the edge of her bed and replaced the phone into the cradle and then, turning to her daughter Jenny who stood motionless in the bedroom doorway, smiled at her curious face.

"It's okay darling, it was young Andy Brownlie, the guy I work with. He's on day shift and was only calling to find out how I…" she stopped and smiled again, "how *we* were doing."

Jenny nodded and without a word, walked over and sitting beside her mother, threw her arms about Susie.

"If only there was *something*," she sighed, "it's this not knowing. It's doing my head in, Mum."

Susie suppressed a giggle at *'Doing my head in'*. Thank goodness Jenny can't guess what Peter's disappearance is doing to *me*, she thought.

Jenny pulled away from her mother and stared at Susie. "Mum, do you think Dad stole that money?"

"So, you know then, what he's being accused of, I mean?"

"It's kind of hard not to hear what's going on, I mean with those two detectives visiting us yesterday then there was the newspaper headline in the 'Glasgow News'."

"Ah, did you buy a copy?"

"No, one of my school mates phoned me on my mobile about it and I downloaded the article on my I-pad," she replied, then quite unexpectedly and to Susie's surprise, added, "It's a load of shit, isn't it?"

"*Not* that I approve of my young daughter using such language, but yes," she grinned, "it *is* a load of shit."

The phone rung again, startling them both.

Susie snatched at it and said, "Hello?"

"Missus Gibson; it's Detective Superintendent Lynn Massey. I apologise for calling so early. Is it convenient to speak?"

"Yes, Ma'am, of course" she replied and glancing at Jenny, she wedged the handset between her chin and shoulder and used both hands to make a T sign. Jenny nodded and skipping from the room, loudly stomped down the stairs towards the kitchen.

"Missus Gibson, I'm calling to inform you that we have found your husband's car."

Susie unconsciously grabbed at her throat, a cold chill enveloping her and involuntarily made a soft, throaty sound. She couldn't let Massey know that Arlene Baxter had already informed her on the

QT knowing that to do so would land the younger detective in more than a little bother.

At the other end of the line, Massey heard her and mistaking Susie's gasp for shock, said, "Missus Gibson, I'm so sorry. I phrased that terribly. I should have first told you that there is no news of your husband, but that we found his car. I owe you an apology. I certainly didn't intend to scare you like that."

"Oh, yes. His car," she slowly repeated and to add credence to her surprise said, "But not Peter. There's no news yet of my husband?"

"No, I'm afraid not. His car, the Mercedes I mean; we found it parked and secured in the long stay car park at Glasgow Airport."

"Glasgow Airport?" Susie repeated, her mind racing as once more she wondered. "Whatever would he…" then she stopped as a new thought occurred to her. "Please, wait a minute," and placed the handset down onto the bed. Crossing the room, she pulled open her husband's sock drawer within the fitted wardrobes and almost with a sigh, retrieved Peter's brown, stressed leather document wallet. Returning to the phone, she said, "I have my husband's passport, Ma'am. Whatever he was doing at the airport, it wasn't to depart on an international flight and as I understand it, these days there aren't many airlines that will permit passengers to travel even to Ireland or the Channel Islands, without some identification and usually a passport."

"Good point, Missus Gibson," admitted Massey with a grin to herself, thinking it should have been the question *she* asked.

"However, obviously because of the location of the car being discovered, I'm having the Ports Control Unit research all the airport CCTV footage, just in case your husband might have travelled under an assumed name." She paused, allowing Susie to consider what she had just said and then added, "You're an experienced detective, Missus Gibson, so I'm certain you must understand the lines of inquiry I have to pursue."

"Yes, Ma'am," Susie flatly replied and then continued. "In light of this new information, I presume you might want to speak with me again?"

"That's another reason I'm calling. Obviously, because of this new development, I'd like the opportunity to again have you interviewed and if you wish, I can have my officers' call upon you at home or, so as not to embarrass you at an office where you might be known, my officers will meet you at a police station chosen by you."

A slight pause ensued, broken when Susie asked, "Am I a suspect, Ma'am?"

The few seconds' delay it took Massey to respond didn't escape Susie. However, she listened intently when Massey replied, "I choose to think not, Missus Gibson."

Or not for the time being anyway, Massey privately thought before continuing, "I'm certain you will be aware that media headlines are attempting to link your husband's disappearance with the murder of a young woman who worked in the same bank…"

"Is that a definite line of inquiry being pursued by the investigating team, Ma'am?" interrupted Susie.

Again, there was that almost indiscernible hesitation by Massey, who slowly replied, "To be frank, it's a line of inquiry we can't dismiss Missus Gibson. However, if there is a definite connection between your husband and the deceased Carol Meechan, then you have my word I will *personally* inform you or make an arrangement to have you kept apprised of any development. But only, and I must stress this in the strongest possible terms Missus Gibson; *only* if such information does not compromise the ongoing investigation. Are we quite clear on this issue?"

"Quite clear," replied Susie, who then continued. "So for now Ma'am, from what you *are* telling me," or *not* telling me, Susie shook her head, "there *is* a presumption that my husband Peter is your primary suspect for the theft from his bank and there also exists the presumption he is *possibly* a suspect for murder?"

Massey took a deep breath. This was not going as she had planned and was developing into a telephone interview, something she did not approve of.

"Missus Gibson," she replied, a little sharper than she intended, "I would rather my officers spoke personally with you than continue to conduct this conversation over the phone. So," she asked again, but now with a little edge to her voice, "your home or a police office of your choosing?"

"I'm not known at Uddingston office Ma'am," Susie replied with a brittle edge to her own voice, "so if you don't mind, I'll meet DI Cameron and DS Baxter there."

"Ah, *yessss*," drawled Massey, "Mister Cameron is currently off duty, apparently unwell; however, DS Baxter, who you have already met will be accompanied by another officer."

"Oh, anything to do with abandoning his neighbour?" Susie frostily asked and then bit at her lip and squeezed her eyes tightly closed, almost immediately regretting her small and petulant outburst.

"I'm sorry? I don't understand?"

"Perhaps DS Baxter hasn't told you," said Susie, now deciding that the arrogant shit that had come into her home and been rude deserved a little bit of payback. "I had to ask the Detective Inspector to leave my house."

"No," Massey paused, "I wasn't aware of any *difficulty* you had with DI Cameron. Perhaps you might wish to explain?"

"Well, Ma'am, let's just say his interview technique is a little outdated," she tactfully responded.

"Indeed," replied Massey, deciding not to press the issue on the phone, but determined to find out from Baxter just what the hell was said to annoy Gibson.

"Well, Missus Gibson, as I said, DS Baxter and her neighbour will meet you at the Uddingston office. Shall we say, midday?"

"Fine Ma'am, I'll meet them there at midday," replied Susie, before concluding the call.

Seated behind Bobby Franklin's desk in his office at Cranstonhill, Lynn Massey stared at the telephone, her eyebrows knitted in concentration, wondering what Alex Cameron had said to upset DS Gibson. And what did she mean, she further wondered, abandoning his neighbour?

With a sigh, she sat back and rubbed at her forehead with the heel of her hand.

It was, she guessed, likely to be a long day and then reached again for the telephone.

Des Mooney parked the CID vehicle in a parking bay in Holland Street, pleased that it being Sunday they would not be arguing with one of the numerous traffic wardens that haunted the area during the week.

Willie, the commissionaire at the West Regent Street entrance to Pitt Street police office was behind his desk, speaking with a tall, slim and suited man in his early forties who was leaning across the desk when Mooney and Waz entered through the glass doors.

The man was clearly angry about something and wagging a finger at the pale faced commissionaire as Mooney and Waz passed by the desk, their warrant cards on thin plastic beaded lanyards about their necks, now held up and flashed at Willie.

Walking to the lift in the foyer, they were stopped dead by the man calling out, "You two!"

They both turned and saw the man striding the short distance towards them, who stopped and putting his hands on his hips, barked out, "Who are you two?"

Waz, suspecting the man to be a boss, was about to reply, but Mooney stepped forward and thrusting his card in the man's face, replied, "That's who I am. Now who *exactly* are you?"

The man's face turned red and in a Northern Scots accent with a slight London inflection, he snapped back, "I'm Assistant Chief Constable MacPhail. Don't you know your senior command officers, Constable?"

Waz stared silently at the man, inwardly praying *'don't bite, Des, for fuck's sake don't bite'*, but his silent plea was, he thought, like throwing petrol to douse a fire.

"Perhaps," Mooney replied through clenched teeth, taking a step towards MacPhail, "if my *senior command officers* visibly wore their warrant card as dictated in the Standing Orders for security purposes for all police offices, then I might be able to recognise you, *Mister MacPhail*, but as you *don't* seem to be wearing any identification, I'll ask you to produce your warrant card to prove *you* are who you say you are...sir!"

A tense few seconds passed before MacPhail, tight-lipped at Mooney's challenge and his face now a rosy shade of beetroot, rummaged in his inside jacket pocket and producing his warrant card, thrust it to within a foot of Mooney's nose.

Mooney leaned forward a further six inches and peering through narrowed eyes at MacPhail's warrant card nodded, as though in approval.

"Now, like I asked, who are *you* two and who's your boss?" MacPhail literally screamed at Mooney.

"Oh, I think that will be the Chief Constable," smiled Mooney, "or were you thinking of someone a little more junior...sir?"

"Don't get flippant with me!" thundered MacPhail.

"Oh, I'm not being flippant…sir. In fact, I'm being cool, calm and collected. It's you, I fear that's losing the plot, though for the life of me I can't think why," Mooney, shaking his head, calmly replied. Waz, standing completely still, just wished the floor would open and swallow him whole for his career, he gulped, was now sliding towards the toilet.

"Where are you stationed!"

"That will be Coatbridge…sir," Mooney cheerfully replied, but smiling now.

"You haven't heard the last of this, Constable!" MacPhail hissed and then turning on his heel, stormed out through the glass doors. Waz, still stunned by the confrontation, exhaled with relief, seeing the commissionaire behind his desk, mouth tightly closed, but his body shaking as he fought to refrain from laughing out loud. Mooney, pressed the button to open the lift and turning, called out to the commissionaire, "If he asks, Willie, you don't know us, okay?"

"Fair enough Des," replied Willie, waving and finally giving in to the laughter, the sound following them both as the lift doors closed.

"What the *fuck* was all that about?" demanded a still stunned Waz.

"Beats me, pal," sighed Mooney, pressing the button for the fifth floor, "though I don't think you are aware that dickhead there," he nodded towards the closed lift door, "is the new ACC for crime."

"That's it," Waz shook his head, "my career's over now. Bloody hell Des; was there any need to wind him up like that?"

"Like what?" Mooney turned towards his younger colleague. "He started it. All I did was to ask him who he was and tell him where we worked."

Waz was confused. "But you told him we worked at Coatbridge."

"Did I?" Mooney feigned surprise. "Now, why would I say that?" The lift doors opened at the fifth floor and they began to make their way round the building towards the Laboratory.

"What if he contacts Coatbridge office looking for us," wailed a worried Waz.

"Who will he be looking for? Did you give him your name? I know I didn't give him mine," Mooney chuckled.

"But he saw your warrant card."

"Aye, so he did. You're right, he saw my warrant card, but the stupid bugger was so angry he didn't read it. I mean, how many people do you know take the time to actually *read* the name that's on warrant cards? Do you?" he asked, holding a fire door in the corridor to permit Waz to pass through.

Waz's eyes narrowed and suddenly he grinned. "You smart bastard," he dug Mooney in the ribs with his elbow, relief sweeping through him, but still feeling a little weak at the knees.

The harassed Lab assistant Ina Young asked Waz and Mooney to wait a few minutes while she completed working on a DNA inquiry. "Bit of a hurry up order from a couple of cops at Shettleston. Drunk driver they think gave a bum name," she said by way of explanation. "Are you just on yourself today, Ina?" Mooney called after her.

"No, Des, there's two of us, but it's the usual story," she called out over her shoulder. "Because we cope, well barely cope," she added, concentrating on the intricacies of the machine in front of her, "we become victims of our own success. Management won't bring anyone else out knowing that the work gets done even though it runs two of us ragged." Then with a hint of sarcasm, she added, "If you guys would stop arresting criminals, it might make our work that wee bit easier."

Waz, standing listening with the grinning Mooney, again marvelled at the number of police personnel known to his neighbour.

Ina rummaged among the paperwork on her desk and at last, with a cry of, "Here it is," brought the two page report to Mooney who immediately handed it to Waz while he continued to chew the fat with Ina.

Then turning towards the younger man he asked, "Is it enough for us to go on?"

Waz smiled and blowing a kiss towards the under pressure Ina, they headed for the lifts.

DS Arlene Baxter saw Lynn Massey beckon with her head and followed her from the incident room to Bobby Franklin's office. Now seated in front of her boss, Massey instructed the younger officer to meet at midday with Susie Gibson at Uddingston office. "Shall I take somebody with me," she asked, "I mean, with DI Cameron being off unwell."

Massey nodded and replied, "I phoned Laura Scott, she's a DS in the Fraud Squad. I believe that you know each other?"

"Aye, Ma'am. I know Laura," confirmed Baxter.

"Laura is already working on the Peter Gibson side of the inquiry, trying to find out how he managed to work the fraud, but I think it would be useful if she were to be present at the second interview with DS Gibson. There might be some questions that Laura can ask that will assist her and besides, I want you to request Gibson's approval for Laura to research her and her husbands bank accounts and any other financial dealing that they might have. I also wish to know if any accounts might have been opened in any other names, but controlled by them and I want you to include their daughter's name too."

Baxter, inwardly aware of the tentative rapport she had developed with Gibson, took a deep breath and asked, "Is DS Gibson to be treated as a suspect, Ma'am?"

Massey stared thoughtfully at her and finally replied, "The outcome of the interview and DS Gibson's attitude towards your request regarding her and her husband's financial affairs *might* possibly determine her status in this inquiry, Arlene. At this time, she is to be treated as a witness," Massey slowly exhaled, then added, "in fact, a witness who is missing her husband and in all probability, is worried and distressed. However, I urge you not to be swayed by the fact that Gibson is a colleague nor any feeling of sympathy that you might have for her, is that clear? If DS Gibson's relationship with her husband is strong and, dare I say, loving, then she will be extremely protective of him and we might *not* be getting told the full story."

She saw Baxter flinch and her intuitive suspicion was aroused. "Arlene, is there something that you wish to tell me?"

She took a deep breath, knowing that what she was about to tell Massey would earn her a bollocking, yet more concerned that she was about to betray a confidence.

"It's about DS Gibson's relationship with her husband, Ma'am. There had been some acrimony. Things between them weren't too good and, well," she bit at her lower lip before continuing, "DS Gibson suspected there might have been another woman in her husband's life."

Massey stared hard at her before replying and then icily said, "I don't recall reading about this in the statement you took, Arlene. Didn't you think it was relevant?"

"I submitted DS Gibson's statement, Ma'am, with what I believed to be all the information relevant to the ongoing inquiry regarding her missing husband. I didn't think it necessary to expose her private anguish, the domestic issues that she is having with her husband."

"Those *domestic issues*, DS Baxter," stormed Massey, "might very well be the reason that Peter Gibson committed the theft from his bank and the other woman quite possibly might have been our murder victim, Carol Meechan!" she slammed her hand forcefully down onto the desk, then added, "Bloody hell, Arlene, what were you thinking?"

Baxter didn't reply, realising that anything she said in mitigation of her failing would be seen to be just that; an excuse for fucking up. Instead, she simply replied, "Sorry Ma'am."

Massey sat back in her seat and rubbed with the heel of her hand at her forehead. "Is there *any* likelihood that DS Gibson might suspect Meechan *was* the other woman?"

Baxter shook her head. "She had never heard her husband mention Carol Meechan's name and can't recall ever having personally met the woman at any of the bank's functions. For what it's worth, Ma'am," she shrugged, "I believe her, that she hadn't heard Meechan's name before."

"But that doesn't mean *he* didn't know Meechan, does it?"

"No Ma'am," agreed Baxter, "but who's to say that he didn't know Meechan as a colleague when he was at work? I mean, there are plenty of cops I know, but it wouldn't occur to me to mention them to my hubby, Darrel."

Though she didn't respond, this time Massey had to agree.

A short silence fell between them, broken when Massey softly said, "Today, when you re-interview DS Gibson, I expect to receive a full and complete report, Arlene. Leave nothing out. If there is any hesitancy, anything at all or you believe that DS Gibson is prevaricating, I order you to treat her as a hostile witness and if it means she then becomes a suspect, you will treat her as you would any other suspect and by that, Arlene, I mean applying the law. Do you clearly understand?"

"Yes, Ma'am, I understand."

"Right then," nodded Massey, handing Baxter a slip of paper, "here's DS Scott's phone number. Contact her and arrange to uplift her from home prior to attending for your midday interview with DS Gibson."

Baxter took and the slip and standing, turned towards the door, only to be stopped when Massey said, "Arlene, you have a bright future. Don't let your emotions or any misplaced feeling of sisterhood with a colleague who just *might* turn out to be of interest to us, get in the way of your career."

"Yes, Ma'am," nodded a chastened Baxter who then left the room.

Within a twin patient room on the fifth floor of the Western Infirmary, Patrick Gallagher, wearing an old black coloured turtle neck sweater and jeans, sat on a rigid plastic chair beside his father's bed and held his hand while a young nurse busied herself at the old man's drip bag. His father had returned to full consciousness, but still required the intravenous medication within the bag being replaced by the nurse.

"Thought we'd lost you for a while there, Da," Patrick smiled, stroking his father's forehead with his free hand.

Magnus, his face pale, slowly turned his head to stare at his son. "I saw our Lord," he whispered to Patrick, his throat still aching from the oropharyngeal airway removed just a few hours previously.

Patrick stared at his father, his faced creased in disbelief.

"Sorry, Da, you saw who?" he uttered, unwittingly squeezing his father's hand that little bit tighter, then seeing the old man wince, said, "Sorry, Da. You saw who?" he asked once more.

"Our Lord, I saw our Lord," Magnus again whispered.

Patrick was aware the young nurse had stopped what she was doing and was now stooped over his shoulder, hardly daring to breathe as she strained to listen to his father.

"I was standing at the gate to heaven when He spoke to me," Magnus whispered, his voice hoarse as he fought against the rawness in his throat.

The nurse leaned across Patrick and held a small cup with a straw at Magnus's mouth.

Patrick and the nurse watched as he sipped at the cool water, then the nurse dabbed at the slight dribble from the corner of his mouth with a clean white pad.

"Da," said Patrick, his eyes opened wide, "What are you saying?"

"He said God spoke to him," the nurse interrupted Patrick, clearly in awe at this revelation and desperate to hear more.

"I know what he said," Patrick impatiently replied, then turning to his father, asked, "What did our heavenly Father say, Da? What did God tell you?"

Magnus weakly held up a hand and in a soft voice, said, "He told me, not today Magnus, we're a wee bit busy. Can you come back another time?"

Then the old man mischievously grinned.

"Aye, very good Mister Gallagher," said the nurse, affronted that he had taken in both his son and her. "I do the jokes round here," she added, getting back to replacing the bag. Turning to Patrick, her face deadpan, but her eyes betraying her humour, she told him, "Any more nonsense from your Da, Father Gallagher and I'm getting him discharged. That's him yellow carded, okay?"

Patrick smiled and nodded, relieved that not only was his father undoubtedly on the road to recovery, but that his sense of humour had returned too.

Taking a deep breath, he decided now was the time; that his Da was fit enough and ready to receive the bad news about his brother Leigh and steeled himself to break his father's heart.

Philip Saunders, comfortably seated within the large, rear conservatory of the sprawling detached house, shrugged more comfortably into the cushions of the wicker chair and prepared to enjoy his Sunday morning edition of the 'Glasgow News'. The faint strains of his daughter's music could be heard coming from her open bedroom window while from inside the house he could hear his wife rattling crockery as she prepared their Sunday morning brunch and sniffed the air, enjoying the tantalising smell of fried bacon wafting through from the kitchen.

He smiled to himself and reached for his coffee sitting on the small occasional table by his elbow, eyes narrowing and wondering if he'd heard correctly.

Yes, he had heard correctly for the doorbell rung again.

A few seconds later his wife with an expression of surprised concern upon her face, called him from the doorway and led him into the lounge.

To his surprise, the two men wearing suits who stood there introduced themselves as police officers.

"What the devil do you people want at this time of the morning," he irately asked.

"Detective Constable Ahmed, sir," said the dark skinned one; another jumped up Paki, Saunders thought to himself. Give these *bloody* immigrants an inch, he inwardly snarled.

"We're part of a team of officers currently engaged in the investigation of a murder and…"

Waz got no further.

"Murder?" interrupted Saunders, his own face now registering surprise while his wife stood timidly behind him, her hands wringing the dishcloth she held. "Why the hell would we know anything about a murder?"

"Perhaps if you let me explain…"

"Yes, please do so and quickly; we *are* about to sit down to eat," Saunders haughtily again interrupted.

Aye, lucky you, Mooney inwardly thought, his nose wrinkling at the smell of the frying bacon, conscious he had left the flat without breakfast and knowing there was no chance of an invite from the fat bastard to join them.

Beside him, Waz was almost certain he could hear Des Mooney's stomach growling.

"As I said sir," continued Waz, "we are part of a team investigating a murder and a series of street robberies in the Partick area of Glasgow."

"Partick? Glasgow?" Saunders repeated and then inhaling as if tolerating a child, added, "Why is that of interest to us? This *is* Newton Mearns, for God's sake man," he sniffed. "You're a little off your, what do you call it? Your turf, are you not?" and then sniggered at his little joke.

Mooney was getting more pissed off at the paunchy guy's attitude than Waz realised and turning to Saunders wife, he said, "Missus Saunders, are you Celia Saunders who was three years ago arrested for drunk driving?"

Pale faced, the woman was about to respond when Saunders snapped, "No, that was my first wife. What the *hell* is this about?"

"Do you have a daughter, aged about seventeen to twenty years old, Mister Saunders?" this time, the short and sharp question came from Waz.

"Eh, yes, Emma, she's eighteen," he replied, taken aback by the double act and surprised by the change in questioning. "She's in her room."

"Turning to his wife, he said, "Get her down here right now. The sooner this is settled, the sooner these *people*," he waved a hand at the two officers, "are gone."

When the woman hurried from the room, the three men stood in awkward silence.

A minute later, Missus Saunders returned with a petite, but pretty blonde young woman, wearing a dressing gown over what looked like pink pyjamas covered with Disney characters.

"Who are these people," Emma asked, acutely aware that both the men were staring at her bandaged left hand. Self-consciously, she put both hands behind her back but was unable to mask the reddening of her cheeks.

"We're the police, Miss Saunders," replied Waz Ahmed with a smile, "and we're very, *very* interested in how you come to injure your hand."

"She fell on some glass," Saunders spoke in defence of his daughter.

"Fell on some glass?" repeated Mooney, then turning to the younger woman, asked, "Is that what *really* happened, Emma?"

Instinctively, she realised that they knew.

It was then her father saw her face turn from red to a shocked pale colour and guessed that he had been lied to. "Emma? Isn't that what happened? Emma!"

"Perhaps your daughter might feel more comfortable speaking with us alone, Mister Saunders," Waz smoothly suggested.

Tears formed in Emma's eyes and she bit at her lower lip, her chin quivering as she fought to stop herself from crying. Slowly, she shook her head.

"Would you like to tell us what really happened, Emma?" Waz softly said, taking a step toward the young woman.

"Get away from her you...you..." Saunders snarled, his hands clenching into fists.

"Philip," his wife cried out a warning, but he turned on her and angrily shouted, "Shut the fuck up, woman!"

Emma began to cry and lowered her face into her hands.

Fuck this, thought Mooney. "Mister Saunders!" He stepped towards him, the venom in his voice evident to them all, "you've a choice to make here, *sir*. We speak to your daughter alone or in your presence, but that's her choice, *sir*. If your daughter refuses to speak with us, we're taking her with us and detaining her under Section 14 of the Criminal Procedure (Scotland) Act, 1995 and if you even think of preventing us, *sir*," his face now barely inches from Saunders and his voice openly menacing, "you'll be coming with us too, *sir*." Saunders gulped, his bluster now spent and stared tight-lipped at the floor. It was all he could do to nod in agreement.

"Now Emma," Waz turned so his back was to Saunders and politely asked, "Do you wish your father to be present when we interview you? I understand you're eighteen, so there's no need for a parent to be present. You do understand that Emma, don't you?" he stared at her and then to her surprise, winked.

The tearful girl got the message and turning to her father, said, "It's all right dad. I know something and I have to tell these officers. It'll be all right. Can we have some privacy? I'll explain it all to you later."

Her father, now completely deflated, simply nodded and trying to regain some dignity, pretended a cough and told her, "Yes, by God, we'll speak later young lady. This isn't finished," he shook his head, "not by a long chalk. Come my dear," he beckoned towards his wife, "we'll eat."

When they had left the room, Mooney turned towards the young woman and smiling, said, "I take it there's no chance now of a cuppa and a bacon butty then, hen?"

Half an hour later, with Emma Saunders statement noted and informed that she might later be required to attend an identification parade to identify the man who attempted to rob her and cut her with his knife, Waz Ahmed sat back in the passenger seat of the car and said, "Nice one, Des. How *do* you manage to be so tolerant?"

"Years of practise, old son; years of practise," he nodded and smiled without a trace of guile at the younger man.

"What do you think she'll tell her father, then?"

"Whatever she wants," shrugged Mooney, "but I'm guessing that racist blowhard will be happy to accept any excuse for us interviewing her. He'll not want to admit, not even to himself, that his daughter put one over on him." He shook his head and continued, "He's nothing but a bag of shite. He'll probably rant and rave for a while and I'm guessing, unless I'm adding two and two together and getting five, that his wife will bear the brunt for most of his rage." He shook his head again, but this time with a little more force and a touch of sadness to his voice. "I'm no expert, but I'm also guessing that bastard isn't beyond handing out a slap or two now and again, just to make himself feel like more of a man."

Waz remained silent for a moment, reflecting on his own happy marriage and once more wondering about his neighbour's domestic situation.

"Handy wee tip she gave us about the guy in Dumbarton Road selling the eccies, eh?" he said, at last.

"Aye, Billy who lives one flight up," Mooney grinned and then stopping the car at a red light, turned towards Waz, grinned again. "We'll save that wee turn for a quiet day."

Uddingston police station, constructed in 1925 and still bearing the title 'County Police Office' engraved above the main door, stands at number one, Old Glasgow Road, just off the junction with Main Street. Once open to the public twenty-four hours, seven days a week, the office had faithfully served the local Uddingston and Bothwell community through the amalgamations that commenced with the merger of Hamilton Burgh Police to Lanarkshire Constabulary, then the newly formed Strathclyde Police and finally in April 2013, the amalgamation of all the Scottish Forces who together unified to become Police (Scotland).

These days, the sturdily built office was opened through office hours only, with a civilian bar officer manning the station through the traditional working week and a free phone located by the front door for emergency calls, when the office was closed to the public. However, patrol officers in the area continue to use the office for rest periods and report writing, but budget restrictions being as they are, the local residents fear the office is now in its twilight years.

That Sunday, aware that out of hours access to Uddingston office was restricted to Divisional personnel, DS Arlene Baxter wisely contacted Hamilton police office and made an arrangement with the duty Sergeant for a duty patrol constable to meet her and DS Laura Scott at the office and permit them entry.

On the way to Uddingston, Baxter and Scott had talked over who would take the lead and decided that as Baxter had already spoken with Susie Gibson, she would commence the interview. She didn't confide to Scott that she felt a little uncomfortable, having developed a slight rapport with Susie, but later felt the wrath of Lynn Massey when having to admit excluding details of the Gibson's marital issues from the statement. Now she determined that she would be totally professional, that she owed Susie Gibson no favours and worried that perhaps the woman had coned her; that Gibson just might after all be colluding in the theft with her reputedly missing husband.

She arrived with Scott in the passenger seat of the CID car a little after eleven-thirty and was met at the office a few minutes later by a fresh-faced, but very affable young constable. The cop admitted them to the foyer area of the office then led them around, with a smile pointing out the kitchen and suggesting they avail themselves of the tea and coffee. With a polite and slightly embarrassed cough, he then showed them the female toilet and thereafter the cupboard like interview room. Excusing himself that he had a call to attend the cop left Baxter with a spare front door key, requesting she lock up and post it through the letterbox when she and Scott departed.

They had just shrugged off their jackets and were preparing themselves coffee when the outer door of the office was knocked. Baxter admitted a pale faced Susie Gibson, her hair loose about her shoulders and dressed in a plain, black coloured sweat top, jeans and walking boots and carrying a blue coloured anorak over her arm. After introducing Susie to Laura Scott, Susie declined coffee and curtly said, "I'd rather we just get this over with, if you please." Scott, dressed in a light pink coloured, flowery kaftan, tight jeans, open-toed sandals with her customary bulging canvas bag slung on her shoulder, nodded to Susie.

"Sorry to be meeting under these circumstances, Susie," she grimaced. Then with an open smile, said, "How's your wee girl these days? She must be what, twelve or thirteen now?"

Susie instinctively knew that there was no guile behind Scott's question, no underhand motive and returning the smile, replied, "Not so little these days. Fifteen now and going through her teenage angst and prelims, so you can probably imagine the atmosphere in the house," she sighed and then added "and of course this business with my husband. Well, it's put a hell of a strain on us both."

Baxter had decided that the kitchen was too open, too friendly and that the bleak, impersonal interview room was the best place to re-interview Susie Gibson and with Scott at the rear, led her along the narrow corridor to the small room.

While Scott fetched a third chair from the kitchen, Baxter and Susie occupied the two wooden chairs in front of the dusty table that was littered with a scattering of police forms and A4 paper that presumably, Baxter thought, was there for note taking. A rusting metal rubbish bin in the corner that was half full oozed the odour of a rotten piece of fruit. With a scowl at the laziness of the cops in the office, Scott gingerly lifted the bin and placed it outside in the corridor.

Now at last settled with Baxter and Susie facing each other across the table and Scott sitting in the corner at Baxter's left side, the interview commenced.

"So, what am I then; a witness or a suspect?" Susie opened the conversation, her voice flat and even.

Baxter, her eyes betraying her discomfort, said, "DSU Massey was quite specific when she told me that you are a witness, that nothing untoward has been alleged against you, that unless there is evidence to the contrary, that's how you are to be treated."

It took less than ten minutes of stilted conversation, primarily because Susie realised that the understanding she previously enjoyed with Baxter was now gone and a more formal atmosphere was in place. This she inwardly reasoned, had to be at the instruction of Lynn Massey.

"So, Missus Gibson, you have nothing further to add to your original statement, noted by me?"

Tight-lipped, Susie merely shook her head.

Baxter smiled sadly and said, "Then I see no reason to detain you any further unless," she half turned towards Scott, "my colleague has anything to ask?"

Scott sat forward, hands clasped in her lap and her eyes on Susie.

"You'll have guessed I've been brought in because of the financial aspect of the inquiry to try and determine if your husband is indeed *allegedly* guilty of committing the fraud and if so, how he *allegedly* did it."

Susie nodded her understanding, having already made the connection and inwardly smiled. Baxter, she thought, must have told Scott of DI Cameron's straight out accusation against Peter and the younger woman was taking no chances, but stressing Peter was, for the time being anyway, a suspect and *not* an accused.

"So," she said at last and gave in with a smile, "If Peter is allegedly guilty, what is it that you need from me?"

"Well, it would help if your man Peter has kept anything at home; files from work, a laptop, any kind of recording or calculating device. Anything at all that he might have used to record the transactions that he allegedly made and might relate to the loans were granted."

Susie turned towards Baxter. "Is there a suggestion here that if I don't cooperate, your boss might consider applying for a warrant to search my home?"

Baxter shifted uncomfortably in her chair and softly exhaling, nodded. "The truth is Susie," she reverted to her forename, "I had to admit to Lynn Massey that when I typed up your statement, I excluded the issues you admitted you are having with your husband." She stopped and bit her lip and continued, "And if you're thinking I betrayed your confidence, you're absolutely correct and I feel a shit for doing it. But I didn't just let you down, I let myself down. I'm supposed to be a Detective Sergeant and I let my sympathy for…" she paused, grasping for the correct word, "your situation, influence me when I noted your statement. For what it's worth, I'm sorry."

Susie stared at Baxter then slowly nodded. She recognised the unenviable position the younger woman had been in and remembered during her own career, being intimidated by senior officers who held sway over her career. Lynn Massey, a woman she had not previously worked for, but heard good things about, was supposed to be a fair boss, but no fool. Baxter, she inwardly accepted, had done the correct thing and Susie, as a fellow detective, recognised this. In a sense, she empathised with Baxter and finally said, "It's okay, Arlene." She smiled at the younger officer and then softly added, "I just hope Massey doesn't hold it against you."

"It's unlikely that she will," interrupted Scott and then with a smile dancing about her own lips, pointedly said, "so, if you two sisters have stopped bonding, maybe we can return to my question. Susie, is there *anything* in the house that Peter might have used to record any kind of transactions, anything at all?"

Susie's forehead furrowed and she briefly recalled Peter's small electronic notebook in the black, leather wallet that he kept hidden in his sock drawer; the notebook that recorded the passwords for their various computers, serial numbers for the televisions and computer equipment, their bank account numbers, life insurance details, the family passport numbers and all the minor minutiae that her husband believed vital should there be a break-in and the items stolen. She had teased him more than a few times about his obsession with recording all these details.

Staring at Baxter, she shook her head and said, "No, nothing."

"There is just one other thing. DSU Massey asked if you would cooperate and provide us with details of your bank accounts or any other accounts that you might have. She made it clear to me that the inquiry would be conducted by Laura here and would be for no other purpose than eliminating any possibility that your husband might have transferred funds from the bank to those accounts."

"Can I just say something here," Scott interrupted and leaned forward in her chair. "Susie, the only person seeing those accounts will be me and if there's nothing to report? Well," she half-smiled, "that's exactly what I'll be telling Ma'am."

Susie inhaled and simply nodded, then said, "We've nothing to hide so I'll forward you the details if you give me your e-mail address, Laura."

Scott nodded and sat back, inwardly pleased there had been no argument to the request.

"Anything you might wish to ask us or anything you want DSU Massey to contact you about?" asked Baxter.

She was about to shake her head when it occurred to her. "Ask Ma'am how long I've to remain off work. I can't sit about the house all day," she quietly said. "I have on-going cases and inquiries. I need to get into the office. Will you do that for me?"

"Yes, of course," replied Baxter, but a little hesitantly and enough for Susie to notice.

"What? What are you not telling me?"

Baxter took a deep breath. "I don't think I was supposed to hear," she stared at Susie, "but I overheard Lynn Massey talking about gardening leave. I think that's the polite way of…"

"I know what it means, Arlene," Susie sighed, "so, in essence, wait till I hear something?"

"I'm afraid so," nodded Baxter.

Less than five minutes later, Susie stood outside the office main door while Baxter locked up and posted the key through the letterbox. They took their farewell of each other with a formal, 'Goodbye.'

On the short drive home, Susie was aghast that she had lied to Baxter, trying to persuade herself that there was nothing in the notebook that might implicate Peter in the fraud.

The truth was, she very well knew, before she declared its existence, she needed to get into his password protected notebook and find out for herself what it contained.

CHAPTER 21

He had slept in again and knew that his boss would sack him this time if he was late. He guessed it wasn't the vodka, because he could handle his drink, but the line of charlie he had taken at the party that had kept him awake the remainder of the night. *"Come on! Come on! Come on!"* he hissed through gritted teeth, angrily slapping his hand against the dashboard, willing the red coloured Volvo's driver to get the *fuck* out of the way. He wrestled with the other hand at the van's steering wheel and drove the vehicle almost on two wheels, nearly clipping the Volvo as he overtook it, the bemused driver staring wide-eyed at the young man as the van passed by, wondering what the hell the white Transit driver was up to.

The van driver shook his head and wondered at the law that allowed old farts onto the roads on a quiet Sunday morning when they should be in their fucking beds and pushed down on the accelerator, trying to urge a few more miles per hour out of the screaming engine.

He raised his backside off the driver's seat and groped in his left hand denim pocket for his mobile phone.

Des Mooney and Waz Ahmed were still laughing at Emma Saunders plea, that if her father phones them at the office they're to pretend she's a witness to a robbery and not the victim; that she tried to intercede and *that's* how she was injured and to suggest to Saunders she might be in for a bravery award.

"It's the final year dance," she had wailed, "and he'll ground me if he knew I was popping eccies. *Pleeeeeease!*"

While not *actually* promising to lie on her behalf, the two cops did promise to consider dizzying her father's calls.

"There's a newsagents in Arden that's open on Sunday morning and does the filled rolls," said Mooney, "so my treat. We'll see if they've got anything halal for you," he grinned at Waz.

"I hear you're a Partick Thistle fan, Des. So what, that makes about *four* of you, does it?" Waz grinned at his insult and continuing to grin, continued, "Are you going to see the Jags play the mighty Glasgow Rangers at Ibrox this Wednesday night then?"

"I'm guessing where *your* loyalties lie," Mooney shook his head and then added, "No, I'm strictly a home game fan. Why would I want to travel over to Castle Greyskull when I can watch my team pulverise yours on the tele in the comfort of my flat, with a can of Mick Jagger in my fist?" he jokingly sneered at his younger colleague.

Mooney turned the CID onto Stewarton Road and changing down to third gear as he approached the small roundabout, slowing as he changed gear to approach the roundabout and preparing to drive straight through towards the roll shop.

He glanced at the time on his mobile phone screen and licked his lips. The boss had warned him that if he was late….Shite! With a gasp, he sharply turned the wheel, narrowly avoiding the stationary bus. How the fuck did I miss *that*, he inwardly thought, but grinned at his reflex action. Jesus, but he was thirsty.

He threw the phone down onto the passenger seat and then it buzzed with an incoming message. Grasping at it, he scrolled down to read the text.

Waz was relaxed, feeling comfortable working with Mooney and decided he liked the older guy. That companionship prompted him to ask the question that had been bugging him since seeing Des with the good looking redhead. Tongue in cheek, he turned towards his neighbour.

The driver slammed the phone down onto the passenger seat, annoyed at this boss's text and had time to comment, "Fuck's sake, Marty, I'm nearly there…." as he pushed down on the pedal and sped the van through the roundabout.

Mooney had no time to react and the van struck the CID car squarely on the passenger side, crushing the front and rear doors as well as the central pillar and overturning the vehicle as it ploughed the car into the middle island.

According to a nearby resident, a woman hanging out her washing over one hundred and fifty yards away, the sound of the collision and the scream of tortured metal was loud enough to startle her into dropping her clothes peg-bag.

The van driver, who had not worn his seat belt, was catapulted through the front windscreen and bounced across the front passenger door of the CID car. His almost immediate fatal injuries, later listed among numerous others, included crushing to his chest, multiple internal injures caused by colliding with the van's dashboard, numerous facial abrasions and cuts that were attributed to the fragmentation of the shattered windscreen, a broken left arm (two places) that was assessed to have occurred when he landed on the roadway and a severely crushed skull. The pathologist who conducted the post mortem examination concluded that any number of the young man's injuries might have resulted in his death.

Such was the force of the van's collision with the CID car, the car was now upended and lying on its driver's side with the unconscious driver, Des Mooney lying huddled on the shattered glass of the driver's window.

The car's passenger, Waz Ahmed was partially hung suspended from his seatbelt and nestled against Mooney's left shoulder, blood from a head wound and his nose dripping onto his neighbour. In a state of extreme shock that was exacerbated by the extensive blood loss from the head wound, it took several minutes for Waz to succumb to his injuries and he did so with a gentle sigh, dying with his eyes open and staring sightlessly at Mooney.

The Volvo driver, a retired plumber, stopped at the junction with the roundabout and stared with horror at the scene in front of him, recognising the white van with the idiot of a driver as the vehicle that had sped past him just a minute before. Only now, the steam rising from both engines clouded the area about the accident. He later recounted that what struck him most was the silence. With a presence of mind that was later commended, the Volvo driver did not immediately leave his car, but remained seated in his Volvo and with shaking fingers, punched in the digits that alerted the emergency services to the accident, then with faltering voice telling the operator where he was and begging that someone come quickly, that there was bound to be at least serious injuries to the occupants of both vehicles. The experienced operator coaxed further information from the driver, assuring the man that help was on its way.

Though it was early morning, other passing cars began to arrive at the scene and while some driver's stood looking on in shocked horror and staring at the calamitous accident, a few with presence of mind tried to resuscitate the young man who lay on the road, even though it soon became obvious he was dead.

A brave young woman, dressed in her favourite top and skirt and walking towards an early morning church service, completely disregarded the threat that the vehicles might catch fire and attempted to reach the two occupants in the car that lay upon its side through the broken windscreen of their vehicle, but heartbreakingly realised the passenger was dead. However, upon hearing a murmured groan from the driver and realising that alone, she was unable to free the unconscious man, the young woman lay upon the blood and the broken glass and held his hand, speaking softly and reassuring him until the arrival of the Fire Service, who ushered her to a place of safety while they took over the rescue. The young woman was herself later treated by the ambulance personnel for shock as well as minor cuts to her legs and forearms, suffered when she lay upon the broken glass to comfort the injured man.

The Traffic Department officers who attended the scene quickly re-routed passing vehicles away from the general area to permit the Fire and Ambulance personnel to conduct their rescue and medical care of the sole survivor of the crash.

While their sister services worked at extracting and treating the injured Des Mooney, the Traffic officers with stoical professionalism, commenced their investigation.

The Volvo driver and the stationary bus driver both provided statements that prior to the collision the van driver was travelling at an inordinately high speed, with the Volvo driver opining in excess of sixty mph and the bus driver thinking it was rather faster.

There was no tyre skids marks found that indicated any attempt by the van driver to slow the vehicle on the approach to the roundabout. As was normal in these incidents where death occurs, both vehicles would be hoisted and removed by trailer to a covered area and examined for any structural defects that might have contributed to the accident.

Later that day, the first tentative examination would disclose no noteworthy problems with either vehicle and for the time being, the cause of the collision would remain undecided until such time the veracity of the other driver's statements and those of nearby residents were collated and a medical examination of both drivers completed.

In the incident room, DI Bobby Franklin was sharing a coffee and joking with one of the civilian analysts when the news arrived that a CID car registered to his Cranstonhill Department had been involved in an accident. The HOLMES operator reached across and handed him the phone, telling him it was the Duty Inspector at the Pitt Street control room. He listened impassively as the Inspector broke the bad news.

"Sorry to be the one to tell you, Bobby," said the Inspector, "but the troops on the ground are telling me it's a fatal. Two dead, one critically injured. As far as I can gather, three males involved and the Traffic has recovered warrant cards from two of the guys. One of the deceased is a DC Waseem Ahmed and the injured man is a cop called Constable Desmond Mooney. I'm sorry, but I've no information as yet as to how serious Mooney's injuries are. He's being conveyed to the Victoria Hospital as we speak. The other deceased, a young guy, well; I believe they're still making inquiry regarding him."

Franklin stood perfectly still, the shock of the news evident on his face, unaware that the room was completely silent as the four others present watched him.

"You know I'm supposed to first kick this news upstairs Bobby to the duty ACC, but you and I go a long way back, so I thought I'd give you a heads up."

"Yeah, thanks, I'm grateful," Franklin quietly replied, ending the call, but his mind elsewhere. He turned his head and with a heavy heart, broke the news to the two cops and two civilians, one a matronly lady who began to quietly weep.

As if in a daze, he made his way to his own office and dialled DSU Lynn Massey's mobile phone number.

At the vestibule door, ACC Jonathon MacPhail, dressed soberly in a plain black coloured suit, wearing a white shirt and Metropolitan Police golf tie, shook hands with the minister and was just leaving the church and approaching his official unmarked police vehicle when the driver, a retired Traffic Department officer now employed to ferry senior staff around, approached him with MacPhail's mobile phone in his hand.

"It's the control room Inspector sir," he politely said, handing MacPhail the phone.

"Yes, Inspector, what can I do for you?" MacPhail said, holding the phone to his ear and smiling at a passing couple.

The smile froze on his face as he listened then tersely asked, "Has the Chief been apprised yet?"

"No sir, as the duty ACC…"

"Okay, I understand," interrupted MacPhail and then instructed, "I suspect that you have more facts at hand than I do right now Inspector, so contact the Chief Constable and then the Deputy Chief in that order. Make them aware that you have told me and that I'm dealing. What station were these officers assigned to?"

"My understanding, sir, is that both were currently engaged in the ongoing murder inquiry being run from Cranstonhill. A DI Bobby Franklin is in charge, but the overall commander is DSU Lynn Massey. Do you wish me to…"

"I'm on my way back to Pitt Street, Inspector so yes, contact DSU Massey and her boss, Detective Chief Superintendent Johnson and have them attend at my office," he curtly interrupted and glanced at his watch, irritably thinking that this was going to take all day and he'd never get that bloody round of golf in. However, his eyes narrowed at the thought, there's always a rainbow at the end of a storm and the press coverage could be useful. He cleared his throat. "Please also arrange to have personnel files for these two individuals and as much detail regarding the accident on my desk that you can muster in," again, he glanced at his watch, "say thirty minutes," and abruptly concluded the call.

'These two individuals' the Inspector inwardly fumed at the insensitivity of MacPhail's comment as he unconsciously slammed the phone into its cradle, startling the nearby operators who stared curiously at him. Aye, and stick a broom up my arse and I'll sweep the ground in front of you, ya callous po-faced bastard, he grimaced.

On the ride back to Cranstonhill, Arlene Baxter and Laura Scott discussed the short interview that they had conducted with Susie Gibson.

"Do you think meeting her again added anything to your first statement?" asked Scott.

"No, not really," Baxter shook her head, concentrating on her driving. "If anything though, I feel a bit better about letting her know that I admitted telling Massey I'd left a bit of her out of her statement; her confidence to me about her personal issues with her husband," she sighed. "Nothing worse than feeling two-faced, particularly when it's somebody you like."

"So you like Susie then?"

"Aye, there's something about her, an honest quality. Call it feminine intuition or whatever, but yeah, I do like her."

Scott gave a sideways grin. "You're not far wrong then. Susie Gibson, if I remember correctly, is a really nice lassie. Treats everybody with respect, regardless of their rank." Her grin widened. "You're testing me, aren't you?"

"Testing you?"

"Don't kid a kidder, Arlene. You want to know how strong my relationship is with Susie. You don't know me *that* well, so before you report back to Lynn Massey, you want to know if I'm going to agree with you or argue that you did or didn't press her enough about her knowledge of her husband's bank activities. Am I right?"

It was Baxter's turn to grin. "Well, it had occurred to me that simply because I hadn't pressed too hard at her initial interview, maybe I was in danger of being too lax today."

She briefly turned her head and asked, "Was I? Too lax, I mean?"

Scott stared out of the side window and shrugged her shoulders.

"She's not your run of the mill witness, for God's sake Arlene. She's a trained detective with more experience than either of us and besides that, what evidence is there that she in any way colluded with her hubby regarding the fraud? None at all or rather none that *we* know of," she shook her head.

"So, you think she just might know something?"

"No, I'm not saying or even suggesting that," she crossly replied. She turned to stare at Baxter. "Look, you know I've been instructed by Ma'am to research Peter Gibson's alleged fraud?"

Baxter nodded.

"Well, I shouldn't be telling you this, at least not before I formally report my findings to Lynn Massey, but the fraud itself is a complicated business. We're not talking here about some lassie in a sweetie shop dipping her finger every now and then into the till. There are protocols in place to prevent the type of fraud Gibson carried out."

"So, he *did* steal the money then?" interrupted Baxter, a trace of excitement in her voice.

Scott sighed, realising she had already said too much. "Put it this way, he couldn't have committed the fraud himself, not with the safeguards the bank has in place. There are individual passwords on some of the systems that he would need to have by-passed to continue the loan applications as well as signatures for some of the documentation and *that* includes documentation that would require to be counters-signed. All in all, Peter Gibson is either a *really* clever individual or more likely, he's colluded with someone else. A second man, as it were. Maybe even a conspiracy of three or more."

"Have you identified his accomplice?"

The car radio burst in with a general message from the control room at Pitt Street that instructed all officers currently engaged in the Cranstonhill incident to report to Cranstonhill office as soon as possible.

Scott, puzzled, turned to Baxter and asked, "Now what the hell is that all about?"

Susie Gibson sat on the edge of the bed, a half-drunk mug of coffee growing cold on the bedside table set of drawers. She stared with frustration at the small notebook, the black leather wallet lying beside it because she thought that the password to permit her entry to the notebook might have been hidden behind the cover.

Never professing to be the best at IT anyway, Susie had in the past laughingly admitted even the TV control confused her and now, the notebook resisted all of Susie's attempts to open it. Fortunately, unlike her computer at work whose passwords for the different programmes changed every few weeks, she was permitted innumerable attempts to open the notebook. The programmes in the PC on her desk allowed three entries then she was locked out and, in the recent past, she had taken to writing her passwords for the different systems down on a piece of paper she kept in her purse. Highly irregular she knew, but preferable to being forced to calling for help from the smirking young IT guy who, she privately thought and had twice caught trying to look down the front of her blouse, was a sleazy bugger and well worth the watching.

It occurred to her to call Jenny into the room and seek her advice, but having lied to Baxter about the notebook, she didn't want her daughter involved in the lie.

Like the methodical detective she was, she had written down the attempts, starting with the names 'Jenny', 'Jennifer', their marriage date, Jenny's birth date, her own name and birth date, Peter's birth date and the list went on for another twelve attempts.

Frustrated at her failure, she tossed the notebook onto a pillow and lay on her back across the width of the bed, her legs dangling over the side and again wondered why she had lied to Baxter. It would have been so much easier to have surrendered the notebook and told Laura Scott: 'Here, take the thing. Get it out of my house and if you find anything, so be it. But if you do find something incriminating, tell my husband when he's found he's not to come home!'

Tears of self-pity bit at her eyes and fought in vain to stop herself from crying out loud. She grabbed the other pillow and sobbed into it, her body shaking as the tears overtook her and fearful lest Jenny in her room heard her mother wailing.

At last, after several minutes, she calmed down, surprised that the burst of emotion had somehow seemed to clear her mind, even made her feel a little less tense.

Peter, where are you, she wondered for the umpteenth time, her gaze falling on the fitted wardrobes.

With a massive sigh, she tossed the pillow away from her and for the second time in as many days, got off the bed and began a methodical search of her husband's clothing and his cabinet drawers.

In the rear garden of the detached chalet bungalow in the small, privately owned housing development at Scotstoun, Harry McPherson perspired and toiled with the lawnmower as sun finally broke through an overcast sky and cast a glow across the faraway hills and Clydebank and the surrounding area.

Harry's arrival at the house earlier that morning had been less than welcoming; he pretending to have just arrived home from a busy overnight session at the bank and found her nursing her whining baby and demanding to know why, when she called the bank through the night, there was no reply nor any reply from his mobile phone. "Don't you check the fucking thing at all?" she had shouted at him. "What if something happens with the baby?" she had accusingly screamed at him and then finally, "Why don't you care about *me* anymore?"

Never an adept or credible liar, he had blustered that the switchboard was not being manned, that he had left his mobile phone in his jacket pocket in the cloakroom, that it was a mere handful of employees who were assisting the Personnel Director, Mister Brewster and Harry with the ongoing inquiry into the theft by that bastard Peter Gibson!

He suddenly found his voice raised, angry that he was being interrogated and that set off the baby again, who wailed at the noise. He had stood there shaking, fists clenched, watching his wife walk off and hushing the baby to quieten her.

He had tired of his wife Tracey's abusive language and screams of hatred and now she sat fuming and withdrawn inside the darkened house with their baby child.

How he had gotten himself trapped into such a loveless marriage he would never understand.

Tracey had at first been an amusing creature, alluring and always flirting with him when he made a purchase in the small shop where she worked as an assistant, permitting him just a glimpse of her deep and full cleavage, then luring him into their first date. He had bedded her that first night, amazed at her insatiable sexual appetite that blinded him to her marital ambition.

His parents, affluent through their own business acumen, had warned him that marrying such a vulgar, coarse young woman would end in tears. He already knew, but never disclosed to his parents of her family history of drink and domestic violence, of a father-in-law who had a criminal past and, Harry suspected, continued to be involved in crime. It would be alien to his parents, mixing with such a family. He had quickly come to regret that he paid heed to their warnings and now, to his regret, Harry wished he *had* listened.

He pushed savagely at the lawnmower, growing increasingly frustrated, feeling angry, forever trapped in a loveless marriage. The romance had lasted a mere three months and then the shocking news. If only the stupid bitch hadn't got herself pregnant, he thought. Tight-lipped, he shook his head as though to clear it.

He stopped and glanced at the rear of the house, at the overflowing bin Tracey had again forgotten to put out onto the pavement for the Friday morning collection. He snorted at the weeds that grew between the flagstones because she can't be arsed getting herself to do at least *something* in the garden. At the bedroom windows where the dirt streaks clearly showed in the sunlight, his glance taking in the untidy bundle of gardening tools; the garden shears, the little used shiny handled small axe, the hoe and the spade and the rake, all lying in an untidy heap in a corner with the metal showing signs of surface rust; then finally at the fence that needed painting and was leaning over into the garden where an upright post had broken at the base.

He sighed, a deeply unhappy sigh and realised that his hesitancy in answering Morven's question had been a mistake; a huge mistake.

'Will you leave your dowdy little wife for me, Harry?' she had asked of him.

Standing there in his garden, right there and then, he glanced about him and grimly smiled.

Yes, he had made a mistake, but it was a mistake that he would now put right.

There was nothing here to keep him anymore.

Yes Morven, he thought and unconsciously nodded, I *will* leave my wife for you.

CHAPTER 22

ACC Jonathon MacPhail sat behind his large, ornate desk studying the brief report that lay before him and contained the synopsis of the accident that had occurred, the accident that claimed the lives of two young men and injured a third man.

Detective Chief Superintendent Frankie Johnson sat silently with Lynn Massey waiting for MacPhail to finish. Johnson, his legs crossed in front of him was informally dressed in a black coloured polo shirt, navy blue corduroy trousers and a pair of old walking shoes, simply because he had been quickly summoned from his favourite armchair, two bacon rolls and a mug of tea. Lynn Massey, he saw was her usual smartly dressed self, wearing a navy blue trouser suit with not a hair out of place and sat demurely, her ankles crossed and legs bent back beneath her chair. He was impatient, anxious for MacPhail to get a move on and for the sad news to be broken to Missus Ahmed before the media went calling on her and intruding, causing her more grief.

The door knocked and MacPhail sharply called out, "Come!"

DI Bobby Franklin, with hesitancy in his eyes, opened the door. Massey stood, greeting him with a smile.

Introducing Franklin to a bemused MacPhail, she explained, "DI Franklin was DC Ahmed and Constable Mooney's immediate line manager, sir. I thought it appropriate that he be present when you make your decision as to which officers will call at their homes to break the news."

"Good idea, Lynn," Johnson quickly added and nodded, throwing his support behind her decision.

It was evident from his scowl that MacPhail didn't agree, but realised that this wasn't the time to question his senor management's decision. However, he wasn't a man to forget.

"Yes, well, take a seat DI Franklin," he idly waved at a chair, pretending to concentrate on the report. Then, taking a deep breath as though the very thought of relating such a tragic accident moved him, MacPhail opened with a brief summary of the circumstances of the collision. As he continued he related the opinion of the attending Traffic Inspector whose initial findings, based on witness statements, seemed to indicate the fault lay with the deceased van driver. He again glanced at the paperwork in front of him and said, as if by way of explanation, "It seems that the driver of the van drove his vehicle at excess speed through a roundabout and collided with the CID car."

He turned towards Johnson and said, "Needless to say, Mister Johnson, as there is a police vehicle involved, I will as a matter of routine instruct a representative from the Police Standards Unit to oversee the inquiry to reassure public opinion that we will *not* cover up any alleged failings by the police vehicle's driver or the passenger."

"You are talking about my *dead* officer Waseem Ahmed and my *injured* officer, Des Mooney," interrupted Franklin, his face pale and voice coldly brittle with emotion.

Johnson and Massey were aghast that MacPhail could be so coldblooded and particularly as the initial report seemed to clear Mooney of any wrongdoing; nor did it escape their attention that Franklin's fists were clenched and he seemed to be leaning ever so slightly towards MacPhail's desk.

"I'm sure that you know I meant no offence, DI Franklin," MacPhail soothingly replied, but unable to tear his eyes away from the large and bulky man who now stood almost over him.

A tense silence followed, broken when Johnson said, "Perhaps we should hurry things along, sir. It will be entirely inappropriate if Missus Ahmed should hear of her husband's demise from anyone other than the police."

"Agreed," snapped MacPhail, breaking eye contact with Franklin. "If you, Mister Johnson should visit Missus Ahmed…"

"I'm not exactly dressed to make such a call, sir," interrupted Johnson, indicating with his hand his casual attire.

"Ah, yes, of course," and turned towards Massey. "Then perhaps, Missus Massey you and DI Franklin might be better suited to inform Missus Ahmed. Yes," he nodded, "I think it will be better if a woman were present, don't you agree?"

Massey shrugged and nodded, too upset to argue with him and turning towards Franklin, indicated with her eyes that they should leave.

"What about you sir, what's your plans?" asked Johnson.

"Ah, I'll attend at the hospital," he smiled at Johnson, "the Victoria Infirmary according to the report here, and check on the injured officer, Constable Mooney."

"Right then," replied Johnson and turning in his seat, asked Massey and Franklin to wait for a few minutes while he spoke with them.

In the corridor outside, Johnson wished them luck with Missus Ahmed and agreed to have a family liaison officer meet them at Ahmed's home address.

"After I've done that, Bobby," he laid his hand on the DI's shoulder, "I'll scoot off down to Cranstonhill and speak with your team. I imagine they'll be in a bit of a state. It's not easy losing one of our own."

"Thanks, Frankie," Franklin nodded his appreciation and left with Massey to carry out their onerous task.

Johnson was about to push open the slightly ajar door to MacPhail's office when he heard the ACC on the phone and hesitated. As he listened, he heard MacPhail speaking on the phone, guessing it was the Duty Inspector at the control room. It went against Johnson's nature to eavesdrop, but on this occasion he had no qualms about quietly standing near to the partially open door.

"Yes, yes, Inspector," he heard MacPhail say, "and if the media *do* contact you, please inform them that I am attending at the Victoria Infirmary where I should be in a better position to personally update them regarding the circumstances. Is that understood?"

Hearing MacPhail replacing the handset, Johnson stepped through the door, pretending that he hadn't heard MacPhail and said, "Right sir, I'll be off. I'm going down to the incident room at Cranstonhill to speak with the colleagues of DC Ahmed and Constable Mooney and reassure them of our support. I assume that you will be calling by after you have attended the hospital?"

MacPhail could feel that golf game slipping away even further and tightly smiling, nodded.

Johnson made to turn towards the door, but stopped and said, "Oh, and one further thing, sir. I'm guessing the press will be all over this, so I'll contact the control room and have them direct all inquiries towards the media department. After all," he paused and smiled without a trace of guile, "that's their job, isn't it?"

Walking through the office towards his car parked in the basement garage, a tight lipped Johnson had one thought; that MacPhail was a devious bastard worth the watching.

Morven Sutherland, dressed in grey coloured sweat top, loose sweatpants and padded gloves, her hair tied back and skin glistening with perspiration after her hour long kick-boxing workout in the basement gym, glanced at the mobile phone screen and smiled.

"So, Harry," she murmured with a smile as she stripped off her clothing, "you've come to your senses, have you?"

She kicked the sweaty clothing into a pile and lifting them, dumped them into the wicker-basket and then turned towards the en-suite shower.

Turning the tap to cold she stepped into the cubicle and gasped as the needle shower lashed at her skin, shivering as her warm body adjusted to the cold.

She was well aware of the effect she had on Harry McPherson and the desire he had for her.

With that thought in mind, she reached for her scented body lotion and began to softly caress her skin with the lotion, experiencing a sensual pleasure when running her hands across her body.

In her mind she had already chosen the outfit she would wear when she greeted him; something light and see though, but would not tear when he tore the clothes from her. She grinned; men were so predictable and could be such little boys at times.

Lathering her body she thought about his visit. According to his text message, he would be arriving in a little over an hour and, she sighed, it would be a busy couple of hours for her, after that.

But in the long term, she inwardly grinned, it was going to be worth it.

She stepped from the shower and dried her body with the rough cotton towel and still completely naked, lifted one foot onto the wicker basket and with a rhythmic motion, began to smooth her favourite aromatic skin lotion onto her, strong, slim legs, but all the while her mind contemplated her future.

When he arrived, poor Harry was in for the surprise of his life; something he would never expect. And after she told him, all she had to do was reel him in and he was hers.

For after all, she smiled to herself, look what she was about to offer him.

The tired and irritable Staff Nurse working early shift in the casualty department of the Victoria Infirmary in Glasgow's south side and dressed in her hospital uniform that included a plastic apron and sterile gloves, pulled aside the curtain to permit the doctor to leave.

The nurse was having a bad day.

Her flatmate had just phoned to admit he had *again* lost the front door key and to tell her the bloody cat had peed on the new lounge rug and, to top it all, the Ward Sister extended her shift for four hours because the fat cow who was *supposed* to be on late shift had *again* gone down with her mystery illness that *always* seemed to occur after a Saturday night out on the town.

The nurse bent over the patient, a detective who was the victim of a road traffic accident, she had been told and who now lay unconscious on the bed.

Though clearly not awake, the nurse had softly spoken to him, explaining what she was doing while she methodically cleaned the dried blood from his face and head and tenderly treated the abrasions and cuts as best she could while she waited for that lazy pair of skiving porters who were *supposed* to be here ten minutes ago to convey the patient to the X-Ray Department.

The curtain was pulled aside and a tall man in a suit stood there, smiling.

"I'm looking for Constable Mooney," he peered at the unconscious officer and then with recognition, his expression changed to one of distaste and he hissed, "*Mooney!*"

The nurse, startled, asked, "Sorry, you are?"

"I'm Assistant Chief Constable MacPhail," he officiously said, then added with a nod towards Mooney, "this officer's boss."

Had MacPhail been more attentive to the nurse, he might have noticed her rebellious eyes and the tightly grim set mouth, but unfortunately for him, he was too preoccupied staring at the unconscious Mooney.

"But you're not a doctor or nurse?" she slowly, but firmly asked. Believing his rank and status to be sufficient, he utterly underestimated his authority.

"No, as I said…" he started, only to be sharply interrupted by the nurse who said, "In that case, please leave immediately. You are in a casualty ward, not a police station," and taking a step back, with a curl to her lip, added, "and God alone knows *what* infection you might have brought in with you."

MacPhail blinked and blinked again. "Now look here…." was all he managed before being interrupted by a stern faced Sister who, with raised eyebrows and hands neatly folded in front of her, suddenly appeared from behind him and asked, "Problem, Staff?"

"No, Sister. This gentleman was just leaving while I treat my patient."

MacPhail stared from one to the other and had the good sense not to argue with the martinet Sister. Turning on his heel, he mustered what dignity remained and angrily stomped off towards the waiting room. "Management, they're the same all over. Give the buggers an inch," said the Sister, shaking her head and then with a sneaky grin, added, "Carry on Staff."

DS Laura Scott turned towards Arlene Baxter, her face registering the shock they both felt at the news.

The staff sat or stood about in the incident room, alone or in two's and three's, but each individual lost in his or her own thoughts. Scott and Baxter felt like interlopers, present in the room because they worked for DSU Massey, yet not quite part of this tight-knit group of divisional detectives and civilian staff.

"I'll get us a coffee," said Baxter, not really wanting one, but needing something to do. Scott walked with her to the table and sat on a vacant chair by the table that held the makings. "Do you know if he was married or single?" she asked.

Baxter shook her head. "I only saw the guy here at briefings and," she was a little embarrassed as she lowered her voice, "I only recognise the name because DC Ahmed was the only Asian guy working on the inquiry. Des Mooney," she shrugged her shoulders, "I don't know at all and right now I have to admit I can't put a face to the name."

"Me neither," admitted Scott with a shake of her head then added, "but bloody hell. A young guy wiped out, just like that? Doesn't bear thinking about," she shook her head.

"I had a word earlier in the toilets with that analyst there," Baxter discreetly nodded towards a middle-aged woman being comforted by a younger colleague while she quietly wept into her handkerchief. "She says Ahmed was married with a young daughter. She liked him, told me that he never passed her by without a smile or a wee chat. Just a nice guy, she said."

"His poor bloody wife," replied Scott, and then got to her feet when the door opened to admit Frankie Johnson.

"Hello folks," he called out, his voice grave, but loud enough to attract the room's attention. "If you could gather round please and I'll tell you what I know so far."

He took a deep breath then related the scant information that had been passed to the ACC and told them that DI Franklin had accompanied DSU Massey to break the news to Waz Ahmed's wife. His widow now, Scott inwardly thought, unconsciously reaching for her throat and caught up in the emotion of the moment. Her lips trembled and she was a little uncertain why she was blinking back tears.

Des Mooney, Johnson continued, was being treated at the Victoria Hospital over on the south side of the city and though his injuries were not known, what was known is that they were not life-threatening.

"Now," Johnson stood with his hands on his hips and licked at his lips, "I guess you'll think I'm a heartless bugger for saying this and that you think in light of the circumstances I should be sending you all home." He paused and stared round the room, then shook his head. "But I'm not going to do that, ladies and gentlemen," he softly said, "for I don't want anyone here going home to an empty house or taking this awful news back to their loved ones. The death of Waseem Ahmed is the worst of news, but I am confident that we will get past this terrible day. Keeping you all here to work through this day isn't about the current inquiry, it's about keeping you here as a group, as colleagues and friends who worked with and knew him well, who can talk about him as the day progresses. Who will support each other because you all," he pointed his finger in an arc, encompassing the room, "you all liked him. It's evident from the depth of feeling I get standing here that he was one of you, one of the team; so, as a team, you *will* get past this," he repeated, then added, "*we* will get past this."

He took a deep breath and with a soft smile towards DS Emma Ferguson then said, loud enough for all to hear, "I'm reliably informed there's a roll shop just opposite the Tesco down the road there, Emma. I think you and I will take a wee walk down there and we'll get lunch for the team, eh?"

"As for the rest of you," he turned to the group, "relax for the minute and once we've all had something to eat and a cuppa, we'll continue to do what young Waz Ahmed and Des Mooney and you guys set out to do; we'll get back to work and find ourselves a killer."

The engine remained switched off as Lynn Massey sat motionless in the driver's seat of her own vehicle with Bobby Franklin sitting silently beside her.

They had left the much experienced family liaison officer, a female cop with over twenty years service, upstairs with the distraught Alima Ahmed and her child. The cop was on the phone as they were leaving, calling Missus Ahmed's parents with the request that they get to the flat as soon as they possibly could, that their daughter urgently needed them.

After they delivered the news, the cop had politely but firmly ushered Massey and Franklin from the flat, assuring them that their presence was no longer needed, that they leave and permit her to do her job.

They didn't argue, both uncertain why, but keenly eager to depart. Sitting in the vehicle, they reflected that during their respective careers they had on several occasions delivered death messages. Sometimes the families were shocked and immediately begun the grieving process, while on the odd occasion they were greeted by indifference to the passing of a family member. On the journey to deliver the bad news to Alima Ahmed, Massey admitted that she had not previously informed the spouse or parents of a colleague's bereavement.

"Me neither," a disconsolate Franklin shook his head, "and by God, I never realised how difficult it would be."

At last, Massey inhaled and reached for the key to start the engine, then with a quick glance over her shoulder, pulled away from the kerb.

The man dressed in wellington boots, a green coloured wax jacket, faded jeans and cloth cap opened the boot lid of the old and battered Vauxhall Cavalier estate car and grinned as the lively Border collie leapt down and began to run excitedly about the grassy area, barking her joy at being released from the confinement of the vehicle.

He reached into the driver's door and from the passenger seat, fetched the plastic carrier bag and took out the tennis ball and then stretching back his arm, threw the ball in a high curve towards the River Clyde.

The ball landed among the high reeds on the waste ground near to the small piers that jutted out into the water, but was almost immediately snatched up into the jaws of the dog that returned and dropped the ball at the man's feet, then with pride at her recovery, immediately sat down in front of him.

The man smiled at the small dog and glanced towards the ruins of Dunglass Castle to his left, his eyes narrowing at the skyline collision of the Henry Bell tower against the ruins of the fifteenth century castle.

"Might be worth a photie, eh lass?" he smiled at the dog and from his pocket, withdrew a small, but expensive digital camera.

While he steadied himself to take the photograph the dog ran off towards the piers, barking excitedly.

"Bugger will fall in again if she's not careful," he sighed and shook his head as he saw her edge out onto a rickety wooden structure, so old it seemed in danger of collapsing even beneath the little dog's weight.

He quickly made his way towards her, fearful lest the wee dog topple over for he knew that despite her brave bark, she had a terrible fear of the dark and treacherous water.

As he approached, the dog ignored him, her head bent down as she stared into the water below and her tail between her legs. Her barking had now curiously turned to a quiet whimper while her body began to shiver.

"What is it that's fretting you, you silly girl," he teased the small dog as he took her collar in his fingers and pulling her back from the edge of the pier, cautiously leaned over to see what had upset her.

"Oh my God, oh Jesus," he mumbled, then pulling the dog forcibly towards the parked car fifty yards away, stumbled across the uneven ground while fumbling with trembling fingers in his pocket for his mobile phone.

Beneath the pier, arms lazily outstretched as though in supplication, the body floating face down gently rose and fell with the swell of the water.

CHAPTER 23

In the corridor outside the incident room, Laura Scott approached Frankie Johnson and asked, "Sir, do you know if DSU Massey will be returning to the office today?"

He smiled and narrowing his eyes as he stared at her, replied, "Sorry, the face is familiar, but your name again?"

"DS Laura Scott, sir," she replied. "The reason I'm asking is…"

"You're the lassie Lynn's always going on about," he interrupted and then guffawed, "I hear your Department has nicknamed you the *happy, hippy fraudie*, am I right?"

Scott blushed and tolerantly grinned as she nodded, surprised when he clapped a hand on her shoulder and guiding her into Bobby Franklin's office, still smiling bade her take a seat while he sat behind the desk in Franklin's chair.

"So, eh, Laura you said?"

She nodded.

"So then Laura, what's this about?" he sat easily in the chair, his full concentration on the young and to his mind, oddly dressed Detective Sergeant, but from what he had heard of this young woman, was wise enough not to let her appearance deceive him.

"Are you aware sir, that DSU Massey set me the task of trying to find out how the missing banker Peter Gibson managed to commit the fraud against his bank?"

"Aye, you mean DS Gibson's husband. I recall meeting him once at a CID dinner dance," he nodded thoughtfully. "Tall, lanky guy and seemed a decent type as I recall. His wife, Susie Gibson," he pursed his lips in thought. "She's a good cop, a good, hardworking and tenacious detective."

He nodded as he stared at Scott. "Lynn did tell me that she had somebody checking the bank's files so I assume because you hijacked me in the corridor, you have something to report, Laura?"

Scott leaned forward, then hesitated, slightly uncertain and asked, "Is it appropriate to give my initial report to you sir, or should I wait for DSU Massey to return?"

"DSU Massey's here, Laura," said the tired sounding voice behind her.

Massey, with Bobby Franklin standing slightly behind her, stood in the doorway.

"Laura," said Johnson, "grab yourself a coffee in the incident room will you and give us a couple of minutes. We'll call you through and you can update us all when we've had a wee chat," he nodded towards Massey and Franklin.

When Scott had left the room and the others seated in the two available chairs, he asked how it went with Missus Ahmed, almost immediately regretting his question that he followed with, "Stupid of me. How else could it go," he shook his head.

"I take it that there is someone with Missus Ahmed when you left?"

"The police family liaison officer was there," replied Massey, "a Constable from the local division. She seemed a very competent woman."

"From the way she dismissed us two, I don't think that's any doubt of *that*," interjected Franklin, but without any malice in his voice. Massey smiled and nodding her head, continued. "The FLO was on the phone when we left, speaking with Missus Ahmed's parents. As far as we're aware, they're on their way round to the flat. The FLO was also going to contact the local doctor, just in case Missus Ahmed needs any kind of sedative. She won't leave Missus Ahmed till she is sure that the poor young woman won't be left on her own."

"Any word yet on Des Mooney?" asked Franklin.

"I called the casualty at the Viccy fifteen minutes ago," said Johnson. "He's got a suspected broken lower right leg, likely has damage to his ribs, torn muscles in his right shoulder and multiple cuts and abrasions on his right side, presumably from the car being overturned and bounced onto the driver's side, but he was still unconscious when I phoned. The nurse I spoke with said the attending doctor had arranged a CAT scan, so," he glanced at the wall clock, "I presume that's being done as we speak." He spread his hands out and added, "Just a matter of time, waiting to find out what's happening now, I suppose. I left the phone number here on your desk with the hospital Bobby, should there be any change in Mooney's condition."

"Oh, and one other thing," he continued speaking to Franklin, "the Chief intends visiting the incident room some time this afternoon. I've asked that he gives us a heads up before he arrives; the opportunity to gather all the staff to be present. He asked about calling in on Missus Ahmed and visiting Des Mooney, but I've suggested that we wait a day or two before he calls upon her and visits young Mooney, if that's agreeable with you, Bobby?"

"Whatever you think best, boss."

The phone on Franklin's desk rang and Johnson nodded that the DI take the call.

They watched as Franklin listened, saw him nod and heard him say with a smile, "Thanks, nurse, yeah. That's a relief. Aye, it is good news, eh? Thanks again, nurse," then return the phone to its cradle.

"The hospital," he nodded towards the phone and exhaled with relief. "The nurse says that Des is awake and fully conscious. Initial assessment by the doctor is that there is no head trauma, other than the obvious lacerating injuries, but they're not too serious and should heal within a week or two if he takes care of them."

"What family has Mooney got and have they been told?" asked Johnson.

"Des was widowed a number of years ago, now. I know he has two grown-up kids, a boy and a girl. The girl's a serving soldier and could be anywhere and the lad, I think he's working in London somewhere, but I'm not certain. I'll contact HR and try to get contact numbers for them to let them know about Des."

"He's no significant other half then?" asked Massey.

"Significant other half?" chortled Johnson. "In my day the *other half* was called your bird."

"In your day you hunted women with clubs," retorted Massey.

Franklin grinned. "To know Des is to love him. He was a bit of a lad when he was younger and I heard he treated every woman like a challenge. Settled down apparently when he got married, but the wife died, though I'm not sure of the circumstances and though if I recall correctly there was some family pressures to have them live with his in-laws, he kept the kids." He shook his head and continued, "Des might have gone further in the job; he's certainly smart enough, but stayed at the constable rank because it suited his domestic life, having the children to care for I mean. As for someone in his life right now," he shook his head, "I don't know anything about that, but I'll speak with his Sergeant, Archie Cuthbertson. However, if you want my guess, no; I don't think there's another half, right now.

"Has he been told about Waz Ahmed?" asked Massey.

Franklin shook his head. "I don't know and didn't think to ask," his eyes narrowed. "Maybe I should go over there…"

"No, Bobby," Johnson began to rise from his chair, "I'll go. I doubt that Mister MacPhail will still be there and I'd rather Mooney didn't hear it from the hospital staff. It should be one of us that break the news. Also, it's important that you and Lynn are here with the team, particularly when the Chief arrives."

He walked to the door, but then turned. "Oh, there's just one more thing Lynn. DS Scott has an update regarding the fraud at the bank. I asked that you were present for her update, so you can fill me in later. I'll send her along if you're ready?"

"Okay, Frankie. Good luck with Des Mooney."

He nodded and closed the door behind him.

The attending officers from the local Dumbarton Division had sealed off the area with blue and white plastic police tape around the pier where the body floated underneath. The senior officer, a portly uniformed Inspector, wisely decided it was too risky having his own officers try to remove the body from the water, worried that if any fell in, the possibility of catching some God awful disease from the black, oily water was too risky. Instead, he called for assistance from the police Marine and Underwater Unit based in Greenock, across the wide expanse of the Clyde River.

A little over an hour later, the Marine Unit sergeant and four of his available eleven constables, all called out from their homes, arrived to find that the first constable reacting to the dog walkers frantic 999 call had resourcefully procured a length of rope and with some difficulty, lassoed the arm of the floating body to prevent the tide from carrying it away, then tied the rope to an old, rusting metal ring set into the pier.

Attaching their hoist equipment to the tail hook on their six-wheeled van, the sergeant and his men, with some difficulty, managed to raise the body from the oily waters and convey the body over the waste ground to a white forensic tent and laid the sodden body on a large sheet of plastic laid out inside the tent.

The on-call police casualty surgeon, wearing a forensic suit and tight-fighting rubber gloves, knelt low over the body, his opening remarks being, "Well, the poor chap hasn't been too long in the water, I'd say. Maybe a day at the very most but if you want my humble opinion," he glanced up at the Inspector, bent over him, "a matter of hours."

The doctor lifted the dead man's hand and remarked, "You can see the skin is reasonably smooth. I'd expect if he *had* been much longer in the water, there would be at least some wrinkling of the skin and the commencement of bloating. No," he sighed and shook his head, "this man has been in the water for a very short time."

"The tides on the wane," said the Inspector, standing straight and arching his back against the dull ache that had persisted in the last few months, "so I'm thinking he likely entered the water upriver."

"Possibly," agreed the doctor with a nod. "Anyway, Inspector, I'm confirming life extinct and of course, the post mortem will determine cause of death though I'm inclined to think," his eyes narrowing as he turned the body towards the Inspector and wiped with a glove hand at the mud adhering to the hair, "that this large wound at the back of his head *might* be of interest to your colleagues in the CID."

"Oh," replied the Inspector, the ache in his back gone as he bent to take a closer look at the large gash. "My, my, I didn't see *that* when we took him from the water."

He paused with a thoughtful look and continued, "It would be helpful if we could identify him sooner than later. I don't suppose the CID will have any objection to me rifling his jacket pockets."

"Here, let me," replied the doctor, noticing the way the Inspector stood favouring his left side and acutely aware that the portly Inspector might be suffering a back condition and thus have some difficulty getting down onto his knees in the cramped space of the tent.

Gingerly, the doctor opened the dead man's sports suit jacket and withdrew a brown leather wallet that he handed to the Inspector who also wearing forensic gloves, opened and withdrew from within a plastic card that bore a photograph.

The Inspector glanced at the dead man and showed the photographic card to the doctor.

"Seems our man here was a banker then," sighed the Inspector, reading the small writing on the card, "says here he worked for the Caledonia Banking Group."

Frankie Johnson, driving his youngest daughter's old, beat-up Ford Fiesta while his wife commandeered his larger car to convey some of her elderly parishioners to church that morning, slowed to turn into the already crowded casualty department car park, but slammed on the brakes and with a sharp breath, involuntarily cried out,

"Bloody hell!" when a glistening black coloured four by four was driven at speed out from the car park.

The female driver, wearing dark glasses and her red hair tied up in an untidy bun, hardly glanced at the road as with a squeal of tyres, the vehicle joined the traffic and sped away to the obvious irritation of a motorist who was like Johnson, forced to come to a dead stop to avoid colliding with the large vehicle.

Johnson shook his head and exhaling at the near miss and with a little more attention to his own driving, drove into the car park and with good fortune, found an empty space.

The young casualty Staff Nurse was immediately charmed by the courteous, older and casually dressed man with the ready smile who politely asked after Mister Mooney, his injured officer.

Granting him a five minute visit, the nurse led him to the cubicle where he found Des Mooney propped up on some pillows, using his good hand to hold a plastic beaker from which he sipped water through a straw.

Before pulling the curtains closed to allow them some privacy, the nurse with a smile asked Johnson if he would like a cup of tea, thinking to herself it was an offer she wouldn't have considered making to that other police officer with the uppity attitude.

"Here, let me son," said Johnson, assisting Mooney to sit up even further and didn't miss the grimace as the younger man shifted in the bed to a more comfortable position.

"Thanks, sir. The nurse told me that there was another boss here, but she didn't catch his name. I must have been well out of it at the time," said Des.

"Aye, ACC MacPhail called by earlier to see how you were, but he's had to return to Pitt Street to deal with the media regarding…." he stopped and sighed heavily, then turned and drew a plastic chair towards the bed, the metal framed legs scraping nosily on the linoleum.

"Des," he sat down and slowly began, "do you have any recollection of what happened, son?"

Mooney, tight-lipped, shook his head. "All I remember was driving down the road and then," he paused, "nothing," and shrugged or as much as his injured body would permit him to do.

Johnson cleared his throat and said, "There was a collision between your car and a van. It seems that from the statements the cops at the locus took, the van sped through the roundabout when you were on it and struck your car, side on." He took a deep breath. "I'm very, very sorry, Des, but young Waseem Ahmed was killed. As far as we can tell, he died almost immediately from injuries that he suffered. I'm sorry," he repeated.

Mooney could only stare at him, the shock of the news registered on his face. His eyes welled up and his head bowed as he stared at the blankets in front of him. He took a deep breath and asked, "Does his wife know? Christ, I can't even remember the poor lassie's name."

"Here we go then," the curtain was pulled back and the young nurse stood there, a cup of tea on a saucer held in her other hand. She realised almost immediately she had interrupted something, something that caused her patient to be so sad and with a nervous smile, handed Johnson the tea and left, pulling the curtain back into place.

Johnson carefully laid the cup and saucer on the bedside cabinet and said, "Her name's Alima and yes, Lynn Massey and Bobby Franklin visited her to break the news earlier this morning. They took an FLO with them and she's staying with Missus Ahmed for now, or at least till her parents get there."

He didn't think it necessary to add that Missus Ahmed was so distraught that the FLO also arranged for the family doctor to attend to the young woman.

They sat for a few minutes in silence while Mooney composed himself. Finally, he asked, "The van driver, what about him? It was a guy, yeah?"

Johnson nodded and replied, "Also killed at the scene."

"Fucking deserves it!" Mooney spat out with no hint of sympathy in his voice, still too upset at the loss of his young neighbour to even consider the other fatal casualty.

Johnson wisely said nothing, but then said, "You realise that once you're back on your feet, the Traffic will want to interview you?"

"Not much I can tell them, but yeah, that won't be a problem boss."

"Good man. The important thing is to get you well, first." Then he asked, "Your own injuries Des, have they said anything about you?"

Mooney slowly exhaled and replied, "The CAT scan apparently came back positive and yes sir, before you ask," he softly smiled, "I do have a brain. Other than that, broken right leg, some pulled muscle in my right shoulder, multiple contusions to my right side and head, as you can see," he waved at the sticking plasters and bandage about his head, "and two cracked ribs that they're leaving alone to heal themselves. My hand is cut," he held it up, "but apparently just superficial. Might be off for about a week, boss," he attempted a weak grin at his humour, but winced as his ribs reminded him of his injury.

"What, a full week?" Johnson raised his eyebrows. "The nurse told me you would be fit for duty tomorrow?"

Mooney smiled, not risking any further movement and sighed.

"Truth is the doc suggested that once I get my leg plastered, he said if I can cope with crutches, they're going to let me out either tomorrow or the following day."

"So soon?" Johnson was visibly taken aback.

"It's the way it is, boss. If the hospital can free up a bed they'll do so and besides, there's less risk of infection if I'm at home," he sighed. Johnson shook his head.

"Speaking of which, Des, I'm not being nosey, but you're one of my guys so I *do* have a responsibility for your well-being. Is there anyone at home to care for you when you are discharged? I know that you've got two grown-up kids, but I understand they are both working away. You might also need to know that I made arrangements through our HR people to inform them of your accident," and forestalling Mooney's complaint, added, "its protocol, son. The police, as your employer, have a duty for your welfare and to inform your next-of-kin of any life threatening injuries you might have suffered and by God you came very, very close. Don't worry though, your son and daughter is being told your simply swinging the lead," he grinned. "Now, about you getting out of here? What arrangements can I make for you?"

"Thanks, but I can cope, boss. I'm on a ground floor flat over in Pollokshields. Once I'm in and through the door, I'll be fine, honest. My son works down south in Bristol. He's in IT and my daughter's serving in the army. She's in Afghanistan right now, nursing at the base camp in Camp Bastion."

"Pity she's not back here nursing her poor old dad," Johnson grinned at him.

The curtain was pulled back and the same nurse, a little more hesitant, reminded Johnson that his five minutes were up and then smiled when she saw that on this occasion, the two men seemed a little more jovial.

Johnson stood and gently laid his hand on Mooney's shoulder. "Needless to say, Bobby Franklin will be in touch as will the welfare people, so you're not going to be left alone. Stand on me regarding that. Besides, I hear you're a popular man so likely the nursing staff here will be fending off all sorts of inquiries and visitors for you." He turned towards the young Staff Nurse and said, "Right hen, lead on," and with a wink at Mooney, followed the young nurse through the curtain towards the Nurses Station.

"My lad there," he cocked a thumb over his shoulder, "says the doctor might discharge him today or tomorrow, nurse. Once my people have a time and date, I'll make an arrangement to have him uplifted and taken home from here. One other thing; Mister Mooney has two children, but his son is working away in England and his daughter, apparently she's a nurse too," he smiled, "but she's with the army in Afghanistan. Likely they'll phone asking after him and it's more than likely you might expect to receive a large number of calls from friends, maybe some visitors too."

"Oh, his wife has already been in."

"His wife?" replied Jonson.

The surprise must have shown on his face, for the nurse, clearly embarrassed and worried she might have been indiscreet, continued, "Well, I assumed it was his wife or maybe his girlfriend. A slightly younger woman she was and good looking too. Red hair tied in a bun."

The nurse wondered if she had said too much, then explained, "The reason I *thought* she was his wife or his girlfriend was because she was a little upset and they seemed very close," not wishing to disclose that the woman had cried and held the patients hand and repeatedly kissed him.

"She didn't stay too long and left just before you got here," her voice trailed off. She swallowed with difficulty and in a low voice, asked, "I haven't said anything out of turn, have I?"

"No," he smiled and patted her arm to put her at ease, "I hear that Des has always been a bit of a dark horse, so you mind yourself round about him," he winked, then conspiratorially added, "but regarding the woman, I think we'll keep that between us, eh?"

"Aye, of course," she replied with some relief.

It was while he walked towards his daughter's old car that he remembered the large, black coloured four by four that almost run into him and the red-haired driver with the dark glasses.

Laura Scott sat in front of Bobby Franklin's desk facing the DI, with DSU Massey sitting to her left. Pulling her laptop from her cavernous shoulder bag, she sat the machine on the desk in front of her beside her cooling cup of coffee and switched it on. That done, she scrolled to the page of bullet points and prepared to deliver her speech.

"In furtherance of your instructions, Ma'am, what I've found is, in simple terms, a very complicated, but successful series of business loan applications culminating in the total acquisition by fraud of three million, two hundred and sixty thousand pounds sterling."

"Sterling, why do you say sterling?" asked Massey, her brow knitted in curiosity.

"Because once I converted the various currencies, that's what it amounts to," Scott replied, her voice inching a little higher as she grew more intense.

Clearly, thought Franklin as he stared at her, this young woman was a real take-on. Her dress style he inwardly admitted had thrown him at first, but her mind was as sharp as an open razor wielded in a Gorbal's gang fight.

"Right, Laura," he interrupted her and glanced at Massey, "I'm more of a slow-burner when it comes to fraud, so being an old guy, for my sake I'll be grateful if you keep it real simple. Lay man's terms, so to speak."

"My thoughts exactly," nodded Massey and admitted, "I'm no great shakes at keeping *my* bank account in the black, so simple English please, Laura."

Scott nodded and began, but first cautioned them both, "If I sound like I'm delivering a school lesson here, please bear with me. It's the best way I can explain things."

She took a deep breath. "The Caledonian Banking Group is in the business of making money, none of this," and raising both hands in the air, her fingers making pretend italics, said, *"We're your friend* nonsense. It's a business, pure and simple and like any business, its there to make money. It takes risks, but," she stressed, *"calculated* risks. In short, the banking system ethos is that in order to make money; to accumulate you must first speculate. The way that banks accumulate and turn a profit is simply by investing or speculating in opportunities that present themselves. These opportunities in turn permit the bank to make that profit; hence first speculate then accumulate. Now as you are aware, we all use banks for a variety of purposes, whether it is simply a cheque or savings account, mortgage or loan account; whatever the account might be, whether it be for ten pounds or one million pounds, the bank will make a charge against the customer and thus turn a profit."

"Particularly when I get the red headed letter," Massey dryly observed.

"We've all been there, Ma'am," grinned Scott.

"Some of us with a spend-happy wife are *still* there," interjected Franklin. "My missus thinks her credit card is some sort of a high street challenge."

"Indeed," Scott continued to grin and then more soberly, continued. "So, as I was saying, when a bank is approached by a customer who wishes to borrow money, there is a number of procedures the bank *must* follow before making a decision as to whether that customer is a risk or more properly, a speculation worth considering. After all," she shrugged, "who in their right mind, bank or otherwise, would consider lending money to any individual that clearly will not or is unable to refund that money and more particularly, refund the money with a profit for the bank."

She paused for breath. "What I discovered when I researched the Caledonian Banking Group's lending procedures is that the bank has an *almost* foolproof system for lending money. Almost," she repeated, "for like most banks, the system is only as good as the banking personnel who operate the system and this is normally where the most reliable system for lending money kicks in; the human aspect."

"Now again as you will be aware, the bank like most large companies including ourselves the police, relies heavily today on IT computer systems and to protect it's investments, by that I mean its money, it installed a virtually foolproof method of checking and re-checking its accounts; simply put, when and where the money comes in from and when and where it goes out to. This IT computer system is itself protected from invasive interception by hackers and includes all sorts of safeguards, not least personal passwords that are unique and issued to each member of the bank's staff. Each password when used by the individual member of staff, I'm sure you will be aware, records when that individual member of staff logs onto the computer system, what programme in the system is accessed, how long the programme is accessed and what if any changes are made when the individual *is* logged on; for example, if credit or debits are made at that time the individual is logged on. In short, every time the system is accessed, the access is timed, dated and from what computer station the access is gained, yeah?"

Both Massey and Franklin nodded.

"Much the same as our own police IT systems and in common with other companies, it is forbidden for staff to share their unique passwords and is a disciplinary offence, totally against the bank's own policy on data protection. Excuse me," she said and took a sip of coffee.

"Still with me?" she glanced with a smile at them both and saw them nod, almost in unison.

"Now the bank, like other organisations, has a rank structure, therefore the more senior the member of staff is, the more programmes are available for that individual to access. Obviously it then follows that the more senior the individual, the greater autonomy that individual has in making decisions regarding money transactions without having to resort to seeking authorisation from a more senior bank official. That's why for example, a low level manager or supervisor can authorise a five grand loan for a car while a five million pound loan would require a couple of directors approval, if you follow me."

"In essence, a pyramid of fiscal responsibility?" asked Franklin.

"Exactly," Scott shook her head, "and yet, as I said before, for all their IT systems and safeguards the bank primarily relies upon the human aspect; those employees who are trusted to make decisions based upon their professionalism and their experience. Now," she paused and licked at her ruby red lipstick, "nearing the top of this pyramid is Peter Gibson who has been with the bank since he left school almost thirty-five years ago. According to his file, he worked his way up from a lowly clerical assistant through teller, accounts and one or two other departments until finally, arriving at the position he now holds or, I should say, held. Trusted and experienced enough to know the system inside out, he took full advantage…"

"Wait a minute Laura," interrupted Massey, leaning forward in her chair with one hand on the desk to support herself, her eyes suddenly bright, "are you telling us that you have proven Peter Gibson *did* commit the fraud?"

"Yes, Ma'am, according to my research and," she smiled, "I'm pretty good at research; yes, Gibson screwed the bank for all that money."

"You said earlier Laura, sterling; what did you mean by that?" asked Franklin.

Now buoyed and animated by her success, Scott continued, "Most of the business loans that Gibson authorised under dummy company names were local, here in the West of Scotland I mean and primarily in the greater Glasgow area. However, I found a couple of business loans that he authorised for premises in Spain using Glasgow based company names, the alleged reasons being that the dummy company's wanted to expand their export base."

"Why weren't these loans identified as false and why weren't they picked up? Surely there must be some sort of checks in place? I mean, for heaven's sake, Laura, it can't have been that bloody easy, can it?" asked Massey.

Scott shrugged and replied, "When you know the system Ma'am and the way round certain programmes, well, the proof's in the pudding, as they say. But Gibson had two advantages. The first was that he worked to a time scale. Every three months, the bank has regular auditing from a reputable independent company whose sole purpose is to identify any irregularities in accounting in the New Business Investments, Mortgage and Loans Department's, to give it its full title. My research indicates that Gibson commenced his *first* fraudulent transaction the day after the last audit concluded…"

"Giving him a three month window," murmured Massey.

"Exactly," nodded Scott.

"But surely he must have known that at the next audit, the frauds would be discovered?" said Franklin.

"I've no doubt of that," Scott quickly agreed, now leaning forward in her chair, her eyes bright, "but I'm of the opinion that it didn't matter, that by the time the next audit was due and that's *next week*," she pointedly told them, "then Gibson would have gone; flown the coop, so to speak. I'm guessing that he had the fraud already planned and set up, then simply waited for the last audit to conclude before he set his plan in play."

"Very apt, Laura, flown the coop right enough," nodded Massey, the unspoken reminder that Gibson's car had been discovered at Glasgow Airport. She turned towards Franklin, and said, "Digressing slightly, on that point Bobby, any word back from the Ports Control Unit at Glasgow regarding the CCTV there?"

"Not yet Ma'am," he replied, making a notation on the pad in front of him, "I'll get that chased up."

"So where has Gibson hidden it or have you traced the money, Laura?" she asked the younger woman.

"No Ma'am, sorry, not yet; I'm still working on it, but if you want my humble opinion, it's gone. I'm guessing again, but he's probably transferred the money through a couple of off-shore accounts and it's sitting in a lump sum somewhere with Gibson being the only account holder. If I were him," she sighed, "I'd have sent it to a Caribbean bank. Once there I would be able to access the funds from anywhere in the world using a ten digit numbered code and a unique password that would permit me to transfer the money again to an account of my choosing in any bank, anywhere in the world. Well, that's how I would do it," she added a little self-consciously.

"Worth keeping an eye on this one, boss," Franklin joked as he nodded to Scott.

"But wouldn't Gibson have had to *personally* open an account in a foreign bank? I mean, can an account be opened via the phone or an e-mail or by some other long distance method?"

"Different countries have different banking rules Ma'am," she shrugged "and I'm not absolutely certain about that but again, if you want my opinion, Gibson is a Business Investment Manager, a high profile and much respected individual in a prestigious Scottish bank. There's a real likelihood that he might have had previous dealings with the bank he's sent the money to and already be known to them as a trustworthy and credible banking associate, so no questions asked. In his position, he's probably dealt with more banks that I can count. I don't think that he would have much difficulty contacting a foreign bank and opening an account, particularly if say, he told the bank it was for a customer who wanted to move a considerable amount of money to a new account. After all," she opened her hands wide, "business is business and like I said earlier, banks are there to make money so if such a transaction does *not* interfere with that country's banking regulations, why would they suspect or contest such a large deposit?"

"Why indeed," agreed Massey with a shake of her head. "Can you follow the trail of the money?"

"Even if I can and the more I delve into his scam, I'm hoping that I can," she softly exhaled, "we're talking about another country whose banking laws might be so different from what we here in the UK are used to that it might take years of litigation for them to even *admit* they have the money, let alone return it. And not forgetting that during that time, Gibson might be shifting the money around, so the plain truth is, I'm not hopeful."

"Okay," Massey sighed, running a weary hand through her hair, "well, at least we have confirmed that Gibson is now a definite suspect and someone we can pursue for the fraud." She peered closely at Scott. "Laura, you said he had *two* advantages. One you've explained, what's the second advantage?"

"I strongly suspect he had an accomplice."

Franklin leaned forward, both hands on the desktop. "Ah, now it gets a little bit more revealing. Are you going to tell us it was Carol Meechan, the dead girl?"

"Ah, no sir, I'm afraid not. Gibson needed a second authorisation for all his transactions that were recorded on the computer system, a sort of electronic signature; that, as well as written signatures and initialling on the paperwork documentation."

"So, if it wasn't Meechan, who was it then?"

Scott smiled and replied, "The senior assistant Accounts Manager, Harry McPherson."

"Well, that's a turn-up," remarked Franklin, then turning towards Massey, was about to ask what she wanted done about McPherson when the door was knocked and opened to admit Frankie Johnson, who walked into the room, a mobile phone clasped to his ear.

He waved for everyone to remain seated and they heard him say, "Thanks Charlie, that's very useful. Tell the missus I said hello," then ended the call.

"Hello folks," he smiled grimly at everyone. "What have I missed?"

"We just got a break in the bank case, Frankie," said Massey.

"Young Laura here proved that Peter Gibson *did* commit the fraud, but had help from one of his colleagues, a Harry McPherson who works in the Accounts Department. I was just about to get Bobby to arrange to have him hunted down and brought in for interview."

"I wouldn't bother Lynn," Johnson sighed, returning the phone to his pocket and drawing up a chair from the corner of the room. Seating himself heavily down, he sighed.

"That was DI Charlie Miller on the phone there. Charlie's the duty DI today for the north of the city and Dumbarton divisions. He's just told me that the uniform have recovered a man's body found floating in the River Clyde with his head bashed in from the back. Tentative examination by the attending police casualty surgeon indicates the wound is indicative of an assault by a heavy, bladed weapon. Murder, it seems, though of course the PM will confirm that opinion. The wallet and photographic ID found on the body identifies the deceased as a banker employed by the Caledonia Banking Group, a man called Harry McPherson."

He stared at each of them in turn.

"So, ladies and gentleman, just what the hell is going on?"

CHAPTER 24

Monday morning dawned for Lynn Massey earlier than she anticipated, waking with a severe headache and Greg gently snoring beside her. At first, she considered it was her period starting a few days early, but she was as regular as clockwork and still had a couple of days to go. No, she realised, the ache was tension rather than menstrual.

Slipping quietly from bed, she eased out of the door and made her way downstairs to the kitchen, reaching up into the wall cabinet for the paracetamol.

She fumbled two tablets from the blister pack and downed them with a glass of water, then sat at the kitchen table while the hot water jug boiled for her coffee.

Last night's revelation that the dead body fished from the Clyde was Harry McPherson had come as a shock to them all. She had wanted to hotfoot it down to the scene and meet with Charlie Miller, who she knew; a good cop and even better detective, but Frankie Johnson had overruled her.

"It's been a long and traumatic day for all of us, Lynn," he had said, one hand raised and quelling her protest. "We'll convene here tomorrow morning and confer then with what we know. Eight sharp, people, so go home now and get a good night's rest and Bobby," he had turned to Franklin, "that goes for all the team, but have them report a little later, say nine-thirty and that will give them time to avoid the commuter traffic."

They had stood to leave when she saw Johnson wink at her and then say, "Just a couple of minutes of your time, Lynn."

He had waited till Franklin and Laura Scott left the room then first briefly recounted his visit to Des Mooney before informing her that because of this new development, he intended taking over the inquiry. At first she was taken aback, then affronted, believing it to be a lack of faith in her ability and had almost argued with him until he pointed out that it no, it was not a slight on her ability. He then patiently reminded her the circumstance being two murders, a missing banker married to a serving police officer and over two and a half million pounds stolen and with all these incidents apparently connected, it was likely the media and the public would want answers and soon and if no answers were forthcoming, the Chief would be forced by public opinion to serve someone's head up on a plate.

"No, Lynn," he had firmly told her, brooking no argument, "I'm taking charge with you as my second man, so to speak."

She had startled at that and almost immediately realised he was shielding her, protecting her if the inquiry went belly-up.

Further objections fell on deaf ears and what made it worse was he had grinned and said, "I'm in the twilight of my career, Lynn. You've a good few years to go and I've always thought of you as my protégé, so give me the opportunity to do what I believe to be right," then grinned again and said, "and don't force me to make it an order, Detective Superintendent."

She had with reluctance agreed yet still felt like a coward, that she was allowing Frankie to be the face of the inquiry and take the flak if they failed to recover the money or find the killer of Carol Meechan and now, the apparently murdered Harry McPherson; the killer who every indication so far pointed to the missing banker, Peter Gibson.

"Penny for them," said her husband from behind her. She turned to see him lounging in the kitchen doorway, wearing a faded, over stretched once-white tee shirt and his skinny white legs encased in a pair of ridiculously brightly coloured Hawaiian shorts.

He moved towards her and wrapped his longs arms about her shoulders, then bent over to nuzzle at her neck.

"I've never understood why after a night in bed, you can still smell so desirable," he whispered, "while my mouth feels like I've been chewing day old socks."

She smiled at him and grasped at his arms, hugging him tight to her. The kettle whistled and she released him and he turned to make the coffee.

"I take it you've another long day ahead of you?" he asked, carefully handing her a steaming hot mug.

"I've to be at Cranstonhill for an eight o'clock meeting," she sipped at the scalding liquid, "and you?"

"Day trip to London with me representing Border Control at an inter-agency meeting with my opposite number in the City of London Police, but I should be back on the last shuttle," he replied.

"Just make sure you are, Mister Campbell," she teased him, her head feeling a little better with the paracetamol kicking in, "I might have plans for you tonight."

Bobby Franklin was nudged by his wife who stood over him, a mug of tea in her hand and a gentle smile on her face.

He watched as she placed the mug onto the bedside table and saw that her pillow was still firm and bobbed and realised she had not been beside him through the night. He peered at her through sleepy eyes and asked, "Been snoring again, have I?"

"Like a locomotive, but that's not why I was in the spare room," she nudged him to slide over and sat down on the edge of the bed, her hand gently on his brow. "You had a bad night again, Bobby. You'll need to make that appointment with the doctor. I'm worried about you."

"It'll pass," he smiled at her, unable to prevent the wide yawn and then with a twinkle in his eyes, grinned like a schoolboy. "Still early yet, you know."

"Aye," she rose from the bed and stepped away from his reaching hand, her grin equalling his, "but you have to be out of here sharp for your morning meeting, so no shenanigans you bad boy. Up for your shower and I'll have your cereal on the breakfast bar when you come downstairs."

She stopped at the door and biting at her lip, turned and said, "I'm truly sorry Bobby, about your young lad, I mean. If you intend going again to meet his wife, remember; I'm here for you if you want me to come with you."

"Thanks, sweetheart," he sighed. "I probably will want to visit Waz's wife at some point, but I'll wait until such times everything is past, the ceremony I mean. I don't suppose she'll want any visitors just now."

"No, I don't suppose she will. About the ceremony; the lad was Muslim, wasn't he?"

"Aye, the Imam of his mosque has been informed, the Central Mosque, on Ballater Street down in the Gorbals, by the Clyde. The Imam was contacted by our welfare people and he's making the formal arrangements for the funeral service." He wiped a hand across his face and continued. "I'm no expert in Islamic funerals, but my understanding is that the service is to be conducted as soon as possible, with the burial normally within twenty-four hours."

"Won't there be a post-mortem or something for the lad?"

"That's being conducted today, hen; this morning in fact. Lynn Massey herself spoke with the Imam and I believe she's invited him to be present to ensure that the correct practises are observed." He sighed. "I'm also going to be present because Lynn felt that it might be inappropriate for a woman to be there."

A sudden silence fell between them, broken when Franklin continued by intimating, "The cause of the accident was pretty well determined almost immediately, so there won't be any trial or anything like that. The best we can hope for is the Procurator Fiscal ordering a fatal accident inquiry, an FAI they're called. However," he wheezed, "if the witness's statements are correct, the circumstances seem straight forward so I think it's highly unlikely that the PF will authorise an FAI, particularly because of the cost," he said, but with a trace of bitterness in his voice.

"What about the other man that died, the young man who was driving the van. What about his family?"

"Don't know much about them, I'm afraid," his eyes narrowed and he grimaced. "The accident is being dealt with by the Traffic

Department, but I can only assume they'll be grieving like the rest of us."

"Poor Missus Ahmed," she shook her head, one hand on the doorsill. "There's a wee one too, isn't there?"

"Aye there is, a wee girl. She's not even a year old yet. Waz was never done talking about her," he slowly exhaled to relieve the sudden pain in his midriff.

His wife pretended she hadn't noticed and said, "And your man, Des is it? How is he doing? I've met him, have I not?"

"Probably at one of the divisional dances, I think," he nodded. "Nice guy, Des. I didn't get to visit him, but Frankie Johnson says that he should be out of hospital in the next couple of days. I'll take the time to visit him at home."

"I think you said he's on his own, a single man, is that right?"

"As far as I know, yeah, he's on his own."

"Okay, let me know when you're going to see him and I'll make a pot of soup and a few things for his freezer."

His wife stood tight-lipped watching him, worried how the tragedy might affect him and worried even more that it could exacerbate his condition, what they both suspected, a hiatus hernia.

"You'll really need to see the doctor, love," she tried again.

"I'll make you a promise. Let me get this case finished and I'll make the appointment," he smiled at her.

"Okay, it's a deal, now get yourself showered and come downstairs when you're ready."

Susie Gibson decided to walk with Jenny to her school that morning and watching as her daughter shrugged into her school blazer, made the decision and told Jenny that the two of them were going out that night for dinner to the new tapas restaurant in the Main Street, that it wouldn't do them any harm to get out of the house for a couple of hours.

"What if dad phones when we're out?" her daughter huffed at her.

"There's an answer machine and we'll both have our mobiles, so he's bound to get at least one us now, isn't he?" she smiled, trying to instil some positive energy into the lacklustre Jenny.

Walking together along Kylepark Drive, Jenny plugged her earphones in and concentrated on her I-phone while Susie recalled the eight-thirty news bulletin she had heard just prior leaving the house, learning with sadness of the accident that claimed two lives and injured another, one of the dead being a young police officer. The names, the reporter had said, are being withheld till such times that the next of kin were informed.

Susie guessed the relatives will already have been told, that it was the media who were not being given the names in an effort to save the families of the deceased any harassment from reporters eager for photographs.

The interviewer had spoken briefly with the Assistant Chief Constable, Jonathon MacPhail who in 'police-speak', promised that a full investigation would ensure the public were informed and that no cover-up would be tolerated.

Cover-up, thought Susie as she strolled along, what the hell did that mean?

She had never met MacPhail, but of course was aware that he recently was appointed as the ACC in charge of crime.

"I really don't feel like going to school, today," Jenny broke into her thoughts.

"Nonsense, you're just worried about your dad, that's all," she tried to inject some confidence into her voice, but knew she was failing miserably.

Turning into Old Glasgow Road, Jenny waved to two of her friends and with a quick peck on her mother's cheek, was off without a backward glance to join them.

Susie, arms folded, stood and watched her daughter link arms with the two girls and heads together, make their way towards the school gates, pleased that Jenny had such close friends.

She inhaled deeply, her senses enjoying the smell of the freshly cut grass from a nearby swing-park that filled the air, then turned to walk home, her thoughts filled with how she would occupy her day and maybe, just maybe, first grab herself a coffee and spend a little more time with Peter's electronic notebook.

The young and junior casualty doctor probed and prodded at Des Mooney, apparently unaware that his fingers were causing the police officer to grimace in pain.

The Ward Sister, stood behind the young doctor with her face showing her irritation at the examination that was causing her patient discomfort, had had enough and stepping forward, firmly said,

"Thank you, doctor. I think Mister Mooney has more than wore out his welcome on my ward, so if you're quite finished, I'll get him packed up and out of here. I *do* need this bed."

"Ah, yes, of course Sister," replied the doctor, standing up and away from his patient, quite unaware that his ministrations had caused Mooney some distress.

However Mooney, dressed in a loose fitting tee shirt and a pair of football shorts, was not fooled by her remarks and inwardly thanked the Sister for saving him from giving the boyish doctor an earful. When the doctor had gone, the Sister smiled at Mooney and reminding him of the instructions regarding his medication, handed him his crutches and told him that two colleagues waited in the reception area to convey him home.

"Now, one more time Mister Mooney," she stepped back, "let me see you handle those crutches and," her eyebrows warningly rose, "if you can't manage them to my satisfaction, you're going nowhere."

"No bother Sister, the physios spent half an hour with me earlier this morning," he grinned at her and deftly swinging his legs from the bed tucked the crutches under his arms and with the Sister shepherding close behind, slowly made his way through the curtain into the corridor and towards the casualty reception.

DS Emma Ferguson and a youthful uniformed cop stood patiently waiting as he joined them, the cop taking the plastic hospital bag carried by the Sister that contained Mooney's toiletries and medication, as well as a second pair of shorts and tee shirt that had served as his pyjamas.

"So," he winked at Ferguson, "what's the chance of stopping for a pint then?"

"There's as much likelihood of that as you getting your Nat King Cole while you're on those bloody things," she returned his wink, but with an evil grin.

"You never know Sarge," the cop grinned at them both, "there might be a bit of the sympathy vote from some of the women at the pensioners club Des here attends for the tea dance."

"Very funny you cheeky young buggers," he shook his head and turning towards the Sister, thanked her and asked that his thanks be passed to her nurses. That done, he walked slowly between his two colleagues towards the sliding door, reminding them that there was a time, particularly when he had more hair, that the women found him a very attractive man and more than a few had been liberal with their charms.

The Sister, watching him go, acknowledged with a nod the student nurse at her elbow.

"It's a phone call asking when Mister Mooney is getting released, Sister," said the nurse.

"You can tell the caller that his colleagues have just collected him and that's him away home now," exhaled the Sister, her mind distracted by the thoughts of what shopping she needed to get to make that nights evening meal, but then turning, cast a critical eye over the nurse and added, "and *do* try to tuck those stray hairs behind your ears, please nurse."

Outside the glass doors, Mooney stopped and took a lungful of fresh air, pleased to be gone from the antiseptic smell of the ward. Ferguson walking beside him with one eye on Mooney, a little anxious and ready to grab him if he should trip on the uneven ground, continued the banter with, "I understand from my history books that in your days Des, flared trousers, flower shirts and beads were all the rage when going out to the dancing."

"You can joke," he responded, his eyes on the ground as he made his way towards the marked Transit van, "but there's many a female swooned over me back then."

"Swooned?" Ferguson laughed as she turned towards him and held open the van's rear door and stood ready to help inside. "Now you're *really* giving your age away, you old duffer."

The journey to his Pollokshields flat took a little over ten minutes during which time Ferguson, sat in the back of the van with Mooney, told him of the arrangements that had been made for Waz Ahmed's funeral service that was to be conducted the following day.

"It's a bit of a rush, isn't it?" said Mooney, surprised at the haste.

"It's the practice of Islam and the bosses don't want any of Waz's family or friends offended. From what Bobby Franklin told me, Lynn Massey is keen that all the rituals for Waz's funeral are to be observed. It's called," her eyebrows narrowed and then she reached into her jacket pocket and brought out a slip of paper, "I thought you'd ask so I wrote it down," she explained. "It's called a Janazah. Once the PM has been conducted and that's taking place as we speak, Waz will be removed to the mosque over in the Gorbals and…" but was interrupted by the van driver who called out, "What's your number in Mansionhouse Road, Des?"

"Forty-seven," called out Mooney, then turned towards Ferguson and said, "I'd like to go. Attend the funeral, I mean."

She took a deep breath and reaching across the space between them, placed her hand with compassion on his arm and stared at him. "Is that wise, Des? I mean, remember; you've just been through a really traumatic experience, it might be very upsetting for you."

"All the same, Emma, do you think you can fix it with the DI? See if he'll get someone to collect me from the flat? I, well…" he exhaled, "I owe it to the young guy. To be there, I mean. For him," he hesitated, then added, "and for his wife."

"That's us here then," called out the driver as he slowed the van to a halt. "Hang on a minute and I'll get the back doors open for you guys."

"Do you know her, his wife I mean?"

"No, never met the lassie. I didn't even know Waz that well, other than bumping into him in the office and working with him the last couple of days."

He glanced down at his feet and said, "It's important to me, Emma."

"Look," she replied, hands rising as in surrender, "I'll speak with Bobby and tell him what you've said and if he agrees, then *I'll* come and get you." She licked at her lips as the rear doors opened and added, "But think about what you're asking of yourself and if you change your mind Des, give me a call."

The cop stared curiously at them both, knowing something was going on and, reluctant to interrupt, stood patiently and silent.

"Will you need a hand to get dressed in the morning?" she asked.

"What time is the service?"

"We've to be at the mosque at one-thirty in the afternoon."

"Okay, I'll get myself up and be dressed and ready when you arrive at say, one o'clock; if that's okay with you?"

"One o'clock it is then," she smiled at him and handed the hospital plastic bag out to the cop while Mooney shuffled along the wooden bench seat to the open doors.

While the cop stood anxiously watching that Mooney could cope on his crutches and shepherded him to the tenement close entrance, Ferguson fetched two plastic bags from the front passenger seat and said, "I thought that you might not be able to get out for a while, so got you some messages. It's just milk, teabags, coffee, bread and a few other things," she sheepishly explained.

He was touched by her thoughtfulness and could only nod his grateful thanks and at the cop's request, indicated the keys to both the close door and his ground flat door was in the hospital bag.

The cop rummaged in the bag and held both doors open while Mooney and Ferguson passed by.

In the bright hallway of the flat, Ferguson smiled and with a typical woman's nosiness, asked, "Can I have a wee peek at you place, Des?"

He grinned and watched as she poked her head into the lounge, kitchen and three bedrooms, finishing in the glistening white tiled bathroom.

"Well," she sounded surprised, "it's not only immaculately clean, but I like your décor too," she gushed, her eyes opening wide with surprise, then narrowed, "but I see there's a woman's touch in the middle back bedroom?"

"Ah, that will be my daughter Jill's room. She's in the army, but stays with me when she's home on leave," he explained with a smile and then added with a wink at the cop, "and you think and old divorcee of fifty-two can't take care of himself, Emma?"

"No, I don't mean that, it's just that…well, aye. The guy I live with is a slob, darling that he is though. Can I move in with you, Des?"

"Does that mean there will be an intimate relationship, Emma? If it does, I'd certainly think about it because a good looking young thing like you would be great for my street cred."

"Oh no, I wouldn't want to wear you out," she drawled and returned his grin. "An old guy like you, I mean. You'd never keep up with a young thing like me."

"This conversation is getting to raunchy for me," interrupted the grinning cop, his hands defensively raised, "so will we get him settled in then Sarge? I've a beat to patrol, you know."

It took Ferguson and the cop just a few more minutes to get Des Mooney settled into his flat and returning to the van, she joined the cop in the front seat.

Driving away from Mansionhouse Road, neither Ferguson nor the cop paid any attention to the black coloured four by four BMW with the red-headed woman in the driver's seat, who nervously turned her head away as the marked police Transit van passed her by.

CHAPTER 25

Morven Sutherland, dressed formally in a charcoal coloured business trouser suit, closed the door of the Accounts Department office behind her. Uncommonly nervous, she glanced at the clock.

As usual, she was first to arrive, but knew that she had barely minutes to rifle through Harry McPherson's desk and find what she was looking for.

With another glance at the closed door, she sat behind his desk and tried the top drawer on the right. It noiselessly slid open. As she suspected, like many other staff members, McPherson didn't bother remembering his password for the banks internal Internet computer system, but kept a piece of paper sellotaped to the inside of the top drawer on which was typed his unique password that permitted him access.

She switched on his hard drive, again glancing at the door and silently urging the machine to hurry as it fired up and connected with the computer server located in the ultra secure strong room in the bank's basement.

With a short ringtone, the monitor sparked into life and the banks logo appeared on the screen with the small window that required first the users surname and initial then below, the nine digit password.

Hurriedly, she typed in 'mcphersonh' and tabbed to the password box, but in her haste got the sixth digit wrong. "Fuck!" she loudly exclaimed and started again, inwardly cursing her clumsiness and wishing she paid more attention to the infrequent lectures on computing skills the bank occasionally run. She could never admit to be more than adequate in her use of the banks computers and while competent enough to operate the systems within the parameters she had been tutored in, was lost when stepping outside those parameters.

She heaved a sigh of relief when finally the screen flickered into life and left clicking the button on the mouse, created a new folder. Quickly she withdrew a USB from her trouser pocket and inserted it into the hard drive portal. It took but a heart-stopping moment to transfer the file from the USB into the new folder that she then renamed 'private funnd,' but did not notice the misspelt word.

Without properly ejecting the USB from the machine, she snatched it from the hard drive and returned it to her pocket and was about to turn off the screen when she heard the sound of laughter in the corridor outside and realised that some of the female Accounts staff were approaching the door.

With nervous fingers, she pressed the off button on the hard drive and stood up, willing the screen to darken as it powered down and smoothing her trousers down, then lifted a sheet of paper from the desk that she pretended to read.

"Good morning, Miss Sutherland," the two young females called out together, each heading towards their desk and excitedly talking over one another as they returned almost immediately to their respective stories of their Saturday night adventures in the city.

Sutherland smiled humourlessly at the younger women and walked slowly towards her desk, her heart hammering in her chest at the close call. To access McPherson's computer files when he wasn't present was tantamount to requesting an immediate dismissal from the bank.

She knew almost with certainty that today or tomorrow, the police would call at the bank and if nothing else, she was determined to be prepared.

The management meeting that commenced at eight o'clock that morning and took place in Bobby Franklin's office was chaired by Frankie Johnson and, to Lynn Massey and Bobby Franklin's surprise, attended by ACC Jonathon MacPhail.

"The circumstances as they stand," Johnson commenced, "is we have the murder of Carol Meechan and Harold McPherson, the missing man Peter Gibson, who is suspected of the fraudulent theft of over three million pounds. These three incidents are bound by the fact that all three of these individuals were, or are in Gibson's case," he corrected himself, "employed by the Caledonia Banking Group. That is *not* what I would consider a coincidence and with Mister MacPhail's agreement," he turned to Franklin who was not yet aware, "I am assuming charge of the inquiry that will now encompass all three investigations. My first decision is to appoint you Lynn as my second in command. Bobby," he nodded towards Franklin, "I'm bringing all three investigations to Cranstonhill and you will assume command of and run the incident room from here on in."

"Boss," Franklin nodded in acknowledgment.

"Again with Mister MacPhail's approval, I have instructed that half a dozen officers from the Major Investigation Team based here in the city at Govan will be seconded to the inquiry. Lynn," he nodded towards her, "you will organise a team this morning to visit the bank, interview *all* the employees who worked or socialised with McPherson. If there are any problems with the banks management," he stopped and stared at MacPhail, "I assume we'll have your backing if there are any issues there, sir?"

All three stared at the ACC and none of them missed the brief hesitancy that crossed MacPhail's face or the anger that followed as he found himself quite unexpectedly on the spot.

"Perhaps we might discuss that later in private, Mister Johnson?" Johnson stared at him and inhaling, slowly nodded then turned towards Massey, and continued.

"My understanding, Lynn, is that DI Charlie Miller has visited McPherson's wife and broken the news?"

"Yes sir," she formally replied, "and it *was* my intention to accompany Charlie Miller to the PM today. It's set for nine o'clock, this morning," she added and continued, "and if you are in agreement with that decision, thereafter I'll lead the team to the bank and get them settled in for the interviews. I agree that it might be prudent that I be present just in case there is any kind of difficulty with the senior management at the bank. I don't think it would do any harm to have a senior police officer present, sir."

"Agreed, Lynn and while you are at the mortuary, inform DI Miller that I'm taking charge of the inquiry regarding his dead body, Harold McPherson. Please also inform him that he is to assume the duties of acting Detective Chief Inspector with responsibility for both his own sub-division and," he nodded to Franklin, "the DI's sub-division here at Cranstonhill. Tell him he can work out of Maryhill and with your agreement Bobby, I'd like to remove DS Ferguson from the inquiry and have her assume the role of acting Detective Inspector while you are otherwise engaged in the incident room. Emma can deal with the day to day running of your office."

Turning towards MacPhail, Johnson explained Miller and Ferguson's temporary appointments. "With the resources I'm tying up sir, I'll need good people to oversee the general day to day criminal inquiries."

"Yes, I see Mister Johnson. Quite correct," agreed MacPhail.

"Of course sir," Franklin also agreed with a nod, but with a little hesitancy in his voice, inwardly wondering how young Emma would deal with his other two hard-bitten, world weary detective sergeants who might believe themselves to have been a better choice for Acting DI.

"Back to you, Lynn," said Johnson, glancing down at his written notes. "Can you arrange for DS Scott to have whatever she needs when she interrogates the bank's computer system? She'll also need corroboration by another officer, so if you're agreeable, leave young Arlene Baxter to work with her."

"Are you satisfied that Baxter has completed her interview with DS Gibson, sir?" asked Massey.

Johnson's brow furrowed and slowly shook his head as he thoughtfully chewed at his lower lip. "I think we've went as far as we can with Missus Gibson for the minute. I'm reluctant to conduct any further interviewing…"

"Is this DS Gibson the wife of the missing man?" interrupted MacPhail.

"She is sir," Johnson nodded, "but I must stress that there is absolutely *nothing* to suggest that DS Gibson…"

"But we can't dismiss her as a suspect?"

"No, not entirely," agreed Johnson.

Had MacPhail known Johnson as did Massey and Franklin, he might have detected the slight frustrated edge to the older man's voice, but so intent on apparently displaying that he was up to speed with the details of the inquiry, he continued. "Then perhaps you might consider bringing her in, have two of your best officers conduct a real interview, maybe put some pressure on the blasted woman and…"

"Could you give us a minute, please," Johnson interrupted this time, while smiling tightly at Massey and Franklin.

He waited till the officers left the room and turned to MacPhail, his face pale with anger.

"While I realise, Mister MacPhail, that you are my senior officer I must *insist* that you allow me to do my fucking job as *I* see fit. I am a Detective Chief Superintendent, a rank that I *earned* on the streets of

Glasgow and beyond. I have accrued more than a modicum of experience and frankly, I *know* what I'm fucking doing!"

In the corridor outside, Lynn Massey, her right hand holding her left elbow, worriedly chewed at the fingernails of her left hand while Bobby Franklin, leaning slightly with both hands and his brow flat against the wall, grimaced as they listened to Frankie Johnson's angry voice clearly heard through the closed door and paper thin walls.

Quite suddenly, the door was pulled opened and ACC MacPhail stormed from the room, his face grimly set and chalk white as he wordlessly brushed past Massey and made his way quickly towards the stairs.

Taking a deep breath, she glanced at Franklin and they both re-entered the room to find Johnson seated at Franklin's desk and breathing hard, his head bowed and scribbling on his pad.

He looked up and stared at each of them in turn, before calmly asking, "Now, where was I?"

The bulky figure of Acting DCI Charlie Miller stepped out through the wide doors of the Mortuary at Glasgow Southern General Hospital and taking a tissue from his pocket cleaned away the small blob of scented hand cream from beneath his nose. He had a quick word with the young DC who then left with a large number of paper bags that contained among other things, the deceased's clothing and personal effects as well as some glass sample bottles containing blood, body tissue and samples.

Miller took a lungful of fresh air and leaned on the metal railing that surrounded the doorway while he waited for Lynn Massey who had remained inside the hot building having a quiet word with the duty Fiscal and the pathologist. As he did every day, Miller wished he could take a deep mouthful of whisky to wipe away the smell and taste of the building, but almost immediately regretted the thought. Those days were gone now that he had his wife Sadie and step-daughter Geraldine.

No stranger to violent death, Miller had some time ago realised the part of the job he hated most was attending post mortems. How anyone could work in that atmosphere, he slowly shook his head, he would never understand.

His mobile phone activated in his pocket and glancing at the screen, he smiled.

"Hello Sadie, wife of mine," he grinned into the phone, "what's up?"

"Where are you, can you speak?"

He glanced behind him, but there was no sign yet of Massey.

"Yeah, sure I can. Go ahead," he replied.

"Two things, husband of mine. My mum's taking Geraldine for a sleepover. It's a school in-service day tomorrow, so she's asked if the wean can spend the day with her."

"No problem," he grinned again, "so, what are you planning for us tonight then?"

"I thought if you're not otherwise engaged, *Acting* Detective Chief Inspector, we might go to the late night shopping at the Fort in Easterhouse."

He exhaled, the grin dying on his face. Of the few things that Miller hated, including visits to the Mortuary, shopping was high on his list.

"Oh, yeah, that sounds like a great idea," he replied in a flat tone.

She laughed, understanding his reluctance and teasingly added, "But you don't know what shops we might visit."

"Let me guess, you'll need *this* and Jellybean will definitely need *that*. I've been there before, Sadie. But," he shrugged his shoulders, "if it's time with you, who am I to complain. Besides, we might eat out, so it won't be *too* bad"

The door behind him opened and Lynn Massey stepped out into the sunlight. She was about to speak, but saw him on the phone just as Sadie Miller then said, "I was thinking more of popping into Mothercare."

Miller held his breath, slightly uncertain about what she had said and then the significance of those few words suddenly struck home.

"Mothercare?" he softly repeated, his eyes widening and his throat suddenly dry. "You mean…"

"Yes, husband of mine. I've just been to the chemists and bought the test kit; two kits, in fact, just to be sure. We're pregnant, Charlie. And I *mean* we; you and me. We're going to have a baby."

He swallowed hard, a sudden emotion sweeping through him, his breathing suddenly rapid that turned into a gasp. Then he smiled.

Lynn Massey at first thought Miller was having a seizure until she saw the huge grin and suspecting it to be good news, waited till he ended his call.

She smiled when he told her and congratulated him and his wife on their good fortune, but was surprised at the tightness in her throat, for she did not expect the small twinge of envy that swept through her.

They walked together to their cars, their conversation now professional while they discussed the findings of the pathologist; his confirmation of a killing blow to the back of Harry McPherson's head from a heavy, sharp bladed implement.

"I understand that McPherson drove a car. Has it been traced yet?" she asked.

"A silver coloured Qashqai, boss," he replied. "No, not yet, but I've got the registration number circulated, so unless it's in the water where we found him, it should turn up. Kind of leaves open the question of where he was dropped into the Clyde and there *is* the possibility that if the car was used to take him to the riverside and if it turns up near the water, it might be fair to assume that's where he was dumped into the drink."

"How did his wife react to your news, Charlie?"

He pursed his lips and his eyebrows knitted.

"Tracey McPherson," he mused, his mouth twisting and eyes narrowing as he considered the question and then continued. "Surprisingly well, Lynn. You've been there yourself, delivering the worse kind of news. It can be difficult to gauge how people will react, some with surprise, horror, disbelief and others who are quite happy that the dead person has turned their toes up. Missus McPherson just sat on the couch, fussing over her baby daughter while I told her and to be honest, I thought she might be half doped. On reflection, however, I think she was maybe suffering sleep deprivation; with the baby I mean. Just sort of shrugged her shoulders when I broke the news and at first I reckoned maybe she either wasn't taking in what I was telling her or she was in shock or something. I wouldn't *quite* describe her attitude as indifferent, but she didn't seem overly concerned. However, when the young police woman I had taken with me offered to hold the baby while spoke with Missus McPherson; well, nearly tore the face off the wee lassie with her language and fair made even me blush," he exhaled, his eyes widening at the memory.

Her brow creased as her thoughts turned to the previous day's visit to Missus Ahmed and other such visits she had made to deliver such news. You just never could tell how people reacted, she wondered. Miller stood with his back to Massey's car, his arms folded and continued, "This is going to make me sound judgemental, but the state of the house and her attitude caused me to think that maybe things weren't too good between her and her husband. Mind you..." he didn't finish, but slowly shook his head and shrugged at memories from his distant past; a happy, if chaotic house with baby clothes on radiators and toys always underfoot. Then, almost in defence of Tracey McPherson, he added, "The lassie's not long had a baby, so these things take a bit of getting used to. Getting organised about the house, I mean."

"Could she be a suspect?"

"Hard to say," he paused and then shook his head. "It wasn't the right time to get into her with the heavy questioning. I thought if that's needed, we'd better wait a day or two to let the news of her man's murder sink in. One thing though and it might be nothing," he stared at Massey as though cautioning her not to take it too seriously, "but just after I told her that her man had been murdered, McPherson's wife asked the young cop to call her father and tell him the bad news and to ask him to get himself down to the house. The wife didn't want the young cop to stay with her and her father arrived in a wee van just as we were leaving. He didn't stop to speak with us, other than a quick 'hello, cheerio', if you know what I mean. Said he wanted to see his daughter and rushed into the house. Understandable, I suppose, given the circumstances. The thing is though," he licked at his bottom lip, eyes narrowing and brow furrowed, "her father's face seemed familiar so I took a wee note of the van's registration number. I've still to run it through the system. It might be nothing, but acorns and oak trees, if you get my drift and besides, the number of people that I've dealt with in the job," he ended with a sigh and shake of his head.

"So back to my original question; we can't discount her as a suspect, Charlie?"

He shook his head again. "At the minute, McPherson's murder is an open book of suspect's, boss."

She glanced at her watch. "Aye, you're not far wrong there," she sighed and then added, "Sorry Charlie; got to go. I've a team to meet at the bank."

He watched her drive off and recalling his news from Sadie, grinned; oblivious of the strange glance a passing nurse gave him and who suspiciously thought that the large, rather dishevelled looking man with the scar on his left cheek seemed just a little *too* happy to be out without a carer.

DS Arlene Baxter, sat in the driver's seat of the CID car glanced again at her wristwatch.

"Time yet?" asked Laura Scott, sat beside her.

"Nearly," Baxter replied, "the boss said to meet her there at ten-thirty so why don't we just get there. I know it's only ten minutes, but I don't want to be late," and starting the engine, smoothly drove out from the rear yard at Cranstonhill.

"So," Scott turned in her seat and stared at Baxter, "what's the story about your neighbour, this DI Cameron then?"

Baxter shrugged and said, "Nothing to tell, really. The guy's a wanker and thinks that bullying suspects is the way to get to the truth."

"Met a few of them in my time too," sighed Scott, who then smiled and added, "and dated one or two as well."

"Aye," grinned Baxter, skilfully overtaking a lorry that swung out and veered into her path as it turned left into Elderslie Street, "I remember one guy that I thought was 'the one' until we had our first date. He took me for dinner to a fancy Italian place in the Merchant City then, when the waiter handed us the menus, looked lovingly into my bright blue eyes and said how do you feel about going Dutch?"

"I'd worn my best dress and made a real effort for the twat, too," she shook her head.

"But you're married now?"

"Oh, aye, he works in insurance."

"My man was an HGV driver in the army," smiled Scott. "He's in Health and Safety now. Took me to the Caribbean on honeymoon," she smiled at the memory.

"How does he feel about you being a copper?"

"I was a detective when we met, so I don't think he even thinks about it, " replied Scott, "but I suppose like most men, he probably worries about me sometimes. Worries about the bampots that we sometimes have to deal with, I mean. How about your man? Does he worry?"

"You kidding?" snorted Baxter. "He's seen the size of the baton they've issued us with. I think he's more worried about who I'll use the bloody thing on."

The van that transported the six members of the inquiry team was parking outside the bank when Baxter smoothly drew up alongside an empty bay and reversed into it.

Opening the passenger door, Scott saw a parking attendant hurrying towards them and wagged a warning finger at the red faced man and said, "Police on an inquiry, pal."

"Doesn't matter, officer," he blustered and reached for his ticketing machine, said, "You're parked in a no parking zone. I've got a job to do, you know."

Scott lazily got out of the car and slung her bag over her shoulder as she closed the door behind her, then turned towards the attendant and taking a deep breath, quietly replied, "And so have I pal, so go ahead and stick a ticket on that windscreen when I'm not here. But," she leaned towards him, so close that even Baxter couldn't hear her and whispered, "If you do, I'll find you, ya pompous wee shite and I'll make your fucking life miserable for the rest of your life; are we clear?"

The attendant gulped and, staring at the mad, steely-eyed, weirdly dressed hippy polis, he mustered as much dignity as he could, turned and marched off.

"What did you say to him?" asked a curious Baxter.

"Politely asked if we could get some kind of dispensation as we are all in the same job," replied Scott, who smiled and brightly added, "Right, ready to rock and roll then?"

Des Mooney, unshaven, wearing a frayed and threadbare Scotland rugby top and knee length gray coloured training pants, was fed-up watching daytime television, reading newspapers and drinking tea. He longed for a good, stiff drink, but realised that with the medication it would be foolish and besides, he argued with himself, he wanted to be sober and alert for Waz's funeral the next day, already dreading the sympathetic back-slapping and goodwill from his colleagues.

He sighed and manoeuvring himself from the old but comfortable green coloured, stressed leather Chesterfield couch and hobbled over to the small CD player on the low table, selecting a Motown compilation disc from the pile beside the player that he inserted into the machine. If he was asked to explain it, he knew he wouldn't be able to find the words, but the sound of Marvin Gaye singing *'Let's Get It On'* washing over him, went some way to chase the sombre mood he was in.

He turned the volume down and stood unsteadily leaning against the wall, reluctant to return to the couch and the temptation of the painkilling pills that sat beside the jug of water on the coffee table. He needed a clear head to remember what had happened, how his young friend Waz had died and rubbed hard at his forehead with the heel of his hand.

It was when Marvin was finishing the song that the doorbell rung, startling him.

Bugger it, he thought; I'm in no mood to speak with anyone.

The next record to be played, Tina Turner's *'Let Stay Together'*, had barely begun when the doorbell rung for a second time, but on this occasion, the caller was more insistent and kept a finger on the button.

"*Shit!*" he loudly and angrily exclaimed and awkwardly reached out for the back of the couch to steady himself, almost falling as he grabbed at one crutch and irritated by the doorbell continuing to ring. Now madder than a Paisley housewife that's been short-changed, he shouted out loud, "I'm coming!" and hurriedly hobbled on the one crutch through the lounge door and into the hallway.

He fumbled with the lock and at last, dragged the front door open, tensing himself to give the caller a mouthful.

He wasn't prepared and didn't expect it to be her and couldn't know that she would visit him here, at his flat.

She stood as tall as he in her expensive, deep green coloured Gucci heels, her red hair bunched on top of her head, her face that of an angel, her pale skin clear and unblemished. He could not to know that she deliberately avoided the use of make-up because she had wept for most of the day. The simple white blouse complemented the bottle green two-piece skirted suit that reached to just above her knees and she carried a matching clasp bag in her left hand.

The bell stopped ringing when she removed her finger from the buzzer and staring at him in the sudden silence, she drew a breath, her eyes smarting with unshed tears and simply said, "I'm not going away, Des. No matter what you tell me, I'm not leaving you again. Besides," she tried with difficulty to smile through her tears, "I have some news for you, for us both."

Wordlessly, he shrugged his shoulders and shuffled to one side to permit her to pass by into the hallway, the scent of her perfume causing him to involuntarily inhale with a sudden desire for her. For the moment all thoughts of the deceased Waz Ahmed had gone and slowly closing the door, he slowly followed her towards the lounge and pondered this new problem.

Lynn Massey, her arms folded as she stood in the centre of the opulent foyer of the Caledonia Bank, irritably shook her head and said, "Mister Brewster, I don't think you quite follow me. One of your employees, Harold McPherson, your senior Accounts Manager, has been *murdered*! Another employee is suspected of stealing a *significant* sum of money from this bank! Now, whether or not you willing assist my officers…"

"I am not used to being threatened Detective Superintendent Massey…" the HR Director hissed at her, only to be cut off in mid-sentence when she snarled, "And I'm I am *not* used to having members of the public, no matter *who* the hell they think they are, interfering in my murder inquiries, *Mister Brewster*!"

"It is not my intention to interfere…" he began, now visibly shaking at the vehemence in her voice, suddenly aware of the curious interest they were attracting from both staff and customers.

"Then, as I have already requested, you may either provide my officers with accommodation in these premises to conduct their interviews and I will permit the bank to continue its day to day business or I will close the doors there," she pointed with an outstretched forefinger towards the entrance, "then arrange for a *very* visible uniformed officer and marked police vehicle to be present outside and I will instruct that officer to inform any customers that might call that this bank is closed pending a police investigation. Do I make myself clear, Mister Brewster?"

She watched the Adams apple in his throat perform an Irish jig, aware that her detectives stood nearby, discreetly ignoring the confrontation between their boss and the bank's bumptious Director. In his mind, he already guessed the harm that closure on a banking day would cause, not only to the bank's reputation, but could also provoke the possibility of a catastrophic fall in shares if word reached the Glasgow Stock Exchange, let alone the Stock Exchange in London.

Slowly, pale-faced he nodded his head and quietly replied, "Unequivocally, Madam," and turning on his heel, walked a short distance and curtly beckoned towards him a middle-aged woman who stood waiting patiently.

Head bowed towards the woman, he turned towards Massey as he gesticulated to the detective.

Massey watched the woman continually nod as she received instructions then Brewster, without a backward glance, made his way towards the nearby stairs while the woman nervously approached Massey.

"Good morning Madam, I believe you and your, ah, colleagues require some rooms to ah…."

"That's correct," Massey interrupted, surprising the woman with a smile. "Might I ask who you are?"

"Who me?" she startled, eyes widening as she peered at Massey through thick lens spectacles. "I'm Miss Fraser, secretary to the Board of Directors. Mister Brewster has instructed that I be of service to you," she formally responded.

"Well Miss Fraser, I'm Missus Massey," she continued smiling, noting that Fraser did not wear a wedding ring and was dressed in a starched white blouse, hand knitted pink cardigan buttoned to the throat and dark tweed skirt, thick brown tights, sturdy polished brown laced shoes and unconsciously labelled the older woman as a prim spinster.

"So," Massey continued to smile at the bemused Fraser, "why don't we get started by showing my officers where they can set up to conduct their interviews, then you and I can sit down with a nice cup of tea and you can tell me *all* about the bank and who is doing what to whom, eh?"

Ushering the bemused woman alongside as they walked, Massey discreetly nodded to her team to follow and the dozen detectives in the group made their way towards the stairs.

CHAPTER 26

Alima Ahmed held the child to her breast, her daughter making slight gurgling noises as she slept nestled against her mother. Alima's mother watched from the kitchen doorway, her husband standing silently behind her with one hand resting lightly on her waist.

"The police, they called while you were out fetching some shopping," he whispered to her, but his eyes were fixed and staring over his wife's shoulder at his daughter, wrapped in a multi-coloured woollen blanket, her lengthy black hair braided and lying over one shoulder as she sat slumped and slowly rocking back and forth in the old fashioned wooden rocking chair Waz had bought for Alima, when his daughter had been born.

"What did they want?" asked his wife without turning her head for like her husband, she too was deeply concerned for her daughter's well-being.

"It was a Mister Franklin, Waz's boss. He wanted to know if we, Alima and us I mean; if we needed a lift tomorrow, to the mosque. He also said if there was a problem with getting someone to care for little Munawar," his voice broke, but he struggled on, "when we're at the service. He said his wife would be happy to babysit with the little one. Here in the house or anywhere we choose."

His wife turned and stared up into his face. "That was very kind of him. What did you tell him?"

Her husband shrugged. "I wasn't certain, but I thought if we take the little one to the mosque, the crowd that will be there and everything. It could be overwhelming for the little one and too upsetting for her. Perhaps we should consider asking the lady to babysit Munawar here?"

"Perhaps," his wife nodded, then added, "but we must first ask Alima. It is her daughter and she must choose."

She took a deep breath and turned back to stare at the younger woman and sighed. "If only she would sleep, even for a few hours."

"Do you think we should call the doctor again, maybe ask him to give her another sedative?" he asked.

"No," she shook her head. "Alima would not thank us for involving him again. She would not want to be drowsy when she is caring for the little one."

"She is already drowsy from lack of sleep," he pointed out, "and besides, we are here to care for Munawar."

"I'm tired, not deaf and I can hear you," Alima startled them, turning her head to glance at them both, "and you're quite right, mum. I don't want the doctor calling again."

She took a deep breath and rising from the chair with the sleeping Munawar in her arms, continued, "But what I will do is hand you this precious little bundle and go to bed for a lie-down. Even if I don't sleep, I promise you, I will rest."

Her mother reached for the little girl and smiled sadly at Alima. "Then go to bed, my darling child. Go and rest now, for my sake. Your father and I will be here caring for Munawar."

"And caring for you, as long as you need us," he added, his heart aching as he reached across his wife to hold and hug his precious daughter.

Across the city, Tracey McPherson lay in bed listening to the bustling noise coming from downstairs. Her head ached from the half dozen whiskies her father had made her drink the previous evening, assuring her that it was purely medicinal and would take away the shock of hearing that Harry had been murdered. She sniggered, remembering that her dad must have been in shock too, for he finished the rest of the bottle and that was definitely more than she had drunk.

Evidently, from the noise of clattering pots and pans, her dad was cleaning up the disaster that was the kitchen while her kid sister, bribed into caring for the baby by the promise of ten quid and a day off school, now sat in the lounge watching television, though how she could hear the wean above that fucking racket, God only knew. She sighed and wriggled uncomfortably in the bed, her bladder reminding her she needed to pee, but reluctant to get out from beneath the warm quilt. Finally, she gave in and in a fit of pique, stumbled from the bed to the en-suite.

She dropped her pyjama trousers to her ankles and settled herself onto the pan, wincing at the coldness of the plastic seat.

Then she groaned as with a sudden clarity, she remembered the telephone call from Harry's parents, demanding to know what had happened to their son and insisting *she* jump a taxi and to bring *his* child to their house.

Tracey placed her elbows on her knees and lowered her head into her hands, recalling his father's increasingly raised voice while Harry's mother had been weeping in the background.

She knew too well that they didn't like her and would never, hated her even and never approved of her marrying their precious fucking son. She snorted, recalling the one visit they had made to the house, both casting their eyes over every little thing and she had even seen Harry's mother sneakily wiping a finger along the television unit checking for dust.

Cow!

Harry though had been falling over himself with, "Yes dad, no dad, three bags fucking full dad." It sickened her to watch him, desperate for their approval.

They had hardly even glanced at the wean and his mother had refused to hold her granddaughter, worried that the baby would throw up on her new blouse.

Cow!

She took a deep breath, her lips tightly closed in angry memory of the visit.

The telephone conversation had turned into an argument that ended with her father snatching the phone from her hand and shouting that Harry's dad *fuck off*, that it was *his* place to come and visit his distraught daughter-in-law and granddaughter, adding that the wean was going *nowhere* without her mother.

She thought about yesterday's visit from the cops. The big guy, the detective Miller; he had been all right and that wee lassie in uniform that looked like she had just left school. Her shoulders heaved and she sniggered, but then quite unexpectedly and abruptly the snigger turned to a worrying thought and her lips began to tremble.

Feeling sorry for herself, Tracey wept then as the enormity of the situation finally hit her and tore at the toilet tissue to wipe away her tears and the snot from her nose.

Calm now, she sniffed and slowly exhaled and standing, pulled her trousers up, disposed of the tissue and flushed the toilet.

She took a deep breath and leaned against the wash basin, both hands flat against the wall on either side of the mirror, turning her head back and forth as she studied herself. Her glance took in the engagement and wedding rings on the third finger of her left hand. "The widow McPherson," she murmured and smiled a little uncertainly at the mirror.

She stood a little back from the mirror to obtain a better view of her figure, turning her head left and right and critically studied her reflection, frowning at her slight post-natal paunch then through the thin material of her silky pyjama top, weighed both breasts in her hands, each breast still heavy with milk. Slowly, she compressed her breasts together and bit at her lower lip as she leaned slightly forward and admired the cleavage she created; the cleavage that had hooked Harry.

Once I get my figure back, she mused, continuing to smile at the mirror and a sudden thought struck her.

The smile turned to an almost secretive grin when she remembered with an increasing excitement that there was bound to be insurance money.

In the unusual quiet of the Tesco supermarket store in Uddingston, Susie Gibson was pushing the shopping trolley down the aisle looking for the coffee she preferred when the mobile phone in her tracksuit trousers chirruped. The screen indicated the caller's name to be her neighbour, Andy Brownlie and smiling, pressed the green button and held it to her ear.

"Hello Andy," she said, "how is everything with you? How is Janice doing; is she keeping okay?"

"Whoa boss," Andy replied, "one question at a time. First though, can you speak?"

Instinctively, she glanced around her and said, "Yeah, go ahead. What's up?"

From the whistling noise of the wind in his background, she guessed he was outside and knowing he was on dayshift, thought it likely he was calling from the rear yard at Baird Street office.

"Pal of mine at cranny hill office gave me the head's up, Susie. Seems there's another body turned up and it's somebody that worked in your man's bank."

She flinched, but Andy must have guessed her anxiety and he hastily added, "Sorry, Susie it's not Peter; bloody idiot that I am. Sorry hen; that was me being a stupid arse. I didn't mean to scare you like that."

She slowly exhaled and replied, "Don't worry. If it had been Peter, I'd have been informed by now," and probably been arrested, she inwardly grimaced, but decided that was a comment she would rather not share. "When did this happen, the body turning up I mean?"

"I don't know all the details; hold on," he said and holding the phone away from his mouth, she heard him shouting, "I'll be with you in a tick, Jimmy."

"Sorry Susie, I need to go. I'm neighboured up with Jimmy Paterson while you're off."

She heard his puffing as he quickly made his way across the yard and hurriedly said, "Anything you hear Andy, anything at all, okay?"

"Right, boss, I've got to go. Don't forget now, that info's on the quiet. Tell the wean I said hello," and the call died in her hand.

She stood still, the news of another death having taken the wind out of her.

Leaning with her forearms on the push bar of the trolley, she activated the internet on her I-phone and scrolled down to the BBC local Glasgow and West of Scotland news reports where she saw the third item on the list was the reported discovery the previous day of a man's body, in Dumbarton. Reading the sparse information didn't tell her much more than what Andy had intimated and there was of course the obligatory 'police investigating' conclusion to the few details that was listed.

"Can I help you madam?" said the voice beside her.

The young teenage girl wearing the Tesco uniform stared uncertainly at Susie.

"Oh, no, thanks, I'm fine," she smiled and returning the phone to her pocket, reached for the coffee, annoyed with herself that she hadn't pressed Andy how the pregnant Janice was getting on and resolved to phone her tonight.

Morven Sutherland, wearing a new and fashionable light coloured pink blouse and a darker pink trouser suit sat behind her own desk. Earlier forewarned by the office grapevine that a number of detectives had arrived in the bank foyer, she expected to be among the first to be interviewed and took the few minutes respite within the women's cloakroom to expertly apply her make-up and to prepare herself. Stepping out the door, she took a final glance in the cloakroom mirror and patting lightly at her hair, was satisfied she looked presentable. No, more than presentable, she smiled at her refection; very, very smart and professional.

Now seated opposite her was the detective who had introduced herself as DS Baxter. Casting a quick glance over the younger woman's business suit and hair tied back with a bobble, she mentally dismissed her as an off the peg shopper who hardly even bothered to properly apply make-up to work this morning. As for the other woman detective; she risked a glance at Laura Scott, who was now seated behind Harry McPherson's desk. She recognised her as the one who had previously been in the office; what the *fuck* is she all about, she wondered?

Scott sat a few yards away at McPherson's desk, ostensibly interrogating the desk top computer, but listening to every word that passed between the two women and hoped Baxter had heeded her warning; that Scott had formed the opinion that Sutherland was a conceited woman and likely believed her own hype about how smart she was.

"Now, let me make it quite clear, Miss Sutherland. Or is it Missus Sutherland?" smiled Baxter, her notebook in her left hand and a pencil poised in her right hand.

Returning the smile, Sutherland held up her left hand to indicate the absence of a wedding ring and staring into Baxter's eyes, cautiously replied, "Miss Sutherland."

"Miss Sutherland," repeated Baxter. "As I said, let me make it quite clear that you are not a suspect, but I do need to interview you and ask questions of you about the Senior Accounts Manager, Harold McPherson."

"Harry; he preferred Harry," Sutherland corrected her and already believed she was taking the initiative in the interview "and joked that Harold was too old fashioned for a young, go-getter like him."

"Harry," repeated Baxter, continuing to smile. "I understand you were his deputy?"

"Yes, for the last…" she hesitated and shrugged her shoulders, "Well, really since I commenced working here at the bank."

"And that was when?"

"Almost two years ago. Well, it will be two years this coming October."

"And what was your previous position?"

"I worked for a commercial accountancy firm in London, Campson and Baker; in the City, of course."

"Of course," Baxter replied with her smile fixed to her face. Working at McPherson's desk, Scott swallowed hard. '…*of course,*' she almost guffawed out loud and choked back a grin.

"How long where you at, ah," she glanced at her notebook, "Campson and Baker, Miss Sutherland?"

"Just over one year," she said, then her eyes narrowed, "I thought you said you wished to discuss Harry, Mister McPherson, I mean?"

"Yes, well, I'm just getting some background on you as a witness…."

"Witness to what? What is it that I can tell you," she asked, her voice now slightly raised in pitch, both hands flat on the desk as she leaned slightly forward to stare at Baxter.

Scott forced herself not to turn, but to concentrate on the blank screen monitor. She reached down to press the 'on' button on McPherson's hard drive, but listening intently, realised what was happening. Sutherland was pretending anger and baiting Baxter, subtly trying to dominate the conversation by asking the questions.

"Please Miss Sutherland," Baxter smoothly replied, determined not to be riled, "I won't take up any more of your valuable time than is necessary if you permit *me* to ask the questions, okay?"

Nicely done, Arlene, Scott inwardly grinned as the monitor burst into life with the bank's logo prominent in the centre of the screen and a rectangle box that demanded the user's identification and password details.

Guessing that Sutherland was again about to protest, Scott forestalled her by turning slightly in her chair and asking, "Don't happen to know Mister McPherson's log-on details do you, Miss Sutherland?"

Sutherland half smiled. This was the opportunity she had hoped for and replied, "Well, *of course*, it's strictly against the bank's security protocol, but before he signed on each morning, I would see Harry open that drawer there," she pointed to the top left hand desk drawer. Scott pulled the drawer open and almost immediately saw the piece of paper sellotaped to the inside of the drawer with the password typed upon it. She immediately realised that Sutherland knew fine well that the log-on details were there. Well now, she inwardly grinned, that in itself is a useful wee bit of information.

"I've got what looks like a password," Scott said, "but what's his log-on identification; do you happen to know that?"

"It'll be the standard bank employee log-on," Sutherland smiled at Scott, happy to be seen helping the police. "It will be his surname and then his first initial, all lower case."

"Thanks," nodded Scott, her eye meeting Baxter's, who gave her the subtlest of nods and turning towards Sutherland, asked her, "So, Miss Sutherland, you were just over one year at Campson and Baker. What made you return here to Scotland?"

"It was a promotional sideways move. Previously I was an accounts assistant; here I'm the deputy." She shrugged again as though the question was of no significance. "This job pays more money and provides better career opportunities."

"And did you know Harry outside of work?"

The change of tactic almost caught her out, but not quite. She smiled and shook her head. "Harry was a married man with a young child; a daughter, I understand," then a sudden thought occurred to her that other staff members being interviewed might be a *little* more forthcoming, so decided on a half truth. She smiled, "Of course, Harry was also a rather tactile individual, if you know what I mean?"

"Tactile? How so?"

"*Well*," she drawled, "sort of touchy-feely with some of the female members of staff, if you get my meaning."

"Do you mean he was friendly or promiscuous?"

Sutherland raised a hand to her breast as though shocked by the very suggestion that McPherson was anything other than a faithful husband.

"I'm not suggesting he, ah…"

"Played away I think is the term you might be looking for," Baxter dryly suggested, then added, "and what about you, Miss Sutherland? Was Harry ever *tactile* with you?"

Sutherland turned pale and her lips whitened when she compressed them tightly together with anger. "Never," she curtly responded.

"I find that odd then," smiled Baxter, "for you are a very good looking woman Miss Sutherland. Don't *you* think that's odd for a man that was, how did you describe him again? Touchy-feely I believe you said."

"I would *never* encourage that sort of behaviour," she retorted, "Never!"

And that's a bloody lie, thought Scott, busying herself with the horde of small file boxes down both sides of the monitor, each of which she saw was individually labelled, but it was the file labelled 'private funnd' that immediately took her attention.

"Moving on," Baxter resumed her fixed smile at Sutherland, "you will likely be aware that one of your other colleagues, Peter Gibson has been reported missing to the police. How well did you know Gibson?"

"I thought this interview was about Harry?"

Baxter stared at Sutherland, suspecting the question was a deflection to give her time to think and respond with a suitable answer.

"I'm simply trying to connect the dots, get the bigger picture Miss Sutherland and it would be useful to me, you being in the unique position of middle-management, to garner your knowledge of both men. So, how well did you know Mister Gibson?"

Sutherland shrugged again and pursed her lips. "Not too well. Of course I *knew* who he was, but other than work related issues, I didn't know Peter… Mister Gibson, I mean, *that* well."

"But enough to know him as Peter?" Baxter pressed the point.

Sutherland exhaled, angry that this little bitch was being so difficult. "So I called him by his forename," her voice again rose by a pitch, "that doesn't mean I knew him that well. Isn't his wife one of you, a police officer? Are you questioning her?" she irately replied.

Baxter watched as Sutherland defensively folded her arms and had the gut instinct that the increasing angry woman wasn't telling the full story, but decided without any information to indicate otherwise, she wouldn't press the issue just then. It also occurred to her that maybe the anger was being stage-managed, an attempt at some kind of diversion.

Relaxing, she smiled and glancing down at her notebook, she pretended to read for a few seconds before asking, "The young woman who was murdered, Carol Meechan. She was also am employee of the bank and I understand she worked with Gibson. Was Meechan known to you?"

Careful now, thought Sutherland and smiling, replied, "Yes, I knew Carol; a lovely young woman. It's so sad what happened to her. Are you anywhere close to catching her killer?"

"How well did you know her?" Baxter again ignored the attempt to deflect her questioning.

"Hmmm, not *too* well" she replied, brown knitted as if trying to recall. "I would sometimes see her in the women's locker room and we might exchange courtesies, but of course I'm a grade above her so we didn't socialise or anything like that."

'...*of course I'm a grade above her*...' Scott gritted her teeth at the comment, her increasing dislike for Sutherland now compounded by the woman's conceit.

Staring at Baxter, Sutherland granted the detective a wide smile, knowing she was on safe ground. The conversation she had with Meechan was not recorded anywhere, so the police could not know of it and inwardly gave a sigh of relief that at the meeting she had with her, she had sworn Meechan to silence.

Laura Scott read and re-read the file marked 'private funnd' and then from her spacious canvas bag, fetched a memory stick that she inserted into the computer.

"I'm sorry," Sutherland curtly called out to her, "you can't do that."

"Do what?" Scott pretended surprise.

"Copy bank files. That's a contravention of the Data Protection Act as well as being totally against company policy.

Scott smiled tolerantly and replied, "Miss Sutherland, I'm the CID engaged in a murder inquiry. If I want, I can trip downstairs to where your server is located in the basement and seize the bloody thing, lock, stock and barrel but that," she pursed her lips, "wouldn't be good for the bank and its customers I think. As it is," she nodded towards the computer, "I'm copying files," then she pointed at the monitor, "and God help anyone who tries to stop me. So, do you have a problem with that?"

Neither Scott nor Baxter could know that Sutherland's protest was planned, that it was her secret delight the police were seizing Harry's files.

A sudden thought occurred to Scott who narrowed her eyes as she stared at the monitor.

"Changed my mind," she said almost to herself and whipping the memory stick out of the computer, fetched a pair of forensic gloves from her bag and slipping them on, added, "I'm taking the whole thing," and began disconnecting the computer hard drive leads from the monitor, the mouse and the leads that connected the computer to the server.

"There, all done," she grinned good-humouredly at Sutherland.

Baxter didn't know why Scott was removing the hard drive, but reasoned there must be a some justification and turning to Sutherland, said, "Was Carol Meechan one of Harry McPherson's touchy-feely victims, Miss Sutherland?"

"I really couldn't say, detective, but *if* she was and *if* she complained, I'm certain that our HR department would have a record of it. Why don't you ask *them*?" she suggested, her voice patronising and dripping with sarcasm.

It seemed to Baxter that Sutherland was, curiously and suddenly very relaxed, an instinct she had but couldn't explain. Something had changed; something had occurred but Baxter had no clue as to what it was. What she did realise was that there was no likelihood of her getting anything of value out of the interview now.

She glanced at Scott and raised her eyebrows to indicate she was wrapping the interview up. Snapping her notebook closed, she stood up and smiled at Sutherland.

"Thanks for your time," she nodded and stepped towards the door, but stopped to permit Scott carrying the computer to pass through first and then turning, almost simpered, "I do like your suit Miss Sutherland. You know, such a young and fashionable style like that looks *amazing* on a woman of your age," and with a wave, added, "Cheerio for now."

Baxter could almost sense the shock then rage that followed her. Outside in the corridor, with the door closed behind them, Scott turned towards Baxter and quietly said, "Nice one, neighbour."

"Bitch deserved it," scowled Baxter, but her mind still wondered at Sutherland's sudden change and her unexpected confidence.

As they made their way towards the office designated by Lynn Massey as the satellite incident room in the bank, Baxter's mind turned over every little thing, every word she and Sutherland had exchanged, trying to figure out at what point cause the sudden change in attitude; wondering if she had inadvertently given something away, said something to cause Sutherland to relax. Following her neighbour who strolled ahead of her, her eyes narrowed as she stared at the computer Scott carried.

Could it be, she wondered?

My age? She gritted her teeth; her fists clenched and face red with anger.

Morven Sutherland stared with hate at the closed door; the fair headed detective's slight still ringing in her ears.

Cheeky bastard, she thought and slowly exhaled, but then forced a smile. They has taken Harry's computer away with them and, she smiled even wider, were bound to examine the file she had inserted.

The muster room at Stewart Street police office in the Cowcaddens area of the city centre was a cacophony of noise as the dozen or so traffic wardens all gossiped and laughed among themselves while they waited on the senior warden arriving to delegate their beats for that day's shift.

Agnes McKenna had managed to get herself a seat beside the new guy, pretending not to have noticed he was sitting there, yet anxious to engage him in conversation and trying to work up the nerve to maybe even invite him to her sister's birthday party on Saturday night in the Counting House. Taking a deep breath, she licked at her lips and was about to turn towards him when the door opened and the supervisor walked in, loudly calling out, "Settle down people. Right, beats for today are…" and proceeded to delegate the beats to his shift.

Taking a note of the streets and new roadwork diversions in her notebook, Agnes's thoughts were still on asking the new guy out when she half heard the supervisor add, "…and I've had a wee request from the murder incident room down at cranny hill office," he cleared his throat. "Further to the look-out for the convertible Mercedes they're looking for, they have asked us to keep an eye out for a silver coloured Qashqai," and read out the registration number, sighing and slowly shaking his head as though the request was an extra burden to his already over-worked shift.

Agnes was about to whisper her invitation to the new guy when she stopped, her ears prickled, brow furrowed and eyes narrowing.

As a child, Agnes had attended a Glasgow council school in the Priesthill area of the city and left at sixteen years of age with the minimum of qualifications. A succession of jobs had culminated in her employment with the Council's Parking Unit and though not a higher educated individual, the one thing she was noted for and prided herself on was her razor sharp memory.

"What was that reggie number again, Jimmy? For the Qashqai I mean," she called out, flipping through the pages of her notebook. The supervisor repeated the number to a now hushed room, all eyes trained curiously on Agnes, who wide-eyed stared at him and in a nervous voice, said, "Jimmy, that's one of mine. I put a ticket on that car a couple of days ago."

DI Bobby Franklin sat ill at ease behind his desk, rubbing at his desk while he again read the tick list in front of him, but his sombre mood was not one of pain, but of self-recrimination.

Waz's father-in-law had thanked him, but declined tomorrow's offer of a lift to the mosque for Missus Ahmed and her parents, then surprised the detective by asking if the offer to have Missus Franklin care for little Munawar still stood?

He was more than surprised, having already believed that the family would likely prefer to have one of their own look after Waz's daughter, then almost immediately regretted the thought.

One of their own?

My God, he inwardly rebuked himself, I sound like a bloody racist. Waz was one of us, a cop like me as well as like his daughter, being Scots born; just like me.

One of their own?

He shook his head, angrier with himself than he had been for as long as he could remember. He inhaled and reaching for the phone, dialled his home number, forcing himself to smile when his wife answered.

"Hello hen, you know we discussed the chance that young Waz's wife might need someone to look after his daughter tomorrow, for the ceremony I mean? Are you still up for it?"

"Aye, of course I am," she immediately replied.

He told of her of his conversation with Waz Ahmed's father-in-law and explained the family would prefer the child to be cared for at the Ahmed's house, that he would drop her there an hour before the ceremony and give her time to bond with the wee girl before Waz's wife left for the mosque.

"Are you all right, Bobby? You don't sound too happy love," she worriedly asked.

"Oh, I'm fine," he lied, "just needing a cup of tea and a wee dose of understanding and humility," then with a sad smile, said he would explain when he got home that evening.

The phone had hardly reached the cradle with his hand still on it, when it rung.

"DI Franklin," he answered and listened closely to the nervous sounding woman who some days previously, issued a penalty parking ticket to the Qashqai car he was looking for.

CHAPTER 27

Detective Chief Superintendent Frankie Johnson sat bent over at his desk in his office at Pitt Street, his suit jacket slung over the back of his chair, a cold and empty mug by his right hand and, wearing his new glasses, engrossed in reading the computer print-out summaries and statements so far accumulated in the three inquiries he was now charged with solving as the Senior Investigating Officer.

It made sense, ACC Jonathan MacPhail had agreed that drawing in two murders and a missing banker suspected of the theft of over three million pounds from his place of employment, to collate all three inquiries under the same banner and was now allocated the operational name Midas.

The phone at his elbow rang.

Removing his glasses, he sat back smiling and said, "Hello Lynn, what's new?"

"It's confirmed by the pathologist, Frankie. I quote 'a heavy blow with a sharp bladed implement.' According to the pathologist, its unlikely even immediate medical assistance would have saved him. The blow was murderous and that's his unofficial quote," she grinned into the phone, then asked, "Anything new from your end?"

"Not so far. I'm sitting here going through all the statements. It's worrying that we can't trace this Peter Gibson," he rubbed with a weary hand at his forehead. "I realise that the Ports Unit at the airport trawled through all the CCTV, but there was no trace of him departing. Is it possible he might have gotten through without having been monitored?"

"Anything's possible Frankie, you don't need me to tell you that, but since the terrorist attack at Glasgow Airport back in two thousand and seven, there's a host of cameras everywhere except the toilets, or so I understand," she said, yet not quite certain if even the toilets were unmonitored. "One suggestion I had from one of my team is that Gibson might have skipped the country in disguise with a false passport."

"Is that a credible suggestion?"

"We can't discount it and frankly," he heard her sigh as she added, "we can't discount anything."

"Where are you at the minute, Lynn, are you still at the bank with your team?"

"Yeah, I'll be here for another hour or so, but we're not getting much information," then her voice dropped a little as she continued, "but I'm looking over at my two sergeant's, Baxter and Scott. The two of them are huddled over a box, a computer I think. Hang on Frankie, I'm getting waved over. Give me a couple of minutes and I'll phone you back."

He returned the phone to its cradle, but it almost immediately rung again and thinking it was Massey, he said, "Yes Lynn?"

"No boss, it's me, Bobby Franklin."

Johnson could hear the excitement in Franklin's voce as the DI continued, "Think we might have gotten a break, boss. Two things; I've just had the divisional controller on from Clydebank office regarding the lookout for McPherson's Qashqai motor. It's been discovered lying abandoned behind a disused shed over in the Scotstoun area. According to the controller, it's been dumped and torched; all the windows have been blown out and there's extensive fire damage to the interior. Apparently the area's frequented by the local neds, so it's a fair assumption how the car incurred the damage. Scenes of crime are en route as we speak."

Johnson could feel Franklin's excitement rise in his own chest and inwardly praying to God this was a breakthrough of sorts, asked, "And the second thing, Bobby?"

"Ah, that's a little more interesting," he smiled at the phone as he teased him, knowing that Johnson would be desperate for some good news. "I've not long had a city centre parking warden on the phone. Seems that on Sunday morning she issued a parking ticket to the Qashqai because it was parked in a parking bay designated for residents only."

"And that was where?" Johnson asked with just a hint of impatience in his voice.

"Sorry boss," sighed Franklin, now aware that he was making a hash of the call, "in Brown Street, in the city centre."

"That *is* good news Bobby; well, of a sort anyway." Then a thought struck him. "Two things Bobby; what time was the ticket issued and do we have any idea why McPherson would be parked there?"

He heard the rustle of paper and Franklin answered, "The ticket was issued at zero nine thirteen hours on Sunday morning. As for why the Qashqai was parked there? I've got my analysts chucking through what we know of McPherson's personal history to see if he's got any mates living there. Certainly, it's not his home address; he lives in a wee housing estate over in Clydebank somewhere, that I know for sure. Oh, hang on boss," Johnson heard the phone being placed on the desk and the muttering of Franklin and a female voice. "Still there boss?" asked Franklin.

"Aye, go ahead Bobby," he replied.

"That was my analyst. It seems from the records that the bank provided us with, there is an employee residing in Brown Street; a woman."

Johnson felt a flicker of excitement, but forcing himself to remain calm, quietly said, "Okay Bobby, get the info to Lynn Massey. She's still at the bank. Maybe it's something that she can use."

"Before you go boss, there's something else you should know. I've *finally* had the written report from the lab delivered regarding the bloodstained knife discovered in the boot of Peter Gibson's car that was found in the car park at Glasgow Airport."

"Please tell me that you are going to tell me the blood belongs to Carol Meechan?"

"No, boss," Franklin shook his head at the phone. "Apparently the car was unusually clean, but the report compared a couple of strands of dropped hair that were found in the car to the DNA from the blood. It's a match."

"Does the report identify whose blood or hair it is?"

"No, it doesn't; sorry boss though the report indicates the hair was found lying in the well of the driver's side of the car and on the driver's seat, so the presumption is that the hair has cast off from the driver's head. However, I'm thinking that if she's agreeable, we might have Baxter and Scott visit Susie Gibson again and ask if she'll permit us to obtain a DNA sample from the house from some item that belongs to her husband; his comb, hairbrush or toothbrush or something like that. It would be even better if she would allow us to obtain a familial sample from his daughter."

He hesitated, knowing that Johnson would be considering the consequences of approaching Susie Gibson with such a request and continued, "I don't need to add that the sooner the better boss, to give us a clue as to what has happened to Gibson."

There was a pause while Johnson mulled over Franklin's suggestion and then he replied, "Leave that with me, Bobby. If the blood *is* Peter Gibson's, we will be inferring to his wife that he has come to harm, might possibly even be dead."

Franklin heard him sigh and Johnson continued, "I'll speak with Lynn Massey and I'll get back to you on that."

Father Patrick Gallagher nervously paced the corridor outside the cardiology ward, giving an occasional glance at his watch; a solid, reliable and costly reminder of his father and mother's sacrifice in saving the money from their meagre wages and presented to him when at last, he had completed his training as a priest at the seminary and been posted to his first diocese.

The door to the ward opened and he took a hesitant pace forward, only to be greeted by the young female cleaner who shyly smiled at him as she pushed the wheeled bucket through the door and past him.

He exhaled and shoved his hands into his pockets when the door again was pushed opened and he was greeted by the smiling consultant.

"Good news Father," said the consultant, "I hope you've brought your dad's clothes with you. I'm discharging him as of now. Just make sure the old bugger doesn't run any marathons or go chasing young women now, eh?" he joked.

Patrick grinned, but more with relief than at the consultant's humour and offering his hand replied, "I can guarantee no marathons, but with his touch of the Blarney, I think the lassies in Maryhill better watch out."

He watched as the consultant turned away and taking a deep breath, opened the ward door and feeling much better than he had all week, went in to fetch his father Magnus and take him home.

"So, what are you telling me here Laura?"

Scott pointed to the computer, now again plugged into a monitor, keyboard, mouse and a socket in the room that connected it to the bank's server.

"It's this boss," she replied, typing in Harry McPherson's log-on and password and accessing his files. Her finger traced the file labelled 'private funnd' and right-clicking the mouse, opened the: 'Properties' box.

"McPherson's body was discovered on Sunday, yeah?"

Massey nodded, not quite following, but now catching a hint of Scott's excitement.

"Well, look at this file here," her finger danced across the screen and settled on the box labelled 'Created.'

"This file was added to the desktop screen of the computer yesterday morning before eight-thirty. Someone with McPherson's log-on and password details inserted this file and I'm guessing it was done for us to find. You can also see that whoever the individual is, they misspelt 'funnd' and I'm of the opinion they were in too much of a hurry to notice their mistake. I'm also of the opinion that the file has been inserted by that individual using a USB, you know, a memory stick, but the IT forensics at Gartcosh should be able to confirm when any such device was inserted though again, I'm guessing it was probably at the time the file was created. Someone," she cast a quick glance at Baxter that Massey didn't miss, "who was trying to frame McPherson."

"Okay, you two, I can see that you're nearly peeing yourselves to tell me, so cut to the chase. Who have you got in mind for adding the file," then her eyes narrowed, "wait. First though, what's on the file?"

Scott, the excitement of her discovery obvious in her eyes, licked her lips and related a summarised narrative that the file contained all the false details of each of the dummy companies, as well as the sums of money loaned to the false companies by the bank. In short, concluded Scott, a detailed account of the scam that robbed the bank of the money.

"Does it tell us where the money is now?" Massey anxiously asked. Scott shook her head. "Sorry, boss, the destination account for the stolen funds seems to have been wiped from the file before it was inserted into the machine. Neither does it say who is involved in the theft of the money, but in my opinion the report, for really, that's what it is, was written by someone well versed in banking matters and in particular, the lending of money, as well as being able to spell properly," she grinned.

Massey inhaled and her eyes narrowed. "So, in short, detailed banking business issues for which both McPherson and our missing man, Peter Gibson are well qualified."

"Yes boss."

"So, the crunch question. Who do you two think inserted the file for us to find"

Again, Scott glanced at Baxter, who nodded and turning to Massey, said, "It's just our opinion, boss and we can't base it on anything other than suspicion, but…"

Scott got no further when she was interrupted by a shout.

"Missus Massey, Ma'am," called out a detective, a mobile phone held to his ear. "DI Franklin would like a word if you can; says it is important."

"Stay exactly where you are, you two," Massey wagged a warning finger at the two sergeants and rising from her seat, went to take the call.

Baxter and Scott sat in silence, each lost in her own thoughts when Massey loudly called out for the detectives in the room to gather around her.

"Who's missing?" she asked.

One of the detectives informed her that two colleagues were out the room, conducting interviews with some bank personnel.

"Right, I'll speak with them later, but for now, that was Mister Johnson on the phone. Couple of things you need to be aware of. The bloodstained knife in the boot of the missing man Peter Gibson's car is *not* that of our victim, Carol Meechan. Secondly, our victim Harold McPherson's car has been found lying behind a derelict building over in Scotstoun. Seems it is burnt out and Scene of Crime is on their way there now. Lastly and importantly, McPherson's car was given a parking ticket early on Sunday morning in Brown Street in the city centre. He lived over in Clydebank and according to our information from the bank there is a bank employee resident in Brown Street...."

"Morven Sutherland," interrupted Arlene Baxter, who seeing the surprise on Massey's face, continued, "you asked us who we suspected Ma'am. It's Sutherland; that's the name we were going to give you. She's the deputy Accounts Manager and we believe also had access to McPherson's computer log-on details."

The light tan coloured curtains shielded the midday sun from fully penetrating the back main bedroom where Des Mooney lay in the bed on his back, wincing slightly at the throbbing pain in his lower right leg, but afraid to move lest he disturb her.

He turned to stare at red-headed woman whose hair billowed out across the pillow and who lay on her back quietly asleep beside him, naked under the single sheet that was drawn up to just below her chin. Her soft breathing caused the sheet to rise and drop and accentuated the swell of her firm breasts.

He wondered for the millionth time why a woman like Shona had taken such an interest in a dead-beat like him. Smart, as well as beautiful, younger by sixteen years and with an affluent lifestyle that he could not possibly achieve, yet she was and willing to give up such a lifestyle to be with him.

He softly exhaled, excited to be near her yet dreading the time when he must persuade her that to be with him was wrong, a mistake that she would eventually come to regret.

He watched with bated breath as she slowly opened her eyes and turning her head towards him, smiled.

"Hi gorgeous," he grinned at her as she fully turned towards him, her left hand reaching up from under the sheet to gently caress the abrasion on the right side of his forehead, now healing but looking worse than it actually was.

He stared into her eyes and then suddenly said, "Ouch!"

Her eyes opened wide and she jerked her hand back in shock, until she saw him grinning, then playfully slapped at his bare shoulder.

"Sod!" she grinned at him, "You gave me a fright. I thought I'd hurt you."

"Take more than that you hurt an old guy like me," he returned her grin.

She continued to smile at him and returning her hand to under the sheet, began to stroke at his penis.

He felt himself become aroused and his breathing become shallower as she continued to gently stroke him then moved towards him so that now, their bodies were pressed against each other, her breasts squashed against his chest and his erection fully pressed against her.

"Not so much an old man, I think," she smiled seductively at him, "as a stand-up guy."

He smiled at her humour and with an inward reluctance, took a deep breathe and reached under the cover to gently hold her hand.

"Shona, we need to talk," he began.

"Maybe later?" she teased.

"No not maybe later; now, please," he replied.

She withdrew her left hand and still facing towards him, raised her right arm and rested her head in her hand, staring down at him.

"Is this about us getting together? You know how I feel, Des. I can't go back. I need you. I *want* you. Don't you want me?"

"It's not that I don't want you Shona, you know how I feel. I'm worried that we…" he paused and then corrected himself, "you might be making a mistake, a big mistake."

"You can't speak for me, Des. You don't know, can't imagine what it's like living with him. I just can't take any more of it," she sighed.

"Then leave him, find your own way. You're smart, bright; you can achieve anything that you set out to do."

"But what use is any of it," her voice began to rise, "if *you're* not in my life?"

"I might not get back to work, Shona," he softly said, staring at her, "now that I'm nearing the end of my service, I could end up being retired because of the accident and out of work, an old crippled guy.

All I've got is this bloody flat; all I've known is being a copper and all I'll have is a constable's pension."

"You'll have me, Des, isn't that what we both want? And as for making our way, I could get a job, another income. I'm not exactly helpless, you know. It's not as if I *need* this bloody life I'm living," she almost spat out. "What I *need*, you idiot, is you!"

He was silent; trying to comprehend again what it was that attracted this woman to him. Finally he said, "There's the age gap, Shona, I mean...."

"Bollocks," she angrily interrupted him, "you're Desmond Mooney, the man I love. Not *Constable* Mooney, not loads of *money* Mooney. It's not anything you *have* or *don't* have Des."

She sighed, calm now and added, "You're just simply Des, the man I love and *that's* all that matters to me. Well, mostly, because Des, what I *really* need to know is that you love me too."

He took a deep breathe again and this time, smiled at her.

Opening his arms, he reached for her and as manoeuvred her body to lie across the top of him, he held her tightly, ignoring the pain in his leg and whispered in her ear, "Yes, I love you too, even though I *still* think you're making a big mistake."

She pushed up from him and sat astride him with her hair falling about her, framing her face as she peered down at him, then resignedly shook her head at his misgivings and lay beside him.

They held each other and quietly discussed her plans to return home, break the news of her leaving and collecting what things she would decide to bring with her to his flat.

But not today, he asked of her. He didn't want any complications before Waz Ahmed's funeral service.

She nodded with understanding and snuggled into him.

They made love once more then an hour later, she dressed and left.

CHAPTER 28

The emergency conference that was held and chaired that afternoon in Frankie Johnson's Pitt Street Office was attended by Lynn Massey and Bobby Franklin and also present was Detective Sergeants Laura Scott and Arlene Baxter.

"So DS Scott," began Johnson, "please explain again to an old fart like me that can hardly work a mobile phone and Laura, keep it in layman English; what *exactly* did you find in the deceased McPherson's computer and if anything is of evidential value that you did discover?"

Once more, Scott explained the finding of the file marked 'private funnd', the insertion of the file after the discovery of McPherson's body and her opinion that the file was inserted in haste, hence the misspelling and the file's content that described the method by which the money was stolen from the bank.

Johnson, eyebrows knitted together, sat with his elbows on the desk chair arms and his fingers making an arch in front of his nose.

"But again I repeat Laura, evidentially, from what you described I understand that the information you gleaned from the computer did not disclose any name or names and so does *not* indicate the guilt of any individual?"

"No sir," she agreed with a shake of her head.

"And you, DS Baxter," he turned towards her, "I also understand have an opinion that this woman Sutherland might be of further interest to us, is *that* correct?"

"Yes sir," she nodded.

"Based on what, your opinion only?"

Baxter drew a deep breathe and nodded, biting simultaneously at her lower lip. "I admit sir there isn't much to go on other than my instinct…"

"Which I support sir," interjected Scott, who drew a sharp almost reproving glance from Massey and inwardly she wondered at her impudence.

"Yes, that might be, Laura," Johnson agreed, "but you have been a detective long enough to know that opinion and suspicion isn't fact and certainly isn't evidence. I assume we agree on that?"

"Yes sir," she nodded, humbly accepting the gentle chastisement.

"So Arlene," he turned again to Baxter, "is there *any* evidence, anything at all, that might indicate Sutherland has knowledge of the murder of McPherson or the theft of the money and yes," he nodded, "I am aware that McPherson's vehicle was recorded as being parked in Brown Street where Sutherland resides, but again that in itself is *not* evidence."

Baxter risked a short glance at Scott and replied, "Sutherland knew where McPherson had noted his log-on details for his desktop computer sir. She worked in close proximity with him…"

"But as I understand it, so also did a number of his colleagues, Arlene and that the log-on details or whatever they're called were not hidden, but easily available to any person and particularly those who worked within McPherson's office."

"Yes sir," she miserably sighed.

"So in summary, what we have ladies and gentleman, is the suspicion that this woman Sutherland, because of the proximity of where she worked in close liaison with the deceased McPherson and his vehicle being discovered near to where she resides, *might* be implicated in his death and also *might* be responsible for the insertion of a misspelled file into his desktop computer."

He paused to draw breath and continued, nodding towards Baxter, "In the statement I have read that you obtained from Sutherland, she denies any kind of relationship other than work related, with the deceased McPherson and there is no evidence to suggest or indicate she is in *any way* directly involved in either incident. Is *that* correct so far?"

Those present almost as one nodded their heads, then turned when the door was knocked and was almost immediately opened to admit ACC Jonathan MacPhail.

The five officers respectfully shuffled to their feet.

"Ah, Mister Johnson, I was unaware you were holding a meeting," explained MacPhail, waving for them to resume their seats. "Just wanted a quick five minutes to discuss the arrangements for tomorrow's funeral for, ah…."

"Detective Constable Ahmed, sir," Franklin reminded him in a dull voice and it didn't escape anyone's notice his voice was just short of a growl.

"Yes, of course. DC Ahmed," MacPhail repeated, then added, "Perhaps Mister Johnson you might oblige me with a quick visit to my office when you have concluded here?"

At Johnson's nod, MacPhail left, closing the door behind him.

"As well as an update on the murder inquiries too," added Johnson with a trace of bitterness in his voice, then turning towards the four upturned faces, added, "Did I say that out loud? Pardon me."

Resuming his seat he inhaled and glancing at each of the officers present in turn, settled his gaze on Lynn Massey and said, "I have come to accept that in all my years in the police, there are times when a detective's gut instinct is so overwhelming that it is almost an indicator of an individuals involvement in a crime or offence. On those few occasions and mostly early in my career when I have *not* heeded those instincts, it sometimes has proven to be my own undoing and an opportunity was missed." He paused as though deliberating and taking a deep breath, continued, "I do not intend to ignore the instinct of two of my trusted detectives and therefore, Detective Superintendent Massey, it is my decision that based on the *extremely* slight evidence that we have," he directed a stern gaze towards the two sergeants, "you will arrange for the craving of a search warrant for the house occupied by this woman Sutherland and such warrant is to obtain any evidence that might be found to indicate a liaison between her and the deceased McPherson."

The few seconds of stunned silence that followed was broken by Massey, who simply said, "Yes sir."

"Now," he turned towards Baxter and Scott and formally said, "If you ladies might return to your duties I would like to have a private word with Missus Massey and Mister Franklin."

As the two sergeants stood and turned towards the door Johnson, with a soft smile, added, "And ladies, regardless of what you might think of an old duffer like me, I'm not *that* much of a dinosaur that I can't get excited at the thought of chasing down a suspect and I too, in my day, have had the occasional gut instinct. My advice to you both is *never* to ignore it."

When the sergeants had gone, Johnson sighed and stared at Massey, then almost to himself, said, "I'm taking one hell of a chance, aren't I?"

He smiled softly then continued, "Right then Lynn, be honest. What is our chance of getting a warrant based on the little that we know?"

She shrugged her shoulders and replied, "My best guess, Frankie? Slim to none I would think."

"What about you Bobby? You got any ideas on this?" he asked Franklin.

Franklin screwed his face in thought, then slowly replied, "Might depend on who we approach, boss. You know as well as I do that a Sheriff will issue a warrant if it looks good on paper and some of the Depute Fiscal's," he also shrugged, "well, let's face it. Sometimes they have to be a little *creative* in the application."

Johnson grinned at Franklin's discreet description and then said, "I don't suppose wee Susan Duncan has returned yet from maternity leave? What was it, her third bairn? Susan's always been very approachable, even if she *is* a little acerbic at times."

Franklin returned his grin and replied, "Her fourth wean; a wee girl this time and yes, I spoke to her this morning, albeit for a short time. She's back to work just today and landed the muggings that I reported. The accused is Leigh Gallagher…"

"The lad that was briefly in the frame for Meechan's murder?" interrupted Johnson.

"That's him boss. Appeared from custody this morning and has been fully remanded, so Susan has the case to prepare and thinks that given the evidence against Gallagher, it's likely we're looking at a quick plea and particularly as she intends putting him before a Sheriff and jury."

"What do you think, Lynn?" asked Johnson. "Is it worth having a word with Susan Duncan and trying to persuade her to support a search warrant application?"

"Can't do any harm, Frankie. Particularly if I take our blue-eyed boy with me," she smiled at Franklin. "I think Susan's got a soft spot for the more mature detective."

"That's me," he grinned, "every woman's dream come true."

"I'd have thought more a nightmare than dream," retorted Massey, then turned towards Johnson. "Speaking of kids, Charlie Miller's wife is pregnant."

"Well, that's great news," replied Johnson, genuinely pleased for him. Miller's personal tragedy several years previously, losing his first wife and child to a drunk driver was known to both the men and they greeted Massey's news with a smile.

"Right, back to the business in hand," said Johnson. "The funeral arrangements for tomorrow for young Waseem; I trust everything's been take care of, Bobby?"

Franklin nodded and said, "Operations here at Pitt Street have everything under control, boss. The service commences at one o'clock and with your permission, I intend closing the incident room at Cranstonhill for a couple of hours or so, to permit those staff who wish to attend."

"Agreed, though I must ask you to have someone, preferably a volunteer to remain behind and man the incident room's confidential telephone line."

"Already done boss; I have a member of the Pitt Street control room staff coming in for a couple of hours. And they can note anything that should be phoned in."

"What about the injured man, Constable Mooney?"

"My DS, Emma Ferguson has arranged to uplift him from home. Des insists on attending and, well, it seems the right thing to do."

"Have you arranged a lift for the Ahmed family?"

"Opted to use their own transport, but my wife will be childminding Waseem's wee daughter at their flat over in Govanhill."

Johnson smiled at this and said, "Tell your wife from me she's a star, Bobby," and added, "Okay, well done. Now, as you both will realise the senior commanders including the Chief Constable will be present tomorrow as will likely be a number of what the media like to call dignitaries. The funeral of a cop and particularly an officer from what the media perceive to be a minority group will undoubtedly make the news, so pass the word to your guys to be on their toes. The three of us know that the majority of officers attending will probably be members of one Christian church or another and likely never have been inside a mosque, so we must abide by whatever values or beliefs the Islamic faith practise. Islam has lost a son as we have lost a colleague and brother officer and in that, we are united." He paused and then said, "In other issues, Lynn, Bobby here has suggested that it might be prudent to obtain a DNA sample from Peter Gibson's house or, if his wife DS Gibson agrees, obtain a sample from his daughter. What's your thought on the issue?"

"I don't see that we've much choice in the matter, Frankie. We need to resolve the question as to whose blood is on the knife found in Gibson's car and quickly; and we have to begin by comparing his DNA for either a match or elimination. I don't relish the thought, but if anyone is to speak with DS Gibson, then," she sighed, "I think it should be me, so I'll make the call."

He stared at her and nodding his head, simply replied, "Agreed. I'll leave you to make the arrangement, but Lynn; the sooner the better, eh?"

"Bobby," she turned towards Franklin, "I've got a rather personal issue to discuss with Frankie. Couldn't give us five minutes?"

"No problem Lynn, I'll fetch the car to the Pitt Street entrance and see you there," he replied, then rising left the room and closed the door behind him.

"So, what's this *personal* issue?" asked a curious Johnson.

"No harm to Bobby," she replied, and reached across the desk for Johnson's copy of Morven Sutherland's statement, "but it involves Greg so I'd rather keep it between us two, Frankie," she said, her head dipped as she quickly scanned the statement. "Ah, here it is. When Baxter and Scott told me of their suspicions and mentioned that Sutherland apparently worked in London in the City for an accountancy firm Campson and Baker, I asked Greg to make a discreet inquiry with his opposite number in the City of London Police. Just to poke around and find out if there was anything of interest."

"And the result is?"

"Greg phoned me just before the meeting here and told me that he should hear from his contact by the end of the day and if there *is* anything of interest, Greg will have the information e-mailed to him and then he'll inform me."

"Okay and as you say, we'll keep this between the two of us," he nodded, and added, "Right, now that is settled," he sighed, "I'll let you two get on and contact Susan Duncan. Good luck and bell me to let me know how you get on," he rose from his seat and shaking his head, said, "As for me, I'm off for my quick visit to *my* boss."

Susie Gibson sat on the kitchen stool and stared at the mobile phone in her hand, her eyes narrowing. The call from Detective Superintendent Massey had taken her by surprise and she wondered why Massey needed to personally speak with her when previously, it had sufficed that a Detective Sergeant noted her statement. She reasoned that it couldn't be that they had located Peter or, a chill swept through her, that he was dead for Massey would have arrived unannounced at her door to break such news and probably to gauge what kind of reaction the news would have provoked.

No, it had to be something else.

Her thoughts turned to the phone call she had received from DS Baxter, the phone call indicating Peter's car was discovered at Glasgow Airport. Susie had not officially been informed and guessed that Massey, like every other SIO she had worked for, would be keeping certain privileged information close to her chest. She also knew that Baxter had taken a chance on phoning her and for that she was grateful to the younger woman and would not divulge her knowledge that the car had been discovered, for it would create real problems for the Detective Sergeant.

Is it something about the car, she wondered some more, standing and reaching to switch on the electric kettle.

Almost like an automaton as the kettle boiled, she spooned coffee into a mug and fetched milk from the fridge, but all the while her mind racing with the reason for Massey's visit the following morning and why, she shook her head with frustration in not knowing, did Massey request that Jenny be present too?

It was as she was pouring the boiled water that it struck her and she nervously placed the kettle down onto the worktop, the mug just half filled and blinked rapidly as her a number of thoughts crossed her mind.

DNA.

Anything Massey had to tell Susie would be for her to know as Peter's wife and with Jenny being a juvenile it would then be Susie's responsibility to inform her daughter of anything that concerned Peter. Jenny had no knowledge of Peter's whereabouts therefore, she reasoned, the only possible reason that Massey wished to speak with Jenny was that they needed something from her and the only physical connection that Jenny had with her father was DNA; familial DNA.

That must be it she felt her stomach lurch and her hand, still holding the kettle, shook.

If Massey and the police needed DNA it must be for comparison or elimination purposes and the first thought that came to Susie's mind was blood.

Somehow or other, they had discovered blood and Massey needed to determine if it was Peter's!

Susie gripped tightly to the edge of the worktop as her knees almost buckled and a weakness overcame her. Her body shaking, she stumbled to the nearby stool and sat heavily down, breathing heavily and slowly lowered her head to below her waist to counter the faint that almost overcame her.

She remained like that for a few minutes while the blood rushed to her head and then, almost tentatively, reached forward to grasp the table top and sat upright.

She didn't know why nor could explain, but suddenly the days of her pent up anxiety and anguished concern for her husband overtook her and the tears began to flow unabated.

Des Mooney sighed as the door bell rung again thinking it was bloody time he disabled the damned thing and with a crutch under his arm, hobbled towards the door.

Pulling it open, his eyes opened wide with surprised delight. The young, suntanned woman standing there wearing British army multi-terrain camouflage uniform, her beret sitting atop of dark coloured hair and perched jauntily on her head and a khaki rucksack hanging from one shoulder grinned at him and said, "Hello, dad. What you been up to that you need a nurse to come and smooth your fevered brow?"

"Jill!" he gasped and wrapping one arm about her neck, pulled her close to him and almost dropped his crutch, such was his haste to embrace her.

She held him close and then still grinning, said, "I could murder a cup of tea, dad. Why don't you let me in and you can tell me all about what happened, eh?"

He didn't know why, couldn't explain it, but suddenly the accident, the death of Waz Ahmed and the sudden unexpected appearance of his daughter brought on an emotional response and he had to blink back tears. Biting at his lip, he could only nod as she lifted her rucksack and he led her through to the lounge.

He rubbed at his eyes with the sleeve of his shirt, at first unable to trust himself to speak as he stared at the smiling Jill.

Taking a deep breath, he asked, "When did you get back? How long do you have? Are you all right? Is everything okay?"

"Slow down dad," she grinned at him, "one question at a time, eh?" She dropped her rucksack to the floor and sitting herself wearily down on the couch, tossed her beret onto the coffee table and replied, "I'm here because you got injured. I'm on a compassionate leave, so it's an open-end ticket. I'm not finished out in Afghanistan yet. My tour of duty has another three months to run, but I'm here for as long as you need me, okay? I mean, what's the use of me being a nurse if I can't be here to care for my old man?"

He could only grin in return, then said, "I'll stick the kettle on and we'll have a cuppa and I'll tell you all about it, love."

Exhaling, he stared with pride at his twenty-two year old soldier daughter and then added, "There's a little more than just the accident that I have to tell you, Jill."

"Right," she slowly drawled, uncertain where this might be leading and then asked, "What about Tom? Has he been in touch?"

"You know your brother, Jill. Work, work, work, but he *did* phone and I assured him that I was okay, that he needn't come home."

"What, like Bristol's the other side of the fu…." she hesitated, the curse dying on her lips. "Sorry dad, but sometimes he's such a selfish sod."

"Look, you're here, that's what counts love and I'm already feeling better for seeing you."

She smiled tolerantly and yawning widely, heaved herself to her feet. "I'll get the kettle and have a cuppa with you first then," she theatrically sniffed at her underarm and added, "it's a shower and if you don't mind dad, I'm going to take a few hours shut-eye to catch up. That bloody flight to Brize Norton then the shuttle to Glasgow seemed to take longer than usual, okay?"

"Okay, love," he said.

She was almost out of the lounge door when she stopped, a sudden intuitive thought occurring to her. One hand on the door, she turned towards him and eyes narrowing asked, "Dad, you said there's a little more that you want to tell me; something else besides the accident. It wouldn't be about a woman, would it?"

She could see the answer in his eyes but before he could respond, she thoughtfully nodded her head and slowly said, "Okay then, let me get the kettle on first. If you can put up with the body odour a little longer, I think my shower can wait."

Procurator Fiscal Depute Susan Duncan sat back in her chair, idly rubbing at the recent caesarean section scar on her abdomen with one hand while the other held the short and hastily typed warrant application that she read, her aching feet resting on the footrest beneath the desk because her wiry, small frame was supported by legs that didn't quite reach the floor.

On the other side of the desk, a pensive Lynn Massey and Bobby Franklin watched her for a reaction.

Duncan turned to the second page and grunted, "Hmmm."

"Is that a good '*hmmm*' or a bad '*hmmm*', Susie," asked Franklin.

Duncan placed the two page application down on the desk in front of her and now twirling her fingers into her dark coloured, frizzy hair, replied, "You two have *got* to be kidding me. You want me to apply for your warrant on the hope of finding evidence based on nothing? How the hell can I put that in front of a Sheriff and ask him to sign it? This," she waved at the application, "is nothing more than conjecture and speculation. There's not even the hint of evidence in your application, guys. You really need to give me something else other than guesswork."

"It's the best we can do for the minute, Susie and to be honest, we really need a break in this case. So far, we've got nothing."

"Nothing's right Lynn. I'm sorry," she emphatically shook her head, "but there's no way I can support this application, not if I want to keep my job."

Massey's mobile phone chirruped in her bag and bending down, she saw on the screen the caller was her husband Greg.

"Sorry, can you give me a minute?" she asked, rising from her seat and making her way into the outer officer where Duncan's blue rinse, middle-aged secretary was at a work station, reading glasses perched on her nose and busily typing at a computer.

"Hi," said her husband, "can you speak?"

"Yeah," Massey replied, glancing at the apparently uninterested secretary, her stomach unaccountably churning with hope it was good news. "Please tell me that you have something for me, something I can use."

"Something you can use?" Greg's voice sounded incredulous as he continued, "Lynn sweetheart, I think you've stumbled onto something pretty sinister. I have an e-mail here from my contact that in turn has some pretty useful contacts in the City. Wish I had the same contacts," he almost wistfully added. "However, my contact made it *very* clear that there is a caveat with this information. It cannot and I stress, Lynn, *must not* be used in evidence nor can the source of this information be disclosed. Is that perfectly clear, Lynn?"

She had never before heard her husband sound so anxious about anything he told her and was slightly miffed that he would doubt her confidence, but then almost as quickly reasoned that if Greg was asking this of her, it must be important to him; perhaps even impact on his own line of work.

"Can I use the information to substantiate the application for a warrant, Greg?"

"Will the warrant be used as evidence in open court?"

"Quite possibly yes, if it should prove that the use of the warrant has resulted in incriminating evidence."

There was a sharp intake of breath then he slowly replied, "I trust you Lynn, so what I will ask of you is this. When I forward the information to you, please use your discretion to cherry-pick what information that you need, but just as long as such information does *not* disclose the source. Is that agreeable?"

She smiled at the phone and said, "Yes."

"Okay, I'm forwarding the e-mail now and Lynn, this *will* cost you."

"In what way," her brow furrowed.

"Well," she heard him sigh, "I'm thinking of that racy little black and red number that you've got in the back of your wardrobe from our honeymoon; that tight little basque with the…."

"Right, yes, I'm at the PF's office," she hurriedly interrupted him, her face beginning to blush, fearful the secretary might have overheard and then added, "If you forward that information I'll get it here. Love you," and quickly pressed the red coloured end button on the phone. Taking a deep breath, she smiled at the secretary and asked if she could access the computer to print off an e-mail.

The secretary nodded and stood to permit Lynn to sit at the work station.

Quickly, she accessed her e-mail address and selecting Greg's forwarded e-mail, pressed the button for it to be printed off at the machine located on the adjacent desk.

Standing to allow the secretary to resume her work station, she quickly scanned through the two pages of closely typed information, her eyes widening as she read.

Turning towards Susan Duncan's door, she pushed it open, but before stepping through, remembered and almost absent-mindedly said, "Thanks," to the secretary.

"No bother," replied the woman, her eyes on the monitor screen, but who then wearily added, "at least *you've* got the figure for a basque, dear. Mine went sideways after my fifth wean," then carried on typing.

Suppressing a grin, Massey closed the door behind her and with a renewed confidence, resumed her seat in front of Duncan.

Bobby Franklin stared curiously at her, then sensing that it might be good news simply asked, "What?"

To determine first that the temperature was correct, Morven Sutherland trailed her fingers through the scented bath water and stripping off the short, cream coloured dressing robe, stepped over the side. Slowly lowering herself into the bath, she lay savouring the warmth of the water and idly traced her fingers along the line of bubbles, flicking at them and watching as they popped.

Her eyes might have been watching the bubbles, but her mind was elsewhere.

The two detectives had not been as easy to handle than she had anticipated and had almost immediately decided the fair haired one was obviously worth the watching while the curiously dressed other one, Scott had been her name; she just seemed plain... *devious*.

She sighed and realised that perhaps she hadn't fooled them as she had hoped and it worried her that the detective called Scott had insisted on taking away Harry's computer. Even she had to admit she wasn't *that* IT aware and worried even further that her planting of the file might not have deceived after all, but reasoned that if the detectives *had* been suspicious of her, she would have been detained in the bank.

She gritted her teeth, recalling the *nasty* slight the one called Baxter had made about her age and her eyes narrowed as like a shadow of uncertainty, self-doubt crept upon her and she wondered; *was* she beginning to show her age?

She glanced down at her naked form, her breasts breaking the surface of the water and she gently squeezed them, fondling the ripe nipples that stiffened as she caressed them. No, they were still firm she decided and slowly let her hand slide down towards her belly; smooth and even, a tribute to the daily workout regime at the building's private gym and to which she rigorously adhered. Eyes half closed, she let her hand slide even further to cover her Venus mound and with the heel of her hand, rubbed at it and gave a small sigh of pleasure as the memories of past lovers came to mind.

Her eyes opened wide and she self-consciously grinned at what she was doing; this was not the time for distractions, she inwardly decided, not when she had to consider what was at stake.

Her thoughts turned to the money and again, she wondered how the hell was she going to gain access it?

Would Peter have told anyone, she wondered for the thousandth time, almost immediately dismissing his policewoman wife and smirked. A copper would have been the *last* person he'd confide in. Or would he?

Again, she wracked her brain, trying to imagine who he might have trusted with the account information and password?

They had argued long and weary that she needed the account information as well as he, arguing that should anything befall him, she would be left high and dry; remembering him laughing and dismissing her argument at her lack of trust in him and promising that when they left together, all their dreams would come true.

The plan had seemed so simple on paper. Dummy companies awarded the bank loans and the loaned money forwarded to the account in the Cayman Islands bank.

The account, she seethed with frustration, knowing where the money was yet unable to access it without the necessary information. Her hands clenched in anger, teeth gritted and unconsciously shaking her head, she made her decision.

The scam was getting out of hand and she could not figure out how to resolve it and rescue the plan that she had so elaborately concocted. There was nothing else for it. She needed to leave, abandon everything other than her identity escape kit and get away before suspicion fell upon her. The money she had deposited in the bank account under her new assumed name would easily tide her over for the next few months and could be accessed from an ATM anywhere in the world. It hadn't been difficult setting up the account for after all, she inwardly grinned; it was her who had approved Miss Alana Beatson's banking application and request for VISA cheque cards that were now with the few items of clothing she kept in the emergency escape bag handily located in the cupboard by the front door.

Tomorrow would be a short drive to Cairnryan to catch the car ferry to Belfast and then she would drive to Dublin, the beauty of the plan being that there was no need to produce a passport. Once she arrived in Dublin she would take a week or so to plan her next move and somehow or other, procure herself an Irish passport and then consider either Europe or maybe even the United States.

She smiled, for the opportunities that lay before her were endless. Pushing herself to her feet she reached for the brilliant white Egyptian cotton towel and began to roughly and vigorously dry herself, but all the while making her plans for departing. The towel wrapped abut her, she made her way into the bedroom and glanced about her. The flat meant nothing to her, just another convenience, another step towards her ultimate goal; complete financial freedom to do whatever she wanted.

Leaving tomorrow morning after a good night's sleep would be best, she decided and as she slipped into her robe and reached down to pull the plug and empty the bath, began to plan her new life.

The phone on Acting DCI Charlie Miller's desk rang just as he was leaving the office. He considered ignoring it, but with a sigh, his conscience got the better of him and snatching at the receiver, growled, "DCI Miller. I hope this is important, I've my wife to meet and she can be a bad bugger if I'm late."

The soft laughter was followed by the female controller telling him, "Its Lesley Gold here, sir. I don't want to keep you from your missus, but you *did* request a PNC check on a registration number?"

"A PNC check?" he slowly repeated, then recalled, "Oh, aye Lesley, a wee van. What you got for me hen?"

"The number you gave me relates to a small Peugeot van, the registered keeper being a Thomas McIntyre of Scaraway Street in the…"

"That's okay Lesley, I know where Tommy lives," he interrupted her, his mind cast back a number of years when as a young Squad member, he investigated Tommy McIntyre, former prolific housebreaker who targeted private properties where the rich and famous lived. If his memory served him correctly, McIntyre served six years for his crimes and according to the last intelligence Miller read, it was recently suspected that while no longer actively breaking into houses, McIntyre was heavily involved in handling and resetting the property that was stolen by others.

Interesting though that Tracey McPherson's father was McIntyre, but likely of no use to the inquiry team, he thought.

"Anything else, sir?" asked the cheerful Gold.

"Ah, no, thanks Lesley. That'll do for now," then a thought struck him. "How you are your postie getting on then?"

"My Andy, you mean? Fine, sir, I'm still working on him, getting him round to my evil ways," he could almost hear her grinning, "and I kind of suspect there might be a wee offer coming my way soon."

"Would that be an offer with a ring attached?"

"Ah, now you're fishing. Away home to your wife and tell Sadie I said hello."

"Right you are," he smiled and glancing at the wall clock, ended the call, but his hand rested on the phone and with a further glance at the clock, sighed and lifting the phone from its cradle, dialled the number of the incident room at Cranstonhill.

Lynn Massey had instructed Bobby Franklin to return to Cranstonhill not only to brief the inquiry team with an update, but to catch up on Emma Ferguson's progress as Acting DI and offer any assistance of counselling during her new role.

But first, she had Franklin drop her at Pitt Street, having decided that she would prefer to brief Frankie Johnson personally with the new information rather than a phone call. Besides, she told Franklin, her car had been left in the underground car park.

Johnson, waiting patiently in his office, had the foresight to have some coffee brewed and waiting ready to pour when she knocked on his door.

"I presume your hubby came through with some good information, Lynn?"

"Good enough to obtain the warrant and have it signed, Frankie," she smiled at him "Bobby Franklin has it and will hitting the house early tomorrow morning."

"So, what's the story?" he asked, handing her a black coffee.

She sat down and sipped appreciatively at the steaming brew, pleased that Johnson remembered she preferred a china cup.

"Well first things first. It seems that Morven Sutherland is not after all *Morven Sutherland*," she began.

"How so?" his eyes narrowed as he sat back in his own chair, his fingertips creating an arch in front of his nose.

"Greg sent me the information his informant in the City of London force obtained, but stressed I was to disseminate *only* that information that neither identified the source, but would permit me to obtain the warrant."

"So, it's a need to know as it were?"

"Yeah Frankie, that's it exactly. So you will forgive me if I ask that you don't disclose all the information?"

"You got the warrant Lynn, that's all *I* need to know," he smiled at her, "but of course I'm keen to know how you achieved that without giving all of Greg's information away and what do you mean, that Sutherland isn't who she says she is?"

"Sutherland was born Gwen Margaret Jones forty-three years ago in Cardiff, so the date of birth on her statement that gives her age as thirty-seven is a few years adrift. According to Greg's informant, Jones comes from a working class background, a pretty dysfunctional family by all accounts and as a teenager in Cardiff accrued a record for petty crime; shoplifting, theft from her place of employment, but more of interest to us, is recorded as a particularly good DSS fraudster. It seems she has a keen analytic mind and started life as a trainee book-keeper, then graduated to become the brains behind a gang producing benefit books and benefit hardship cheques and I'm not talking a few hundred quid here, Frankie. The gang apparently had sufficient resources to produce the books and cheque to be disseminated throughout the UK and could have caused serious damage to the Department's budget that in turn would have affected the genuine welfare of hundreds of thousands of families. When the South Wales Police, with the assistance of the National Crime Agency, eventually arrested the gang, Jones gave evidence against her fellow accused and was rewarded with a conditional sentence. However, immediately after the trial and in response to threats from the families of her co-accused, she fled Cardiff and then the next time she's heard of popped up in London, but this time under the name," Massey glanced at her notes, "Marilyn Morning." She glanced with a smile at Johnson and continued, "According to Baxter and Scott's description of her, she's blonde, very pretty and speaks with a soft, husky voice, so work that one out yourself."

"Anyway," Massey continued, "while in London she came to the notice of the Metropolitan Police as the girlfriend of one of a bunch of violent jewel store robbers. It seems the Met received a tip-off and they arrested the gang. Sutherland, or whatever you want to call her, was caught fleeing her flat with a bagful of the gems and charged as an accessory; however, she turned Queen's Evidence and cut a deal with the Crown Prosecution Service. Needless to say, the mysterious informant who phoned was never identified, other than it was a woman with a slight Welsh accent, so again, work *that* one out for yourself."

"Don't tell me, let me guess," he sighed. "This deal she cut with the CPS in cooperation for her testimony; it provided her with a new identity and background?"

Massey grinned and replied, "Hello Morven Sutherland, junior accounts assistant and employee of Campson and Baker."

His eyes narrowed with curiosity. "You said that the information Greg provided was to be used discreetly, Lynn. Surely what you've told me must be public knowledge through court records and suchlike. I'm afraid I don't quite follow, Lynn, what's so secret about all that you said?"

"Yes, correct Frankie," she nodded, "and I should add that no harm to Bobby Franklin, but that's *all* he knows, up to this point, I mean."

"Okay, I understand that."

"So to continue, according to what Greg has e-mailed me, it seems that Campson and Baker is the premier London accountancy firm for the rich and famous and include as their clients Government ministers and some of the minor and less ranking Royal's."

"Ah, I think I know where this might be going," he took a sharp intake of breath. "But wasn't there any kind of vetting done prior to her starting work at the firm? I mean, surely an accountancy firm *must* have some sort of reference checks completed?"

"The Morven Sutherland identity came with a checkable history that confirmed to her new employer she was squeaky clean and besides, she apparently demonstrated some competency in book-keeping that she likely learned during her apprenticeship as a book-keeper and subsequently through her previous shenanigans when she was counterfeiting DSS benefit books and suchlike."

"How long was she at the accountancy firm then?"

"Long enough to become involved with a Royal," she sighed, "though for obvious reasons, Greg couldn't disclose which one. It seems that a few weeks after commencing work there, she took the opportunity to introduce herself to a visiting Royal and turned on the charm. Pretty soon after that, she's been moved into a 'grace and favour' flat in the Westminster area of London and her *frequent* late night visitor is the said Royal. Because of the liaison, the nameless Royal's Close Protection Officer caused a security background check to be made and Sutherland's true history was disclosed.

Needless to say, there was a risk of scandal and Miss Jones or Morning or Sutherland or whatever you want to call her, was immediately interviewed, ordered to back-off from the relationship and offered a non-disclosure agreement, though frankly, given her previous criminal history, I don't think it's likely she would honour such a deal. The deal apparently was she move on without causing a fuss and she'd be granted a sparkling job reference from Campson and Baker for her new position with the Caledonia Banking Group, as well as a generous gratuity that among other things enabled her to purchase her flat in Brown Street, a fancy car and likely still have a tidy sum left in the bank!"

She stared at a stunned Johnson, who simply muttered, "Bloody hell."

"So," he said at last, "what information did you disclose to Susan Duncan to obtain the warrant?"

"Just the information about Sutherland's previous identities and her cutting deals with the CPS in both Cardiff and London."

"And that was enough to get the warrant?"

"Well, Susan did first find out which Sheriff's were sitting at court at the time and it seems that Sheriff McPhee, who signed the warrant, is married to an accountant who just happens to be a associate Director of the Caledonian Banking Group."

"That was damned fortunate," replied Johnson, who then asked, "What time do you intend executing the warrant?"

"I've instructed Bobby Franklin to take a team and Scenes of Crime personnel for a 7am search tomorrow morning of Sutherland's Brown Street address. He's arranging for the surveillance to watch the place tonight to ensure she's at home. I can't personally go because I'm travelling with DS Baxter to visit DS Gibson at home at eight in the morning."

"Why so early?"

"I thought if her daughter's still at school, I didn't want her keeping the girl off."

"You think she'll cooperate, about the DNA I mean?"

Massey shrugged her shoulders. "If she's telling us the truth, why wouldn't she want to cooperate, Frankie?"

"So you have still a lingering doubt she might be involved in her husband's activities?"

"I really don't know, but we can't dismiss it, can we?"

He shook his head and said, "No we can't, but I don't need to remind you, the woman and her daughter *might* be victims too, Lynn."

"I know, Frankie," she smiled at him, "so trust me. I'll be my usual sensitive self."

With that she left, promising to update him regarding her visit to Susie Gibson and to see him at the 2pm funeral for Waz Ahmed.

Walking through the underground garage towards her car, she blushed and self-consciously grinned, recalling that she had a debt to pay that evening and hoped that the tight black and red basque still fitted.

CHAPTER 29

Bobby Franklin hadn't slept well and rather than disturb his wife, arrived just after five that morning at Cranstonhill. Carefully, he carried his black suit in the bag from the car and hung it in his office. If the search at Brown Street took longer than anticipated, he might not have time to return home to change and his wife would have to find her own way to the Ahmed's flat to care for the wee girl.

The hubbub of noise from the incident room seemed to indicate the officers he had designated as the search team was already arriving and he was pleased to have seen the large blue van in the yard that belonged to the Scene of Crime department.

The note on his desk from the departing nightshift officer that manned the incident room telephone hotline informed him that nothing new had come in other than a call at five that morning from the surveillance team leader, who reported no movement at the Brown Street flat and that the suspect's car remained parked in its bay in the underground car park.

So far, so good he thought.

Across the city, Lynn Massey, fully dressed in a bottle green trouser suit and carrying shoes in one hand and matching shoulder bag in the other, quietly tip-toed to the bed and bent to give her sleeping husband a peck on the cheek.

Turning, she almost tripped over the basque that lay discarded on the floor by the bed and smiled at the memory of Greg removing it from her. She lifted the item and with a self-conscious grin, gently draped it on the bottom of the bed where he couldn't fail to see it when he awoke. With a final glance at her husband, she turned and quietly left the room.

In the kitchen of her home in Alexandria, DS Arlene Baxter sipped at the steaming hot cup of coffee and munched at the bagel while she glanced at the clock. It wouldn't do to be late for the boss and hurriedly grabbed a last mouthful of coffee as she grabbed at her jacket and then closed the kitchen door behind her.

DS Laura Scott again turned the key in the ignition, staring in frustration through the windscreen while her husband Daryl, wearing a jacket over his pyjamas, laboured beneath the bonnet at the engine. "Bugger it," she angrily muttered and glancing at the dashboard clock, got out from the driver's seat and grabbing her mobile phone from her handbag, first urgently phoned for a taxi then called Cranstonhill office to inform DI Franklin she would be late and instead of going to the office, would meet the team in Brown Street.

Susan Gibson hardly slept at all through the night and was in the kitchen before six o'clock that morning, the kettle boiling and her mug with a spoonful of coffee granules awaiting the water.
Time and time again her thoughts turned to Detective Superintendent Massey's pending visit and the purpose for that visit.
Automatically, she poured the boiled water into the mug and stirred in a little milk.
By now, Susie had convinced herself the visit was to obtain Jenny's DNA; it could be for no other reason and guessed that possibly the visit was related to the discovery of Peter's car, the sleek and powerful bloody machine he loved and jokingly referred to as the Beast.
She cradled the mug in both hands and was about to sip at it when she stopped, her brow furrowed as a thought crossed her mind.
Could it be so obvious?
A sudden excitement hit her like a bolt and her chest tightened. She placed the mug onto the worktop, spilling a little in her haste and her slippered feet making no noise, hurried upstairs to her bedroom and closed the door softly behind her.
From the top drawer of her chest of drawers, she withdrew Peter's electronic notebook and fingers shaking, pressed the on button. The

notebook burst into life, startling her with its little jingle. She grabbed at a pillow to subdue the noise, but to her relief it ceased and a password box appeared, but then the screen went dark. "*Fuck!*" she burst out, but realised that her hours of trying to unlock it had exhausted the battery's power supply. Nervously animated, she threw the notebook onto the bed and quickly searched through Peter's side of the fitted wardrobe for the power cable, finding it in his sock drawer and plugged the machine into the socket by the bed. Again the jingle startled her and impatiently, she waited for the password box to appear. When it did, she typed in 'beast', but nothing happened. A wave of disappointment swept over her and almost as an afterthought, she typed in 'the beast'.

To her surprised delight, the screen burst into life and a row of file folders appeared down one side with headings that read 'serial numbers', 'account numbers', 'passport numbers' and other domestic details that were to her, readily identifiable. However, on the other side of the screen, one file folder sat alone and was simply headed 'caymans'.

Later, she couldn't say how long she stared at the folder, whether it was one minute or ten, fearing that if she opened it the folder would make a liar of the man she knew and loved; make a mockery of the trust she had in Peter and destroy twenty years of marriage.

She took a deep breath and slowly exhaled, working up the courage to open the folder.

Her forefinger trembled as she manoeuvred the inbuilt mouse and caused the arrow to hover over the file.

It would be so easy she thought, to switch the damn thing off, destroy the bloody machine, but she knew the genie was out of the bottle, that she would never forget seeing the folder and would forever wonder what it contained.

She double-clicked the right hand button at the keyboard and the folder immediately opened.

Susie was a divisional detective, vastly experienced in the way of the criminals she dealt with on a daily basis and though being aware of the definitions of fraud, would never consider herself to be an expert in the intricacies of the crime for after all, she inwardly reasoned, that is why the specialised Fraud Squad were on call to support the divisional detectives, like her.

As she read the list of companies and the amount each listed company was loaned she realised that what she was looking at was a elaborate scheme to steal a fortune from the Caledonian Banking Group and to her horror, while none of it made any real sense to her, it seemed that it was her husband who had devised the scheme.

Tears welled in her eyes as she continued to read and try to make sense of the details of the fraud, unaware that what she *was* reading was an exact copy of the information discovered by Laura Scott on Harry McPherson's desktop computer.

However, what Susie didn't know was that the file she read contained a sub-heading at the conclusion.

Nor could she know the subheading had been deleted by Peter Gibson from the folder he had copied to a USB and shared with Morven Sutherland; the same copy which was later discovered by DS Laura Scott on Harry McPherson's computer

For the sub-heading that Susie read was sought not just by Morven Sutherland, but also the police and listed the account information and password to access three million, two hundred and sixty thousand pounds that was now sitting in the McMurray Bank of Cayman in the Cayman Islands.

Des Mooney rolled on his back to try and find a more comfortable position in the bed. He thought again of the conversation he had the previous evening with his daughter Jill, now asleep in her own bedroom.

He had worried that she would be judgemental, annoyed that he was so easily giving up the memory of her mother, then surprised that it was Jill who had reminded him that he had been alone for over fifteen years, that he had struggled to raise she and her brother Tom without any real help and held down a coppers job as he did so.

He had never felt so relieved.

They had enjoyed the takeaway together and envied her the bottle of beer she drunk while he had to refrain because of his medicine.

She had related the experiences of her time at Camp Bastion and her uncertainty whether to remain in the army or to pursue a career as a civilian nurse.

No, she had a little hesitantly told him, there was nobody special in her life just now, but he suspected that not to be true; that there *had* been someone, but that it was over and he decided not to press the issue, that if she wished to share anything, she would do so in her own time.

She remained angry that Tom had not come home when told of their dad's accident, if only to ensure that Des was okay.

He had tried to calm her, but suspected there was an underlying dislike for her brother. Though he would never tell his daughter, his wife, Jill's mother had been a selfish woman, but he had loved her and forgiven her that fault and in time reluctantly come to accept their son was more like his mother than he would have wished.

He had told her about Shona, the full truth and held nothing back. How they had met and parted, but recently come together again. He admitted his uncertainty if Shona's decision to live with him had been an avenue of escape for her, but realised that he believed her and that she *did* want to be with him.

He confessed of his concern about the age gap with Shona, but Jill had brushed aside his reservations and grinningly told him that age was a state of mind, not body, that her dad was the youngest man she knew and reminded him that with two vodkas in him, he was the best hip-swinger in town.

Besides, she had snuggled up to him, yawning as the lost hours of sleep crept up on her, Shona sounded like she was a good woman and if she was good enough for her dad, then Des would have no problem with his daughter. All she really wanted, she had told him as she rose, stretched, yawned again and then kissed the top of his head, was for her dad to be happy and with those final words, sleepily stumbled from the lounge towards her bedroom, all thought of a shower forgotten.

Jill's decision to accompany him to the funeral had pleased him more than he thought and early in the evening he had spent over an hour ironing both his and her outfits for the ceremony.

Now today had arrived.

He turned wearily to glance at the sunlight beginning to peek round the edges of the closed curtains and sighed, for today would perhaps be one of the most difficult days of his career.

Des Mooney and Susie Gibson might both have had sleepless nights, but neither compared to the difficult night experienced by Alima Ahmed, who throughout the darkness had wept and sobbed as she lay in her lonely bed and held close a framed photograph of her beloved husband Waseem.

In the guest room, her father lay holding his wife close to him, occasionally biting at his lip with helplessness, as he worried at the suffering of his daughter.

At the foot of the bed, his grandchild lay sleeping peacefully in her cot.

She quietly turned and stared blankly with sorrowful, unseeing eyes at the walls of the spare room. She thought again of the momentous decision she had taken and the impact and far reaching consequences of that decision, but knew there was no turning back now.

She knew he had his suspicions, that there was someone else and two days previously he had challenged her and in fury even raised his fist, but drew back when he saw her flinch as if shocked by what he had intended and turning on his heel, angrily left the room without another word.

He had not spoken of it since, but yesterday curtly reminded her that this afternoon, she must accompany him if for nothing else, appearance sake.

She had reluctantly agreed and slowly turning, stroked away the thick red hair that had fallen across her eyes and stared at the black dress and veiled hat that hung from the wardrobe door.

The officer in the surveillance van with the power company logo signs on the side was bursting for a pee. His partner, who had taken the first shift of four hours, was dozing on top of the crumpled sleeping bag on the floor of the van.

It was unfortunate that after almost three hours of constant staring through the small grill window in the side of the vehicle, the officer chose that few minutes to turn away to pee into the empty, plastic two litre milk jug and missed the fire engine red coloured Audi TT exit the underground garage from the flats he was observing.

CHAPTER 30

A little before seven o'clock that morning, DI Bobby Franklin and his team of three detectives, four uniformed officers, one of whom carried the heavy metal battering ram or 'door opener' and three white paper-suited Scene of Crime officers arrived in a convoy of four vehicles that rendezvoused in the Broomielaw, just round the corner from Brown Street flats.

Franklin spoke into the handset of the car radio and inquired of the surveillance team leader, "Any update on our suspect?" only to be assured there was no change and that the suspect's vehicle was still in the underground car park.

Satisfied that everyone was ready, Franklin gave the word to proceed to the suspects flat and the convoy moved round to the main door of the building, with the forensic team remaining inside their vehicle until the flat was entered and secured.

Waving two detectives down the ramp towards the car park, Franklin and the remaining officers pressed the service button that permitted them entry to the stairwell of the flats, but had hardly reached the target flat when his radio burst into life and one of the detectives in the basement breathlessly informed him, "Boss, the suspect's car. It's gone!"

DS Laura Scott arrived in the taxi to find the two detectives exiting the car park, seeing one heavy-set detective puffing up the ramp while his skinny partner shook his head at the utilities van parked across the street.

"Fucking idiots," the skinny one seethed at her. "Sutherland's away. They said she was in her flat last night. How the *hell* could they miss her driving out? I mean, for heavens sake, it's not like they can't see the bloody ramp!"

"Right, before we start the blame game," she soothingly replied, "why don't we find out what's happening upstairs, eh?" and led them towards the main door of the building.

Scott found Bobby Franklin standing in the hallway of Sutherland's flat and he was not in the best of moods. Angry as he was though but unlike his DC, he didn't want to apportion any blame till he had the facts, but that could wait he told Scott and ordered her to put a lookout for the Audi's registration number and to include it in the Automatic Number Plate Recognition list.

"You think she could be heading south, boss?" Scott asked, aware that ANPR cameras were located along the border area.

"No idea, hen, but one thing's for certain; she isn't here," he pointed to the front door that now hung crookedly and the grinning, burly cop who stood there with the 'door opener' at his feet.

"Right guys," Franklin waved to the three detectives in the flat, "we've cleared the flat but before we conduct a thorough search, I want the Scene of Crime boys in first. I don't want to contaminate the locus any further, so," he pointed to a detective holding a radio, "step outside and call them in."

Unexpectedly he turned to Scott and asked, "What happened with your car?"

"Don't ask me boss," she shrugged her shoulders, "if there's a noise or a squeak, I just turn up the radio. All I can say is that the bloody thing wouldn't start, so my man is having a look at it the now."

Franklin grunted his sympathy, recalling his time as a young DC when every penny was a prisoner and the bald tyre bangers that were the only things he could afford.

He beckoned the other detectives and uniformed officers towards him. One detective and one cop were instructed to stand by the front door of the flat to deal with nosey neighbours or provide any assistance the Scene of Crime needed while the others he dispatched to a van that served morning rolls and hot beverages on the Broomielaw near to Washington Street. He grinned as he saw face's fall and said, "Don't be worrying. I'll have you relieved in half an hour, okay?"

It was then that his mobile phone rung and stepping to one side saw on the screen the caller was Frankie Johnson.

"Morning boss," he greeted him, then related the bad news that the suspect was not at home and the door had been forced, adding the Scene of Crime were now in the flat giving it a once over.

"Any likelihood she was tipped off," growled Johnson, annoyed at the setback, but immediately regretting his words for it would imply that there was a leak or informant in Franklin's team. Before he could retract his question, Franklin replied, "No chance. I think she probably just got the wind up and took off. I've got Laura Scott putting the word out, so with a bit of luck, she won't get too far."

He turned when the detective he'd left on the door tapped his shoulder.

Franklin said, "Hold on boss," and stared curiously at the DC.

"The Scene of Crime supervisor wants a word, boss. I think they've found something."

Franklin felt a slight stir of excitement in the pit of his stomach and said to Johnson, "I'm needed at the flat, boss. I'll call you back," then concluding the call, followed the DC to the front door.

Lynn Massey uplifted Arlene Baxter from the West Regent Street door at Pitt Street and set off through the morning rush-hour traffic towards the M8.

"What kind of reception am I going to get from her?" she asked Baxter.

Baxter didn't immediately reply, but took a few seconds to consider the question.

"Obviously, Ma'am, I can't say with one hundred per cent certainty, but I believe that DS Gibson is as dumbfounded about her husband's disappearance and the theft of the money from his bank, as we are. During my interview with her, I'm confident that she told us the truth or what she perceives to *be* the truth. I mean," she turned her head to reinforce the point, "it doesn't matter if we interview a civilian or a cop, everyone lies to the polis, though for a variety of reasons."

"Explain that to me?" replied Massey, concentrating on the Saab estate car in front that weaved down the Charing Cross ramp towards the motorway, the driver intent on forcing his way past the Fiat Punto, whose driver she could see nervously kept turning his head towards the motorway traffic and seemingly unaware that he was driving in a dedicated lane.

"Well, my experience is that interviewees will lie to avoid telling the truth to protect themselves or others, they'll lie by either adding information or failing to provide information, they'll lie because they believe that's what I as the interviewing officer wishes to hear; as I said, a whole variety of reasons."

"Okay, I accept that, but I ask again; what's your gut feeling about DS Gibson? Is she a credible witness?"

Once more, Baxter inhaled and took her time to respond as though deliberating, then replied, "I think DS Gibson will lie to protect her family," then shook her head, "but only if she thinks her husband is innocent, not if she thinks he has betrayed her and especially not if he has betrayed her daughter. If we can prove that Peter Gibson is the thief we believe him to be, then there is a likelihood she will wash her hands of him because she will *not* want to risk her job and livelihood for him. Not because she's worried about her own career, but her livelihood provides her daughter with the comfort and security and her way of life. No," she shook her head, "I don't think she would risk Jenny's happiness or expose her to a life that she doesn't know."

"Jenny, that's her daughter's name? Curiously," Massey shook her head, "I never thought to ask. Just as well you mentioned it."

Now on the motorway, she nudged through the traffic to the outside lane while wondering how they might prove that Peter Gibson has committed the theft.

Morven Sutherland raced the red car along the A77 towards Cairnryan and the early morning ferry. The radio cackled as the signal became intermittent so instead, she pressed the CD button, smiling as the sound of Genesis blared from the speakers.

She wasn't stupid and had seen the utilities van parked across the street, guessing them to be the police. However, she hadn't been stopped by the cops in the adjoining streets and wondered if maybe, just maybe, she had got it wrong.

But if as she surmised, the two detectives hadn't been fooled by her insertion of the USB into Harry's computer then she was better off out of it and taking no chance.

Ah well, she inwardly grinned, better to try and fail than fail to try as a former boyfriend had once told her and besides, she had plenty of ideas for other scams.

A bus loomed ahead and she swerved round it, laughing as the irate driver flashed his lights at the nutter overtaking him on a bend.

Life's for living, you dumb fuck she thought, mentally giving the driver the finger.

The signpost pointed straight to Stranraer, then she would be almost at Cairnryan and in the far distance, she could even see the early morning sun shining on the waters of the Irish Sea and breathed a little easier.

She would be across the water and over the Irish border before the bastards even knew she had gone.

Susie Gibson shook the sleeping Jenny awake.

"Morning sleepyhead," she smiled at the tousle headed teenager and placed a cup of tea and plate of toast on her bedside cabinet.

"What time is it?" mumbled Jenny with a yawn.

"Gone seven-fifteen, love. You remember we've got the detectives coming this morning at eight?" replied Susie, lifting discarded sweat shirt, pants, socks and a bra from the bedroom floor.

"What you doing mum," asked Jenny, staring with weary eyes at Susie. "They're not coming in here to my room, are they?"

"No, of course not," replied Susie with a confidence she didn't really feel. "But you know me, I'm only doing what mum's do," she cheerfully added and carrying her daughter's washing, closed the door behind her.

In the hallway outside, she stood with her back to the wall, hearing Jenny rustling about and rising from bed, then her en-suite door opening. She sighed as once more, she worried about the decision she had to make.

Would she tell DSU Massey that she had accessed Peter's notebook and that within, discovered the folder that contained details of his theft, the evidence of his guilt?

Jill Mooney was up and showered before her father arose, blaming the early rise on her disrupted body clock and the time difference between the UK and Afghanistan.

In his own bedroom, Des Mooney smiled when he heard the rustling in the kitchen. For the briefest of seconds, he thought about shouting out that he was awake, that he was getting up, but then the smell of bacon assailed his nostrils and he smiled and decided to let Jill have some time on her own, guessing that there was little room for privacy from where she had so recently arrived.

The skipper of the old puffer was well past retirement age and constantly ignored his wife's pleas, telling her, "There's nothing like the smell of the salt or the roll of the sea under my keel. Do you not understand, woman? That's what keeps me *alive*!"

He grinned as he steered the boat through the waves, calling down to old Archie at the bow to get the kettle going, that he fancied a cuppa. Archie, his long time friend raised with him on Skye, grinned up at the wheelhouse and began to wave in acknowledgement but stopped; his arm stiff as he craned his neck to get a better view.

"Look you there, skipper!" he cried out, "To the port side, in the water, there!" he pointed, one hand on the derrick to steady himself against the gentle swell while the other continued to point overboard. The old skipper, his curiosity aroused, rubbed at the condensation in the glass of the wheelhouse and stared into the Clyde, but the sun shining off the water made it difficult. Then he saw what Archie was pointing towards and whispered to himself, "Oh my God," for there less than twenty feet from the boat, floated a body.

Franklin listened to the Scenes of Crime supervisor and asked again, "but you're certain it's blood?"

"Aye, our equipment confirms that there is no doubt about *that* Bobby, but it's been well cleaned and I'm guessing from the smell, bleach was used."

"What about the quantity and is there anything that you can save that might identify whose blood it is?"

"Well," drawled the supervisor, "as I said, there has been a good attempt to clean the blood, but I'm guessing it's all superficial. What *doesn't* seem to have been done is the lifting of the floorboards." He saw the doubt in Franklin's face and using his gloved hands, explained, "Look, whoever has cleaned up the blood spill has wiped *across* the floor and negated any chance of a lift from the floor where the bleach was used, but blood is like any other liquid, only thicker of course. As a liquid, it seeps down through cracks and holes and will always gravitate towards the bottom of any location. That's not to say that some of the bleach might have followed the blood trail down between the joints in the floorboards, but as I said, whoever cleaned the floor has wiped across the floor and likely not considered the blood spill seeping down."

"So you're saying that blood and maybe a wee bit of bleach *might* have seeped down between the joints in the floorboards?"

"Exactly," nodded the supervisor and, now down on both knees, glanced about him then looked up at Franklin. "This flat is part of an old converted warehouse, yeah? These floorboards here," he thrust at the floor with a forefinger, "are likely the originals. You can see they are wider than your modern floorboards. Though they have been cleaned up and polished etcetera and undoubtedly look very nice, they are not as close tight fitting as a tiled floor or a lot of the new laminate floors that are laid. That means that there will be minute cracks where the floorboards, through wear and tear or aging or perhaps maybe even being slightly ill-fitting, will have created cracks between the floorboards. It's my intention to lift the floorboards here in the kitchen to get at whatever is underneath and hopefully, there could be some blood residue that has not been contaminated by the bleach. If there *is* blood there, it's probably coagulated and maybe even crystallised, but fingers crossed, still worthy for the lab people to examine and maybe get some DNA from. My question is, are you okay for me and the guys to rip up the floorboards?"

Franklin smiled at him, a slow and wicked smile.

"Tear the fucking place apart," he quietly replied.

Father Patrick Gallagher, dressed in his old plaid shirt and worn jeans, sat in the diocesan van in the visitors car park at Polmont, watching the entrance to the Young Offenders Institution. He felt curiously nervous and for the umpteenth time, glanced at his wristwatch.

The glass doors were pushed open and two women, cleaners he assumed from their uniforms, exited, busily chatting to each other. As he watched, the women stopped walking and the older, grey haired one reached into the front pocket of her smock and fetching out a packet of cigarettes and a lighter, proceeded to light one. Even from where he sat some fifty yards away, he could see the relief in her face as she drew deeply on the cigarette.

The women walked past the van towards an old Ford Escort, both animatedly talking over each other and through the partially open driver's window, he could hear what he thought must be the local, Falkirk accent.

He glanced in the driver's side mirror, seeing the women enter the Escort and when he looked again towards the front entrance of the prison, his brother Leigh with a plastic bag in his hand, was being escorted out the door by a uniformed prison officer who gave him a small wave before re-entering the building.

Patrick got out of the van and waved towards Leigh, surprised that his brother seemed to hesitate before walking towards him.

"I wasn't expecting anybody to be here," said Leigh, walking to the passenger door.

"Dad wanted to come too, but I thought after his heart scare the best thing is for him to rest up," replied Patrick, getting into the van and starting the engine.

He drove smoothly towards the exit, aware of the uncomfortable silence that lay between them, and quietly asked, "How are you?"

How am I, thought Leigh, his fists bunching in his lap. He swallowed with difficulty, the sudden memory of his first night in the prison causing a chill to sweep through him; the laughing, furtive groping of the older cons in the communal shower, the hissed whispers that he'd better sleep on his back with his mouth tightly shut or a young chicken like him was going to get well and truly fucked; of staying awake all that first night, his back against the corner of his lower bunk, arms wrapped round his knees and sobbing as quietly as he dared to avoid wakening the heavy-set, tattooed junkie on the top bunk, not aware that the junkie meant him no harm at all.

He glanced out of the passenger window and replied, "What, like you mean you fucking care?" snapped Leigh.

Patrick fought the rising wave of anger that coursed through him and as calmly as he could, replied, "Of course I care. Why do you think you were released today instead of remaining on remand?"

"I don't know," shrugged Leigh, "overcrowding maybe?"

"No, not overcrowding Leigh. I contacted the Fiscal's office and spoke with a parishioner of mine, a prosecutor who works there. I explained that you were *not* a risk and that I would be responsible for you. I had to literally beg him to get you what they call a Fiscal's release."

"What," Leigh turned towards him, eyes widening, "you mean I'm not going to trial? I'm free?"

"No, of *course* not," it was Patrick's turn to snap back, "all it means is that you are on bail till the time of your trial and that I'm responsible for you. Didn't they explain that to you when you were released?"

"I signed some forms," he muttered, too embarrassed to admit he didn't even read them nor asked what the forms were, just happy to be gone from the prison.

"Well, like I said, I've put my neck out for you so I expect you to behave until this case goes to court, okay? Any infraction and you're going straight back on remand and that means till your court appearance."

Leigh didn't reply, simply nodded and turned again to stare out of the window, too angry to even contemplate that his *big brother* was once more the hero; once more the big shot; saint fucking Patrick.

Driving towards Glasgow, Patrick experienced a keen sense of disappointment. He hadn't expected Leigh to be overjoyed at seeing him and knew fine well what his brother thought of him. He had always known Leigh to be a selfish boy and now a selfish young man and wasn't expecting a vote of thanks or any kind of emotion from him, but what riled Patrick was not *one* word of concern for their dad.

He gripped the steering wheel hard and angrily thought why the *fuck* do I bother.

Arlene Baxter directed Lynn Massey towards Susie Gibson's house and decided to ask the question that had been troubling her. She waited till Massey was parked and switched off the engine, then asked, "Ma'am, I know of course that our primary purpose in coming here today is to obtain a DNA sample for DS Gibson's daughter, but I've no doubt that you might also have some further questions for her. If that *is* the case and in the unlikely event that you are not satisfied with the answers that she provides," she hesitated, "is it your intention to detain her?"

Massey stared through the windscreen, contemplating Baxter's question and replied, "All I want to do Arlene is satisfy myself that DS Gibson is not art and part of the theft, that she did not in any manner or form collude with her husband nor is she in any way responsible for his disappearance." She took a deep breath and turned to face the younger woman. "The statements that you noted seem to indicate that DS Gibson is innocent and as you *are* an experienced detective, I have to trust that you believe her to have told you the truth," she smiled and added, "regardless of what you previously said about taking a witnesses statement. There is one further thing that I would like to do today, Arlene," and reaching into the rear passenger seat, grabbed at her brown leather folder. From the zipped pocket she brought out a ten inch by eight inch colour photograph of a black handled knife with a serrated edge. "If she's agreeable, I'd like a look in DS Gibson's cutlery drawer."

"Ma'am?" said Baxter, her face displaying her curiosity.

"It wasn't disclosed to the inquiry team, but this is the knife that was discovered in the boot of Peter Gibson's car. That's why we're here, Arlene. Not just to obtain a DNA sample, but if the knife in the photograph is similar to any of the knives in DS Gibson's cutlery drawer, then as you suggested, we might end up by detaining her for further questioning."

The police were waiting with the casualty surgeon and an ambulance crew when the old puffer docked at her berth in Bowling Harbour. The elderly skipper, with Archie the deckhand ready with a rope, skilfully manoeuvred the old boat against the quay and then with the assistance of the Bobbies, the body of the man was lifted onto a waiting stretcher.

Bending low over the body, the elderly casualty surgeon turned the man onto his side and grimacing, glanced up at the two young constables.

"Sorry lads, but this poor soul is going nowhere till you get the CID down here," he shook his head and pointed to the numerous torn holes in the back of the man's jacket. "Unless I'm way off the mark, I don't think this is a drowning. It looks to me like this man has been repeatedly stabbed in the back. I think this is a murder."

CHAPTER 31

Susie Gibson, watching from behind the curtain, saw the two detectives walking up the pathway and, shouting to Jenny to come downstairs, made her way to the front door to open it as Massey and Baxter arrived on the doorstep.

"DS Gibson," Massey smiled and courteously held out her hand, "I'm Lynn Massey and Arlene here you already know."

Susie returned the handshake and invited them into the lounge and offering them a seat, turned to see Jenny at the door.

"Sweetheart, you couldn't pop the kettle on could you?" and turning, offered the two detectives coffee or tea.

Massey smiled at Jenny and requested a white coffee while Baxter asked for water and when the teenager turned and left, Massey said, "Is it okay if I call you Missus Gibson?"

"Susie will be fine Ma'am," she replied, a fixed smile on her face and keen to confirm what Massey wanted.

"Susie then," she agreed and continued, "The reason I asked to meet with you and Jenny today is simply this. I regret to inform you that when your husband's car was discovered at the airport car park, a bloodstained knife was found in the boot," then immediately raised her hands to calm Susie's fears by adding, "So far, we have been unable to ascertain whose blood was on the knife. What I also wish to disclose to you is that two single strands of hair were discovered in the drivers area from which the lab were able to collect some DNA and the DNA from the hair is a match for the blood on the knife. I am *not* saying the hair or the blood belongs to your husband, Susie. Am I quite clear about that?"

Susie, unable to reply, clutched fearfully at her throat and nodded, but shivered as a chill swept through her

Massey waited a few seconds for Susie to compose herself before continuing and then said, "As an experienced detective, I am certain you will be familiar with the advances in DNA technology…"

"You're talking about familial DNA and you want to compare the blood with a sample from Jenny?"

"Yes, if that's possible," nodded Massey. "Obviously we could obtain a sample from a hairbrush that you could identify as belonging to your husband or…"

"No," Susie raised a hand to interrupt and said, "Jenny will provide a sample. We need to know if it's…" she stopped and inhaled, not trusting herself to speak any further.

The door opened to admit a smiling Jenny who walked through carrying a tray upon which was balanced two white coffee's, a glass of water and a plate of digestives.

Baxter rose and helpfully lifted a small occasional table that she sat between the couch and the two chairs and on which Jenny laid the tray.

Susie inhaled and fought back tears then forcing a smile, said "Jenny, Missus Massey here has something to ask you and I've agreed its okay."

"Jenny," Massey began, "as you know we're trying to discover where you dad is and we'd like you to help us by providing a small sample of DNA. It doesn't hurt," she shook her head. "I simply take a swab from the inside of your mouth on a cotton bud and, well, that's it really."

"You think something has happened to him," replied Jenny, her eyes almost accusing, her small fists clenching and her face turning pale. Massey glanced at Susie who gave an almost imperceptible nod and that it was okay to tell her and that her daughter was no fool.

"We hope not," continued Massey, her smile now fading and realising that young as she was, this girl would accept nothing less than the truth. "The sample you provide us with will be used as a comparison sample for anything that we have found or will find that we suspect *might* belong to your dad."

"Mum?" she turned towards Susie, who nodded and quietly said, "I think it's for the best, sweetheart."

Baxter's mobile phone chirruped and leaving Massey to fish again in her leather bound folder for the sample kit, with an apologetic smile Baxter stood and left the room. In the hallway outside, she saw the caller was Bobby Franklin.

"Boss?"

"I called you Arlene because I know you're with Lynn Massey. Is she able to speak?"

"Ah, not right now. She's getting the DNA sample from Susie Gibson's lassie in the lounge. Do you want me to call her to the phone?"

She waited the few seconds for Franklin to decide then almost with reluctance in his voice, he sighed, "Aye, you'd better do that hen. I've got some bad news for DS Gibson."

Frankie Johnson listened intently to Bobby Franklin's account of the discovery of another body in the River Clyde.

"And you're certain it's our missing man, Peter Gibson?"

"According to the cops at the locus he still had his wallet with all his credit cards and bank identification card in the inside pocket of his jacket, boss. Obviously, we need to have a *positive* identification, but for the minute, we're working on the premise it's him right enough."

"Did the attending casualty surgeon give any kind of estimate as to how long he'd been in the water?"

"I only spoke briefly with the doctor on the phone, but he told me that from the time the body was apparently immersed in water, there is swelling to the limbs and there is also facial and body damage from seagulls and what looks like some wounding to the legs, but this he thinks is presumably from a boats propeller. In short, the body isn't really fit for viewing until some work has been done on it. What he is clear about is that there is stab wounds on the back to the upper torso from what he reckons is a narrow bladed weapon."

"Any suggestion there might be a serrated edge to that weapon?"

"I think that PM will likely be the best place for that to be confirmed, boss."

"Aye, you're right Bobby," sighed Johnson. "Have you informed Lynn Massey yet?"

"Spoke to her just before I contacted you," he began to apologise. "I thought as she was at the Gibson's house…."

"You did the right thing," interrupted Johnson. "Better she does it now than have to return later."

Johnson tapped at the folder on his desk with a pen, then hearing the sound of noise through the phone, asked, "Are you still at the flat in Brown Street?"

"Aye, we are that. The SOCO boys are tearing up the floor and so far reckon that what they have found is a 'generous amount of blood'. Their words, not mine, but enough, they assure me, for the lab guys to get to work on so there is already a sample en route to the laboratory out at Gartcosh. I'm also having the flat fingerprinted all over and *all* of the clothes that Sutherland left behind will be going to the lab for analysis. It'll be interesting to discover who Sutherland entertained here."

"Still no word on her whereabouts yet?"

Franklin shook his head at the phone, "Nothing so far, but the good news is the SOCO supervisor agreed that if my guys wore the white suits and gloves, they could commence their search and so far, you'll be pleased to hear, we have discovered a USB in a suit jacket pocket. One of them memory stick things, you know? I had Laura Scott check it on her laptop…"

"Is *that* what she carries in that big bag of hers?" Johnson chortled and then a thought occurred to him. "It's a bit fortuitous that she kept the memory stick, Booby. Call me old fashioned, but surely she would have gotten rid of it if she had thought it was too dangerous to hang onto or maybe even wiped it clean; what do you think?"

"Sometimes boss, I think we give the opposition too much credit. Yeah, I admit people like Sutherland can be really smart and fool us most of the time, but even they make mistakes. Who knows, perhaps she thought that we wouldn't connect the dots or maybe even forgot she had the thing, but no matter. It's in an evidence bag now."

"Anyway," Franklin continued, "don't ask me how she does it, but young Laura more or less confirmed it's the same memory stick that was used to implant the information in the deceased McPherson's desktop computer."

"Now that *is* interesting," agreed Johnson and then asked, "Anything else?"

"Aye, boss. I've saved the last till best. You'll recall the knife that was found in the boot of Peter Gibson's car?"

Hearing the slight raise in the pitch of Franklin's voice, Johnson felt his chest tighten.

"Yes, I remember. What about it?"

"Well," he drawled, savouring the moment, "it just so happens that Miss Sutherland has a set of six of what appears from my memory of it, the same knives, only it seems that one of her set of six is missing."

Among the line of cars and vans that waited to be boarded onto the berthed ferry included a red coloured Audi TT, the good looking blonde driver attracting more than a little attention from two young and unshaven Irish labourers dressed in working clothes who were sitting in the adjacent van.

"Hey missus," called the passenger with a huge grin, his brogue thick and as pronounced as a pint of Guinness, "D'ya fancy a wee drink in the bar when we're onboard, now?"

Morven Sutherland smiled tolerantly and without responding, turned her head away and pressed the button that closed the driver's window, only to be startled when the window was sharply rapped. She turned to give the van's passenger a mouthful, only to see a well dressed young man standing smiling at her and indicating that she roll down the window.

She returned his smile and presuming him to be with the shipping line, pressed the button to lower the window and asked "Yes, can I help you?"

"I'm a Detective Constable with the Ports Control Unit madam, so if you'd lock your car Miss Sutherland and come with me please," he said.

"Oh, I'm sorry, you seem to have mistaken me for someone else," she simpered, and turning from him, began to search through her handbag that lay on the passenger seat, but with a subtle glance at the vehicles around her car. With a sinking heart, she saw she had no opportunity to manoeuvre the Audi through the nose to tail line of vehicles. Almost resignedly, from her purse she took out her bank cards and presenting them to the man said, "Here, this is me. Miss Beatson, Alana Beatson."

The man took the cards from her and inspected them, then with a soft smile said, "Good one Miss Sutherland. The change in name and the cards *might* have worked, but maybe you should have thought about changing the registration number of your car," and with that, he pulled open her door and sharply said, "Out of the vehicle. Now, if you please."

"Hey, what the *fuck* do you think you are all about there, now?" said the adjacent van's passenger, belligerently opening his door and stepping out of the vehicle, challenged the officer in a misguided attempt at chivalry. The driver also left the van and began to make his way round to where the officer stood, sneering and mouthing curses as he walked.

"That wee woman has done you no harm, you arse!" continued the Irishman, his fists balled and beginning to rise for confrontation with the officer.

Suddenly as if from nowhere, a heavyset and older PCU officer appeared beside the first officer, but with a metal extendable baton carried loosely in his hand.

"You had better be thinking twice before you commit yourself to something you can't handle," the burly detective's voice boomed with a soft Highland accent, the baton in his hand now raised and resting lightly on his shoulder as he stared menacingly at the two Irishmen. "You laddies might start it, but *believe* me; I'll be the one finishing it."

The Irishmen's slight hesitancy was all the officers needed and beckoning the startled Sutherland from her car, firmly took their suspect by her arm and marched her through the line of traffic towards their office as a hundred pairs of inquisitive eyes followed them.

Acting DI Emma Ferguson was pleased that she had the foresight to wear her black, formal skirted suit when she commenced work that morning at the office. The phone call from Bobby Franklin, who was detained at the search of the flat in Brown Street, requested she make the visit to Harold McPherson's widow to determine if Missus McPherson was fit to be formally interviewed. The unexpected instruction had disrupted Ferguson's plans for a leisurely morning, checking crime reports and other admin duties prior to uplifting Des Mooney from his flat.

Now, accompanied by a young female DC, here she was rapping her knuckles on the McPherson's front door and getting no response, even though she could hear a wailing child inside the house.

She was about to give the door a good kick when it suddenly opened and she was confronted by an angry young teenager whose middle name, Ferguson thought, must be Insolence and who held the crying child over her shoulder.

"What the fuck are you all about, waking the wean like that," she snarled at Ferguson.

"Is Missus McPherson at home," Ferguson adopted her sweetest smile.

The teenager glanced down at Ferguson's foot in the door and realising the polis were not going away, shrugged and wordlessly walked into the hallway, pointing towards the room that proved to be the lounge.

She stood in the hallway patting the child's back , as the officers passed her by with their backs turned towards her, gave them the finger.

Tracey McPherson, her hair in disarray and wearing a crumpled and stained pink coloured dressing gown, lay slumped on the couch. Upon the coffee table in front of her was a selection of empty spirit bottles, some crushed beer cans and two ashtrays that overflowed with cigarette ends. It seemed very obvious to the detectives that Missus McPherson was either very drunk or drugged.

Ferguson subtly sniffed and detected the sweet and sickly odour of cannabis then turning to her colleague, raised her eyebrows as a discreet warning to say nothing.

She first introduced both her and the DC then said, "Missus McPherson, I'm sorry for your loss. I'm here to determine if you need anything from us and to assure you that we're doing everything possible to find out…"

"Who he was shagging?" interrupted Tracey with a giggle that quickly turned into a hacking cough.

Ferguson waited till the coughing fit passed and then asked, "I'm sorry, are you saying that your husband was having an extra-marital affair?"

"What does that mean?" asked the teenager for the doorway, who proved to be Tracey's younger sister.

"Its fancy talk for asking if he was shagging somebody else," whispered the young DC.

"Oh aye," replied the teenager, nodding vigorously and keen to let the detectives think that she knew everything that was going on by loudly commenting, "Tracey said it was somebody at his work, didn't you hen?"

"You're a grass! Shut the fuck up!" screamed Tracey, trying to rise from the couch, but her legs wouldn't support her and she wearily fell back down.

"Fuck you too and I'm no a grass!" screamed the teenager and with the crying child in her arms, angrily stomped from the room.

Ferguson turned and slightly nodded to her colleague who understanding, left the room to follow the teenager upstairs and quiz her further about what went on in the McPherson household.

"Tracey; is it all right if I call you Tracey?" Ferguson asked the stupefied woman.

"Aye, whatever," Tracey slurred.

"Is that right, your man was having it off with someone at his work?"

"He was always at it, liked big tits; thought he was a ladies man. Wanker," she spat at the memory of her husband.

"Do you know who it was that he was having the affair with, Tracey? Was it *definitely* someone at his office?"

"What's it to you? Who are you?" she peered suspiciously at the detective.

"I'm Emma; it's me and my colleagues who are trying to find out who murdered Harry. You want to know, don't you Tracey, who murdered Harry."

"Who murdered Harry?" she repeated and then with a sigh waved her hands in the air and giggling, waved her hands in the air and replied, "Really? Listen hen; *who* the fuck *cares*."

It was later in the car as the young DC drove away from the house that Ferguson confided her opinion of Tracey McPherson. "She's that far out of her face with the drink or the drugs or both that she doesn't know if it's Tuesday or Christmas!"

She turned slightly to stare at the DC and asked, "How did you get on with the toe-rag sister?"

The young DC shrugged and with her concentration centred on her driving, slowly shook her head. "She's just a wee slanderous gossip, so she is. I don't believe that she knows anything of value and was repeating only what she has overhead with her own slant on it. What *does* seem apparent is that the deceased wasn't liked by any of the wife's family who thought of him as a stuck-up arse," she grinned. "Her words, not mine. As for him being a philanderer, all she knows is what she heard Tracey telling their father; that Harry was shagging about and, this is only my opinion of course," she added, "Tracey *thought* it was someone at Harry's office."

"*Philanderer*," mocked Ferguson, "what are you, some kind of Mills and Boon fan or what? Into the romantic novels are we?"

"Well, you know what I mean," replied the red faced DC. "Anyway, it sounds better than shagger, doesn't it?"

"Aye, well it doesn't get us much further not having a name, but the bit about the wife thinking it was somebody in her husband's office," she mused, "that's interesting."

A thought occurred to her and fetching her mobile phone from her handbag, she rang the preset number.

"Bobby, it's Emma here," she said. "We had a wee interesting titbit when we interviewed Tracey McPherson, the deceased's wife. She was out of her face and not ready yet t be formally interviewed, but it seems she suspected her man was having it off with somebody and thinks it might have been a work colleague. Just a thought but likely his prints will be on his computer Laura Scott seized from his office. Is it worth having it fingerprinted then seeing if any of *his* prints turn up at Sutherland's flat?"

"Good idea Emma," Franklin replied. 'The computer's back at the incident room. I'll have Scott take it to the SOCO office and they can look for a comparative match there. Well done, hen. Where are you the now?"

"Heading back to the office," she sighed. "I did have admin and crime reports to check, but they'll need to wait. I'm collecting Des Mooney at one o'clock for the funeral, so I'll see you there."

"Aye," he theatrically sighed, "the life of an acting DI is *really* hectic, isn't it?" he wisecracked and concluded the call before she could respond.

"If I might speak with you alone in the kitchen, Susie," said Lynn Massey, her eyes conveying the seriousness of the request.

Closing the door behind them, Susie stood with her back against the worktop, her arms folded and staring at the floor.

Lynn Massey stood some six feet away, hesitantly wondering and a little unsure if Gibson would need comforting when she broke the news.

"This is bad news, isn't it?"

"From the information that I have just received Susie, I'm sorry, but it's the very worst of news." With sudden inclination, she thought it best to be as formal as possible and continued.

"I regret to inform you that a body was recovered a short time earlier today from the River Clyde." She took a deep breath. "From identification that was found on the body, we believe it to be your husband, Peter Gibson. I'm so very sorry, Susie.

"There's no doubt?"

"As far as I'm aware," she chose her words carefully, "what I have been told is that the body has been in the water for some days. It seems the body has suffered…" she hesitated, uncertain how to break such devastating news, "some damage from a passing ship as well as…." she stopped and sighed. "Look Susie, the details are a bit sketchy at the minute but I promise you, I won't keep anything back from you."

Susie took a deep breath, the tears welling in her eyes and she asked, "But why? Why would he drown himself? What possible fucking reason would he have to do this to us?" and placed her face in both her hands as she wept.

Massey drew a sharp intake of breath and inwardly cursed.

"Susie," she said at last and moved towards her. "Susie," she repeated a little sharper than she intended.

She lifted her head and stared at the Detective Superintendent, the tears continuing to roll down her cheeks.

"I'm so very sorry Susie," she softly said, shaking her head, "but Peter didn't drown. Your husband was murdered."

CHAPTER 32

The discovery of the murdered body that was to prove to be Peter Gibson changed all plans for that day made by some of the senior officers in the inquiry team.

Lynn Massey and Arlene Baxter were unable to make the funeral ceremony, for their colleague Susie Gibson had received the worst of news; the death by murder of her husband Peter Gibson and both agreed that they should remain with Susie for the time being, if for no other reason than to support their colleague.

Bobby Franklin, satisfied that the best part of the search for evidence at the flat occupied by Morven Sutherland was well under way, had left the flat and was en route to his office to change into his suit when he received the phone call from Frankie Johnson informing him that Sutherland had been detained by the Ports Control Unit officers at Stranraer.

"We've got twelve hours to interview her, Bobby," snapped Johnson, "and if we can't make a charge stick during that time, she walks."

"We can't be bringing her back here then," replied Franklin, "for it would take an hour and a half in a fast car just to get here and that would be three hours wasted before we did anything. That and common sense dictates we can't deny her a break or rest period during that period and would further cut down the interview time. No," he shook his head, "I'm of the opinion the interview will need to be conducted down there." His eyes narrowed and he hissed with anger, pulling up sharply to avoid colliding with a bus whose driver stopped without warning. "When was she detained and has she asked for a brief?"

There was a slight pause and then Johnson said, "She was captured about twenty minutes ago and no, she hasn't asked for a lawyer. According to the young DC that I spoke with she smirked and I quote," he grimaced and repeated, *"Why would I need a lawyer? I have done nothing wrong."*

Johnson had misgivings at Sutherland's reported indifference to being detained and worried that in some manner she might use her knowledge of the affair with the Royal personage to negotiate a deal; a knowledge that he could *not* divulge to Franklin and bitterly realised would put his DI at a terrible disadvantage during the interview.

Unaware of Johnson's predicament, Franklin's mind raced and he rubbed at the ache in his midriff.

"How about this, boss," suggested Franklin, "you arrange for a Traffic patrol car to attend at the Pitt Street entrance, get me a neighbour from the incident room and I'll head down to Stranraer to conduct the interview myself?"

"How long will it take you to get to Pitt Street?"

"Two or three minutes, boss. I'm just on St Vincent Street now," he replied and to the anger of the other motorists, making a highly illegal U turn.

"Right, I've a neighbour in mind for you, so while he's making his way here, pop into my office for the paperwork so that you're up to speed when you meet this woman."

No sooner had Johnson ended the call with Franklin than he was on the phone to the control room upstairs from his office to summon a Traffic car to Pitt Street and that done, he dialled the DCI's office at Maryhill police office.

"Charlie? It's Frankie Johnson here. I've got a wee job for you."

The uniformed Chief Inspector responsible for organising the hundred and one things that would ensure Waz Ahmed's funeral procession and ceremony go off without any hitches could hardly believes his eyes. Standing on the pavement outside the Central Mosque on Ballater Street, he stared across the road.

The elderly sergeant stood next to him slowly shook his head in disbelief as he too watched the dozen men and women, ranging from late teens to the oldest at nearly sixty years of age, stand murmuring together on the opposite pavement brandishing placards that could clearly be seen to be racist.

One stout, bespectacled cropped haired woman, her arms bared and displaying numerous tattoos and who seemed to be the leader rallying the others, held up a homemade sign that read '*Another One Bites The Dust*' while others in the group held similar themed signs, some of which read, '*Paki's Go Home*' and '*Muslim Means Terrorist*'.

The Chief Inspector took a deep breath and turning towards the sergeant, quietly said, "I don't care if it takes one or a hundred officers. I don't care if they want to go peacefully or if they resist. I don't even care if you baton them into unconsciousness, but I *do* care that we are burying one of our own today, a fine man and a good copper by all account and I will not have these *fucking* racist bigots parading their fascist and vile hatred in my city and mocking our citizens. Take as many cops as you need and sort it out."

The sergeant shrugged and without a word, turned back and walked the short distance to the car park where over twenty uniformed cops stood milling about, some angrily pointing towards the protestors while others wondered why the group waving signs across the road were permitted to remain in full view of the mourners who would soon be arriving at the mosque.

The sergeant stood with hands on his thumbs hooked into the front of his utility belt and beckoned the constables to him. Shuffling towards him, the officers stood in a rough half circle about him. The sergeant cleared his throat and in a slightly raised voice said, "Our society permits freedom of speech and the right of the individual to protest against anyone or anything that they might perceive to be wrong. You have all at various times policed the Irish republican or the Orange order marches and countless political demonstrations through our city or elsewhere in our region." He paused at stared at them. "Today, we are here to police the funeral ceremony of a colleague who happens to be of the Islamic faith. I didn't know Waseem Ahmed and I'm guessing that none of those protesters," he waved a hand behind him, "knew him either. What I do know is that when he was on duty, Detective Constable Ahmed was *not* a Muslim just as right now none of you are Christian or Muslim, Sikh or whatever religion you were brought up in. Today, here and now, you *are* police officers who conduct yourselves without fear or favour. You *are* police officers who are sworn to uphold the laws of Scotland. You *are* the visible presence of decency and safety for our citizens and today," he half turned and indicated with a thumb towards the silent group across the road, "those people wish to remind us that there is a few among our society who will seek to destroy our unity with their spite and ignorance, their venomous hatred for anyone that does not fit their profile of a Scot."

He dug into a pocket of his uniform cargo pants and withdrew a folded leaflet and brandished it towards the officers.

"This was produced by the brothers in the mosque. It's a short obituary for Waseem Ahmed to be handed out to the mourners. It might interest you to know that DC Ahmed like me was born in the maternity of the Southern General Hospital down the road in Govan. The man is…" he paused, "was as Scottish as I am."

He took a deep breath and continued, "It is my intention to move that group across the road and hopefully, they will go quietly. I would prefer no arrests for breach of the peace on this solemn day, however, if there *is* the slightest resistance from any individual in that group, I will expect that we as police officers will do our duty."

The group almost as one took a step forward, but the sergeant with an inward smile, raised his hand and pointing out one young female officer to accompany him, turned towards the protestors.

Still within the kitchen with her daughter now returned to her room to get read for school, Susie Gibson, her face streaked with tears said, "I need to tell Jenny. She needs to know, then hesitated. "You're absolutely certain? There's no doubt?"

Lynn Massey turned towards Arlene Baxter and instructed, "Phone Mister Johnson and ask him from me to confirm there's no doubt that the…." she paused, conscious that Susie was closely watching her, "that it *is* Mister Gibson."

Baxter turned away towards the door, her mobile phone in her hand and concentrating on dialling the number and almost collided with Jenny, who now dressed for school walked into the lounge and seeing her mother distraught, asked "Mum?"

Charlie Miller opened the door of the parked traffic car and climbed in to join Bobby Franklin in the rear seat. No sooner had he sat down than the sergeant in the front seat tapped the arm of the constable driving, who revved the engine and they were off.

"Frankie Johnson said you would bring me up to speed Bobby, that you would have a file for me to read?"

Franklin handed the file to Miller, both swaying against their seat belts as the driver negotiated a line of traffic at a red light on St Vincent Street and with blues and two blaring, screwed round the parked cars and turned onto the ramp for the Kingston Bridge.

Miller, not the best of passenger let alone rear seat passenger, took a deep breath and said, "To be honest, I'd get nauseous trying to read in a moving vehicle. Can you maybe just give me a verbal briefing, Bobby?"

Franklin grinned and for the next twenty minutes, related the circumstances of the inquiry to date, answering Miller's occasional interjected question until both men were satisfied that they each knew enough to question the suspect who currently languished in a detention room at Stranraer police station.

"If you're okay with it Bobby and as you have been at the hub, I'd prefer you to take the lead when we get round to interviewing this woman."

"No problem," replied Franklin then with a smile, extended his hand and added, "Congratulations Charlie, the words out. Seems somebody had it in for you," he grinned at the old joke. "So, how does it feel to become a dad at your age?"

"Don't ask," Miller grinned a little self-consciously, "but suffice to say if I'm going to have a baby, it couldn't be with a better woman."

"Well said," Franklin returned his grin and then, his face a little grimmer at the thought of meeting with Morven Sutherland, added, "Hopefully, we'll wind this up today."

Of course, neither man had been privileged to the information obtained by Lynn Massey's husband Greg, of the relationship between their suspect Morven Sutherland and a member of the Royal family; information that was about to throw a proverbial spanner into their planned interview.

The Scene of Crime team worked methodically throughout Morven Sutherland's flat and at last, glancing around him at the damage wreaked to the wooden floor and the silver, powdery fingerprint dust that was settled on furniture, walls and every other bloody thing in the flat, the supervisor was satisfied for the time being they could do no more.

He stepped into the hallway and called to the senior detective whom Franklin had left in charge and informed him that the blood and fingerprint samples obtained would now be taken straight to the lab and fingerprint department for comparison.

"The boss asked if DNA from the blood and the prints you found could be checked against both these names," replied the detective and handed the supervisor a slip of paper.

The supervisor glanced at the slip of paper and thoughtfully nodded. "How urgent is this?" he asked, conscious that like his team, he wished to attend young Waz's funeral; remembering the likeable young detective who always had a joke for them.

"I'm not privy to the workings of the management," sighed the detective, "but my understanding is that DI Franklin was rushed away to question the owner of the flat, so I'm surmising it would be useful if he had the info when he conducts his interview."

"So we're talking yesterday," sighed the supervisor, but without any malice in his voice. "Okay," he resignedly agreed with a nod, thinking that even Waz Ahmed would agree attending the ceremony wasn't as important as nailing some murdering bastard. "I'll get right onto it."

A light fall of rain was hitting the windscreen of the vehicle as Charlie Miller risked a glance over the Traffic constable shoulder and inwardly took a deep breath, shocked at the speed the BMW was travelling at on the A77 towards Ayr.

"How long do you reckon it will take us to get there now, sergeant?" he nervously asked the front seat passenger, glancing out of the window as the blue lights on the roof bounced off the windows of a bus they raced past and thankful at least the bloody siren was switched off.

The sergeant grinned and turning on his seat towards Miller replied, "The way young Lachlan here drives sir, mindful that he hasn't had an accident for nearly a week, I should say we'll arrive in Stranraer in what, fifty minutes?"

Franklin glanced at his watch and mindful that the detention time was eating away, slightly leaned forward and to Miller's horror, suggested, "Maybe put the foot down son. We're time critical here." Miller could almost feel the thrust press him back into his seat as the engine discovered another few revs and fists clenched tightly, inwardly prayed to a God he had long forgotten.

CHAPTER 33

Emma Ferguson stepped from the passenger seat of the police van and asked the uniformed officer to wait while she collected Des Mooney.

To her surprise, she found him standing just inside the front door of the close with a young woman who, like Mooney, was dressed in a black skirted suit, white blouse and hair pinned up into a bob on her head.

"Emma, this is my daughter Jill. She arrived yesterday from Afghanistan," he introduced her with a hint of pride in his voice, "and asked that she accompany me today to the funeral."

"No problem," agreed Ferguson with a smile and stood to one side as Mooney hobbled on his crutches towards the rear of the van.

The first of the mourners had begun to arrive at the Central Mosque for the funeral ceremony and included a large number of both uniformed and plainclothes police officers.

The Glasgow city council, as a mark of respect for the numbers attending, had for that day relaxed their parking restrictions and instructed the small number of wardens on duty there and in the surrounding streets to assist rather than hinder those arriving by car.

The uniformed constables discreetly located about the area kept a weather eye open for any further dissent that might be displayed and with courtesy, pointed mourners towards the mosque courtyard where some of the younger brothers tasked and supervised by the one of the three Imams, directed those attending towards the building; the men to the main hall and the women to the stairs inside the main doors that led to the upper floor, where a large mezzanine permitted the women to gaze down into the great hall.

Frankie Johnson, accompanied by his wife, stood to one side greeting his divisional detectives as they arrived and watched as a large black saloon car delivered the Chief Constable who similarly was accompanied by his wife.

A number of official vehicles followed as the Deputy Chief and several Assistant Chief's, most of who were accompanied by wives, arrived in succession.

Johnson's eyes narrowed and he took a sharp intake of breath when he saw ACC Jonathan MacPhail and his wife exit their vehicle. He watched as MacPhail walked briskly to join the Deputy while

MacPhail's wife, dressed in a black jacket, skirt and wearing a black hat and veil covering most of her face, hesitantly followed.

"Mister Johnson," a voice called softly, distracting him and turning, he saw the Chief Constable discreetly nod to him.

The discreet nod, however, was not so much a greeting as a beckon for a quiet word.

The two men walked slowly together towards a quiet corner of the courtyard while the wives stood nearby, spoke softly together.

"Sad day, Mister Johnson," opened the Chief and then almost immediately asked, "What if any is the update on your inquiry regarding the missing banker and the money?"

"Our prime suspect has been detained using a false name and while attempting to flee through the port of Cairnryan, sir. I've two men en route as we speak to interview her."

"And I hear that you've had two bodies washed up in the Clyde. What's the story there?"

It never ceased to amaze Johnson that the Chief seemed to have a finger on the pulse, sometimes even before Johnson himself had the information. He inhaled and replied, "Both the men were employed by the bank, sir and I'm working on the assumption that our suspect, herself a bank employee, had a relationship with both men, however, the nature of those relationships is still to be ascertained."

"And the wee lassie Meechan that was murdered over in the close in Partick; was she also involved?"

"That's still being investigated sir and of course, I can't dismiss the theory there was some sort of collusion going on between all four. However, I've an officer attending to speak with Meechan's partner, see if he can add anything that we might have missed in his initial statement."

"But he's not a suspect? I mean, it's not a curious coincidence that she, a bank employee, was killed but might *not* have been connected with the theft or the other deaths?"

"No sir, I'm convinced Carol Meechan's murder is somehow related to the other deaths, both of which are of course murder. The link is definitely our suspect, Morven Sutherland."

A respectful silence had fallen among the large number of mourners who were still stood within the courtyard area, causing Johnson and the Chief to turn around and stare towards the wide gates. A black coloured sedan vehicle had drawn up and from which stepped and elderly man and woman who in turn, helped a younger woman exit the rear of the vehicle.

It seemed obvious to those watching that the younger woman was DC Ahmed's widow Alima and with her parents at her side, saw her walk with dignity through the crowd towards the main doors of the mosque.

The Janazah for Waseem Ahmed, conducted in the great hall of the Central Mosque, was for all those who observed a pious and solemn occasion.

The elderly Imam conducting the ceremony had on occasion to briefly pause to compose himself, for he had known Waseem throughout his life and could never imagine that the likeable young man's life would end so tragically.

From the mezzanine above, the sound of women weeping included not just family members, but police colleagues and to everyone's surprise, the Cranstonhill bar officer, Nicotine Mary who was so distraught she had to be assisted from the mosque.

The prayers ended and concluding the ceremony, the Imam indicated to the congregation that at the family's request, Waseem's interment was to be a private affair.

In the courtyard outside, Des Mooney, ably supported by his daughter Jill and with Emma Ferguson standing close by among the throng, was approached by many of his colleagues wishing him well at this sorrowful time, but all he could feel was the need to get home, uncertain of the conflict that raged within him and unaware he was experiencing a survivor's guilt.

The large crowd began to disperse and as Frankie Johnson watched, the senior officers paid their condolences first to Missus Ahmed and her parents and then stood respectfully aside as the Chief Constable's car drew up to collect him and his wife.

He watched as ACC MacPhail and his wife walked towards their own large, black coloured vehicle parked nearby and a soft smile played about his lips.

The last time he had seen that BMW was when it almost rammed him outside the Victoria Hospital, the day he had visited the injured Constable Mooney.

He watched as Missus MacPhail, now at the passenger door, removed her wide brimmed hat and veil to reveal her red hair bundled on top of her head.

He eyes narrowed and he sighed, slowing shaking his head in disbelief when without doubt, he recognised that the driver of the BMW that day had been none other than the ACC's wife.

John Paterson was still suffering the pain of the murder of his girlfriend Carol Meechan when about the time the funeral ceremony was occurring at the Central Mosque, two detectives from the murder incident room called at his parent's neat, detached bungalow in the Paisley suburb.

Leading them through the hallway his father hastily whispered to them that his son had not been sleeping well, but had refused all attempts to have their GP attend to him and asked if the detectives would bear that in mind, when they spoke with him.

The officers agreed and in the subdued light of the parents lounge sat facing Paterson, whose face was pale and throughout the interview, clenched his hands in his lap and whose left leg uncontrollably shook.

The senior of the two detectives began by softly reminding Paterson that they were there simply to ensure that the officers who initially spoke with him had not missed anything and elicit if he had recalled anything further since that interview.

The second interview was interrupted after a few minutes when believing themselves to be courteous, Paterson's parents entered the lounge together, the father bearing a tray upon which sat three of their best China cups and saucers, milk jug and sugar bowl and a plate of digestive biscuits while the mother carried a teapot encased in a hand-knitted woollen cosy.

The detectives smiled through their irritation at the interruption and then when the parents with some obvious reluctance left the room, continued.

Did John remember anything else, again asked the senior detective? He slowly shook his head and asked, "Are you any closer to finding out who did it, who killed my Carol?"

"We're making headway, but slowly," the detective smiled at him. "Do you know if it was random thing, her murder I mean or a mugging gone wrong or something to do with her job?"

"Why do you mention her job?" asked the detective as she leaned forward a little, her interest peaked by his comment.

He shrugged his shoulders and replied, "I don't know really, just…" he seemed a little confused as he tried to recall. His brow furrowed and he continued, "It was something she said the night before… you know."

"The night before the day she died?"

"Yes," he softly replied, his voice a hushed whisper as though the death should not be openly spoken of. "She said something about being worried, something at her office causing her concern." He apologetically shrugged his shoulders again and explained, "To be honest, I was so wrapped up with the news of my new job I only half listened."

Just like my hubby, thought the detective; selective bloody hearing, then tolerantly smiled and closing her notebook, stood and said, "It might be helpful John if you *do* recall what was giving Carol cause for her concern. Here," she opened her shoulder bag and handed him a business card, "give me a call if anything else comes to mind," and nodded to her neighbour that there was little else they would get for now.

It was as Paterson was showing them to the front door he stopped and his eyes narrowed.

"She spoke with one of her bosses, a manager I think she said. It was something about accounts that she didn't understand."

The detectives stared at him and the senior detective gently asked, "Can you recall the name of the manager? It would be very helpful."

He squeezed his eyes tightly shut, trying to force the memory to the forefront of his mind and said, "A football team. Some name like a football team," then with a sigh, shook his head.

"A football team," sighed the detective and was about to reach out and pat his arm reassuringly when he burst out, "Sunderland. I think she said the guy's name was Sunderland."

The detective swallowed hard, not wishing to deflate him now that he seemed to be remembering and asked, "Are you certain the manager was a man?"

"Eh, no, I'm not certain," he hesitatingly replied.

"Well, you have my card," she reminded him and smiled as she stepped through the front door.

The detectives walked along the garden path to their car parked on the roadway outside, her neighbour repeated, "Sunderland?"

She felt that tingling sensation she always got when something good popped up out of nowhere and with a grim nod of her head, reached into her handbag for her mobile phone. She scrolled down the names and stopped at Bobby Franklin's number. While her neighbour stepped round to unlock the driver's door, she placed her bag on the roof and leaning with her free hand on the car, pressed the green button.

"Boss," she said, eyes narrowing when she heard the high pitched sound of a car engine, "We've re-interviewed Carol Meechan's partner John Paterson and he didn't remember much, but did recall she was worried about some accounts, though couldn't tell us anymore about the accounts. However, he did tell us she spoke with a manager and thought it might have been a man, but isn't certain. What he *did* recall was the manager's name sounded like a football team, Sunderland."

She nodded and grinned then said, "That's what I was thinking; it's too close to be ignored. For *Sunderland*, maybe read *Sutherland*."

The Traffic car pulled into the car park of the police office at Port Rodie in Stranraer and came to a sudden halt outside the front door of the one-storey, oblong shaped, flat roofed building.

Neither Charlie Miller nor Bobby Franklin had previously visited the office and exiting the vehicle, Franklin told the Traffic officers to find themselves a cuppa somewhere, but to check back at the office in a couple of hours.

Miller and Franklin entered through the front glass doors to be met by a burly Port Control Unit officer, who watched by a pretty young female bar officer, introduced himself in a north of Scotland accent as DC Fraser McIntyre and led them through to the security door into a cramped CID office.

"We share accommodation with the local detectives," he explained, "though we have our own secure filing cabinets."

"We've no time for a conducted tour son, we're under some time constraints," snapped Miller, then almost immediately raised both hands and apologised, explaining, "Sorry, Fraser. My knees are still shaking from that bloody road trip. Where's the suspect the now?"

"She's in the detention room sir, but I've already set up our interview room and the tapes are there waiting for you. I'm guessing that you might want to proceed as you've got less than ten hours, but there's something you need to see first."

Franklin turned towards Miller, but could see the acting DCI, though anxious to get on, was as mystified as he was.

"Is it important?" he asked McIntyre.

"Sorry, sir, but you'll need to be the judge of that," and walked back towards the CID door, locked it and then made towards the seated side of one of the six desks in the room.

On top of the desk was a black coloured, hard shell suitcase that lay partially open.

They watched curiously as McIntyre took a set of keys from his trouser pocket and bent over to unlock a desk drawer from which he withdrew a small leather wallet that he handed towards Miller.

"While my neighbour processed Miss Sutherland at the uniform bar, I went through her luggage to check if there was anything else that might indicate any other identities and I found that," he nodded towards the wallet that Miller now unzipped and opened.

Inside was a dozen six inch by four inch colour photographs.

"Eh, I never mentioned this to my neighbour, sir," added McIntyre, who then stood quietly while the two detectives stared curiously at him.

Miller laid the wallet on the desk and one by one, went through the photos, handing the ones he examined over to Franklin, who exhaled through pursed lips and then whistled when he saw the content.

"Fuck me," was his only comment, turning the photos back and forth to examine each one from a different angle.

"Does *anyone* else know about these?" Miller asked McIntyre.

"No sir," McIntyre vigorously shook his head. "I'm Special Branch, or I was until they changed the bloody name," he grimaced, "so let's say that I'm familiar with the need to know concept and well, it's easy to guess the damage that these could do," he pointed to the photographs, "if they got into the public domain."

"You are *not* kidding, son," agreed Franklin, nodding and unable to hide his grin at the sexual positions of the two naked subjects who featured in the photographs, the blonde haired one McIntyre named as Sutherland while the other needed no identifying, but who featured regularly in the media.

"I didn't think the Royals did such *common* things," Franklin continued to grin and handed the photographs back to Miller, adding with a sly grin, "particularly the *women*."

Miller examined the rear of one of the photos and said, "I'm no expert, but it seems to me that this might have been printed on a home printer. It's not very professional and," he glanced with narrowed eyes at a second and then a third photograph, "they all seem to have been taken from the same angle."

"I was guessing a fixed camera sir," suggested McIntyre, "probably a hidden camera because I can't see *her*," he pointed to the photograph, "agreeing to have these taken and I agree it's probably been a home printer. I mean, who would risk putting these into the local chemists for developing?"

"Aye, you're probably right Fraser. What it does, though, is it opens up a can of worms," then he turned to Franklin and said, "Bobby, I'm thinking that she wouldn't just have the one set of photographs, that likely she has probably got back-up photos on one of those wee….what do you call them?" he turned towards McIntyre

"I think you mean a memory card, sir."

"Aye, a memory card and *if* I'm right, she will have it on her somewhere, be travelling with it I mean. I don't see her trusting anyone else with this kind of information."

He ground his teeth, a habit Sadie was always chiding him for and shook his head as he continued, "It won't be at her flat in Glasgow, because she's abandoned that place and unlikely has any inclination to return, I'm thinking."

He glanced at the opened luggage case.

"Bobby, you tear that apart and Fraser, you turn her car upside down. That card will be somewhere, so *find* it. We need to have it before we can interview her or else she'll have the upper hand and something she will believe she can use to deal with us. We need to demonstrate to her that she's got nothing to play or use against us."

"What are you going to do Charlie?" asked Franklin, moving towards the case.

"Me? I'll give Frankie Johnson a phone to update him regarding these," he held the photographs up, "but unless I'm way off the mark, I think with that sly bugger the photographs might not be *that* much of a surprise to him."

CHAPTER 34

Lynn Massey and Arlene Baxter had returned to the car and both sat slightly numbed from their experience.

"All in all, Ma'am, I don't think she expected *that* kind of news. I got the impression she thought her man had done a bunk and that eventually we would find him and that as far as she was concerned, whether she continued with the marriage or not, at least there would be some kind of closure for her."

Massey sighed and said, "I think you're right, Arlene. I'm convinced her reaction to the news of her husband's murder was genuine. God," she sat back in the driver's seat and rubbed with the heel of both hands at her forehead. "That poor wee lassie, she's taking it very badly. I got the impression she worshipped her dad."

"The knife Ma'am," Baxter reminded her. "Did you manage to check the kitchen drawer for the knife?"

"Damn, I forgot," she replied and then added, "Bit redundant anyway. It seems that there is a similar set of six in Morven Sutherland's kitchen, but one is missing."

"Now why would I be happy to hear that," Baxter grinned just as her mobile phone sounded in her handbag. She withdrew it and pressed the green button.

"Hello sir," Massey heard her reply and then, "Yes sir, she's here in the car with me now."

Turning towards Massey, she handed her the phone and said, "Mister Johnson."

"Frankie, I've just informed DS Gibson that you have had the identification confirmed by comparing the DNA from the body to that of the head hair discovered in her husband's car, that the lab is satisfied it *is* her husband, Peter Gibson. There's not been a development about that has there?" she anxiously asked.

"No, it's as I told you Lynn, I'm perfectly satisfied the second body fished from the river *is* Peter Gibson. The lab boys and the Scene of Crime have done a remarkable job and the sample that you've taken from the daughter will further simply corroborate it. However, right now I need you to step out of the car. I don't want to be overheard," he told her.

She realised immediately it must be about the information that Greg had provided for nothing else came to mind that wasn't available to the investigating team.

"Just be a sec," she smiled at Baxter and opening the door, exited the car and walked a few yards away then stopped under a tree, her free arm supporting the elbow of the other arm. "So Frankie, what's up?" she asked him.

Quickly he related Bobby Franklin's phone call, the discovery of the compromising photographs and the ongoing search for a memory card.

"*Jesus*," was all she could softly reply, her thoughts a jumbled mass. "What about the search of the flat? I presume that nothing like that was found there?" she finally asked.

"No, nothing, but Charlie Miller is of the opinion she was unlikely to leave anything like that for us to find and I tend to agree with him. Those photographs are too valuable to her so I also agreed that she will have the memory card with her. However, what you will be pleased to hear is that the Scene of Crime lads found very few *different* sets of prints at Sutherland's flat and at my instruction, two sets were compared against the post-mortem prints taken from the deceased Gibson and McPherson."

She held her breath and asked, "They match?"

"Aye, Lynn, they match. From the location of where the prints were discovered, the SOCO supervisor is of the opinion that Gibson and McPherson were *more* than casual visitors to the flat; he mentioned on the headboard and elsewhere in the bedroom, apparently. It seems with *both* the deceased," she heard him stifle a chuckle, "that our Miss Sutherland was apparently liberal with her charms."

"Too much information for me, Frankie," she grinned down the phone," then asked, "The blood discovered under the floorboards? Is it McPherson's?"

"No not McPherson's, however I'm told there was sufficient blood to enable the lab to obtain DNA and what they have so far discovered is that the DNA *does* match that of Peter Gibson. From what the SOCO supervisor told me, his opinion based on experience is that the volume of blood was and I quote, '*consistent with massive haemorrhaging.*' It is also the opinion of the supervisor that our missing banker was if not actually stabbed to death in the flat, then must have been at least seriously assaulted. However, if you want *my* opinion, I believe the flat was the locus for Peter Gibson's murder."

Morven Sutherland was growing impatient. Nobody had come near her detention room in an hour and she needed to pee in a closed cubicle, not that fucking pedestal concreted to the floor with the flushing chain on the outside of the door. There was not even a toilet roll!

She raged with anger knowing the bastards just didn't realise who they had locked up; didn't realise what power she could wield.

She stood up from the concrete bench seat and hammered with her fist at the inside of the metal clad door, shouting loudly, "*I NEED TO PEE!!!*"

Down the corridor, the young and pretty, dark haired bar officer standing hunched over at the public counter heard the scream and inwardly smiled as she idly flicked though her glossy magazine. She cocked her head as once again, the beating on the detention room door continued and the plaintive cry resumed, then muttered to herself, "And I need a shag, hen, but my lad's working abroad, so that's the two of us well and truly buggered, eh?"

In the CID room, Bobby Franklin sat sipping at a cup of tea among the clothes and debris that had been Morven Sutherland's suitcase. Charlie Miller glanced at his watch as a grim faced Fraser McIntyre came through the door and shook his head.

"I can't say it's not there sir, because it would take an exhaustive check of every nook and cranny in that Audi and to be honest, we just don't have the time."

Tight-lipped, Miller nodded, unconsciously realising that McIntyre was not just correct, but his accent seemed to be more pronounced the more stressed he was.

Then his eyes narrowed.

"The local CID, Fraser; they guys do their own scenes of crime down here, don't they?"

"Aye, usually they do unless it's a big case, a murder or something like that; then they get the big boys down from the city. Why?"

"Where do they keep their camera equipment?" Miller thoughtfully asked.

Alima Ahmed returned home, her parents by her side to be greeted with a laughing Munawar who sat cradled in the arms of the grinning Missus Franklin.

Alima forced herself to smile for the little one, though her heart broke.

As quietly as she dared, Bobby Franklin's wife took her leave of the bereaved family, but not before her hand was thankfully shaken by Alima's father while a tearful Alima's mother almost crushed her with a grateful embrace.

Outside the flat with the door closed behind her, she couldn't explain why and would never tell her Bobby, but stood for several minutes on the half landing leaning against the cold, stone wall and unashamedly wept for the little, fatherless girl.

Susie Gibson had finally, stopped crying, but realised that today was the first of the many tears that she would shed.

Curiously, she had been unwilling to accept what she had already guessed; that Peter was dead.

Jenny had asked to go to her room, for no other reason than she needed some time alone and, though desperate to console her daughter, with a heavy heart Susie reluctantly agreed.

Her thoughts turned to the visit by Massey and Baxter and with some reluctance, inwardly admitted that the solicitudes of both women had seemed genuine.

She sat quietly rocking back and forth in the lounge armchair, her hands clenched in her lap and brushing a loose strand of hair from her face, realised that with a start that though Massey had confirmed Peter was dead, she had not disclosed the circumstances of his murder nor if there was anyone arrested or suspected.

Susie inwardly cursed her lack of questions for the DSU and shaking her head, gritted her teeth in anger. She *should* have asked questions.

Thoughts of Massey brought to mind the electronic notebook upstairs and she wondered why she hadn't mentioned it?

Her stomach twisted with tension. She knew full well why she had not brought it to the Detective Superintendents attention; the notebook would simply have added to the evidence in any case the police might have brought against Peter.

She swallowed with difficulty and tears formed in her eyes for now that he was dead, such evidence would be totally irrelevant.

She wrapped her arms around her body against the pain of tension and then inhaled, letting her breath slowly release through pursed lips.

She had to think ahead, work out what her next move would be; what decisions that she would need to make, but no matter what she decided, it would *all* be for the benefit of her daughter Jenny.

"When you brought her to the office, was Sutherland *thoroughly* searched?" asked Charlie Miller.

Fraser McIntyre shook his head. "Just a cursory search sir, by the female bar officer. We don't have a permanent female turnkey here at Stranraer; the size of the office doesn't justify it."

"Is there a police woman on duty?"

"Aye, there is. I just saw a panda crew going for their break in the canteen and one was young Betty McKinnon."

"Right, you and McKinnon fetch Sutherland out of the detention room and bring her to the interview room. Let her use the toilet and while you're both watching her at the loo, Bobby and I will give the detention room a turn to ensure she hasn't secreted the memory card there. When she's in the loo ensure that McKinnon stands over her. I don't think she'll have the memory card banked, but I don't want it flushed away. Not if this is going to work."

McIntyre's eyes narrowed. "Banked?"

Franklin grinned at Miller and said, "It's the manner in which the customer's care of HMP get their drugs and other items into the prisons, Fraser. The cons usually use they wee plastic eggs that weans buy; you know, the ones with sweeties and a toy inside?"

"Aye, I know what they are."

"Well, let's just say that some of our more *determined* prisoners have the ability to secrete the eggs in what I can only describe as their natural orifices. Female prisoners are quite adept at the ruse and our information is that Sutherland has previously served time on remand, so it's likely she'll be aware of the routine."

"Right," McIntyre slowly drawled, wondering how he was going to explain *this* to the probationary police woman.

"Five minutes, Fraser," Miller interrupted his thoughts, "and then I want her in the interview room."

Emma Ferguson waved goodbye to Des Mooney and his daughter Jill, who silently opened the close door and stood to one side to permit her father to pass by.

Mooney cautiously hobbled along to the front door of the flat, but stopped and quietly said, "Okay Jill, it's just the two of us now. What's on your mind?"

"Let's get inside first," she replied, "and I'll get the kettle on."

"Right," he softly inhaled and stepping through the door, made his way to his bedroom where he removed his jacket and tie and then limped into the lounge.

Sinking wearily onto the dining chair, the most comfortable seat for his injured leg, he patiently waited for Jill who a few minutes later came through from the kitchen with a mug of tea in each fist.

"That was her at the funeral, wasn't it?" asked Jill without preamble, handing her father a mug.

He took the tea from her and nodded with a soft smile, "What gave it away?"

Jill sat on the arm of one of the armchairs "While you were down in the hall with the other men and I was up on the balcony with the women, I suppose I was naturally curious and looked around me. I couldn't help but notice the woman that kept staring down at you. Bit of a looker I'd say, though at first it was hard to tell in the mosque until I saw her outside when she was leaving and taking her hat and veil off." She paused and stared at him. "The man who was with her at the car, when they left the mosque; is that her husband?"

"Yes," he nodded and deeply inhaled as though the very thought repelled him. "Assistant Chief Constable Jonathon MacPhail. They've been married for, oh, must be about eight years now."

"How did you two meet, you and Shona I mean?"

"She was a probationary cop at Cranstonhill," his eyes narrowed at the memory and a smile played across his face, "must be over ten years now. I liked her then, but things were," he paused, "difficult for me then. You'll remember, hen, I was in a bad place at the time, having lost your mum and trying to cope with work and two precocious teenagers. I knew Shona liked me and she made it clear was keen for us to get together, even." He bowed his head at the memory of that time. "The thing was, I was too scared of becoming emotionally involved and I had you guys to consider too. I couldn't just move a young woman into my life. It would have been too upsetting for you and Tom…"

"Don't be using me and Tom as an excuse dad," Jill interrupted, her hands defensively raised.

"No, you're right. I don't mean it that way, love. It was me; I was the one who was scared. Anyway," he shrugged, "one thing led to another and," he paused then with an ironic grin, said, "you've seen her. You can guess she was a much sought after and there was always guys hanging about her, trying to nip her. Anyway," he loudly exhaled and shook his head, "a few weeks before her probation finished, she quit then up and married MacPhail. I can't begin to describe how gutted I was at the time."

"You sound as though you don't like him."

"I don't *really* know him," he admitted, "other than from what I heard and none of that is good. The man's a career cop, a uniformed politician flitting from force to force when a promotion opportunity arises and according to what I've heard, never met an angry man," he almost spat out. "I got an e-mail a couple of years ago from Shona; just a general 'hello and how are you doing' sort of thing." He shrugged and continued, "I responded and when she travelled north to Glasgow to visit her family, we met for coffee and, well, told me that she missed me. Then about a year ago I received a letter asking if I would meet her, but out of the blue she turned up at my door."

He took a deep breath and sipped at his tea.

"She told me that she was desperately unhappy, that her marriage was a sham and she wanted out, but her husband refused her a divorce because it would impact on his career."

"Do they have kids?"

"No," he shook his head and then turned his head towards the bright light that shone through the large front windows and stared for a few seconds before adding, "but Shona has just discovered that she's pregnant."

Jill stared at him and then the penny dropped.

"*Jesus* dad, are you telling me…bloody hell," Jill stood sharply and almost dropped her mug onto the coffee table, spilling some of the hot liquid on the varnished surface, but neither noticed, such was the shock of his statement. "How…when…I mean… Dad!"

"I'm sorry that you had to learn the news like this, Jill. Truly, I am." He paused, gathering his thoughts. "All I can say is that I love her and she loves me. Yes," he nodded, "the baby is a bit of a shock…"

"Bit of a shock? It's a fucking disaster!" she interrupted. "Dad, you're what, fifty four?"

"I'm fifty-two if you don't mind and no, I'm *not* past it."

Jill slumped down into the couch, her face pale and still registering her shock at the news, but then quite unexpectedly, she grinned.

"You, Desmond Mooney, my balding father, are telling me that aged twenty-two years; I'm going to be a big sister?"

He grinned self-consciously at her.

They sat in silence for a minute then Jill asked, "Your job, dad. Her husband is a boss, isn't he? How will this affect your job?"

"That, Jill," he slowly replied, "is just one thing that worries me."

Charlie Miller sat in the corner to one side of the room with Bobby Franklin occupying the prominent seat behind the desk; both chairs facing the door in the small, square, windowless room. He glanced at his wristwatch and saw there was now just over eight hours till the detention concluded and wondered if this was sufficient time to get to the truth of the three murders and theft of the money.

Franklin glanced towards the bottle green painted wall upon which a notice screwed to the wall warned visitors that any damage to the room or equipment would result in prosecution while a second notice beside it advised detainees of their rights under the Criminal Procedure (Scotland) Act 1995.

Ironically, Franklin saw, both notices were badly defaced.

A red coloured emergency bar situated at waist height run horizontally round the walls that when struck anywhere on its surface, activated an audible alarm throughout the station.

The equipment mentioned in the wall mounted notice consisted of a twin tape recording machine that itself was securely fastened by screws to the desk and in which were placed two unused recording tapes.

As previously agreed with Charlie Miller, Franklin would conduct the interview with Morven Sutherland. On the desk in front of him was placed the file he had obtained from Frankie Johnson to remind and prompt him during the interview process.

The door was knocked and opened by Fraser McIntyre who directed Sutherland into the room. A young, fresh faced policewoman stood behind McIntyre in the corridor and in Franklin's mind, looked as though she was on job experience from the local high school.

Catching Franklin's eye, he saw the young officer discreetly shake her head, indicating that nothing had been secreted on Sutherland's clothing or in her body.

Franklin turned towards Miller and saw from his raised eyebrows that he too had seen the silent message.

Neither Franklin nor Miller stood as Sutherland entered and haughtily stared at both men then, at McIntyre's beckoning she sat on the single chair facing Franklin, while McIntyre left the room, closing the door behind him.

"Miss Sutherland, I'm Detective Inspector Franklin and this," he continued to stare at her as he waved behind him, "is Detective Chief Inspector Miller."

He reached across the desk and pressed the button that activated the tapes and began to read the prepared script from the laminated sheet in front of him that included a formal caution and reminding her she had declined the services of a solicitor, all the while ignoring the scowling Sutherland who stared fixedly at him.

At the conclusion of his short speech, he was about to speak when Sutherland, sat straight backed in the chair with her arms crossed and her face a mask of fury, snapped at him, "Why am I here. What right do you have to detain me?"

Franklin was determined not to be provoked into engaging her in argument and softly replied, "You are suspected of being involved in the theft of a large sum of money from your place of employment…"

"Nonsense," she snapped at him, then turning her head away, added "that's nothing to do with me!"

With a slow and derisive smile, her arms now unfolded and both hands flat on the desk, she said, "If anything, that's all down to Peter Gibson and Harry McPherson. If you need me to tell you anything, it will be about them both; how they tried to involve me."

"Are you telling me that you had known of the theft, but were not involved?"

He saw her throat bouncing as she swallowed, then she nodded and replied, "As far as I am aware, knowing about a crime in Scotland is *not* indictable, it's the participation that *is* indictable."

He smiled and replied, "You seem to have some knowledge of our criminal law, Miss Sutherland," then bent over the file and as though studying it, flicked a page onwards and added, "or do you prefer I call you Miss Jones?"

She flinched as though struck, then a slow smile crossed her face and with a strong Welsh accent, replied, "You seem to have some knowledge of my previous life, Mister Franklin. Just how much *do* you know?"

Bobby Franklin was no fool and recognised that she was trying to take the initiative, that it was her aim to have him disclose the information in the file. He smiled and countered, "I understand when you were detained you assumed the name Alana Beatson. Why was that?"

"I simply outgrew Morven Sutherland," she returned his smile, "and again, I understand in Scotland it is not a crime to change one's name."

"You're right, it's not a crime. You can call yourself whatever you like unless you seek some pecuniary gain and *then* we, the police take an interest. But I'm more concerned with your relationship with Peter Gibson. What exactly was that relationship?"

She shrugged as though the question was irrelevant and said, "Peter pursued me and tried to involve me in his scheme to steal money from the bank. Of course, I refused."

"Did you inform your employer?"

She shook her head and answered, "Why would I? It was none of *my* business what Peter got up to."

"This pursuit of you by Peter Gibson; did you have a sexual relationship with him?"

She smiled seductively and replied, "Why Mister Franklin. What a question to ask a lady. Are you a little jealous?"

"No, Miss Sutherland," he smiled tolerantly, "but I am interested to know why you murdered him in the kitchen of your flat?"

Her face turned pale and her lips tightened.

"I don't know what the fuck you mean," she snarled.

"Oh, come now, Miss Sutherland. Our fingerprint analysis of your flat indicates that you *were* having sexual relationships with both Gibson and Harold McPherson and we also discovered Gibson's blood under the floorboards in your kitchen, after you stabbed him in the back with the steak knife and even though you tried to clean it with bleach; curiously, the very bleach by the way that our forensic laboratory confirms is *also* the same liquid that we found in the bottle under your sink. We're *very* thorough, you see," he smiled at her.

"You don't know anything and there's nothing you can prove," she sneered at him, but he could see that the mention of the blood found under the floorboards in the kitchen of her flat had shaken her confidence and, he thought, she wasn't quite so cocky now.

"After you murdered Gibson, Miss Sutherland, you placed his body into the boot of his car along with the steak knife, drove the body to the River Clyde and dumped him into the water. But you forgot to get rid of the knife, for we found that in the car when it was discovered at Glasgow Airport. I'm curious, why did you leave the knife in the boot of the car?"

She didn't reply, just stared wide-eyed at him and inwardly cursed, for he could not know that in her haste, she had forgotten to get rid of the knife.

"Why did you kill Carol Meechan?" he asked.

She was blindsided and did not expect the change of tactic.

"She got…" then stopped and continued to stare at him, but now through narrowed eyes.

"What makes you think I killed her?"

"We know that Meechan came to you, that she was suspicious of the accounts," he said, aware as was Miller that the question was a bluff based on the supposition of the detective who had just a few hours previously interviewed John Paterson. "I believe you made a mistake, Miss Sutherland, when you left your flat this morning. You see, you abandoned quite a number of clothing items in the wardrobe of the flat that I had checked for blood residue and I've now learned that our laboratory discovered a dark, hooded top with some staining. Turned out to be blood that to be honest, we still haven't had identified, but we will," he slowly nodded, his slow speech and confidence shaking her to the core, "and I'm guessing that with the advances in DNA technology, it *will* prove to be Carol Meechan's blood."

He could not see her hands that were below the level of the desk top, but Franklin would not have been surprised that they were tightly clenched to prevent them from shaking.

White-faced, she replied, "She was suspicious of the accounts that we…" she gulped. "Peter I mean," she hastily added, "was creating accounts that didn't seem to have any financial credibility and she came to me to report her suspicions…"

"And you saw her as a threat and stabbed her," he quickly interrupted.

"*I'm admitting nothing of the sort!*" she hissed at him, but then just as quickly, calmed down, her hands still clenched tightly beneath the level of the desk while her stomach churned.

"Well, time will tell when the blood examination is completed," he said with some finality.

He glanced down at the file. "Now, let's discuss Harold McPherson and help me out here. We got his body out of the River Clyde, but we're not quite certain where you killed him…"

"I didn't kill him," she said through gritted teeth.

"Why would I believe you? Tell me something that makes me think you're telling the truth, Miss Sutherland?"

"You have to believe me, I…did…not…kill…Harry," she hissed again.

"But you did involve him in you and Peter Gibson's scheme to steal the money?"

"No, you have to understand," she banged her fists down on the table, her face almost pleading, "Harry wanted *me*; he didn't care about the money…at least, not at first."

"Did you care for him?"

The question took her aback and she blinked rapidly, trying to decide on how to respond before finally replying, "He was…useful."

"And is that why you used a memory stick to implicate McPherson in your scheme?"

She smiled slyly. "I never could get to grips with computer technology. I suppose that sour faced, weirdly dressed woman worked that out?"

"Yes," he nodded, forcing himself not to smile at her description that he immediately recognised, "Detective Sergeant Scott is *more* than adept with computers," he agreed.

"But let's get back to Mister McPherson. After you killed him…"

"You're not listening, I told you; I did not kill Harry!" she almost screamed, but he ignored her interruption and continued, "…like

Gibson, you dumped his body into the River Clyde. Just how much did he know about the scam, the theft of the money?"

She crossed her arms and turned sullenly away, staring at the blank wall to one side.

He reached across the desk and with his finger hovering over the top button on the machine, said, "I'm switching the tapes off to permit Miss Sutherland a comfort break."

She hadn't asked for a break and puzzled, stared at him.

Then he said, "Let's talk about these," and reaching down to his feet, lifted her leather wallet from which he withdrew the photographs that he tossed onto the table.

She turned and a slow smile crossed her face as almost with reverence, she lifted the photos and began to look through them.

"So that's it," she said as if with understanding. "It's time to make a deal, is it? My silence guaranteed and my famous lover's name *not* disclosed to her adoring public."

"I understand you have already made some previous deals with the Crown Prosecution Service in Wales and in England, Miss Sutherland," he replied and glancing at his file, read aloud, "First in Wales when as Gwen Jones, you informed on your associates," he looked up and added, "your true name, I understand," and glancing again at the file, added, "then in London when as Marilyn Morning, again you turned Queen's Evidence to turn on your associates."

"I always liked that name. Don't you think, Mister Franklin, I look a little like her," she pouted, the assurance of a deal restoring her confidence, bringing her back from the brink of despair.

"Indeed you do, Miss Sutherland," he nodded and quickly ushered from his mind the thought that arrived. "However, I regret that on this occasion," he reached across and almost gently took the photos from her and began tearing them up, dropping the shredded paper into the waste bin held by Charlie Miller.

The last one torn, he smiled and said, "I'll be burning these when I'm finished here."

She returned his smile and shrugged her shoulders. "I still think that there's a deal to be made, Mister Franklin. You might wish to inform your superiors that the destruction of the photographs is irrelevant. I *can* make copies," she smiled almost sweetly at him. "Your superiors must decide what's important. Locking me up for the murder of some irrelevant people or you and I arriving together at a deal that will prevent me exposing the hypocrisy of the Royal family. You know Mister Franklin, the knowledge that I have and the photographs *might* just bring them down. The world wide public outcry would be…" she stretched her hands out as if in supplication and with a smile, softly sighed, "catastrophic for the Royals as well as the great British public. Now, is that not worth considering?"

"And how would you do that?" he coaxed her.

"Let's just say," she teased him, "I have the photos recorded."

"Recorded on what?"

"A little memory card, Mister Franklin."

He let her enjoy her moment of victory, then with a shrug of his shoulders and a smile, fetched a memory card from his jacket pocket and brandishing it at her, said, "You mean this one?"

Her face turned pale and her eyes fluttered as if in disbelief.

The atmosphere in the room was suddenly electric and it was unfortunate that neither Franklin nor Miller had known or even considered that the svelte and very fit Sutherland was a keen kick-boxing fan.

The first indication that they might have a problem with her was when quite unexpectedly she leapt across the desk at Franklin to grab at the memory card clutched in his hand.

Taken completely unaware, Miller could only stare in shock as her body weight, though a lot slighter than Franklin, carried both of them to the floor with her on top and using her elbows to smash at his face. Miller leapt from his chair, first banging on the emergency bar with a fist and grabbing at her with his free hand, missed and slipped to his knees, only to see Franklin's nose explode in a violent burst of red that sprayed blood on the three of them.

The audible alarm screeched loudly and drowned out the grunts and groans from the three of them, now struggling and rolling about the interview room floor.

Franklin's instinct was to close his hand holding the memory card, but he yelped in pain as Sutherland sank her fine white teeth into his wrist and caused his hand to fly open.

They watched almost in slow motion as the memory card slid across the floor of the room into a corner.

Miller, now back on his feet, stood astride Sutherland with both hands on her shoulders to lift her from Franklin, only for her to kick back at him and land her heel squarely on his genitals.

He crumpled over her with a quiet sigh.

She struggled to get out from under his weight when the door burst open to admit the young female constable who seeing her two older male colleagues struggling with the female prisoner, reached down and taking a handful of Sutherland's hair, screamed at her, "*Fucking calm down, you!*" and crashed her head against the leg of the desk. Sutherland, stunned, almost immediately went limp and the cop released her grip.

Turning towards the two detectives writhing on the floor, a groaning Franklin, holding his bleeding nose, tried to sit up while the whimpering Miller had both hands wrapped round his groin.

The baby-faced cop stood over the two men with her hands on her hips and grinning at their discomfort, said, "I thought you guys were the big city cops? You should come down to Stranraer on a Friday night," she added, "that's *real* fun and games at throwing out time. Now, do you lads want a doctor or a cup of tea?"

CHAPTER 35

Frankie Johnson glanced at the personnel file that lay upon his desk and took a note of the home address, then lifting the phone from its cradle dialled Lynn Massey's phone number.

"Hello Lynn," he began, "I've just spoken with Charlie Miller and I'm pleased to report that he and Bobby Franklin got a result down at Stranraer. Seems our suspect has more or less admitted to the murders of the young woman Carol Meechan and Peter Gibson, but is denying murdering Harry McPherson."

"Odd that she denies killing McPherson, him being discovered like Gibson in the River Clyde and all," she replied.

"Yes, too much of a coincidence," he agreed, thoughtfully nodding his head. "She's blaming the idea for the scam on Gibson, but Charlie is of the opinion that she is the brains behind it and that she seduced him into it. As for McPherson, it seems he sort of stumbled into a relationship with her and she's used him, then when he became too interested in the money, Charlie believes that's when she killed him."

"What about Carol Meechan. Was she involved?"

"Therein seems to be the tragedy of the whole affair. Sutherland, or whatever name you wish to call her," he sighed, "admitted that

Meechan was suspicious of the scam and Charlie thinks she's obtained Meechan's address, followed her home and stabbed her to death in the close to prevent her bringing the scam to the managements attention. She hasn't openly admitted to Meechan's murder, but Bobby Franklin is convinced that a stain on a sweat top found in Sutherland's wardrobe will match Meechan's blood type or hopefully, her DNA."

"So, what's she been charged with?"

"At this time, she's charged with the murders of Gibson and McPherson and collusion in the theft of the money from the bank. When the result of the staining on the sweat top is confirmed, if Bobby's opinion is correct, she'll likely be charged with Meechan's murder too. Charlie and Bobby have arranged for her to be brought this evening to Cranstonhill police office and she'll appear tomorrow morning at the Sheriff Court, here in Glasgow."

"Did she confess to where the money is?"

"Inferred she knew, but according to Charlie, just grinned and told him to eff off."

Massey grinned at Johnson's old fashioned chivalry, consistently unwilling to use foul language to a female colleague.

"What about that issue we discussed, the information that Greg obtained from his source down in London?"

He realised that Massey would not yet know about the photographs discovered in Sutherland's possession and quickly sketched to her a description of what the photographs contained and the assumption she would have a back-up in the form of a camera memory card, as well as her attempt to make a deal.

Massey was aghast and asked, "Where are the photographs now?"

"Destroyed by Bobby Franklin," he replied.

"What about the memory card?"

"Unfortunately that wasn't found, but Charlie's making arrangements to have her car taken to Meiklewood Road garage and thoroughly searched and will tell SOCO that the memory card has information pertaining to the theft of the money from the bank."

"So she still has the advantage of knowing that she can cause havoc with the photographs if we don't find that memory card?"

She listened, hearing Johnson chuckling then replying, "Well, there's a story. Charlie and Bobby worked a flanker on her. Borrowed a memory card from the local CID's Scene of Crime kit and pretended they had found hers."

"And she fell for that?"

"Apparently, because she kicked off and attacked Bobby Franklin and burst his nose and, when Charlie tried to intervene," he begun to laugh, "he got a boot in the balls for his troubles."

"Are they alright?" she was aghast that Johnson found it funny.

"Oh aye, just a bit humbled because Charlie said it was a young policewoman, a slip of a lassie according to him, who apparently saved them."

Even Massey had to smile at that and then Johnson asked her, "How did you get on with his widow, DS Gibson I mean?"

She spent a few minutes relating the circumstances of her visit with Baxter to the house in Uddingston and told him she was convinced that DS Gibson knew nothing of her husband's activities at the bank.

"There is something I'd like to ask you, Frankie. It will come out that her husband was having an affair with Sutherland. How do you think I should handle it; tell her now before she learns from someone else or just let her find out on her own?"

"If you were in her position, Lynn, how would *you* prefer to find out?"

He heard her inhale and then she replied, "I'll leave it for tonight and then phone and make an arrangement to visit her tomorrow morning."

She asked how the funeral went and he spent a few minutes describing the ceremony and how pleased he was at the large turnout.

"No problems then?" she asked.

"I did hear that there was a small protest before the ceremony commenced," he said, "one of these anti-Islamic groups waving some banners, but the uniform boys cracked down on it and lifted some female for a breach."

He didn't think it necessary to mention that before going home that evening, he had a visit to make.

The call concluded with both agreeing to meet early the next morning in the incident room at Cranstonhill for Bobby Franklin's briefing to his troops.

It was later that evening when Jill Mooney answered the door bell to the polite, middle-aged man with the charming smile who carried a box of doughnuts and introduced himself as Frankie Johnson, a colleague of her father and asked if Des was available for a wee chat?

Jill's intuition led her to suspect that Johnson was more than just a colleague and led him through to the lounge, where her father sat watching the television and nursing a cup of tea and.

He tried to stand when Johnson entered the room, but was quickly waved back down into his seat.

"Do you hear that?" Johnson said to Jill, his eyes narrowing and head cocked to one side as though listening, but she wasn't fooled.

"You're just like my dad," she grinned. "He can hear a kettle boiling at fifty yards," and taking the hint, left with the doughnuts to make a brew.

"Nice young woman," Johnson smiled at Mooney, "and if I correctly recall, you said she is in the army?"

"Aye sir, she's a nurse and currently serving in Afghanistan. They let her come home on leave to take care of me. I'm very proud of her."

"Understandable. Des," he took off his overcoat and sat down on the armchair opposite Mooney, "I'm not here in any official capacity, so I'd be grateful if you would use my given name. Most people call me Frankie."

Mooney's eyes narrowed and nodding, then said, "Okay Frankie. Why *are* you here then?"

Johnson inhaled and blew through pursed lips. "There's no easy way to broach the subject and please forgive me if you think I'm overstepping the mark, but when I visited you at the Victoria Infirmary that day, I was nearly rammed by a car in the car park driven by a woman and I got a good look at her. Used a few expletives too," he smiled. "On the way out of the casualty ward, the nurse said that a woman with red hair had just visited you and she mistakenly thought the woman was your wife. She described the woman who I believe was the driver of the car I nearly collided with. I saw the same woman today, but she *seems* to me to be married to ACC MacPhail."

He slowly shrugged and continued, "You have my word that nobody else knows, Des, but you must realise that it places you in one *hell* of an awkward position if word does get out."

"Right guys, tea up," said Jill, carrying a tray into the lounge, then seeing both men's faces, added, "and when I've put this down, I'm away to my room like a good wee girl to play with my dolls."
Johnson grinned while Mooney simply smiled.
After Jill had closed the door, Mooney said, "I'm not giving her up, Frankie. I made a mistake many years ago and let Shona go then. I will not let her go again."
"Does MacPhail know?"
"He knows she's leaving him, but I don't think he knows who I am."
"Have you met him?"
"Oh aye, we've crossed paths, Mister MacPhail and I," he grinned and added, "but there's no love lost there."
"How's the leg, by the way?"
Mooney pursed his lips and said, "Healing, but slowly. I might find myself on light duties for some time to come."
"What about the other injuries?"
"Not causing any problems," Mooney shook his head.
Johnson's brow knitted as an idea crossed him mind, an idea so outrageous that he baulked at even admitting to it.
"I'll not kid you, Des," he slowly said, "but when I got your home address from your personnel file, I saw that you're sitting with almost twenty-eight years service. That's correct, isn't it?"
"Aye, Frankie, twenty-eight years this coming November," and now it was his brow that furrowed as he stared curiously at Johnson. "Why do you ask?"

EPILOGUE

The day following her detention at the Port of Cairnryan and subsequent arrest at Stranraer police office, Gwen Jones appeared at the Sheriff Court in Glasgow, at her own request, under her pseudonym Morven Sutherland.
Prior to her appearance, the police laboratory were successful in obtaining DNA from the blood stain on the hood sweat top that had been discovered in the wardrobe of her flat in Brown Street. This sample was compared with a DNA sample taken from the deceased Carol Meechan and proved to be a match.

In consequence, the two murder charges already libelled against her for the murder of Peter Gibson and the murder of Harold McPherson now included a further indictment for the murder of Carol Meechan. Aside from these charges, Sutherland was also charged with colluding with the deceased Gibson and MacPherson in the theft of three million, two hundred and sixty thousand pounds from her place of employment, the Caledonia Banking Group, 148 West George Street in Glasgow.

By mutual agreement, DCI Miller and DI Franklin decided that charges of assault against them both seemed unnecessary, considering the more serious charges that were libelled and both also privately agreed the public humiliation of taking a kicking from the slighter built Sutherland would be more than they could bear.

At the urging of DI Bobby Franklin, the case reporting officer Detective Chief Superintendent Frankie Johnson attempted to persuade Crown Office, who prosecuted the case, to consider an additional charge of Breach of the Peace, arguing that by murdering Carol Meechan, the accused caused the death of the elderly neighbour, Violet Cairns, whose demise resulted by a heart attack brought on by the shock of discovering the body of the unfortunate Miss Meechan. While the Crown Office agreed in principle, the charge was not libelled against Sutherland, but throughout the trial, much was made of it by the Prosecuting Counsel. To Franklin's delight, he saw that many of the jurors were moved by the issue of the old lady's death and firmly believed this contributed to their final decision when the trial was finally concluded.

On the advice of her solicitor, Sutherland pled not guilty to all charges and was remanded in custody to the women's prison at HMP Cornton Vale, pending her appearance for trial at the High Court in Edinburgh.

Several attempts were made by Sutherland's solicitor to the Crown Office, pleading that his client was willing to make a deal to dismiss the charges; that his client had privileged information concerning a prominent member of the Establishment and that failure to release Sutherland would cause her to disclose such information to the media.

Regretfully for Sutherland, she was unable to substantiate this allegation and when contacted, the arresting officers were unable to provide any information regarding this allegation and reminded the Crown Office that *if* Sutherland was in possession of such information it should have been disclosed at the time of her taped interview. Needless to say, the taped interview did not disclose any such discussion regarding this alleged information.

In due course, the trial commenced and almost from the commencement of the three weeks of evidence, Sutherland screamed abuse at the witnesses until finally, unable to take any more outbursts, His Lordship ordered her to be taken down and incarcerated in a cell below the court.

The trial proceeded without her presence.

As expected, the local media reported every facet of the case that included Sutherland's shouted allegation of a salacious affair with a leading member of the Royal family. This allegation suggested to His Lordship that the accused was seriously deranged and he ordered a psychiatric evaluation that curiously, resulted in a finding that her mental state was exemplary, with the psychiatrist later and very privately commenting that Sutherland wasn't mad, just bad.

In any event, the jury apparently took no notice of her outburst and finally returned verdicts of guilty for the murder of Carol Meechan and for the murder of Peter Gibson.

However, the jury was undecided regarding the evidence against Sutherland for the murder of Harold McPherson and, arguing among themselves there was insufficient proof to convict her, subsequently returned a verdict that is unique to the Scottish judicial system; Not Proven.

Almost as an afterthought, Sutherland was also found guilty of being art and part for the theft of the *considerable* sum of money from the Caledonian Banking Group.

In his summing up prior to sentencing, His Lordship described the accused as a manipulative and conniving, wicked woman before awarding her a total of two life imprisonment's for the convicted murders and ten years for the theft of the money; such sentences to run concurrently and no parole to be considered until a period of thirty years had passed.

Head held high, Sutherland departed the dock grinning and waving a single digit at the jury, still firm in the belief that her allegation of an affair with a Royal personage would set her free.

She also remains unaware that her flame red, beloved Audi TT now lay in bits and rusting in the police garage at Meiklewood Road with the undiscovered memory card secreted in a small, hand-sewn pocket within the underside rear seat lining.

The hard work and favour called in by Father Patrick Gallagher to have his brother Leigh released from remand proved to be of no avail. His brother was unable to resist the easy money made from robbing women and after robbing three women in two days, was identified, arrested and returned to prison to await trial on the previous and new additional charges.

Leigh later pled guilty and incarcerated for three years; however, in the first month of his sentence his father Magnus Gallagher, shamed by his son's actions, suffered a massive coronary and died whispering Leigh's name.

Father Patrick Gallagher dutifully attended on a number of occasions to visit Leigh in prison, but on each occasion his brother refused to see him.

Charlie Miller resumed the rank of Detective Inspector and with his wife Sadie, eagerly awaits the arrival of his child. DI Miller refused point blank to be told the gender of the unborn child, but grows suspicious of the number of pink baby clothes Sadie continues ordering on-line.

Bobby Franklin was finally coerced by his wife into making the long overdue doctors appointment about his suspected hernia. However, the doctor was unhappy with Franklin's self-diagnosis and referred him to the Western Infirmary, who in turn referred Franklin to the oncology clinic at the Beatson West of Scotland Cancer Centre. Franklin and his wife were devastated to learn of his tumour, however, he almost immediately underwent treatment that included an operation and shortly thereafter, the consultant was pleased to inform him that the prognosis is good.

When later asked by his wife how he coped with the post-operative pain, Franklin assured her it was less traumatic than being belted by an elbow on the nose.

The Caledonian Banking Group did not fare so well.

The loss of the money was severe, but did not compare with the loss of prestige and trust by both the customers and banking industry.

In consequence of the adverse publicity the case generated, the Directors at their board meeting reluctantly agreed to a takeover by a Chinese conglomerate that sought to add a prestigious Scottish banking name to its list of international companies.

The takeover resulted in a streamlining of the bank's Glasgow office during which almost one third of staff lost their jobs.

However, one member of staff retained was the elderly commissionaire Max McFarlane, who guiltily took secret delight in watching almost half the board members, including the HR Director John Brewster, march down the front steps for the last time.

Detective Sergeant Susie Gibson, in consultation with her daughter Jenny, decided that she had had enough of the police and with the reluctant agreement of Detective Chief Superintendent Frankie Johnson, took early retirement, citing emotional stress as the reason for her departure.

A sympathetic Assistant Chief Constable who was not only in charge of Personnel issues, but also a long standing friend of Frankie Johnson, agreed that as DS Gibson had achieved the statutory twenty-six and a half years service, her pension would be made up to the full thirty years.

That money and the life insurance payments she received upon confirmation of her husband Peter's death, assured that she need not work for the foreseeable future and could concentrate on both her daughter Jenny's and her own welfare.

Besides, she reasoned with an inward smile, if she needed money *that* badly, she could always access Peter's small, electronic notebook and transfer funds from the Cayman Islands account.

Some days after meeting with des Mooney, the same ACC (Personnel) met with Frankie Johnson for a quiet drink at their favourite watering hole, the Old Toll Bar located on the corner of Paisley Road West and Admiral Street, in the Plantation area of Glasgow's south side.

It was there that in confidence, Johnson broached the issue of Des Mooney's affair with their colleague Jonathan MacPhail's wife and it was also there it was agreed that to avoid a public scandal and humiliation for both MacPhail and the police, Des Mooney would be quietly retired on ill-health grounds resulting from his near death experience and receive his full superannuation.

Later that evening, Johnson phoned Mooney with the good news and learned that Shona MacPhail was now living with Mooney.

Slightly less than two months later, Jonathon MacPhail successfully applied for and was later appointed as the Deputy Chief Constable of a small, provincial English force and almost immediately departed Glasgow to take up his new post.

Des Mooney's soldier daughter Jill returned to Camp Bastion to complete her tour of duty during which she successfully applied for a nursing Sister post at the newly built Southern General Hospital in Glasgow; the position to be taken up upon completion of her military service in six months time.

"After all," she told her happy father and Shona, "if I'm going to be a big sister, I'll need to be around, won't I?"

Harry McPherson's wife Tracey was deliriously happy.

The insurance payout on Harry's death meant the house was hers, lock stock and barrel and there was still enough money in the bank to see her through the year; well, at least until she found herself a new man.

Her daughter was now being looked after by her parents for most nights of the week to permit Tracey to 'come to terms with her grief' and thank God for that, she shook her head. The wee bugger's constant whining was beginning to get on her nerves and she really needed the break to get herself together; most evenings of which were now spent celebrating her new found widowhood in the city centre pubs and clubs with Gaz, who worked as a bouncer in her favourite bar.

She peered again at the mirror and dabbed daintily with her left pinkie at the slightest of smudges on her lower lip. Gaz was due to arrive at the house for a drink any time within the next half hour and she wanted to *dazzle* him.

She sat at her mirrored dressing table, studying her makeup and trying to decide if she was going to shag him on this, their first full night together.

Her breathing became more pronounced when she thought of his muscles rippling through his tight shirt and yes, she smiled; she liked the traditional celtic tattoo sleeves that he had on his arms and right round his neck and imagined running her hand across his shaven head when he was…her breathing became a little faster and she sighed with anticipation and drew her knees tightly together.

He was a real man, was Gaz; not like that wanker Harry, she sniffed. She stared critically at her tight, blood-red coloured low cut top, uncertain if instead she should wear the lacy, front opening wired bra and using both hands, plumped up her breasts; always her best features, she grinned and leaned slightly forward to examine her deep, milky-white cleavage.

Standing, she turned towards the full length mirror affixed to the wardrobe door and pulled at the hem of the black leather mini-skirt, tight enough to reveal the bump of the suspender buttons on her upper thighs and half turned to ensure the seam of her silk stockings were straight. She pouted at the slight post-natal bump, but figured membership of the new private gym would soon get rid of it, already imagining herself attired in the sports clothes she intended buying.

Stepping back from the mirror Tracey seductively run both hands down the sides of the short skirt and grinned again, conscious that she looked like a right tart, but didn't care. Her mind was made up. Tonight, she decided with a firm nod to her reflection, Gaz was getting lucky.

She left the bedroom and tripped downstairs, walking first into the lounge to turn the music up full blast and *fuck* the neighbours, she thought.

Her eyes narrowed for she had something to do and in her excitement at what the evening promised to bring, couldn't quite remember what it was; but then she smilingly recalled. In the kitchen, she ignored the sink of dirty dishes and pulled open the fridge door. She frowned, for the fridge was so full of foodstuffs there was no more space and decided to leave the dozen cans of Gaz's favourite beer in the cool box outside the back door, but thought it would be nice to have one ready for him when he arrived. She glanced nervously at the clock and biting her lip, made her way to the back door.

Stepping out into the shadowy back porch, Tracey bent down to retrieve a can from the cool box and glanced at the overgrown garden, staring with distaste at the mess it was in and thought she would get her father to organise somebody in to cut the grass and weed it. Maybe put the house on the market, she mused. It wasn't the first time she had thought of selling the house and getting herself one of them nice, modern city centre flats; somewhere central where the life was. After the half dozen or so lessons, she knew she could drive, but maybe now she would finish the lessons and get a licence and a wee motor. One of they sporty types, she thought.

After all, she inwardly grinned, she could afford to now she had a big pile of money in the bank.

The front door bell startled her and standing, with the icy cold can of beer in her hand wetly gripped in one fist, she used her free hand to again smooth down her leather skirt and taking a sharp breath, hurried through the house to greet Gaz.

Behind her, in a dimly lit corner of the garden, abandoned and rusting with lack of use, lay some discarded hedge trimming shears and other tools.

What no one would ever know nor Tracey ever tell was that until recently, among these tools had also been a small, hand axe, but now that hand axe, with minute traces of head hair still attached to the blade, lay alongside the rusting keys of her husband Harry's Qashqai vehicle in the mud at the bottom of the River Clyde.

******

Needless to say, this story is a work of fiction.
If you have enjoyed the story, you may wish to visit the author's website at:
www.glasgowcrimefiction.co.uk

The author also welcomes feedback and can be contacted at:
george.donald.books@hotmail.co.uk

Printed in Great Britain
by Amazon

41067226R00218